TRIUMPH TO TRAGEDY

Book One

Intrigue – Romance – Betrayal
And The Haitian Revolution

DANIEL J.D. BAYARD

Edited by Shawn McAskill
Illustrations by Dian Triyasa

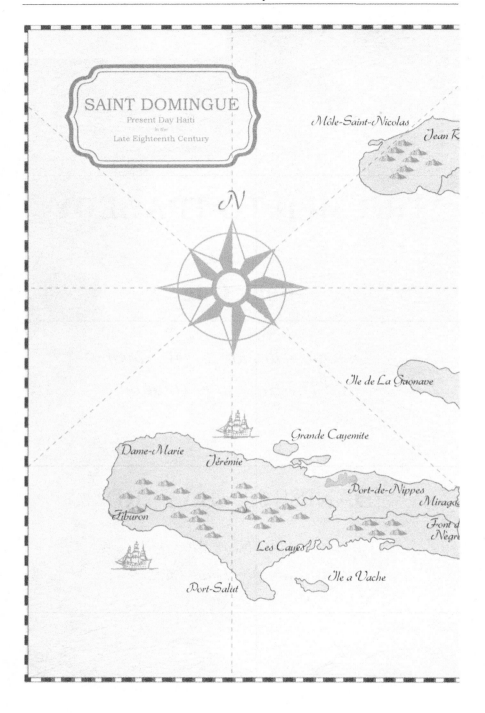

Triumph To Tragedy
Book One

First Edition

Fourth Printing, 2023
L&D Publishing

Email: Author@TriumphToTragedy.com

Paperback ISBN: 978-1-961297-00-5

Hardcover ISBN: 978-1-961297-01-2

eBook ISBN: 978-1-961297-02-9

www.TriumphToTragedy.com

Dedicated to the strong women in my life:

My loving wife Lily
My sisters Marie-Denise and Mica
With Wonderful Memories of Mom, Dad and Jackie.

Inspiration and Creative Input:
Lily LaPlace-Bayard

Special Thanks for Support and Encouragement:

Paul Simon

Chris Meigher III

Jean-Bernard Bayard

Frantz Ludecke

Parental Discretion Warning

This novel is an excellent historical education for youth.
However, adult sexual content exists on pages 89-92.
Please remove these pages for younger readers.

CONTENTS

PREFACE

As the French Ancien Régime (Old Regime) reached its end between 1788 and 1789, St. Domingue, the western part of the island of Hispaniola which is now the country of Haiti, was considered the world's most productive and valuable industrial plantation economy and was called the "Pearl of the Antilles" due to its wealth.

Saint Domingue exported 72 million pounds of raw sugar, and 51 million pounds of refined sugar which accounted for 40% of all sugar consumed in Europe; plus 1 million pounds of indigo, 2 million pounds of cotton, and 60% of all the coffee consumed in the entire world. The Colony employed 1.587 great vessels and 24.000 sailors. At any given time, there would be over 60 ships in the port of Cap-Français alone.

Haiti's exports were larger than that of the entire American colonies combined and worth far more than the golds of Brazil or the silver of Mexico and kept the entire navy of France in business. It became the jewel of the French Colonial Empire and supplied France with over half of the wealth it derived from all its colonies combined! The livelihood of millions of inhabitants of Europe depended directly on the colonial trade centered in Saint Domingue.

Dependent upon half a million African and Creole slaves, its 3,097 indigo, 2,810 coffee, 792 large sugar, and 705 cotton plantations; Saint Domingue produced today's monetary equivalent of $65 billion US per year; $5.5 billion per month; or $219 million per day worth of commodities destined for both Continental Europe and the United States of America.

Comparative 2020 GDP numbers of the US would put the colony slightly above Rhode Island ($63 billion) and under Maine

($69 billion). However, considering the colony's small population of 578,000 (inclusive of 500,000 slaves), the per capita GDP would have come to $112,456; nearly double the $65,280 per capita GDP of the United States. This massive wealth was the revenue of the less than 100,000 free population and would have resulted in an annual per capita income of over half a million dollars per free man, woman, and child.

Between 1763 and 1789, the colony's export exceeded those of all colonies combined and was the driving force behind the French "commercial revolution" of the second half of the 18th century. French plantation owners hailing from Nantes, Bordeaux, Paris, La Rochelle, Bayonne, and the Loire Valley found dynastic fortunes in St. Domingue.

Of little historical record during this period was the significant wealth and contributions of people of color (GENS DE COULEUR); the Negro, Mulatto (half Black and half White), and Quadroon (some parts of Black in their ancestry of ¼ or less). This group constituted a larger population than French Whites, who were categorized as Grands (Big) and Petits (Small) Blancs (Whites)—depending on property ownership, wealth, and social status.

The revolutionary period of Saint Domingue spanning from 1789-1803 was a violent, ever-changing dichotomy resulting in much death and destruction; however, the pre-revolutionary and post-revolutionary periods are as impressive, intriguing, and as important as the revolution itself.

I began this project with the goal of learning more about my own family's history. As I immersed myself in the number of notarized French documents and archived files, I found more questions than answers, and revelations that alternately shocked and intrigued me; I had one ancestor who'd been kidnapped by pirates and another who owned slaves on a successful coffee plantation.

The unexpected slavery revelation hit me hard. How could I have one of my own family members engaged in the evil, racist industry of slavery? Through further research, I came to understand that slavery was an economic practice engaged by all colors within colonial society. There were large numbers of freed Negro slaves who in turn became slave owners themselves.

Slavery itself dates back to when the first tribe of men conquered a neighboring group and enslaved their people to provide forced labor. It was not based on ideas of race but imposed on the conquered for exploitation. Roman slaves were drawn from all over Europe and the Mediterranean, including Gaul, Hispania, North Africa, Syria, Germany, Britannia, the Balkans, Greece, and more. Egyptians enslaved the Jews; the Greeks enslaved those captured in war, and so on.

Previously, I had naively believed slavery to be solely a racist issue, which in reality demeans sub-Saharan Negroes as inferior—as if they were the only population to be enslaved. This is of course untrue. The colony of St. Domingue was supplied slaves from those captured by rival tribes in Africa; by criminals who kidnapped their neighbors and sold them to slave traders as property to be exported off the continent. These unfortunate souls were doomed to an existence of forced labor, torture, and submission by those slave owners who viewed them either equal to, or oftentimes less than livestock.

This historical fiction novel will introduce real members of my family, the Bayard's, as well as notable characters of this period so the reader may be enlightened by American, French, and Haitian colonial history—while also being entertained and captivated by a story of war, family, inter-racial tension, sex, murder, religion, voodoo, love, and most every possible form of good and evil that man has to offer.

The names of my ancestors and historical figures are real, but I cannot confirm their actions exactly as I relate them. For example one of the principal characters, Henry Christophe, was present at the battle of Savannah fighting for the American Revolution as a soldier under the French Flag, worked for the Hôtel de La Couronne, was born a slave, purchased his freedom, became a General in the army and did indeed ascend to become King of Haiti. However, the attributed personal thoughts and sequence of events and accomplishments may not be. This is the challenge and reward that comes with filling in the blanks of history.

I make no attempt to be entirely accurate but intend to utilize these fascinating events as cornerstones of a story and interject persons of interest within context. I hope you enjoy this enlightening and exciting glimpse of heretofore untold history.

Daniel J.D. Bayard

BOOK One
PRE-REVOLUTION
1771 - 1793

St. Domingue
Present-Day Republic of Haiti

Ay-ti
'Land of Mountains'
The indigenous Taíno-Arawak name
for the entire island of Hispaniola

Mwen se Ayisyen
Paske nan tan lontan
Boukmann te fè yon rasanbleman
Nan bwa Kayiman

Sydney Noel

I am Haitian
Because in ancient times
Boukman had a gathering
At the Bois Caiman

Sydney Noel

One

HENRI & COMTE D'ESTAING

Savannah, Georgia
September 1779

The roars of cannons in the distance were muffled by a light but bitter fall wind. Henri counted the cannon fires…Un – One. Deux – Two; and so on, while Jean-Baptiste listened and corrected his pronunciation every now and then. The corrections came in the form of both French and English. Henri was learning the language after recently being thrust into the world of the French from his prior home on St. Christophe—an English colony in the Caribbean. Henri was turning twelve in a few days but had already seen so much for one so young.

Henri was a good boy, Jean-Baptiste thought. How he got here was a story all its own. Yet they were now in a land, fighting for the freedom of a colony to which neither had any loyalty. *"America"* it was called—was owned by the British, though those living here were now fighting to govern themselves. Jean-Baptiste was a French army, Captain. Henri was originally enlisted as a slave drummer boy, but after being wounded in a valiant battle was assigned to him for all things that he could assist with. Though sometimes more trouble than help, Jean-Baptiste could honestly say Henri always tried his best.

He'd grown accustomed to the boy's company, like that of a little brother in need of nurturing, protection, discipline—and much more. But here, in the middle of a war, it was a task easier said than done; during the previous day's battle, he'd found himself ignoring his own well-being while constantly making sure Henri remained in sight as bullets and cannonballs rained down upon them.

Alas, Henri had already tasted the worst of battle. Drummer Boy was no easy task. They acted as the communication chain from officers to troops. *Charge, retreat, flank,* and a host of other practiced maneuvers were well-orchestrated and synchronized as part of the war machine. Thus drummer boys were a prime enemy target, who sought to kill them and paralyze the infantry. Cannons and guns continuously rained peril on the young drummer boy soldiers.

Henri gained his reputation and promotion from just such an encounter.

During their third attempt to overtake Savannah, a combined force of 3,000 troops marched on the city. The British attempted to disrupt signals to the troops by way of heavy cannon fire. Of the six drummers, three were killed, one was wounded and another ran away in absolute terror. Only Henri remained, banging his drum louder than ever to compensate for the loss of his comrades.

Throughout the day, Henri sounded continuous rolls for the infantry's full-on attack; beat signals for a flank attack by the cavalry; and more rolls to signal to the artillery when and how far to hurl their cannonballs. After hours of toiling work, he was ordered to sound the retreat from the bloody skirmish as men from both sides were exhausted. His day's mission finally complete, Henri collapsed. As soldiers hurried to his side, they discovered his torso had been ravaged by shrapnel. Henri was soon rendered unconscious from the loss of blood. He was picked up and rushed to the field infirmary.

Admiral Charles Henri Hector, Comte d'Estaing himself, owner of the slave drummer boy, came to Henri's bedside to commend him and pronounce his elevation to Captain Jean-

Baptiste Bayard's young assistant—an honor to be admired by all. He chose Jean-Baptiste knowing that he too was a father, and had been personally convinced by the Admiral to join this expedition to the British colonies. Jean would have the patience to guide the boy through the hostilities. He felt that something about this boy was special—but just what it was, he had no clue. Only the future would reveal his instincts true.

Henri was fast asleep when the Admiral arrived, so he procured a stool and sat beside the bed, observing the calm on the boy's face as he slept. He clearly remembered the day the boy entered his life six months ago, as he stood on the deck with Captain Henri-Louis de Boulainvilliers de Croy aboard the powerful Languedoc, an 80-gun French Navy ship of the line, and the flagship of the fleet Admiral d'Estaing commanded.

At the time, d'Estaing was in the West Indies following France's 1778 entry into the American War of Independence as an ally to the colonies. He commanded a fleet of 12 ships of the line and a number of smaller vessels. A fleet under British Admiral John Byron began engaging in a series of skirmishes with the French forces, culminating in the British capturing the French-held island of St. Lucia in early 1779. In return, d'Estaing seized the British isle of Saint Vincent in June, followed by Grenada in July.

During the summer of 1779, both fleets received reinforcements. Admiral Byron's fleet now consisted of 22 ships to d'Estaing's 25. The French Comte set a brilliant trap for the British in Grenada by weighing anchor when the British fleet was first spotted at 4 am one morning. He ordered his ships to form a line of battle in order of speed and head northward. This masked the true strength of the French fleet as it left the anchorage. Believing his force superior, Byron gave the order for a general chase, approaching the cluster from the northeast.

When Byron finally realized the ploy, he desperately attempted to reform a battle line, but the British attack was now disordered and confused. The British ships *Fame, Lion,* and two others were separated from the main body and badly mauled by the French. D'Estaing lost no ships and was quickly recognized as a brilliant Admiral.

The fleet stopped briefly in August to take on fresh water in St. Christophe. Most ships were at sea, leaving the island generally unguarded. It was the beginning of their voyage to Martinique and d'Estaing and his captain was counting their blessings for having not sustained any trouble from the British when leaving the port.

Suddenly, a commotion disrupted their calm musings. A sailor was chasing what appeared as an animal of some sort—darting here and there across the ship's deck. Closer observation revealed the quarry to be a scared young boy; one who nearly avoided capture before finding himself surrounded by three sailors and at last surrendering. One of the hunting parties grabbed the boy and marched him before the Captain and Admiral.

"We are still not far from land Captain. If I throw him overboard, he can maybe swim and make it back to shore?" the sailor offered.

Capitan de Croy turned to the boy and inquired "Qui es-tu garçon (Who are you boy)? Comment es-tu monté à bord (How did you get aboard)?"

The boy looked dumbfounded as the Captain repeated the question, this time forcefully as a command, not a request. Hearing nothing from the boy, the Captain retorted "Jetez-le par-dessus bord (Throw him overboard)."

Without hesitation, the largest sailor hoisted the boy over his head and stalked toward the ship's edge to hurl him overboard.

"Non, Attendez!"

The sudden command emanated from the Admiral. The sailor instantly obeyed. After all, Charles Henri Hector, Comte d'Estaing was the Admiral of the fleet and supreme commander of the expedition. On top of that, the Comte was a Nobleman, a member of the privileged French social class which ranked him just below royalty. Nobility granted d'Estaing increased power and wealth over the average citizen and was well respected in the military. In this instance, his word was law.

"Bring him here! " d'Estaing commanded. The Captain provided an unnecessary nod to the passing sailor simply out of habit. He respected the Admiral greatly and would unquestioningly follow him into battle out of respect not only for his achievements but his capable leadership.

"Qui es-tu garçon? (Who are you boy?)" asked the Admiral.

This was once again met with a look of puzzlement from his captive.

"I don't think he speaks French" suggested another sailor. "As he was running, he was babbling in another language. It resembled a sort of broken English" he continued.

"What is your name boy?" inquired the Admiral, this time in French-accented English. The boy looked no older than ten or eleven.

"Slave." came the trembling reply.

"No boy. Not what you are, what is your name? Do you understand me? Your name. How are you called?"

"Me Slave. No name. Just Slave" the boy mumbled.

"Your name is Slave?"

"No, I am Slave"

"You have no name? What did your Master call you?"

"Slave"

"Just Slave?"

The boy's words came more quickly now, though his head bowed and a heavy tear dropped from his eyes.

"Uh huh, just Slave. My master said I didn't deserve a name. I am just a Slave."

"I will not call you Slave," d'Estaing stated in a softer tone. "What would you like your name to be?"

"I do not know. My Master said I was not worthy of such things as a name, as I am worthless."

"Sailors. Come here. What would you name this boy?"

This is what endeared the men to the Admiral. Simple things like a pat on the back after a good performance, eye contact, and a slight smile of appreciation, or in this case, inclusion and input on a decision as important as a name—even one for what they deemed a worthless slave. The three looked at each other and the largest sailor offered "I think Christophe since he stowed away from the island of St. Christophe. This will make him remember that place forever."

"Christophe…quite clever. That will be his surname." The Admiral then addressed the sailor: "That is good thinking." This put a smile not only on the burly sailor's face but on those of the other two, even though they'd provided no input.

"As for his first name, that shall be Henri, after me, so he can remember who saved his life on this day. So, this boy's name is now Henri Christophe, and you, sailor, are to spread the word to all on board that he is my property, and any harm that comes to him shall be addressed forthwith by me." Looking once more toward the large sailor and changing his tone to one of business, the Admiral asked "Do you understand me?"

The sailor shook his head, answering "Oui, Admiral."

D'Estaing walked toward the slave boy and placed his hand under Henri's chin. Raising it, he said in English "Let the world know that from here on out, you shall be named Henri Christophe, and claimed as a slave by Admiral Charles Henri Hector, Comte d'Estaing, who now appoints you a boy soldier for the Army of France under my command!"

He then turned and loudly repeated the announcement in French for anyone in range of his voice. He turned back to the boy. "What is your training Henri? What craft has been bestowed upon you?"

"Mason, my Master. I work with bricks, stone, and rocks," Henri responded.

"We have no work for a Mason on board a ship Henri. But to earn your food and keep, you must have a trade. From now on, you will serve in the military under my command as a boy drummer. Do you understand me?"

"Yes, Master."

"You will go with these men and immediately begin training." He turned to the sailors and commanded "Take Henri Christophe to the drummer corps to begin training immediately in both the French language and drum communication signals."

"Yes Sir!" they saluted, before turning and leaving with the

small boy in pursuit.

Yes, the Admiral remembered that day well, though it now seemed long ago. Since then, Henri had rapidly learned to communicate in French and excelled in his understanding and application of drum roll signals.

A strained moan from Henri brought d'Estaing back from his reminiscing. Henri was beginning to stir. As he attempted to rise, the Admiral could clearly determine his immense pain.

"Down Henri. You've sustained some injuries, but thank God, nothing too serious. I want you to rest and regain your strength."

"What happened to me, Master? Did I fail you and our great army?" Henri asked.

"Quite the contrary, my boy. You were valiant and indispensable in battle." replied d'Estaing.

"Is the battle over? Should I go back and join?" gasped Henri.

"No, Henri. You must rest. That battle has been over for three days." countered the Admiral.

"Three days! I have been in this bed for three whole days Master?" cried Henri.

"Yes, my boy. A well-deserved and much-needed rest. Your wounds will heal quickly as they are superficial and you are young. You collapsed from a loss of blood, so I want you to eat well over the next few days." ordered the Admiral.

"When can I join the drummer corps again Master? I know some of them were hit by cannon. Have they survived?" Henri pressed.

"Three did not make it, Henri," d'Estaing grimly reported. "The fourth was injured but will survive his wounds. The youngest ran like a jackrabbit in fear. When we found him he had pissed in his pants, was crying hysterically, and cowering under a bush. He has been mumbling words of terror and sobbing ever since then. I fear the poor soul may never regain his sanity."

"Please be merciful Master as it can be quite scary in battle— and he is younger even than I." pleaded Henri.

"Do not fret boy. No harm or discipline shall come to him. He is not yet a man and I understand what you say about fear; even worse in such a young soul." responded the Admiral before continuing.

"But never avoid fear, Henri. Fear is a good thing. It keeps you attentive in situations that you must take seriously. As for you, I am here to inform you that you will no longer be a member of the drummer corps. I have a new mission for you,"

"Am I no longer worthy of being a drummer, or even of my new uniform in the army of France, Master?" asked Henri in a sheepish voice.

"That is not it at all. I am proud, no, *very* proud of you Henri. You have proven yourself worthy and I now want you to learn from an experienced officer." stated the Admiral.

"Who will you have me serve, Master?"

"A young officer who I have grown to respect in a very short period of time. His name is Captain Jean-Baptiste Bayard" informed the Admiral. "You will rest for two more days, eat, and gain back your strength. I will inform Captain Bayard of your location and he shall come for you then."

Henri could feel something begin to well up in his stomach.

"Now, get some rest as I have rounds to conduct." finished the Admiral.

"Thank you, Master" Henri mustered as tears burst forth from his eyes.

"What is wrong Henri? Are you in pain? Should I summon the Doctor?" asked the Admiral with genuine concern.

"No, Master. I am not in pain. I do not know why I cry when you have given me the most valuable of gifts. No one has ever been kind to me, and though it should make me laugh, instead I cry. Not a bad cry, but a cry of which I know not why. I do not understand it, Master. Is there something wrong with me? Something more serious than my wounds to bring water to my eyes like this?" implored Henri.

"Henri, this is called emotion. It pleases me that you have not been so broken by your bondage as to have lost that. Emotion is healthy, and will serve you well should you ever be placed in command of men yourself."

d'Estaing stood.

"Aux revoir, Henri. Captain Bayard will come for you in a few days. Now rest."

With that, the Admiral turned and left the tent.

Captain Jean-Baptiste Hippolyte Bayard enlisted in the French army in 1772 at the age of 22. He'd graduated near the top of his class at Louis-le-Grand University in Paris the year prior. He'd have been number one, but the French had no stomach for a colonist like himself achieving the top spot. After all, he was a *Gens de Couleur* – a man of color. Neither White nor Black, but a fair-skinned Mulatto with African blood in his ancestry. He was considered inferior to the Whites yet superior to the Blacks; a race between races in the French caste system. His Grandmother was also Mulatto, while his Grandfather a Frenchman of the *Petit Blanc* category—a White man without wealth and property. This was all well and good by Jean, as he eschewed the pride to care anyway, and loved them both for their differing cultures—one a West Indian, the other European.

Jean was born free, and thus distinct from a freed slave, or *Affranchis;* those born into slavery or enslaved during their lives. This distinction between *Affranchi* and *Gens de Couleur* allowed the latter a higher social and political stature in the French West Indies according to the 1685 French Code Noir. By law, *Gens de Couleur* enjoyed the same rights and privileges as the White colonial population, though in practice strong discrimination by White colonial residents impeded the *Gens de Couleur* from fully exercising them.

Jean never thought he would one day join the army. After all, he was from a rich planter-class family. His father and mother owned and cultivated a successful plantation of coffee and indigo; though not one of the larger coffee or sugar plantations, it was well-run and productive enough to establish the Bayard's as one of the more wealthy families in the town of Jérémie, located on the coast along the lovely southwest peninsula of St. Domingue. Plantation income had provided Jean with a superior education from not only the finest schools in the colony but France as well.

On August 12, 1779, Jean met Comte D'Estaing in Cap-Français. He'd been charged with securing volunteers for the American expedition when the Admiral arrived at the port.

Jean found himself summoned to dinner on the night of the Languedoc's anchor in the Cap-Français harbor, along with three other ships of the French navy.

"Ah, Captain Jean-Baptiste Hippolyte Bayard. Your reputation precedes you," greeted the Admiral upon meeting Jean at the gangway. He continued to address the young Captain with all the honor and respect expected for a fellow officer of the Army of France.

"I understand you have done marvelously well in the recruitment of soldiers for our expedition on behalf of the King and his new American allies."

"It is my pleasure to serve His Majesty," replied Jean, "And in turn serve your cause, Admiral" he added, as he marveled at the beauty and power of the Languedoc's 80 cannons.

He had never seen such a vessel and quickly recognized the Admiral's significant stance in commanding such a stately and impressive warship.

He also couldn't help but notice the upgraded uniforms, polished armor, and seemingly higher stature of the French sailors who busied themselves with their duties around them. "I commend you on this ship, Admiral. She seems an incredible fighting machine."

"That she surely is, Captain. Allow me to introduce her Captain to you." replied the Admiral.

On cue, Captain de Croy appeared in full gallantry—his starched dress uniform a stark background to the gleaming medals on his chest. He bowed his head and clicked his heels in respect for a fellow officer, albeit one from the Army. "Naval Captain Henri-Louis de Boulainvilliers de Croy at your service, Captain," stated Captain de Croy with all the regal protocol learned over his years of service. "It is an honor to welcome you aboard the Languedoc."

"Then gentlemen, let us sit and indulge ourselves for my first feast in this lovely island paradise," invited the Admiral.

The three walked into what Jean considered the most elegant dining room he had ever set foot in of any sailing vessel. A table was set in a formal style with two military servers clad in their best dress uniforms at the ready.

"Let us sit, my two Captains." d'Estaing gestured with both hands toward the chairs. "Tonight, we plan the next course of our American expedition and discuss how France shall play a most vital role in the new American republic," he continued.

"They say that the leader of the revolution is a planter himself, General George Washington," stated Captain de Croy. "It is also said his fighters are a ragged bunch of farmers, laborers, and common folk who arrive with picks and axes as weapons and can be extremely undisciplined," he concluded.

"What they lack in experience and skill I am told they make up in courage and grit," rebuked the Admiral. "The British are a battle-tested army with a superior advantage…but never underestimate a fighting force on their own turf and committed to their country's freedom" he wisely explained.

"Is it a truth or myth that this General Washington attacked in the middle of a violent storm on Christmas night after crossing the Delaware River?" inquired Jean.

"Yes," answered d'Estaing. "He and his party landed north of Trenton, New Jersey, where Washington led the main body of the Continental Army against Hessian auxiliaries. After a brief battle, nearly two-thirds of the Hessian force was captured, with negligible American losses."

"Those Hessian soldiers from Germany have no heart in that war." proclaimed Captain de Croy. "Their government loans them out to the highest bidder. They're mercenaries who fight for money. It is not without reason the Americans were able to defeat them."

The Captain paused to consider his company. "I would even venture to say most were drunk during the Christmas holidays?" he finished with humor.

"Nevertheless, a victory secured by General Washington." d'Estaing responded.

"But not after that British General Howe kicked them out of New York and chased them into New Jersey!" countered Captain de Croy.

"True, my Captain. That is why we are here at this table tonight."

The statement hung in the air as the Admiral sipped the remaining spoonful of his French onion soup before the server replaced the bowl with a dish of raw, finely chopped conch in a light lemon vinaigrette and garlic butter-spiced sauce.

"Ever since I tasted conch during my first visit to Guadeloupe, it has remained one of my favorites" the Admiral decreed. "The flavor is unique and cannot be duplicated."

This was met with curt nods by both Captains.

"Now, where were we? For Captain Bayard's sake, let's start from the beginning."

The Admiral related to Jean the story of how France found itself involved in the revolution. At the start of the war, France had aided the Continental Army with supplies such as gunpowder, cannons, clothing, and shoes—before eventually expanding to weapons, military leaders, and soldiers.

Great Britain was the major power in Europe and throughout the rest of the world. Countries such as France and Spain saw the British as their enemy, especially as both had lost the Seven Years' War against Great Britain in 1763. By aiding the Americans, they were also hurting this enemy. Both countries wanted revenge as well as to regain their lost international prestige.

A free colony of America meant a recapture of territories lost during that war, as well as the development of a new trading partner. France was more focused than Spain on the latter opportunity and in becoming the colonies' primary ally.

The Admiral explained that the new American Ambassador to France, Benjamin Franklin, exercised expert diplomatic skills and had successfully petitioned the King for assistance. Through the

Treaty of Alliance and the Royal Ordinance issued by King Louis XVI in March of this year, France became an official ally of the fledgling country. This also marked the start of direct involvement and led to fighting the British along the American coast.

"One of our key assets with the Continental Army is General Marquis de Lafayette. It was his idea to recruit men from our own colonies to bolster our armed forces."

The server removed the empty dishes of conch and replaced them with a lavish plate of broiled Capon in a wine and mushroom sauce and roasted potatoes in a light butter sauce garnished with a local root called Malanga—a favorite of Captain de Croy and one Jean knew well. The Capon, a castrated rooster that fattened as a result, was a feast indeed. In Jean's estimation, this meal was as delicious as any found in the best restaurants of Cap-Français.

"Unfortunately, our recruitment in Guadeloupe and Martinique have only yielded 40 men, a small number of my ship's capacities," the Admiral stated flatly before turning to Jean. "I understand you are doing better here in St. Domingue?"

"Yes, Admiral. This is a great recruiting ground for men; mostly *Affranchis* that are ex-slaves who went into debt to loan sharks when buying their freedom or paying the manumission taxes. They relish the thought of guaranteed compensation and an advance to pay those debts." Jean responded.

"We also have a good amount of G*ens de Couleur libres* in the ranks, who are more experienced in the matters of armament."

"So, how many in all Captain?" asked d'Estaing.

"I currently have 800 organized into a regiment called the *Chasseurs-Volontaires de Saint-Domingue.* They are in training now and I expect that by month's end when we are ready to sail, they will be an elite fighting force—enough to fill two or three of your frigates when combined with your contingent of 40 from Guadeloupe and Martinique." Jean concluded.

"That is perfect!" shouted the Admiral in true excitement. "With your *Chasseurs*, as you call them, and the additional 3,000 French regulars aboard the other ships, we will make for a substantial fighting force."

"Captain Bayard, I want to transfer the soldiers from Guadeloupe and Martinique under your command to conclude their training and be part of your *Chasseurs*—a name I like very much by the way. It depicts action, the hunting, and the chasing of the enemy. Good choice! I want you to lead these men into battle in America."

Jean was stunned. He knew his next words would require tact.

"But Admiral, my orders were only to assemble and train the *Chasseurs*, not lead them. I was under the impression that another officer would assume command?"

"Nonsense! You have recruited, trained, and led this regiment since the beginning. It is your creation and the men follow you" retorted d'Estaing.

"With all due respect Admiral, how could you possibly possess such confidence in me, having just arrived in St. Domingue?" queried Jean. "You've not any knowledge of my military capabilities to bestow upon me such a heavy responsibility." he continued, carefully.

"Captain Bayard, do you honestly think me that reckless as to assign you to lead this regiment without knowing your abilities? Could I be Admiral of this expedition by being that careless? Do you not think that I had you thoroughly watched and analyzed for the past few weeks by persons whom I implicitly trust?"

He picked up the leg of his Capon and loudly sucked the remaining meat from the bones. "Forgive me officers for being so informal, but this fowl is so succulent that none of it should be wasted. Feel free to do the same." he offered.

Jean was shocked by this revelation which he had never once suspected. He looked over to Captain de Croy, who simply shrugged his shoulders, picked a wing off his plate, and smiled as he enjoyed its taste.

Jean remained frozen at the thought that he'd been spied on, and quickly searched his memory for any missteps he may have committed. Noting his alarm, d'Estaing chimed in once again.

"Let me tell you what I have learned Captain Bayard: You are firm in your discipline but extremely fair. Your men follow you because they trust you and know you will not act outside of their best interests. You meticulously manage your regiment so provisions are plentiful, and your charges eat well and are well-equipped. Most of all, you lead from the front so your men know who to follow."

Another brief pause to indulge in the delicacies on his plate.

"I could go on about your virtues, but I prefer not to swell your head too much!" he laughed.

"You are too kind, Admiral, and I appreciate your compliments. However, there is another reason I must decline your kind offer." ventured Jean.

"My commission ends in two months and I am in the preparations of expanding a new business enterprise here in St. Domingue."

"Is that so?" inquired d'Estaing. "I thought you to be in the French military as a career officer?"

"No, Admiral. I am not a military man for life. My father wished for me to run our family plantation in Jérémie, but as much as I like to drink coffee, the planter's life is a little slow-paced for me. I have moved my family here to Cap-Français to expand our import and export business with my wife Marie."

"Tell me more about this enterprise Captain." the Admiral commanded.

Jean explained how he and his wife had arranged for the accumulation of coffee, sugar, and indigo stocks from farming cooperatives throughout the island; how they would transport them overland to the ports, navigate them to their warehouses at Cap-Français for loading onto freight carriers, and finally ship the goods to France. Then, the return importation of essential and French luxury goods for the island secured better round-trip rates.

The Captain smartly neglected to include his contraband trading with other countries—especially the American colonies— as this was illegal under the French system called the *Exclusif*— which required St. Domingue to sell 100% of her exports exclusively to France, while purchasing 100% of her imports from the country as well.

The *Exclusif* meant prices for imports and exports were extraordinarily favorable to the crown and French merchants, and in no way competitive with international markets.

"A-ha!" exclaimed the Admiral, banging the table and causing the dishes to clang in a way he would never dare back in France. "This is why it must be you! Your skills in procurement cannot be duplicated, and this is what we need when fighting a war in a foreign land."

"Respectfully, Admiral…" began Jean.

"The matter is settled, Captain. You are being short-sighted. When the war is over with the British and the Americans are our trading partners, you will benefit greatly from this expedition. This is a once-in-a-lifetime, albeit temporarily inconvenient, opportunity for you Captain Bayard!"

Capitan De Croy was nodding his head in agreement with the Admiral when Jean once more looked to him for support.

"Do not give me your answer tonight," d'Estaing went on. "You will contemplate your future and provide me with your response in three days' time. What does our chef have for dessert after such a magnificent meal?"

The servers smiled and hastily left the room to fetch more delightful treats.

Jean was taken with the excitement of a military venture such as this, and leading hundreds of his men into battle. However, he was torn by equal excitement for business plans in St. Domingue, and the prospect of enjoying life with Marie and their 4-year-old son Jean Junior in their new home in the bustling community of Cap-Français.

What was he to do? It was all good, but all converging at once!

It was a Thursday evening and the next morning would bring him home. While he slept at the barracks during the week, every Friday he'd spend the weekend with Marie and Junior. He'd always confided in Marie and sought counsel from her. She was his rock and business and life partner since they'd met 8 years prior. Despite the Admiral's directive, he would make no decision until seeking her input.

Two

JEAN & MARIE

Jérémie
June 1771

Jean met Marie when he was twenty-one and she was twenty, in Jérémie, on the southern peninsula of St. Domingue. Established early in the 18th century as Trou Jérémie, the city became an important trading port and produce market for logwood, cacao, hides, coffee, mangoes, bananas, and sugarcane obtained from the fertile countryside.

In 1760, with a population of around 10,000, Jérémie was named the capital of the Grand Anse Department. Relatively isolated, the region is a beautiful area with lovely beaches. The city is divided between the Basse Ville *Downtown*—the commercial center—and Haute Ville *Uptown*, the residential section lined with quaint cottages.

Jean returned from France in June of 1771 to work the plantation started by his grandfather, Philippe Bayard, who immigrated from Lille in the North of France back in 1710. Jean's grandmother, Marie Debreuse, was the daughter of semi-wealthy Mulatto parents who quickly took a liking to her handsome young White Frenchman, as this assured a step up in their social status within the strict caste system.

The elder Debreuse's financed a new plantation for the couple, and in 1725 Jean's father, Jean-Philippe, was born. He grew up to eventually take over management of the plantation, learning and perfecting the farming of coffee. Jean-Philippe married Jeanne Guillemette-Bachelier, of equal age, and also Mulatto. Jean Baptiste Hyppolite was firstborn to the 25-year-old couple in 1750 before being followed by the additions of his brothers Andre in 1754, Julien in 1764, and Rene in 1768.

Jean was home to discover whether farming life suited him, but after a short period of time, it was clear it did not. This frustrated his father Jean-Philippe to no end. He'd long had designs on his son taking over the plantation but was now in a bind. His master plan to retire at the still spritely age of 50 and travel Europe with his loving and passionate wife Jeanne, was in serious jeopardy. They both loved the island so much, but neither had ever ventured from it before.

Jean-Phillippe was excited to put his plan in place the moment his eldest son arrived home. His son, still young at age twenty-one had his father's confidence that four or five years of training under his father would adequately prepare Jean to take over. All that was gone now.

Andre was seventeen and had left for Paris to begin his own University studies. In any case, he was an adventurer not cut out for life on the plantation. His other two sons—six-year-old Julien and three-year-old Rene—would take nearly twenty years to mature enough. Jean-Philippe would be nearing seventy; much too old for the long sea journey.

Should he sell the plantation? Was he willing to entrust it to someone outside the family for the many years necessary for his young sons to mature? Would Julien and Rene even want to follow in his footsteps, or present further disappointment like Jean had?

Still reeling from these important, unanswered questions, Jean shocked his father once more by announcing his intent to join the French Army in St. Domingue!

Jean-Philippe wondered where he had gone wrong. He was confused, disgusted, and outraged at this news. Jean had a successful plantation in Jérémie awaiting him with 22 slaves and three *Gens de Couleur* overseers. His life was meant to be that of a gentleman planter influential in the local politics of the city. What could military service possibly bring him over any of this?

"This is my repayment for sending my son to that cerebral cesspool of *Louis-le-Grand* University in Paris!" Jean-Philippe bemoaned to himself. "They have totally corrupted him. Frigging Parisians! Romantics, all! I never attended a University and have more smarts than these snobs ever will."

"Why are you joining the French Army Jean?" implored the father to his son. "What possible interest do you have in the military? What success can it bring you?"

"Papa, the world is changing rapidly. There is talk that within a few years, the American colonies will be free from British rule. They say they will fight for their independence" answered the son.

"So why is that any of your business Jean?" demanded the father. "You're French!"

"In Paris, there is much talk about support for the American movement, Papa. The British are our enemies and if conflict begins in the American colonies, France will surely be a player!" Jean's passion was now beginning to show.

"And what are your plans for this conflict, my son?"

"To fight on behalf of France, possibly for America, Papa."

The debate on the role France would eventually play in an armed conflict with England was a continuous and contentious topic of conversation, discussion, frustration, and impassioned arguments between father and son during Jean's visit. The two began to drift apart requiring his wife, Jean-Baptiste's mother Jeanne, to serve as a desperate mediator.

She balanced consoling her son with defending his father's stubbornness, pointing out that he was failing to see Jean-Philippe's perspective.

She simultaneously begged her husband for patience and understanding—to recognize that his son was pursuing a cause he believed in, and abandoning the life his father had planned for him was his own choice to make.

Though these conversations continued, throughout the latter

half of 1771 Jean aided his father in special projects around the plantation; a new irrigation system for the crops, expanded quarters for eight more slaves, repair of the barn, and so forth, putting to good use the engineering degree he had obtained.

It was during this time Jean met Marie Jasmine, the daughter of Jérémie Provisions Company owner, Ralph Jasmine. The bustling provisions house in the center of town sold anything one desired—from ball gowns to construction materials, and everything in-between.

It was a successful business begun by Ralph's father, Pierre Jasmine. A French merchant from St. Barthelemy, Pierre earned a reputation during the latter part of the seventeenth century for being a friendly trading partner of famed pirate Daniel Montbars, or "Montbars the Exterminator."

The pirate had a deep hatred of the Spanish, raiding only these vessels. This hatred was derived from the Spanish sailors who captured and executed his beloved uncle in front of him after a battle with two Spanish warships near Santo Domingo. Montbars was known for killing all Spaniards after capture while freeing non-Spanish prisoners in a gentlemanly fashion; even presenting gifts from the spoils on their release.

Pierre had a trusted, exclusive, and financially lucrative arrangement with his pirate friend. After seizing his Spanish conquests, Montbars would sail into *Anse du Gouverneur* or Grand Saline on Saint Barthelemy, a small island off St. Martin. It was here Pierre's men would quickly dismantle the ships for parts, lumber, steel, and anything that could be harvested and sold along with her cargo.

Born to a wealthy family in France, Montbars was well-educated and raised as a gentleman, making the two quite fond of each other. They would spend countless days in deep conversation on politics and women while drinking rum and coconut water. Pierre listened intently to the pirate's exploits and would regale his young granddaughter with his stories. In a way, Pierre was jealous of his friend's freewheeling privateer life.

After Montbars' death in 1707, it was reported that the pirate and his crew had buried their fortune near Grande Saline—though they all died in battle before they could retrieve it. According to local rumors, Pierre found and unearthed the fortune, allowing him to begin a new life and open his business in St. Domingue.

Pierre chose Jérémie not only for the area's natural beauty but because it was an easy sail for the Guadeloupe trade route. With his connections throughout the islands, Pierre could obtain goods—especially new arrivals from France—weeks earlier than other ships bound for the French West Indies. His ingenious strategy relied on small inter-island schooners that were loaded with the prized merchandise, much of it contraband, free of import taxes and diverted to Jérémie to beat out competing merchants. It proved a lucrative venture, indeed.

Being experienced in the business, Pierre's son Ralph took over the scheme after his father's death.

Marie and her older brother Gustav eventually joined their father to work the bustling store from morning until nightfall. Marie loved the fast-paced setting and relished negotiating with customers with the complete trust and confidence of her father and brother. Over a short period of time, she'd honed her business acumen immensely.

During his many visits for provisions and construction supplies, Jean would catch a glimpse of Marie in her element. She was stunning—with long, dark auburn hair which fell over her broad shoulders and ended in the center of her back. Her brow was wide and eyes slightly slanted, courtesy of her French Normandy ancestry. She was slender, with sizable and pert breasts which seemed to point left and right—or East and West as Jean envisioned. Though not tall, her legs were lengthy, and Jean much enjoyed watching her perfectly-rounded derriere as she ascended the stairs to the storage room where the more expensive goods were kept. He was in awe every time he saw her.

Of course, Jean normally dealt with Gustav. The two enjoyed

their joking and haggling, though always arriving at a fair price for both parties. However, on one occasion in the sweltering heat of August, Gustav was not on the property. Instead, Marie came to greet him.

"Monsieur Bayard, how can I help you?" she asked, approaching him from his rear before he'd had a chance to notice her. "Construction? Food? Clothing? What is your pleasure today?"

Jean was caught by surprise and quickly spun around towards her voice, nearly bumping into Marie as their faces ended just inches apart.

His head began to spin instantly from the combined sweet scent of her perfume and perspiration, which produced an intoxicating aroma so divine he could not form a response to her query.

As he glanced away from her face, he could not stop his eyes from venturing toward her chest no matter how he commanded them away. He noticed her sweat had formed crystal droplets freckled upon her neck and bosom. He'd nearly lost all control before quickly turning his gaze back to hers—just in time to see her mouth tense in disgust at his leering.

"Do women intimidate you Monsieur Bayard or do you simply have no self-control when you see one?" she stated coarsely.

Her hair was wet and glistened shiny ebony and her now furrowed brow filled with moisture from the unrelenting August heat.

Jean was caught off guard—a wholly unfamiliar situation. "I uhh, I was, um, I…"

"For a man destined to take over his father's plantation and who I understand earned an education from the best University in Paris, you certainly have a limited vocabulary Monsieur Bayard" she continued, looking around at other employees. "Giles, come here and take care of this customer. He requires a little more time and attention than I have to give. Good day, Monsieur Bayard."

Marie briskly walked away, calling over to another customer;

"Monsieur Gagnon, please forgive me for making you wait so long. We are a little shorthanded today."

Jean was shaken back to reality to Giles repeating "Monsieur Bayard, how can I help you? Monsieur Bayard. Monsieur Bayard, are you alright?" as Jean kept his eyes on Marie, with her long brown dress down to her ankles exposing rugged men's work boots as she walked.

"Excuse me Giles, my apologies. It must be the heat" responded Jean as he took the kerchief from around his neck and wiped his face and brow. "Let me give you my order."

"Can I get you something to drink?" offered Giles.

"No, that's fine. Please, let's continue."

Feeling a total fool, Jean was apprehensive to return several weeks later for fear he would repeat his juvenile behavior in front of Marie. Luckily, he found Gustav waiting, though his wide grin belied his motives.

"Jean, you really made an impression on my sister," he said, barely containing his laughter. "She was upset with me for leaving the day you were here, though you made for quite the comical conversation over dinner that night!"

"You've got to be kidding me," sighed Jean. A knot formed in his stomach and instantly began to ache. "What did she say?"

"That if all Parisians acted like jack-asses like you, it would certainly be a horrible place to visit!" roared Gustav with a jovial laugh.

"Ouch," responded Jean. "I was a mess that day. I don't know if you realize this, but your sister is not like other girls—or women I should say"

"Yes, she's a pain in the ass—MY ass! I swear her mouth is like a grenade in a crowded room and her patience level is non-existent" Gustav admitted. "That's probably what got to her. You simply took too long to order."

Jean nodded, not daring to confess to his friend Marie's intoxicating presence, nor his inability to avoid staring at her round derrière; beautiful breasts; or captivating eyes; or admire her entire being.

"Maybe I should apologize, Gustav?"

"I don't see the need, but if you insist, we will be at *Le Phare* this evening for an engagement party. Why don't you come after dinner? I will buy you a brandy and sing your praises as a customer so I can put our drinks on my father's business tab" quipped Gustav.

"Why not?" replied Jean. "After all, it is Saturday night. I'll see you around eight."

"Sounds good. And if you're a good boy, I'll make sure my sister is nice to you and doesn't have you thrown out of the place. She knows the entire staff!"

"Please." Jean thought to himself. "I can't stand another round of humiliation like the last time."

That evening, Jean saddled up Whiskey, his thoroughbred, and directed him toward downtown Jérémie at a fast pace. It was nearly eight by the time he arrived, and the restaurant *La Phare* was in full swing. As he entered, he could already hear Gustav's laughing voice over the crowded bar and scratch band. He quickly gestured to Jean to join the engagement party.

"Attention everyone! This is my friend and a customer who I take merciless advantage of, Monsieur Jean-Baptiste Bayard. Jean, this is the beautiful Marguerite and her fiancé George. They just got engaged today!"

Bowing his head in respect, Jean stated with formality, "Please accept my congratulations. It is my honor to meet you."

"Thank you, Jean," replied George as Marguerite nodded with a broad wide smile showcasing her beautiful White teeth.

George lifted a carafe and poured Jean a glass of a ruby-red substance.

"Have a drink of this fabulous Bordeaux."

Jean lifted his glass, but as he turned to make a toast, he nearly spilled the wine on the person seated next to him. He recovered just in time to recognize the near-victim as none other than Marie. All eyes awaited his words of wisdom, but Jean found himself once again intoxicated. He stood paralyzed, unable to utter a single word.

Marie looked upon him oddly. "Has the cat gone off with your tongue again Monsieur Bayard?" she asked in an amusing tone.

Her hair was an Auburn sheen, minus the sweat of the August sun from the other week. Her complexion was delicate and smooth and her red lips resembled a delicious cherry. Her dress hugged the curves of her body, naturally sculpted by the hard work at the provisions store.

"Give me that!" Marie commanded as she stood up and grabbed the glass from his hand. "You're making a fool of yourself—again."

She raised the drink and spoke to the group: "To my best friend Marguerite and her handsome choice of a future husband, George! I know her well and can attest to her sheer joy for the next chapter of her life together with her husband. Let us toast their engagement with our love and affection!"

The crowd joined in a cheer and lifted their glasses in salute.

As she took a swig of the fine wine before handing it back to Jean, saying "You're welcome for my saving your ugly moment in the limelight."

With that, she began to make her way to another group in the corner of the room.

"Now wait a minute. You don't get to do that!" he exclaimed as he followed her.

Marie spun around "Do what?"

"That!" Jean said. His mind had still not fully returned.

"What?" she asked, pointedly.

"What you are doing…right now." he sputtered.

"And what is that?"

"This!" he said.

"What?" she asked, a sly smile tugging at the corner of her lips.

He recognized she was toying with him, and undoubtedly had the upper hand—a fact not lost on Marie either. She was powerful in her presence and knew what it was doing to him. "What is it, Monsieur Bayard?"

"Call me Jean."

She stared deeply into his eyes. Her voice softened.

"Alright, Jean. What is it that I am doing to you?"

He felt she saw through his soul as he was held hostage by her presence. He needed to break away but could not. He desperately searched for a way to change the course of this encounter. Nothing in his past dealings with girls in Paris had prepared him for this woman. Her poise and confidence were beyond any he'd ever experienced.

After what felt like an eternity, he mustered all of his courage to ask, "Can we start completely over Miss Jasmine?"

Without skipping a beat, she responded "Hello, my name is Marie. Marie Jasmine. And yours?"

"Jean-Baptiste Bayard. But please call me Jean."

"Alright Jean and you may call me Marie."

"May I offer you a glass of wine or brandy, Marie?"

"Most definitely, Jean. Shall we take a seat at the bar?"

Without waiting for his response, Marie turned and walked towards the bar as Jean followed.

Her dress exposed her tanned skin to her mid back, and Jean admired her wide uncovered shoulders. He carefully placed his hand on her naked skin as a guide while they walked.

The warmth of Jean's hand instantaneously shot a sensual shock through Marie's entire body. She had never felt anything like it and it startled her. She looked back, catching and locking his eyes with hers. His palm felt like it had penetrated her skin, going deep inside, finding her heart and holding it tight. Their eye contact deepened.

She stopped.

"What are you doing?" Marie asked in a soft and sensuous voice.

"The same thing you do to me," he dared. Surely this man had to know he was venturing into dangerous territory.

"Why are you doing this to me?" she asked him.

"What?" he coyly responded.

"That."

"And what is that?" Jean retorted. Marie found herself trapped in the same game of words she'd sprung on him only moments ago.

Marie made a split decision—rash even; and certainly out of character. Egging him on, she ventured: "This."

"We are doing it to each other," Jean answered. "And for me, I cannot break the trance you put on me. Are you somehow saying that you feel this too?" It appeared her gamble was met with one of his own.

"I don't know what this is," she replied honestly.

"Shall we try to find out, together?" he offered.

Marie suddenly realized they'd made it to the bar. Finding two seats together, they embarked on a conversation lasting for hours, discussing any and everything and only pausing when they noticed the bar was shuttering for the night and they were the only souls left.

In typical fashion, Gustav had taken the carriage, which was to be her ride home. He'd once again abandoned her, no doubt to pick up a girl for a sexual toss and leave Marie to fend for herself. Women couldn't resist her brother and he always responded in kind.

"Well, it has been an interesting evening Monsieur Bayard, or shall I say, Jean," she said. "I better be getting home as it's late."

"Please allow me to escort you, Marie. It is far too late for you to be walking the streets alone." implored Jean.

"It is only two blocks away. Our residence is in the back part of the business compound" she explained.

"Well then, would you like some company for the walk?"

Marie knew he would never let her walk alone, but was nonetheless providing her the first right of refusal.

"So Jean, you *are* a gentleman after all," she said. "Let us take our leave."

Jean untied his horse Whiskey, who was patiently waiting for him. Marie felt bad that the magnificent creature had been left outside for so long, though he dutifully trailed behind Jean at the full length of his bridle.

The horse's hooves made a soothing clip-clop which slightly echoed under the moonlit sky. They walked in silence, both talked out but also enjoying the quiet of the night and the closeness of each other's company.

They arrived at a small door built into the huge wooden gate of the compound, and Marie took a skeleton key out of her purse.

"Thank you for a wonderful evening," she said with sincerity. "I truly misjudged the sort of person you are Jean."

Before he could respond, they both moved their lips in unison to lock onto the others. A soft kiss at first launched into a passionate, primal, and deep exchange of desire and need until they both pulled back to stop the trance of mutual emotions. Marie was shocked by her impulse yet had seemingly lost her self-control momentarily.

Upon pulling away, she stared at him, only to be met with the same sense of surprise and embarrassment across his face. Their arms dropped from each other's grasp. Neither made an attempt to move.

Jean found his voice first. "I don't know what this is, but I do know I want more of it. Can we do an evening together again…only the two of us?" he asked.

"Yes. I would like that a lot" Marie responded.

"Then I will be in touch. Thank you for a wonderful evening Marie. I never knew a feeling like this; the feeling I had with you tonight. Thank you for that."

She gave him her most sensuous look. It was beautiful and seductive, yet with a genuine innocence that exposed a childlike joy she'd long forgotten.

"I will see you soon Jean."

She turned and quietly disappeared into the compound, his name still on her lips.

Jean was frozen solid for what seemed ages before he was able to mount Whiskey and guide him home. The night had done little to provide any clarity for his future.

On the one hand, he had a genuine interest in the military despite the grief it brought to his father, but on the other, he somehow knew Marie was destined to be an important part of his life. There was no future without her—he was certain of it.

Lost in thought, he rode Whiskey until the cobbled street turned into a dirt road leading out of town. Suddenly, he gave the horse a slight kick as the command to run like hell. Jean felt the horse's strides and both man and beast synchronized their rhythm. Jean felt the wind in his hair and heard Whiskey's mane flapping in the wind over the sound of his thumping heartbeat. He belted out a huge laugh and let loose a full, primal yell toward the heavens as both hurried home under a beautiful starry sky.

The following Monday, Jean busied himself planning the property's new drainage system, meant to irrigate a one-quarter-hectare field so more coffee crops could be planted. He broke from his project only to send a note to Marie, assigning his slave Hector to deliver it to the store.

Dear Marie,

I think it goes without saying that I am infatuated with your presence and desire for your company. In our conversation this past weekend, I sensed that you may be inclined to maybe seek the same as well? I would very much enjoy your company for dinner this Saturday evening at six o'clock If you are inclined to enjoy the same.

I will have Hector, my hand who delivered this note, return on Wednesday for a response. I so hope that both your schedule and like interests allow us to once again meet and exchange pleasantries and become more acquainted?

My heart awaits your reply.
Jean.

Though he could barely wait, there was work to be done meanwhile. Jean hired eight of the usual 100 *de jure* slaves looking for day jobs from their makeshift camp on the outskirts of town. *De jure* slaves formed a temporary workforce that local planters drew upon for project labor.

De jure slaves were those that many masters told were free to go, without executing the required formalities for various reasons. This mostly revolved around manumission taxes. If an owner had too much slave inventory or believed a slave to be unproductive, or simply felt compelled to set one or more free, manumission taxes were to be paid. As these taxes increased, it became both costly to free or keep slaves, as they needed food, clothes, and boarding. Instead, owners would equip these slaves with a pass permitting them to circulate freely.

Some *de jure* slaves did not owe money to their former masters, while others were required to remit a substantial future payment for this conditional freedom. Slaves would find work on their own, and submit a portion of their revenues owed to their master. The slaves were also responsible for raising the necessary cash for the manumission liberty tax, at which point the master would go to the authorities and file the appropriate papers for permanent freedom.

So as to not waste time with daily transportation, Jean set up two tents adjacent to the work area to house the eight *de jure* slaves. Jean also ordered food cooked for them from the main slave kitchen and brought to the camp, and supplied them with water and bunks. For the most part, the food and accommodations were far better than what the slaves were forced to pay for in the *de jure* camp, enabling them to save more money to buy their freedom and pay the manumission taxes.

The slaves were well-fed and amicable with each other. Their work was productive and they appreciated a long-term and lucrative opportunity as the project would likely last two months. The labor was hard and the sun hot, but anticipating a good meal and rest at the end of the day motivated them. Jean was similarly impressed by the daily improvement of the project and his father was complimentary as well.

Most of the slaves were Creoles born in the colony and of African Congo descent, typically 3 or 4 generations removed. They still practiced the passed-down folklore of their homeland, celebrating in song and dance. Every night, drums could be heard with cheerful melodies emanating from the Bayard plantation slaves, and the eight would often answer with drums of their own, though co-mingling was not permitted in case any of the *de jure's* carried disease.

On Wednesday, Jean sent Hector back into town for two machetes and four picks for the men; but most importantly to receive Marie's response to his invitation. His anticipation turned to delight upon Hector's return with a note scrolled simply with a large 'Yes' and signed in smaller writing with 'Marie'.

That Saturday night marked the beginning of the two seeing each other often over the following weeks. The couple relished their company and found their thoughts drifting to the other whenever apart. Long talks over lunch, dinner, picnics, and social gatherings produced spirited and enlivened conversation.

Having spent years exploring France, Jean was well-versed in all things European, particularly the roots of his ancestors in the town of Lilles in the Northern part of the country.

Marie spoke of her life in Jérémie, her family's history, their business, the customers and the thrill of the deal, and especially the colorful past and stories of her Grandfather Pierre's pirating days. She even confided her desire to own a business herself, as her father would no doubt assign Gustav responsible for all matters of the Provision house.

They knew they were in love, and both freely admitted it began the night of the engagement party. Their hearts were passionate, and while Jean was the ultimate gentleman, he longed for her at night—and she for him. Although passionate in their talk, embrace and kiss, they remained celibate.

Three

BIASSOU AND THE MARÉCHAUSSÉE

Jérémie
September 1771

Around mid-day on a Wednesday during the third week of the drainage project, Jean heard the thunder of an approaching herd of horses nearing the work area. The slaves stopped their work at the impending rumble. Within seconds, a dozen horsemen had encircled the area. Six of the eight slaves dropped their tools and froze; two began to run but were chased down by the horsemen, lassoed, and brought back to the gathering before Jean could even gather his thoughts.

He knew instantly this was the *Maréchaussée* police force. Their effective training and skilled horsemanship struck immediate fear within his workers.

The history of the *Maréchaussée* began when slave owners began violating the ordinances that required their plantations to employ a group of armed Whites proportional to their number of slaves. At the start, the proportion was 1 to 10, before being reduced to 1 to 20 as slave owners appealed the high expense. However, owners rarely followed this law, which encouraged attempts for slaves to flee their posts.

This was further exacerbated by the harsh treatment the French White planters levied on their slaves. Whippings, rape, torture, mutilation, and at times underground burial of slaves alive in locked boxes all served as potential punishments. They were even used as sport, hunted like prey, or burying them in the dirt before using their exposed heads as targets for rock throwing.

Newly imported slaves were often the victims of these harsher crimes against them as they were more likely to resist subjugation. Unlike those born into captivity and never knowing freedom, these African *Bosals*—the newly imported stock—were understandably bitter toward their new and unfamiliar predicament.

These poor souls were typically captured from villages in the Congo by warring tribes or profiteering kidnappers, sold to slave traders, and jailed in forts to await export to foreign countries on cramped vessels designed to maximize efficiency over humanity. Upon arrival they were subjected to hard labor, foreign diseases to which their bodies had no immunity, and either beaten into submission or forced to run for their lives.

Those who managed to escape retreated deep into the mountains to join the *maroon* colonies. The *Maroon* inhabitants would practice subsistence farming supplemented by occasional raids on local plantations. They also maintained active defense systems to resist planter forays to re-enslave them. These colonies of runaway slaves represented a significant problem for the St. Domingue colonial authorities during the first half of the 18th century.

As more and more slaves sought—and found—salvation, fines were instituted to punish planters for non-compliance with the armed ratio. This revenue came to represent a substantial portion of the colonial government's budget, and with their establishment in 1760, served as funding for the *Marechausee* Corps. The *Marechausee* consisted mostly of free Blacks and Mulattos, and proved extremely effective. Thus, the Corps had grown in power and influence since its creation over ten years prior.

"By whose authority do you trespass on my property?" Jean demanded in a commanding tone. "Who is in charge here?"

Clearing the bushes, three mounted Black men emerged, two flanking what appeared to be their leader on a humongous White stallion. His ebony face was large with menacing eyes to match. His physique of hard muscle—all bulging chest and huge arms—sweating through his tan *Maréchaussée* Corps Officer shirt. His two accomplices were nearly as well built, with uniforms clearly indicating their own officer status. All were armed with swords and side arms, and the two lesser carried long discipline whips. They immediately flanked Jean to his left and right side, cutting him off from the workforce.

"I am Commander Georges Biassou of the Southern Region *Marechausee*. I have signed warrants from the Colonial Authorities to search all properties for the apprehension of runaway slaves," the man shot back. "I need to see the papers of all of your workforce both here and at the main house." he concluded.

"Whose slaves have escaped?" Jean asked. "I haven't heard any local news regarding runaways."

"Two slaves belonging to the Garnier plantation are on the run" Biassou balked. "Male, first generation *Bossale* Congos."

"That does not surprise me. What does is that the Garnier's entire workforce has not fled for their lives. Their treatment of slaves is worse than that of their livestock. And that is very bad indeed"

Jean confidently retorted. "And on top of that, I hear they are sadistic and…"

"That is of no matter to me," interjected Biassou. "It only becomes my concern when these slaves escape, and I am charged with bringing them back." he continued.'

"But certainly the proper treatment of slaves would lighten the obligations of the *Marechausee,*" reasoned Jean. "We have never

needed your services because we treat our slaves like humans, not animals."

"Monsieur Bayard, you are lecturing someone who doesn't give a damn, and you are wasting my daylight. Now, get your workforce here to present their permits immediately, and then accompany me to the main house for an inventory of your slaves so I can be on my way." Biassou said forcefully.

The *Marechausee* officer to Jean's right ordered the rest of the party to escort the slaves back to their camp to inspect their papers. However, one of the eight immediately began running through the bushes in the opposite direction. The officer who had given the order nodded at one of his comrades, who galloped off in pursuit. Two other horsemen also followed.

Within seconds, the lead had caught up with the runaway, drawn his whip, and expertly wielded it at the slave. It wrapped around the poor soul's neck, throwing him down immediately and violently to the ground. Jean was certain it had snapped the man's neck.

"Obviously we have a paperwork problem with you!" yelled the officer. "I gather you are a paperless runaway." he continued.

"Wait! cried Jean. "All papers are with my head foreman slave TiLou," he explained. "He went with the others to retrieve them for you."

"Then why did this one run, Monsieur Bayard?" the *Marechausee* officer shot back.

"Perhaps it is best we ask him," responded Jean, approaching the slave. "Why did you run?" he gently inquired. The man stood still, head down, avoiding eye contact with Jean. "Speak, you lousy piece of shit!" bellowed the officer. "If not, I will have you deal with the business end of this whip!" he added.

"Give me a moment, *please*" implored Jean in a gentlemanly tone. "Let me have a word with him."

"Make it quick, as we are on a schedule and cannot wait longer than necessary" the Officer replied with a more professional voice.

Jean preferred to avoid escalating the situation with the *Marechausee,* nor did he wish to see any harm come to the petrified man in front of him. The slave's body was hard and leathered, betraying a lifetime of work under the sun. His hair was balding with strands of White. The deep lines of his face showed worry, despair, and pain, and his clothes were nothing more than a tattered collection of rags.

"What is your name?" Jean asked.

"Fatra, Monsieur Master. Fatra Regale" replied the slave.

Why would anyone name this man *Fatra*, the Creole word for garbage? wondered Jean.

"How old are you Fatra?"

"Thirty-one years next month, Monsieur Master" he replied.

Though older than he, Jean couldn't help but be taken aback by how this still young man could look so worn, beaten, and demoralized. He looked older than his own father.

"Why did you run Fatra? Why did you not go back with TiLou to retrieve your papers?"

"I do not have papers, Monsieur Master," he replied.

"Why not? TiLou assured me that all of you had proper work permits and that he had reviewed them personally," responded Jean quizzically.

"He did review them weeks ago, and they were all in order. But they were stolen from my belongings after I had forgotten them to hurry to a job Monsieur Master."

"He's lying," interrupted the *Marechausee* officer. "That is what they do when caught."

At that moment, Commander Biassou rejoined the men. He immediately addressed his junior officer.

"Reginald, report on the situation here."

"We have one without papers and the rest have gone back with the foreman to retrieve theirs, Commander," he replied.

"Monsieur Bayard, why does this *de jure* slave not have his papers on hand for inspection?" demanded Biassou.

"He claims they were stolen, Commander. He says my foreman TiLou did originally see and inspect them." Jean explained.

"This is unacceptable. Work permits must be available for inspection at all times. No more lies, slave!" His thundering orders visibly shook Fatra.

"Reginald, fetch this TiLou and bring him to me. Speak nothing of this conversation." He then addressed the other *Marechausee* officer: "Stay with your men, watch this one, and don't let him out of your sight."

"Can I offer you and your men some water, Commander?" Jean interjected, hoping to soften Biassou a bit. "It is cool water as we have it in the shade."

The ploy appeared to work. "That would be appreciated, Monsieur Bayard. May I also request some refreshment for my men and our horses?"

"Of course. Come with me."

Jean turned and headed toward the large mahogany tree on which the water was suspended in a goatskin container from the lowest branch. It was late in the afternoon and he could see that the commander was weary from his travels. He offered a gourde of water which the commander took, briefly smiled, and lifted for a long drink. His large gulps made it seem as if he had been dehydrated for days. 'Ahhhh, he said, after the long swig with much delight and a smile finally crossing his face.

Then after his final swig, he smiled more broadly, revealing straight and bright White teeth. "Thank you." he paused. "Where are you from, Monsieur Bayard? Your accent has a touch of, shall I say, nobility to it?" he chided.

"I have just returned from Paris. I was in University there for a few years. That's perhaps where I developed this bad accent," Jean smiled back.

"How fortunate for you" replied the Commander. "Have you returned for good or are you leaving for abroad once more?"

"I am here for good, though not home for long. I have been helping my family for a while, but I am no planter."

"That is regrettable. I would give anything to be in your shoes." retorted the Commander before turning to spot Reginald and TiLou approaching them "Reginald, bring this foreman to me. Where are the others?"

"With our men. They were instructed to await our return."

TiLou stepped forward and handed the Commander a pack of worn papers containing the permits of the *de jure* slaves. "Reginald, go to the main house. Find someone in charge to inventory the slaves and prove ownership," Biassou ordered.

"My father, also Monsieur Bayard, is at the main house and will assist you in gathering the necessary documentation and assigning someone to perform the inventory. Please inform him of our activity here." added Jean.

Reginald, the *Marechausee* officer, looked at the Commander waiting for a nod of confirmation to accept Jean's input. Receiving it, he turned his steed and galloped toward the main house.

Turning back to TiLou, Biassou demanded "Show me the permit for this man behind me."

"I do not have this man's papers, Commander. He claims they were stolen one day after we left to work at a different plantation." TiLou replied.

"But TiLou, you assured me all of these men had work permits!" Jean shot back.

"They do, Master. I can assure you this man has a legal permit to work as a *de jure* laborer," answered TiLou.

Biassou allowed Jean to continue the questioning out of respect to the kindness he'd extended to his parched men and their horses.

"How can this be, TiLou? I pay you extra to assure me of such things" countered Jean.

TiLou went on to explain. "This is not the first time that a slave's papers have been stolen from a camp. To try and prevent this, I require them all to remit their papers to me for safekeeping but they do not always comply. As customary, prior to the theft, I took them all to *Notaire* Bacicoupe and had him certify and register the papers in a master ledger. They are notarized in a permanent record in case of an incident such as this."

Jean was impressed by TiLou's initiative. He glanced at Biassou, who gave a neutral nod through pursed lips.

"I gather that if we visit the *Notaire*, he will collaborate this story and show us the notarized documents?" asked Jean.

"Yes, he will," replied TiLou.

"He is our family's *Notaire* as well," Jean said, turning to Biassou. "May I have a word with you in private?"

The Commander followed as Jean turned and walked slowly back to the shade of the tree. "I have a proposition for you, Commander," Jean stated matter-of-factly.

"And what is that?" inquired the Commander. "I am not one to take bribes if that is what you are offering, Monsieur Bayard."

"Not at all," Jean quickly countered. "I'd like my cooks to slaughter three chickens, procure a bushel of fresh sweet potatoes from our garden, boil some rice and beans, and prepare a feast for you and your men before continuing on your journey."

He continued: "Please make tonight's camp here on the property as it is late in the afternoon. Your men will certainly be refreshed and in appreciation of your leadership."

The Commander remained stone-faced, yet was impressed with Jean's political savvy.

"Tonight, you and I will meet with the *Notaire* to examine and verify the permits. Presuming your full satisfaction, I also invite you as my guest to *Lakay* for a feast of our own, paired with the finest rum and wine. We can return early enough for us both to be rested for tomorrow's work ahead. We will then consider this matter settled, and you can cross our plantation off your list. What say you, Commander Biassou?"

Biassou eyed Jean with a slightly suspicious eye and digested his offer. His officers would be well fed, saving on the cost of provisions. Since *Marechausee* were forbidden from accepting gifts, his men would assume the gesture pre-arranged by Biassou personally, thus solidifying their gratitude and loyalty.

More than that, he deserved a good meal himself—and the taste of rum would be a fine treat. He was pleasantly surprised with

Bayard addressing him as an equal, despite being a well-educated Mulatto from the richer planter class. He on the other hand was *Affranchi*, born into slavery and freed during his lifetime; not necessarily commanding the respect and stature now being afforded to him by a free man of color in the French West Indian caste system.

"Monsieur Bayard I accept your offer. But only to facilitate the confirmation that you are *not* employing a runaway slave. You are indeed aware of the fines associated with such an activity?"

"Yes, I am aware," replied Jean.

"Furthermore, our dinner is a purely business matter. It is in no way a gift of any kind, as this is unacceptable for officers of the *Marechausee.*"

"I would never dream of such a thing. That would be equal to a bribe, no?" Jean said, impressed with Biassou's professionalism and statement of intent as to avoid any potential repercussions. Very clever, indeed.

"Then it is done. I will inform my men and give them orders to strike camp. Is adjacent to your workers' tents acceptable?" asked Biassou.

"Yes, that is acceptable. I will retire to the main house, make preparations for your men's meals, and meet you here in one hour." Jean answered.

"Perfect. That will allow me time to update my journal and wash up. I would not wish for this officer to embarrass you and the *Marechausee* Corps with soiled clothes and an odorous scent this evening." he laughed.

Jean mounted Whiskey for the ride to the main house, and though he couldn't help but think what a hassle this all was, he was also grateful as it could have gone much worse. He decided to give the slaves the afternoon off and allow them to indulge in the special dinner as well. A couple extra chickens was a small price to pay for loyalty and continued dedication to their work.

Upon arriving at the main house, Jean found his father fuming at the disruption the incident had caused. The *Marechausee* had forced a work stoppage, tossed the slave quarters for runaways, and now he was expected to reward this intrusion with a feast?

"Jean, what are you thinking?" the elder Bayard bellowed.

"Papa, it could have been worse," Jean explained hastily. "No matter what, they would have inventoried all of our slaves as they are doing so on every plantation. I have however struck a fledgling relationship with their Commander, which I intend to solidify this evening to avoid any further incursions on our property."

"What is the name of this Commander?"

"Georges Biassou. In our brief interaction, I am already quite impressed with his professionalism."

"Never heard of him." replied the father.

"I'm escorting him to the *Notaire* now to clear this matter up before treating him to dinner. There, I will see whether we can attain common ground for the future." Jean reasoned.

Jean-Phillippe studied his son for a moment before breaking into an appreciative smile. "You are a politician after all! I told you that you'd have a bright future here in Jérémie, my son."

"Papa, we have been through this already." sighed Jean.

"Ah, but you cannot blame your father's love and wanting what is best for his son," chided Jean-Phillippe, knowing this particular battle was all but over.

"Yes, Papa," said Jean as he left the room.

He was suddenly struck by the realization of how much his father cared for him and only kept his best interests at heart. He felt a twinge of shame over his steadfast resistance and the tense arguments it had spawned during his time here. Perhaps he hadn't fully considered his father's intentions and feelings.

Walking through the family home, his thoughts brought him to pause and admire its regal beauty. The thick red tile floors contrasted brilliantly with the White-washed interior walls. Dark polished Mahogany beams accented the baseboards, ceiling coves, and each door frame. The enormous windows were large enough to walk through, welcoming in the sunlight and breeze. Lanterns weren't often necessary until the early evening.

The lower level consisted of the formal dining room, which could sit twelve; a sitting room, the living room, the library, Papa's study, and Mama's business office—all connected by a huge foyer. The kitchen was in a separate structure behind the house. A twelve-foot covered porch wrapped around the exterior, keeping the sun from entering the home directly, and connecting all three wings.

A wide mahogany staircase sat just inside the front entrance, curving to the right and ascending to the second floor and living quarters. The double-sized master bedroom was separated from the upstairs sitting room and the remaining bedrooms by a large hallway. More dark, polished mahogany served as flooring throughout.

Jean headed toward the office to inform his mother of the day's activities, the promised dinner, and his evening whereabouts. The two shared an understanding that she always remained aware of his comings and goings.

"You are too kind, Jean." she counseled upon hearing of his handling of the situation and promise of dinner. "I hope it brings its rewards."

Jean then hurried to wash off and put on a casual evening suit. Making his way down to the stables he discovered Jacques had Cocktail saddled for the ride to Jérémie, providing Whiskey a needed night off. The beautiful Arabian Mare's jet-Black mane reflected the rising moonlight. She was fast and steady; the perfect mount when speed and agility were necessary. No sooner had Jean climbed into the saddle that Cocktail's legs began to move in anticipation of one of her beloved runs. Jean gripped her reins tightly for control.

The two galloped back to the *Marechausee*'s makeshift camp, finding Commander Biassou addressing his troops and charting out the next day's work. Jean was again fascinated by Biassou's leadership and stature. The Commander was impressively dressed in a pressed uniform and high shiny boots, which Jean could not fathom how he'd accomplished in the field. His men were attentive and engaged as he laid out his instructions. He then addressed one of his officers:

"Reginald, you will hand out guard duty and morning assignments. We embark at dawn."

Reginald immediately began calling each soldier by name, handing out two-hour guard shifts, assigning breakfast preparations, and delegating which would break down camp in the morning.

Biassou turned to approach Jean on his White stallion. The huge horse startled the smaller Cocktail.

"Do not worry, my beautiful Black beast" said Biassou. "He is a lover, not a fighter."

"What's his name, Commander?"

"Tabou" he responded.

"Are you and Tabou ready to depart?"

"Yes, let's go!"

The Commander gave his steed a hard backside whip. The magnificent stallion jumped several feet, and darted off, leaving Jean and Cocktail in a cloud of dust. Irritated at being held back, Cocktail snorted her protest and jostled impatiently from side to side. With only a second's hesitation, Jean commanded her forward at full sprint.

Cocktail caught up with Tabou in no time, and all four found themselves running full speed down the dirt road. They continued for a full mile until Biassou pulled back the reigns, acknowledging that they could not outrun Jean and Cocktail. Jean took the opportunity to point out interesting aspects of the land, which plantations were located where, and who was suspected of abusing their slaves.

It was nearly five when they reached the offices of *Notaire* Bacicoupe and dismounted. The staff was readying for closure and shuttering the windows.

"I am here to see *Notaire* Bacicoupe," Jean informed the young, pretty Mulatto girl behind the front desk.

"I am sorry, Monsieur?" she inquired

"Jean-Baptiste Bayard."

"Monsieur Bayard, *Notaire* Bacicoupe does not take appointments after four pm. May I schedule you for tomorrow morning?"

"Madame, we cannot wait until morning. I ask that you inform Notaire Bacicoupe that Jean-Baptiste Bayard from Plantation Bayard is here with urgent business." Jean replied, striking a practiced balance between decorum and insistence.

"Please wait here, Monsieur Bayard," she said, turning toward the hallways behind her.

Soon, a short man in a dark business suit appeared walking ahead of her toward them.

"Jean, is that truly you who has come back to St. Domingue all grown up?" *Notaire* Bacicoupe announced, much to Jean's embarrassment in front of the Commander.

"Yes Monsieur Bacicoupe. It is me. Allow me to introduce you to Commander Biassou of the *Marechausee*." Jean replied quickly—eager to move past the awkward reunion.

"It is my pleasure to meet you, Commander. To what do I owe the pleasure of this, as I'm told, urgent matter?"

"You inspected, verified, and notarized permits for several slaves a few months ago" stated the Commander, curtly. "I need to verify these and take inventory of the names on those documents."

"Josette, please bring me my journal ledger," Bacicoupe asked of his assistant, before turning back to the two men. "What is the name of the party who requested verification of the permits, and do you have an approximate date?"

"The name is TiLou" answered Jean. "Probably within the past six months.I trust it should not be too difficult to find?"

"Correct—quite easy actually, which is a blessing for me. My wife does not tolerate my arriving late for supper, young Bayard." the *Notiare* replied.

Josette had returned with the ledger at this point, and Bacicoupe was already expertly flipping through its records.

"Here it is! April 14 at nine am. He must have been here waiting for us to open."

Bacicoupe went on. "He brought documents for eight slaves,

all with legal working permits to seek employment apart from their original owners. Please review the list of names and expiration dates quickly so I can depart for home."

Jean's eyes lit up as he perused the ledger. "Commander, look—here is the missing name: *Fatra Regale*. He has a permit to work expiring in December of 1795."

"Good. I consider this business concluded. Let's be on then." Biassou conceded. "Monsieur *Notaire*, I thank you and bid you farewell."

"Thank you *Notaire* Bacicoupe," Jean added. "And I apologize for the inconvenience. Also to you Josette. Thank you for being so efficient and organized."

Bacicoupe and Josette smiled in reply.

"*Au revoir*, Jean. My fond regards to your fine parents!" ended the *Notaire*.

The two men exited the office and headed for their horses. "Restaurant *Lakay* is two blocks over." stated Jean, pleased with how well their excursion was going.

"Indeed. I have dined there before. Excellent food." answered Biassou.

The dinner rush had not yet begun, and the two found themselves immediately seated upon their arrival. Two glasses of rum were delivered rapidly, and a pretty slave girl in clean peasant clothes no older than sixteen recited the menu: a solid selection of fresh fish, lobster, lean fried pork griot, and chicken; all served with fried or boiled plantains, White rice, and beans in a sauce.

Biassou smiled broadly, revealing those dazzling White teeth. "You are a class act, Monsieur Bayard. You know the way to a *Marechausee* officer's heart: food!"

The Commander took a swing of rum and studied the young waitress.

"What is your name, Mademoiselle?"

"Labelle, Sir" she answered.

"Well Labelle, I will have both the fish and lobster with the trimmings of fried plantains, rice, and beans," he said.

"And I will have the griot, fried plantains, rice, and beans,

Labelle. If you don't mind, bring me a little of that chicken sauce also, and of course, some Pikliz on the side," added Jean

"*Bien Sur*" replied Labelle as she sped off to have the food prepared.

Jean turned to Biassou. "Commander, please just call me Jean. I consider us nearly friends at this point."

"If I were to indulge my imagination, I would think you are playing politics with me, my new friend Jean," the Commander slyly retorted.

"What makes you think I'm not?" Jean countered, taking a drink of his own before holding up his glass toward Biassou's.

"To God, King, and Jérémie." toasted Biassou. "And you may call me Georges, except in public and only when we are alone."

"I will drink to that," replied Jean. He took another sip of rum, enjoying the warmth it brought through his body. "So, where do you go from here, Georges?"

"West to Dame-Marie and Anse d'Hainault, then Southeast to Port-Salut and Les Cayes. Of course, after we have performed our duties at all the plantations in and around Jérémie," Biassou said.

"How long will that take you? To get all the way to Les Cayes?" inquired Jean.

"Four, maybe five weeks by the time we inspect all of the properties," Biassou replied.

The rum beginning to loosen the Commander's polished exterior, he went on.

"It's a pain in the ass when these slaves run away. By the time we catch them—if we do—they are in bad shape, and one shan't imagine what punishments await them on their return to their owners."

The aroma from the wood fire caught in their nostrils, intensifying their anticipation of the meal. Their conversation flowed easily; Biassou pontificated upon the affairs of St. Domingue, and related stories of incursions into small villages on the Spanish side of the island.

Jean told him of France, which Biassou found most interesting, and the idiosyncrasies of the Parisian residents contrasted with his preference for those born and bred outside of Paris and throughout France's provinces.

"How old are you Georges, if you don't mind?" asked Jean at one point, curious to see whether his wager of late thirties was accurate.

"Just turned thirty this past January," Biassou responded with no hesitation.

"You look rather mature for your age, Georges," Jean stated carefully.

"Bondage will do that to you. Even though, I had it relatively easy compared to others."

"You are an *Afranchi*?" asked an incredulous Jean. "You were born a slave?"

"Yes. Plantation Dupont in *Limonade*. A third-generation Creole slave—and lucky to have had a benevolent master." responded Biassou in a flippant tone. He had told this story many times before. "I owe my freedom to the wisdom of my Grandfather and father."

"Tell me more," pushed Jean

"My Grandfather's father was brought to this island after being captured by a rival tribe in the Congo. They sold him to Portuguese slave traders who shipped him here. Master Dupont's Grandfather purchased him and he worked the sugar fields. However, he was quite skilled at making things back in the Congo and soon graduated to perform maintenance on the equipment. Gradually he moved away from assignments in the sugar fields and life became less laborious. He and his wife had three children, one being my Grandfather."

Jean took a sip of rum but kept his eyes trained on Biassou, enraptured by his story.

"Upon the senior Dupont's death, the plantation passed to his son, also Master Dupont, after his father. Master Dupont was lonely after divorcing his wife, who sailed back to France with their two young sons.

He was a kind man to his slaves. He would visit our quarters and enjoy our folklore music. He even began to take meals with us and we welcomed him and became more and more comfortable together, treating him almost as family. The plantation overseers followed suit, becoming more gentle; and production went up, and we were happier.

Master Dupont's children would visit from France during the summer months—brats the both of them. Their treatment of the workers was degrading, which troubled the old man terribly. They argued constantly over it. He knew his two sons only cared to inherit and sell the plantation, slaves, and livestock upon his death.

When Master Dupont took ill, he drew up a will calling for the freedom of all 39 slaves, as well as the sale of the plantation—with the proceeds going towards the manumission taxes. He also bequeathed to each slave an amount equal to their market value as a gift toward their new life. The balance of the remaining funds was divided in two and split evenly between his two sons and the church. The sons were pissed" Biassou finished, laughing.

"What was it like, Georges? Did you have contempt for your Master? I often wonder whether our slaves have contempt for me." asked Jean with sincerity.

"Why would I have contempt for Master Dupont?" asked Biassou back. "He was not the reason behind mine or my ancestors' bondage. That contempt is kept for my African brothers in the Congo who sold my family into slavery—*that* is who I have contempt for!" the Commander's voice rose with emotion before he could regain his composure.

"Master Dupont's father regarded slavery as a simple business transaction. If my family had not been sold to him, would I be enjoying my good fortune today? Or would I still be owned by an abusive Master? This is all fate, Jean."

Arriving to break the tension, Labelle delivered plates of delicious-smelling hot food. Biassou's first plate displayed a lightly-battered whole Red Snapper, grilled and served in a tomato and onion sauce. His second contained a massive one-pound lobster; its cavity was filled with butter and bread stuffing, grilled over an open fire for a charcoal flavor, and accompanied by melted butter in a side bowl.

Jean relished his griot—six large chunks of tender fried pork meat accompanied by a bowl of hot onions and served aside hot peppers marinated in vinegar called Pikliz.

Labelle then placed steaming hot bowls of rice and kidney bean sauce, as well as the chicken sauce next to Jean as he'd requested.

"Ah, Jean. Tonight I dine better than the King of France! What a grand idea you proposed." Biassou praised, immediately returning to a more genial demeanor.

"Where are you going to put all of that food, Georges?" teased Jean.

"Watch and find out!" Biassou replied before taking a large bite of fresh bright pink snapper.

Madeline, the wife of *Lakay's* owner, appeared as they began to eat.

"Is everything to your liking, Gentlemen?"

"Madeline, you have outdone yourself once again" replied Biassou. "I came on the invitation of my new friend, Monsieur Bayard, and I am taking full advantage of his kindness by eating two of your most delicious meals."

Madeline chuckled. "Don't feel bad, Monsieur Bayard. Whether he or anyone else is paying, the Commander eats like a bottomless pit every time he dines here. Allow me to provide you each another round of rum, or perhaps some wine, on the house. What is your pleasure?"

"Thank you, Madeline, that is very kind. A glass of your red wine please, and for you Geor—I mean, Commander Biassou?" Jean stumbled.

"Rum, please," Biassou said, hardly looking up from his lobster tail. Madeline smiled at Jean, made a comical nod to Biassou which escaped his notice, and turned back toward the kitchen.

"Do you know that Madeline is a slave?" Biassou asked, pausing between bites.

"I believe you are mistaken. She is the wife of Monsieur Delva, the owner," replied Jean.

"That she is—and he is also her master," said Biassou.

"But they appear deeply in love!" protested Jean.

"Indeed they are. He adores her and her, him. He purchased her from her previous owner because of it. She is no prisoner." explained Biassou.

"Then why does he not set her free?" Interrogated Jean.

"He spent all his money on her purchase and cannot afford the manumission tax."

Madeline returned with their rum and wine, Labelle trailing her with a pitcher of water.

"Here you are, gentlemen. How is the meal?" asked Madeline.

"Fantastic," replied Jean. "As for the Commander, I hope his horse can carry him after this!" Biassou's mouth was full of snapper as he nodded in agreement.

Swallowing as the women left, Biassou began again.

"You see, the issue of slavery is a complicated matter. Many, especially those of the British colonies to the north, believe it is rooted in racism; slaves are Black, and Whites ventured to Africa to steal them against their will. The truth is not so straightforward.

Tens of thousands of our fellow citizens here in St. Domingue are Black but are not slaves. If those tribes in the Congo had come across a bunch of Frenchman and didn't know any better, they'd just as quickly sell them to the Portuguese." Biassou concluded. "Black, White, or Purple."

"Why are more slaves Black, then?" challenged Jean.

"Master Dupont taught us that slavery has been around for thousands of years with all peoples. It's just that in this particular period of history, we find those who are Black like me subjugated," replied Biassou. "If not true, that would imply that my race and even myself as inferior to you and all Blancs. For that matter, one day, your descendants may be slaves of mine," added Biassou.

The two chewed their meals, considering the conversation.

"Tell me more about Master Dupont." prompted Jean after a moment.

"He was the White patriarch of our slave family. On most

nights we would gather after dinner around a fire and he would educate us on matters of the world. I think he always knew he would free us, and knew being free may end up harder than being a slave, which I can tell you at times, is the case firsthand!"

"In what possible way is it easier to be a slave than a free man? Enlighten me, please?" chided Jean, convinced he had backed Biassou into a corner.

"Let me ask you a question, Jean: If one of your slaves falls ill, very ill, and cannot work for a month, would you still feed him?" asked Biassou.

"Of course I would! What sort of person do you take me for?" protested Jean.

"And why is that?" continued Biassou, scooping up a helping of rice and kidney bean sauce.

"Because I am compassionate." Jean boldly responded.

"Bullshit!" the Commander suddenly slammed his fist on the table.

"You want to protect your investment. Your property. If there were 50 slaves in need, and you only had enough food for ten, you would pick the ten best slaves to save over any free man you didn't know."

Jean was caught off guard by both Biassou's outburst and his realization that the Commander was right. "Then what is your point?"

"One of my soldiers, Francois, got sick a few months ago and had to take leave. Three months out of work. He went through his savings and was thrown out of his dwelling. Forced to live in the streets like a dog—he nearly starved in the rain and cold. By the time I returned to his town to look in on him, I found him begging in the streets with perhaps days left to live. No slave would suffer as such, because they are valued property." He paused and looked away from Jean.

"In this particular instance, slaves are treated better than a free soldier of France!" Biassou spit his final words out.

"So sad," was all Jean could muster.

"Jean, there are many Black slave owners in St. Domingue—

some were slaves themselves. One day, I hope to own property of my own with slaves to work my own fields," admitted Biassou.

Never before, despite all of his schooling and conversations with abolitionist friends, had Jean learned more of slavery's complications than he had over this brief dinner. He was grateful for the conversation even though it impugned upon beliefs he'd once held steadfast. He had not even realized the two had finished their plates.

Labelle came then and began clearing the dishes with a smile on her face, unaware of the journey the two had just found themselves on.

"Labelle, this food is absolutely fantastic. Have you ever tasted the lobster here?" asked Biassou.

"It is one of my favorites, Commander," she replied.

"What are your thoughts on the fish and the griot?" he further inquired.

"I love the snapper, but my favorite is the fish called *Morue*. The griot is delightful, as is the menu in its entirety. You should come back more often" she said.

"Can I provide a coffee or dessert? We have Pain Patate covered with heavy cream which is quite tasty," she said, lowering her voice to a coy whisper. "I've already had a piece!"

"*Cafe noir avec suc rouge* for me" replied Biassou. "See whether you can find some beans from Monsieur Bayard's plantation. His crops look pristine indeed—sure to make a fine cup." he chuckled.

"Very funny, Commander," Jean allowed. "Make me a cup as well Labelle, and two servings of that divine dessert you described." Labelle smiled again and scurried off to the kitchen.

"Now see this, Jean: here is a slave who eats better than most Whites. She smiles and jokes, even stealing off with dessert without her Master's permission. Is this not happiness?" Biassou proposed.

"But what of the abused?" countered Jean.

"Unfortunate, of course," replied Biassou with a shrug. "But not uncommon among free people, Black or White."

Biassou adjusted his seat, leaning toward Jean.

"Jean, I do not condone the raiding of a village, kidnapping, or shipping captors to a different country and selling them. But this was the destiny my great Grandfather was given. His was a transaction that would have happened whether by that rival tribe or another. The evil is in his African brothers who burdened him with that destiny by kidnapping and selling him to the highest bidder. That is the system of slavery."

He went on. "My master freed me, even though his family had bought my ancestor. I am charged with chasing runaway slaves and returning them to their owners. That is my job, and I do not consider myself evil. I am just part of the system." Biassou concluded.

Jean's feelings about slavery had always caused him consternation. Growing up on a plantation lent him the perspective of an owner rather than a slave, even though he considered himself a devout abolitionist.

However, his parents had always treated their slaves with kindness and respect; he considered the room, board, and occasional stipends or rewards an equal exchange for a job well done. Over the course of an hour, however, Biassou had revealed new points of view on this complicated subject.

Labelle arrived with two strong cups of coffee and their two huge helpings of the desert. "Here you are, gentlemen," she smiled, broadly.

"And I'll take the bill," Jean hastened. "We both have a long day ahead of us tomorrow."

As he paid for dinner, he slipped her an extra coin, not knowing whether the house confiscated tips.

"Merci." Labelle smiled and bowed her head as a gesture of gratitude and respect.

Outside, the men mounted their steeds and rode away; mostly silent until the head of the trail leading to the Bayard plantation.

"This is a beautiful property, Jean" Biassou stated, breaking the long silence.

Jean peered down the Palm and Coconut tree-lined path, again taking in the beauty he had often taken for granted. He marveled at the distant mountains which lent a mosaic effect, framing the main house as the sun descended, bathing the entire landscape in crimson.

"That it is," he replied.

"Will you follow in the footsteps of your father?" prompted Biassou.

"No, Georges. I am going to join the military" Jean replied.

"Fool!" snorted Biassou. "You have no idea what you have here, do you?"

Jean sighed.

"Perhaps I am, Georges. Maybe I am making a terrible mistake. But it is something I have to do."

"I do not have the time to discuss the subject as I need sleep for tomorrow's exploits. But I do suggest you take stock of what you have, lest you regret giving it up. Thank you for your hospitality, and I consider our business with your slaves concluded. *Au revoir,* Jean-Baptiste."

Biassou clicked his heels, and he and the massive stallion disappeared down the path toward the *Maruchesse's* temporary camp.

Jean continued home. His parents had already retired to their bedroom, as was typically the case seeing as they enjoyed their early morning coffee together. Reaching his room, Jean slipped his clothes off and reached for his book, *Lettres Persanes*. It detailed a fictional set of correspondences between two Persians making their first visit to Europe. They satirically describe a Paris in transition between the dogmatic absolutes of monarchy and religion and the freedoms of a new age.

The Persians' experiences touched upon a wide range of moral, political, economic, and philosophical issues—all centering on the link between the public good and the regulation of individual desire. Jean was certainly intrigued by his chosen literature, but his mind kept wandering back to Marie and her dream of a business of her own. The reality was, under French law, men were the only proprietors allowed.

Jean wondered why a woman shouldn't be allowed freedom of choice, without the permission of a male.

"If Marie and I were married, we would be equals in business together," he thought to himself.

This unprovoked thought of marriage surprised him. He was coming to the realization that Marie would be a significant part of his life. But why were his views on all manner of things changing so fast? What of his plans for the military?

It was now mid-September and enlistment was scheduled for October 7th. The military recruiters were planning a one-week effort at the post office downtown. With Jean's degree, he would become an officer upon joining. Three short weeks remained for him to decide what to do, but he could not help but feel a conversation with Marie was necessary.

The two had planned a picnic after church the next Sunday. He was to pick her up after her family dinner at 3:00 pm. They'd go riding in the hills and return before sunset at around 7:00 pm.

That morning, Jean made sure Cocktail and Whiskey were well bathed, pampered, and manicured for his picnic with Marie. The horses were saddled an hour before he was to meet her. Jean mounted Whiskey for the jaunt to pick up Marie, trailing Cocktail behind him with an attached bridle.

Upon arriving at the Jasmine compound, he gave the reins to the gatekeeper and walked toward the entrance. The front door was already open, Marie eager to greet him.

"Come meet Papa and Maman," she said. Outside of business transactions, Jean realized he had never much spoken with either of the senior Jasmines. It would be the first time he entered the main residence behind the store.

"Maman, Papa! This is Jean-Baptiste Bayard." Marie called out. "I know you are familiar with his family, but I just wanted to formally introduce him to you both."

Jean smiled in greeting.

"And this is the lesser part of the family, my brother Gustav."

"Shush Marie, I likely know him better than you. Hello Jean," Gustav greeted him. "I can't believe you still have the stomach for her abuse. What are you, a glutton for punishment?"

Marie turned to look at Jean, eyes wide and awaiting his response. Monsieur and Mrs. Jasmine also looked his way. Jean felt all the family's eyes upon him and noticed a slight frown grow across Monsieur Jasmine's brow.

"With all due respect Gustav, I think you are quite mistaken concerning your sister. I find her extremely charming; her business acumen is superb, certainly inherited from your father, and her intelligence I predict comes from her mother, along with that natural beauty."

A look of delight spread across Marie's face, matched by Mrs. Jasmine's wide smile, who slowly cocked her head to look at Gustav and her husband. Jean caught Marie quickly turn her head and stick her tongue out toward Gustav.

Gustav paused briefly, considering his response.

"You're a suck-up, Jean!" Gustav burst out.

"Gustav! Mind your manners" reprimanded Mrs. Jasmine.

Monsieur Jasmine then interrupted the playful banter with a more serious tone. "Come and sit with us for a few moments Jean," he stated. "Tell me, how are your mother and father?"

Jean followed the elder Jasmine into the living room, decorated in fine furnishings, artwork, and luxurious appointments from France.

"They are very well indeed, Monsieur Jasmine. We anticipate the harvest to be one of the best and of the highest quality ever. In fact, we are expanding with a new quarter-hectare field, for which I am installing an irrigation system now" he explained.

"That's right—you went to school to study engineering. That is wonderful to hear," said Monsieur Jasmine.

Marie interrupted before her father could ask Jean another question.

"Jean, time to leave. We don't want to hit sunset in the hills." Marie turned to her family. "We are going to ride up the mountain a little and see the view of Jérémie. We should be back by seven."

"Jean you must come for dinner sometime," invited Mrs. Jasmine as the two made to leave.

"It would be my pleasure, Mrs. Jasmine. Thank you both for your hospitality." Jean managed to reply as Marie grabbed his arm, leading him out the door more quickly than normal.

"See you later Gustav!" he called back.

Out of earshot, Marie scolded him quietly.

"Are you crazy? If you sit down and Papa begins a conversation, you will be stuck for at least an hour! Let's get out of here while we still can."

Jean smiled as they approached the horses. Marie greeted both like old friends.

"Hello, Cocktail my sweet. To you too, Whiskey," she said, before turning back to Jean. "I just love the beauty of Cocktail. Such a beautiful Arabian she is."

Marie expertly mounted the steed and Cocktail moved her legs in anticipation of the upcoming exercise. Jean mounted Whiskey, and off the four raced towards the hills above Jérémie.

About halfway to the summit, they stopped at a grassy area under a huge mahogany tree. Jean dismounted and tied up Whiskey. He turned to find Marie still on Cocktail admiring the view. Helping her down from her saddle, he again reveled in the sweet scent of her perfume. Before moving any further, they could not resist embracing and kissing gently. Jean retrieved a cotton cloth from his saddle and spread it across the grass for them to lounge. There, they began their usual lengthy and interesting conversation.

Twenty minutes in, Jean brought up the subject of enlisting in the military, informing Marie that recruiters were coming to town on October 7th.

"And why do you want to do this, Jean?" Marie asked. "Why do you need this when you have a plantation to run?"

"I have thought much about that. Being home again has made the decision all the more difficult. Especially, now that I am with you." he said, gazing deep into her brown eyes. "But I have always fancied the military and had many friends in France who were soldiers. I want to—no, I need to serve, Marie," he finished, breaking away from her enchanting stare.

"Then you must do it, Jean. You cannot let your feelings for me stop you from achieving your dreams."

"But those dreams have changed now. You are what I dream of these days!" he retorted passionately, surprising even himself.

Marie paused.

"How long is the enlistment, Jean?" she asked softly.

"Four years. From January 1772 through December of 1775."

"That can be overcome. Do it, Jean."

"What about you? I can't lose what we have built, even in such a short period of time," Jean protested.

"I will wait for you, Jean," Marie replied before moving even closer to him. "There is no one else I wish to spend my time with but you. While you are away, I will apply myself fully to the business, and we shall return to a life together better than either of us could have ever imagined."

The two sat in a melancholy silence before Marie again broke the tension.

"But you better write me always, and let me know that you are safe and will come back to me, Jean-Baptiste," she quipped.

Jean took her hand in his. The two young lovers put their heads together and gazed out over the town below, both wishing for this one moment to last a lifetime.

Four

❦

THE MILITARY AND
THE WEDDING

Port-au-Prince
September 1774

Jean enlisted in the French military in October 1771 and left for training and deployment in January 1772. He would spend the next three years of his life aboard ships, fighting across far-flung lands to maintain order on behalf of France.

His regiment put down an insurrection in Guadeloupe, kept vital shipping lanes open from pirates, and was briefly sent to fight in a skirmish with the British off the Canadian coast before finally heading home to St. Domingue. Over the course of his tenure, Jean earned the rank of Captain.

He and Marie attempted to maintain correspondence, but the constant movement and deployments made it nearly impossible. He'd not even sent a letter announcing his arrival home for the winter of 1774. He landed in Port-au-Prince for three months' leave at the end of September, with orders to report back for his last deployment on January 10th the following year. Though he knew not where he'd be sent on that final voyage, nothing could damper his elation at being home after so long abroad.

He purchased a horse in Port-au-Prince and headed for Jérémie 250 clicks away; a journey that would take him the better part of four days. He could not wait to be together with his family and Marie again.

Jean hugged the coast, making an overnight stop along the shore of *Petit Goave*. He checked into a small guest house overlooking the Kokoya Bay beach. He ordered his new horse well taken care of for the next day's 12-hour ride before deciding to go for a brief swim.

The water was still warm from the summer and he could see clearly to the bottom. Colorful fish swam around him and pelicans fished in the afternoon sun along the shoreline. He loved this island; peaceful, and beautiful, and it was his home. He later enjoyed a delicious dinner of freshly boiled whole fish smothered in onions and tomatoes, corn meal, plantains, and peas—washed down with dark rum.

Jean stared out at the sunset and listened to the sound of the surf. The scene mixed with the rum soothed him immensely. Images of battles haunted him constantly, but for now, were muffled by the wind chimes hung on the rafters of the outdoor porch swaying in the fresh salt breeze.

The next morning he reveled in a cup of rich southern coffee and a breakfast of eggs, smoked herring, boiled sweet potatoes, and tomato. He marked the day's destination at Port-de-Nippes, about 70 clicks away. He had been once before and found it a slice of paradise.

He again found a tiny guest house, this one with a talkative owner who relished Jean's company while he ate his dinner of conch, White rice, and beans. The apparently lonely proprietor continued talking and questioning to the point that Jean finally faked falling asleep in order to excuse himself and retire to his room. Once again he was rocked to sleep by the calming waves of the surf and warm, salt-tinged air.

The next day his mount would only cover 50 kilometers to the small town of Corail, owing to bad pathways and near non-existent roads. That night he fell asleep almost instantly despite his excitement to reach Jérémie the following day.

He reached town mid-afternoon on a warm Friday, finding it exactly as he had left it. He could feel his heart begin to accelerate at the thought of seeing Marie again as he turned a corner—her family's store finally coming into view. He entered the commerce compound amongst customers busy loading lumber, sacks of food, and other hardware into various carts and wagons. He spotted Marie, invoice pad in hand, speaking with a client next to a large wagon. She shook the man's hand as they exchanged the invoice, and turned to head back inside the store.

She suddenly froze dead in her tracks. Marie could feel Jean's presence deep within her, whipping around, her breath catching in her throat.

When she spotted him, a flurry of emotions cascaded throughout her body. He looked similar, yet somehow more mature. His Captain's uniform was starched solid and his boots were still polished under the dust and mud from his journey. The widest smile she'd ever felt burst upon her face. Wasting no time, she sprinted to him, jumping into his arms and wrapping her legs tightly around his waist. The two nearly fell to the floor.

Jean spun Marie around and around and rocked her back and forth for what seemed an eternity, neither daring to let the other go or utter a single word. He felt her warm tears through his uniform as he carried her over to collapse on a bench, still embracing her tightly. Their lips locked together, breaking not even as Marie's dog Max barked and licked them both in a greeting of his own.

He was home. She had waited. He was alive. Nothing could possibly feel better than this.

The two spent most evenings and every weekend together. She demanded to know everything he had experienced over the prior three years. Over time, he recounted story after story of his adventures, always careful to leave out any instances he was ever in danger.

The two families were perhaps even happier than they when the couple was together. For the next several weeks, Jean and

Marie were either dining at the Jasmine's or the Bayard's on weekdays and reveling in the local restaurants and nightlife on the weekends. Marie came out of the shell she found herself in over the three years since his departure. Even Gustav commented on how happy Jean made his sister, as the two men developed an even stronger familial bond.

At home he found his younger brother Julien, now ten, had grown significantly and was taking on chores around the plantation. Rene was no longer a baby either at seven. Both were eager to hear stories of the military and their big brother's exploits.

Time passed quickly, and before any of them realized it, Christmas was upon them. In St. Domingue, Christmas was a twelve-day-long celebration of merriment; as much an excuse for socializing, drinking, dancing, gambling, and numerous parties by its inhabitants as it was religious. Family and friends visited, filling the extra rooms of both the Jasmine and Bayard homes, with others staying downtown at the *Sarah* or *Auberge* Hotels.

During their courtship, Jean's mother Jeanne, and Marie's mother Odette had become good friends. Both adored the other's child and easily developed strong relationships with them. With the love affair in full swing, Mrs. Jasmine and Mrs. Bayard began plotting as match-makers. They decided on nothing less than a full onslaught on their children to open their minds up to the idea of a move forward. As it turned out, in matters of the heart, the women of St. Domingue commanded more power than their husbands could ever imagine.

"Jean," Jeanne Bayard called to her son while he was passing through the foyer one day.

"Yes, Maman?" responded Jean.

"It has been so wonderful having you home, Jean." She said. "I almost want to lock you up so you don't leave in January to join the military again."

"Maman, you know I have to go. It is my duty and I made a

commitment," he replied, though he could not help but smile.

"I know, my son. But a mother can always make a wish." She paused a beat, hoping to belie her intentions for the conversation. "Speaking of commitment, what is your understanding with Marie? I really like that girl."

"What do you mean Maman?"

"You haven't made your status clear to us. I do hope you have at least made it clear to her," she offered.

"Uh, I don't know" Jean replied, unsure of what his mother was getting at.

"What do you mean you don't know? Do you love her, Jean?" Jeanne pressed.

"Yes. So much that I can see myself with no other."

"Do you want to spend your life with her?"

"I do."

"What are you waiting for then?" Jeanne prompted.

"Maman, I am still committed to the military," Jean answered, though his voice wavered a touch.

"What does that have to do with love? You said you love this girl Jean and you want to build a life with her. Why would you wait to put a ring on her finger?"

The idea of a proposal hit Jean over the head. "Do you approve of her, Maman?" He responded in a bit of a daze.

"I currently like her a lot, Jean. But if she was your fiancé, I would love her as my daughter." Jeanne said.

Her son may have been an accomplished military Captain, but she had lured him right into an ambush. The seed planted, Jeanne found an excuse to leave him to his thoughts. The next step was up to him now.

Across town, a similar scenario was playing out in the Jasmine household.

"Marie, could you come and help me with something please?" Odette called to her daughter.

"Of course Maman," Marie answered, coming around a corner. "What is it that you need?"

"Help me arrange these flowers I have chosen for tomorrow

night's Christmas Eve reception. I want everything to be perfect as we have invited the Bayards and their visiting family to meet ours," answered Odette.

"And when did all this planning occur, Maman?" Marie asked, wise to her mother's practiced ability to pull strings.

"Jeanne…Mrs. Bayard—and I thought it might be good for our families to celebrate the season together with Jean in town as we don't know when we will all be together again."

"That's a wonderful idea, Maman," said Marie.

Odette plumped the flowers a bit before casually continuing.

"How shall I introduce him to the family Marie? What is he officially to you?"

"Well, we had spent a lot of time together before he left, and are doing so again now that he has returned, but neither of us has had much time to think about it like that," replied Marie.

"Marie," Odette said turning to look her daughter in the eye. "Do you love this man? Is he whom you intend to spend your life with?"

"Yes, Maman. I love him and want to spend my life with him."

"Then commit to it, Marie!" Odette went back to tending the arrangements. "Why do you young people waste so much time on the inevitable?"

Marie was suddenly flustered. "Do you like him?"

"From the first time I saw how he looked at my daughter with such adoration, respect, and awe," answered Odette. "You do not find that easily in life. I know he loves you."

"Do you really think that Maman? That he loves me?"

"Have you bedded him, Marie?"

"MAMAN!" Marie was aghast at her mother's frankness.

"Look at me. Have you had sex with this man?"

"No Maman."

"Well, maybe it is time you did. But a good Catholic girl must be wed first." Odette briefly turned her back to her daughter in an effort to hide her slight smile.

"What are you saying Maman?"

"Put a lock on him before he leaves for more of his adventures. Jean should spend the next year of his service thinking of two things: staying alive, and his prize for doing so—*you!*"

She began to walk away. "I have much more to do. We will talk later."

"Maman…wait. I…"

But her mother was already through the door. Odette smiled to herself as she went, leaving Marie to her thoughts.

The morning of Christmas Eve, Jean had an official conversation with his mother and father regarding his plans for a proposal. Jeanne was delighted with the results of her plan—Jean clearly believed this to be an idea of his own origin. Both of his parents were pleased with the announcement, agreeing that he makes his declaration prior to his upcoming January departure.

"There are many single and attractive men looking for a woman of her caliber, Jean" warned his father. "For God's sake, commit to her! You should speak with Mr. Jasmine and ask for her hand in marriage prior to leaving."

Jean had not noticed his mother's absence during this conversation until she reappeared with an old jewelry box. She took out a small parcel that contained a humble yet beautiful diamond ring.

"This was my Grandmother's engagement ring, given to her by my Grandfather. Take it for your wife-to-be, Jean" she said, tearing up and giving it to him with trembling hands.

Jean felt like a different man; one with a defined purpose like never before. A purpose that would be the foundation of his life moving forward. He mounted Whiskey and made a fast pace for the Jasmine store. As it was Christmas Eve, he knew Marie would be navigating brisk business with last-minute shoppers looking for gifts. He also knew Mr. Jasmine would be home helping to prepare the gardens for the evening's party.

He arrived at the Jasmine compound through the residential entrance rather than the commercial one so as to avoid Marie seeing him. Odette caught a glimpse of Jean and instantly knew what his mission was, despite having not spoken with Jeanne since they'd hatched their scheme.

"He's out back setting up the tables in the garden, Jean," she yelled out.

Jean wondered how it was she knew he was looking for Mr. Jasmine and not Marie, but paid the thought no mind as he turned and headed for the garden. He found staff cleaning, arranging, and otherwise engaged in party preparation before spotting Mr. Jasmine.

He began by declaring how much he loved and admired his daughter; how over the past several weeks he felt their two families had united, and finally that he wished to ask for Marie's hand in marriage. Ralph Jasmine was a sphinx, reacting only to interrogate Jean regarding his military service and the real danger of leaving Marie a widow.

"I need to speak with Mrs. Jasmine about this Jean before I render my decision." Mr. Jasmine said as his wife came round the corner.

"Speak to me of what, Cherie?" asked Mrs. Jasmine to her husband, coyly.

"Young Mr. Bayard here has asked for Marie's hand in marriage, Odette," Ralph replied, not taking his eyes off of Jean.

"How wonderful Ralph! Jean, it's about time. I knew this was coming—you both have that look in your eyes!" she exclaimed, hugging Jean.

"But Odette, we have not discussed this yet!" protested Mr. Jasmine.

Odette waved him off. "What is there to discuss when two people are in love in this way Ralph? When are you planning to propose Jean?"

"I'm not sure yet, Mrs. Jasmine," he said.

"Well, then you should do it tonight." Mrs. Jasmine stated, as though the matter weren't up for debate.

"Tonight?!" asked Jean and Mr. Jasmine in unison.

"Yes, the engagement! It's perfect as both of our families will be here. Let the three of us keep this secret—our secret—and you can surprise Marie. She will love it!"

That Christmas Eve proved a magical night indeed. Both families were in a jubilant and festive mood for the season, listening to and engaging in song and conversation. A grand dinner was served with speeches and toasts given to family unity by Mr. Bayard, Mr. Jasmine, other elders, and distinguished family guests.

At the conclusion of the traditional formalities, Jean asked for all in attendance's attention and locked eyes with Marie from across the room. She was dressed in a dark violet dress cut to accentuate her broad shoulders and expose her beautiful neck. The dress hugged her torso, highlighting her slim body with her breasts slightly mounded at the top. Below the waist, it puffed outward before gracefully falling to the ground. To Jean, she was the most beautiful creature on earth.

Marie was surprised by Jean's commandment and wondered what he had to say which had not already been said by the parade of family members before him. She had to admit being the only one present in uniform not only enhanced his manly appearance but added a touch of pageantry from the bright red, White, and blue colors of France. He was the most gorgeous thing she had ever laid her eyes upon.

Jean began to speak. He professed in no uncertain terms his unwavering and eternal love for Marie. His speech extolled her virtues in a loving ballad, enrapturing all.

Marie was shocked, but could not take her eyes off him. He slowly approached her as he continued to speak. Her heart stopped and she felt the air escape her lungs as she realized what was happening. She saw her mother in tears somewhere beyond him, catching her nod of endorsement and seeing her father join her before returning her full attention to Jean.

Jean-Phillippe and Jeanne Bayard joined the Jasmines to stand together in solidarity. The world began to move in slow motion.

Jean got down on one knee and a gasp and silence gripped the crowd. Jean pulled his great-grandmother's engagement ring from his pocket and spoke once more.

"Marie Jasmine, I offer you my great grandmother's

engagement ring, a cherished symbol of the Bayard family, and ask of thee: will you forever make me the happiest man alive and marry me?"

Marie modeled a shocked expression on her face before blurting out, "Yes…Yes, yes!"

The couple embraced to the loud cheers of their families. On cue, twelve waiters popped corks from champagne bottles and poured them into glasses to be dispersed through the crowd. The evening quickly filled with music from the small orchestra playing lively tunes. Guests took to the dance floor, wishing each other Merry Christmas and congratulating the newly-engaged couple.

The next day, the Jasmines were invited to the Bayards for Christmas supper. There, Odette and Jeanne, of course having long ago contrived the idea, suggested a wedding while all were still in town. Jean and Marie, still caught up in the romance of it all, were in favor of the idea. The date was set for four days hence; December 29th, 1774.

Nearly five hundred guests attended the grand affair, including family, friends, clients, and business relations; professionals, politicians, soldiers, and other notables of Jérémie. To Jean's incredulous surprise, Commander George Biassou himself arrived, accompanied by a dozen *Maréchaussée*; all dressed in their finest parade uniforms.

The ceremony was officiated by the priest of the local Catholic church in the decorated garden. Upon completion of the nuptials, the couple walked down the aisle under a formal tunnel of swords held aloft by Biassou's men.

The evening was filled with food and drink; toasts, speeches, and merriment which lasted through dawn. The couple was then whisked away in a carriage to the town of Bonbon 15 kilometers away. A friend of Mr. Jasmine's had gifted a well-appointed beach home, outfitted with provisions and staff, for the new couple to honeymoon in.

However, the staff hardly saw their charges, save for when they appeared to take their meals on a table overlooking the sea. Making up for lost time, Jean and Marie spent their days making love and memories for both of them to remember over Jean's upcoming deployment. When not in bed, the two splashed like children in the waves, eating crackers, and cheese and drinking wine on the beach, and taking long walks paired with even longer conversations along the shore.

Alas, their time together was fleeting, and Jean soon had to report for duty. The farewell was difficult for both, but the memories they had made on his leave would last a lifetime. Almost as suddenly as he had arrived, Marie realized that Jean was gone once more.

Jean spent the next year on patrol from Guadeloupe to St. Domingue. On a stop in French St. Barthelemy, he picked up a piece of driftwood to bring home to Marie—a souvenir from her ancestral home.

Skirmishes with British forces were always a threat, as news had reached England that the American colonists were courting France. An Ambassador named Benjamin Franklin had traveled to Paris and was apparently quite persuasive; appearing to steer public opinion and the French monarchs toward assisting the Americans in a potential bid for independence.

There remained among the French military a great resentment for the British as France had lost the Seven Years' War twenty years prior, being humiliated in defeat. As such, the soldiers found any excuse a good one to menace the British. There was no love lost for the Crown among their brothers back on St. Domingue either. During the same war, the British had sent ships to intercept French merchant convoys outside of Cap-Français, leading to a fierce sea battle in the fall of 1757.

France calculated it is in their best interest to assist the American colonists in their revolution years before the formal proclamation. Prior to any Royal ordinance issued, the King ordered all military personnel into the reserves for four years post their final tour of duty. Jean would thus be on call to serve his country through December of 1779.

On December 3rd, 1775, Jean and his 110th Infantry Regiment of Port-au-Prince sailed into Cap-Français to deliver injured soldiers from the 109th. The ship was to be at port onboarding supplies for the next two days.

This was Jean's first visit to Cap-Français, and he marveled at the vibrancy of the seaside city. It was far more crowded and sophisticated than the capital of Port-au-Prince, let alone Jérémie and the exuberance were palpable. Whites and free people of color mingled together in restaurants, bars, and night cabarets which would spill over with crowds of revelers.

Jean picked up that morning's copy of the *Gazette of Cap-Français* which announced all manner of interesting highlights from around the city. There were theaters with visiting artists from Paris and other parts of Europe performing plays, operas, symphonies, and comedy shows. He sat down for lunch at *Chez Antoine* and busied himself deciding between attending performances by Le Devin du Village, Le Cadi Dupe, or The Marriage of Figaro.

He glanced up across the street to see none other than Commander Georges Biassou peering through a storefront window. He nearly dropped his fork in his hurry to catch him— pausing only to inform the server that he would return to finish his plate.

Catching up to Biassou, the two men heartily embraced as brothers.

Jean invited the Commander to join him for lunch, commenting that he hoped his friend hadn't lost his appetite. They caught up as much as time allowed before making plans to meet again that evening.

Rather than return to camp with the rest of his regiment on the outskirts of the city, Jean booked a room at The Grand Hotel and spent the rest of the day reading the *Gazette* and planning the sites he would like to visit. He met with Georges to enjoy a delicious meal of goat stew at the *Barik* restaurant, and upon the latter's insistence stayed out late listening to instrumentalists, which Georges pointed out were also happy slaves, at a bar called *Muzak*.

There were five in the ensemble playing violin, cello, flute, bass, and oboe which produced excellent music that the crowd appeared to enjoy nearly as much as the jubilant musicians playing it.

Georges was gone early the next morning for his next mission with the *Maruchausse,* and true to his plans, Jean toured the city. The food was fabulous, the entertainment captivating, and the general hustle and bustle of the city engrossed him. He now knew why Cap-Français was nicknamed the *Paris of the Antilles*. Its wealth and sophistication—expressed through its architecture, artistic lifestyle, entertainment, and vibrancy—rivaled nothing else outside of Paris. He made a promise to himself to come back with Marie for a visit together. This was a place in which he could imagine them living the rest of their lives together.

Five

A NEW BABY AND
A NEW BUSINESS

Jérémie
December 1775

Jean rejoined his men onboard their vessel the following day, setting sail to their barracks in Port-au-Prince. Upon arrival, the General addressed the regiment with a lengthy speech exulting the call of duty and emphasizing the French government's appreciation. Only a day after being dismissed, Jean purchased a horse for the trip back to Jérémie, the thought of reuniting with Marie the only thing on his mind.

He followed the same route as before—now a therapeutic tradition of sorts. His first destination upon reaching Jérémie was naturally the Jasmine general store. It had been eleven months since he had seen her last. Oddly though, she was nowhere to be found inside the store. Inquiring as to her whereabouts, Jean was directed not to a back office or storage area—typically where he might expect Marie to be if not on the floor with customers—but to the main house within the compound. He found this strange considering the action of the mid-afternoon rush of the store, but paid it no mind as he rushed toward the family home.

Jean hoped to surprise Marie as he had before. She had her back to him as he entered the door, fiddling with something on the living room table. His footsteps interrupted her, and upon identifying her husband, she immediately lept into his arms, wrapping her hands behind his head and passionately welcoming him home with a longing kiss.

Dislodging from their embrace, Jean stepped back, wishing to admire her beauty. Marie wore a light blue dress with a loose White shirt, unbuttoned and exposing the top of her chest. Though her blouse was wrinkled and stained, her hair was loose and uncombed, and her feet bare, he somehow found her more enrapturing than ever. He pulled her in tight once again, noting for a moment that her chest felt more substantial than he'd remembered.

"I have a surprise for you, Jean" she whispered in his ear. "Come with me."

Jean followed her upstairs, pausing in confusion when she turned and placed her finger on her lips. They quietly entered one of the bedrooms, startling Odette—who was cradling a bundle of cloth. Composing herself, Odette smiled broadly, walked to Marie, and presented her what Jean could now see was a small, barely awake baby. As Marie coddled the child, Jean noticed it clearly and looked at him.

"Meet your father, my child," said Marie, softly. "Jean, meet your son, Jean Junior."

The ability to speak suddenly left him. He could not move. All Jean could offer in response was a tear that welled up in the corner of his eye. As it ran down his cheek he regained some measure of control. Looking back and forth between Odette, the baby, and Marie, he finally asked, "This is our baby?"

"Yes, my husband, a healthy boy. Here, hold your son."

Marie placed the baby into Jean's arms and stepped back. A deep love as he had never experienced before engulfed him as he locked eyes with his son. His feelings for Marie, which he wagered impossible to grow stronger, somehow matured into newly profound emotions. They not only shared their lives together— they now shared that of this beautiful creation.

Jean held Jean Junior for a long time, only relinquishing him as he began to fidget and move his head left and right, his lips sucking at the air. The baby cried out for his mother's milk while Jean tried to calm him. Marie held back just briefly, overwhelmed with tears at the presence of Jean with their newborn, and not wanting the moment to end.

As though a primal response to the child's cries, one of Marie's nipples gushed a flow of warm milk, exposing the hard wet breast under her soaking blouse. Jean now understood the stains on her blouse.

Marie and the newborn sat on the rocking chair in the corner of the room. With a practiced ease, Marie unbuttoned her blouse and offered her breast to Jean Junior, who immediately latched on. Jean felt as though he were seeing God's own work up close; mother and child bonded together—and he was lucky enough to witness the long-coming unification of their family.

Odette fetched a new cloth for Marie, touching Jean's arm reassuringly as she passed.

"It is so good to have you home, Jean," Odette whispered.

The young family stayed that night at the Jasmine's before moving to the Bayard plantation the next day, which provided a more relaxed environment for all—particularly with the Christmas holidays and corresponding festivities fast approaching once again.

Marie and Jean spent every moment together, enjoying each other and marveling at Junior. As the new year of 1775 dawned, they found themselves settling comfortably into life at the plantation. Discharged, and with no standing orders to return, Jean found himself free to plan his family's next steps for the first time in years.

He first struck a deal with his father to work the plantation and oversee several expansion projects. Marie enjoyed her time away from the store, embracing her role as a mother and nurturing Junior. However, both parents were the ambitious sort, and often their conversations would turn to business opportunities that would provide their family with much-needed income.

During this time, conversations across St. Domingue centered on the events taking place in the American colonies. The Coercive

Acts imposed by the British in the wake of the Boston Tea Party in December 1773, finally led to armed conflicts erupting in the Massachusetts towns of Lexington and Concord in April 1775. Jean knew that should France be drawn into the conflict, he would likely be called up as a reservist, and that worried him.

Thankfully, the year proved quiet and life remained fun and easy for Marie and Jean. His father's plantation projects were supervisory in nature, with nearly all labor handled by *de jure* slaves. The crops were healthy, and another full ten hectares were planted thanks to Jean's excellent irrigation engineering and construction.

While the harvests remained bountiful, Jean's father grew ever-frustrated with the coffee brokers of Jérémie. Their bids for his plantation's product were far lower than the more competitive prices of Port-au-Prince and Cap-Français, but Jean-Phillippe had no way to efficiently transport them to those markets. Overland routes were impossible due to bad roads, and small sailing vessels were all leased by local sugar brokers shipping their cargo to Port-au-Prince.

Marie and Jean saw the fortuitous potential behind a solution that would allow the Bayards' crops to take advantage of the more popular markets elsewhere on the island. They hatched a plan to convince the captains of the ships used by her father's import business to take a side trip to Cap-Français prior to heading back to Guadeloupe.

The coffee would be loaded onto the ships in Jérémie and then sold in Cap-Français where the coffee market was far more lucrative. The profit would be split between the younger and older Bayards, and the shippers would benefit from a local run of business and increase their overall value of the voyage.

Marie devised the final piece of what was shaping up to be a rather fruitful scheme; her father employed a system of marking down inventory older than ninety days by five percent per month until it hit the rock bottom value of 25% of the original cost. By loading up this overstocked merchandise on the same ships and selling it in Cap-Français, her family business would raise additional cash and reduce unwanted inventory. Similar to Jean and his father, Marie would split the profits with hers. Both pairs of parents agreed to go along with the enterprising plan—now all the two young lovers had to do was enact it.

In October of 1775, A small sloop arrived from Guadeloupe with hardware goods for her father's store. Jean and Marie approached the Captain, who agreed to a round-trip sail to Cap-Français for a reasonable fee. The test run would consist of fifty 60kg sacks of coffee beans and assorted old hardware from the store, overstocked from twelve to sixty months.

"If you don't sell it at Cap-Français, drop it in the ocean somewhere," Gustav chided as the couple boarded the ship with their cargo. "Don't bring it back here!"

The trip took three days as the captain had never navigated the passage between Jérémie to Cap-Français before, and insisted on stopping in small bays overnight. The crew slept in the cargo hold, but Jean and Marie elected to sleep under a makeshift tent on the deck and enjoy the balmy and pleasant fall weather.

"Look at the sky Jean," remarked Marie one night. "It is so beautiful here on the ocean with only the moon to provide light."

"Yes, Marie. It is. Almost as beautiful as you," Jean replied.

They lay in silence for a long while, each contemplating their thoughts. Jean knew that should this voyage prove a success, the two would speak again about how they could further expand their entrepreneurial endeavors.

The sloop docked in Cap-Français late on a bustling Tuesday afternoon. Jean and Marie immediately ventured out to scout the area. They'd need to identify coffee merchants, warehouse facilities, hardware stores—and perhaps most importantly—a hotel where they might clean the salt from their pores after the voyage.

Neither had bathed in fresh water in days, only taking a swim each morning and afternoon.

Though primarily a business trip, Marie was like a child in a candy store, experiencing the sights of the big city for the first time in her life, and enjoying every moment. They decided to splurge that evening on dinner and a show. They arrived at the hotel in the early morning hours and made passionate love until they both collapsed.

Jean and Marie enjoyed a full breakfast the next morning as well as a strategy session to review what they had learned the previous day. Deciding to divide and conquer, Jean would meet with the three top coffee brokers, while Marie would pitch the proprietors of the three largest hardware stores. They would reconvene at the sloop no later than 4:00 pm that afternoon.

His breakfast finished, and Jean left to purchase the day's *Gazette* and *Lumiere* while Marie went over her list of inventory. He and Marie quickly scanned the newspapers for information relevant to both their business and personal interests. Once satisfied, they shared a quick kiss and left the restaurant on their individual missions.

The first hardware store was named *Matériel Blanchet et Fils* on *Rue de la Croix,* and, based on inspection and approval of the merchandise at the sloop later that day, Marie promptly unloaded half her inventory. Under the same arrangements, the other two stores scooped up the rest of the inventory between them. She purposefully gave each of the buyers the same meeting time; should one back out, she'd take the opportunity to discount the rest of the inventory or place it on consignment with one of the others.

Marie felt good with what she'd accomplished in less than three hours, deciding to treat herself at a local outdoor cafe on *Rue Faustin.* She then did some window shopping on *Grand Rue,* finding a beautiful outfit from Paris inside the window of one of the stores she passed. Her mind briefly wandered, imagining both how it would fit her—and the look on Jean's face if he saw her in it.

Across town, Jean was in the midst of visiting the three coffee brokers—finding each more hard-nosed and uncooperative than the last. While their offers were for more than his father was receiving in Jérémie and Port-au-Prince, their numbers seemed insultingly low compared to what Jean felt they would be worth in Cap-Français. There would be little profit remaining after accounting for transportation. Unsure of Marie's progress in selling her inventory, he held out, gambling on finding higher prices for his family's crop.

As he strolled past the warehouses along the wharf, he noted that coffee beans were quite plentiful—likely contributing to the prices he was being offered. Due to that year's booming harvest, the large supply dictated lower prices. Then, he spotted an empty warehouse with its doors wide open. Peeking inside, Jean found a young man in his twenties. With nothing to lose, he inquired as to the nature of his business.

His answer provided Jean with his first bit of good news of the day; it so happened he had stumbled upon another coffee wholesaler—albeit one who was nearly out of product. The young man and his brother were new to the business and lacked the long-term relationships enjoyed between their competition and the popular planters of the area. If they were lucky enough to even procure any stock, it was typically rejected inventory or of lower quality. This was Jean's chance—but he was careful not to show too much of his excitement.

"I am Captain Jean-Baptiste Bayard, and you are..?" he asked the man.

"Renald. Renald Chevallier" came the response.

"Call your brother over, Renald. I may just have an answer to your prayers." Jean said, smiling.

Both proprietors now present, Jean shared a sample of his beans. In growing delight, he watched the brothers' eyes light up as they experienced the southern-sourced beans—usually of much higher quality than those found in the north.

Gerard, the older brother who had wandered over at Renald's behest, was the first to speak.

"Where did you get these?" He asked, holding the beans to his nose and inhaling deeply in appreciation of their robust scent.

"Come with me." Jean offered.

The three walked to the nearby sloop and jumped on board. Jean opened the cargo bay and took a step back. The Chevallier brothers took one look at the fifty bags of beans, looked back at each other, and smiled in unison.

"How much?" asked Renald.

Jean feigned ignorance at the question, responding instead regarding the quantity.

"Fifty 60kg sacks of the finest beans from south St. Domingue." He paused and offered a sly smile. "I am currently taking offers."

Gerard immediately offered the highest price Jean had heard all day, but the cunning businessman in him forced a rebuttal.

"You clearly have no appreciation for the espresso you can make from our fine product, Gerard." Jean retorted. "If that is the case, you should go back to peddling inferior beans. I am looking for a broker who appreciates quality and will properly represent our brand of Southern beans. You will need to increase your offer by twenty percent."

"Seven percent" scoffed Gerard without missing a beat.

"Sixteen and no less."

Just then, Marie appeared down the wharf, a brilliant smile on her face.

"I'll allow you one last chance to inspect the cargo, Gerard. Renald, perhaps you can talk some sense into him." said Jean, walking away to reunite with his wife on the dock.

Marie recounted her successful morning, letting him in on her plan for the three customers arriving shortly. Jean nodded his head toward the two brothers, now deep in conversation with each other, and expressed his hope to soon join in her triumph.

"Mr. Bayard," Gerard called down at that moment. "Ten percent, and no more!"

Jean looked at Marie once more before turning to respond.

"You gentlemen should count yourselves lucky to be in the presence of the finest woman in all of St. Domingue! Allow me to introduce my wife, Marie Jasmine-Bayard," Jean said with formality.

"Marie, these gentlemen may be the newest brokers of Cap-Français's finest coffee: Gerard and Renald Chevallier."

Still, atop the deck, the brothers bowed in unison.

"Our pleasure to meet you, Madame Bayard. Welcome to the great city of Cap-Français," responded Gerard, Renald nodding in agreement.

Adjusting his tone and approaching the brothers back on the sloop, Jean quickly transitioned back to business. "Because I wish to conclude our business so I may indulge in the presence of my bride, I will split the difference with you. Fourteen percent it is!"

Gerard quickly responded "Mr. Bayard, I believe the split between sixteen and ten is dead on thirteen percent, rather than fourteen."

"Please, call me Jean. And I accept your new offer of thirteen percent over your original." Jean extended his hand toward Gerard.

Gerard of course hadn't increased his offer; he was simply correcting Jean's arithmetic. Somewhat confused as to what had just transpired, he had to admit the beans he had just held in his hands were certainly worth the figure proposed.

"Provided we have the first option for your next shipment at the same price, then let us consider the deal made, Jean." Gerard offered.

"I will grant you the first option, but not the price. However, I will cap any increase at twenty percent and suffer the loss should there be any." concluded Jean.

"Then we have a deal."

Jean could hardly believe his turn of fortune. By his rough calculations, he'd just secured a 37% increase over the highest price his father had ever received back in Jérémie. With he and Marie splitting the profits with his parents after deducting expenses, it was a great start to their new partnership.

Arrangements were made to finalize the transaction the following morning, allowing the brothers time to procure a line of credit and transportation. As they made their way down the dock from the sloop, Marie's three hardware store owners arrived in succession. The first two transactions were seamless. Bank checks in hand, Marie then turned her attention to her final potential client. This man was older than the others and had owned his store for decades. He inspected each piece in detail, spotting and complaining of rust on some of the more weathered items. After a brief negotiation, however, she too struck a more than fair deal and the day's business was finally done.

Jean quickly located the sloop captain to inform him of their success. "Captain, I believe we will need to discuss your schedule for future shipments!" Marie effused. "Our business will be concluded tomorrow morning. When can we depart for home?"

"There's no need to await the tides as we have no cargo," the Captain answered. "We can leave port as early as you'd like."

"Excellent! The hardware is paid for and can be transferred to the buyers, but the coffee stays aboard until I give you the word. See you in the morning." replied Jean as he and Marie exited the sloop and made their way toward *Grand Rue* on *Avenue Simone*. Jean locked his arm in hers as they walked.

"Congratulations, Mrs. Bayard. You are one hell of a businesswoman."

"Thank you, Captain Bayard. You're rather impressive yourself—for a soldier." Marie chided. "I particularly liked that 'split the difference' line you pulled on Gerard."

"I call it the Indian Split—and it works every time!" Jean chuckled in spite of himself. "What do you say we celebrate tonight? This morning's newspaper advertised an opera at *Le Soleil* called *Le Merveilleux*."

"I've never been to the opera, my husband, but I'd love to attend it with you."

Turning onto *Grand Rue*, Marie hoped Jean didn't notice as she briefly glanced over to the shop window she'd passed earlier that day. However, she felt him gently steer her in that direction. Nearing the window, she heard him clear his throat.

"Then you will need a fine dress to wear, my love. What do you think of this one?"

Marie attempted to hide her emotion, instead softly replying that she'd never worn something so formal or expensive.

"My love, we have just made the first of what will surely be many lucrative business deals together. We can afford to splurge a bit," said Jean. "Come, try it on for me before we buy it."

Marie couldn't help but burst into a wide smile—the same one, Jean noted, that had struck him senseless that night at the engagement party. The dress fit her like a glove, and the two got a little carried away adding all the accessories the shop owner suggested—in between spilling local gossip and providing her recommendation for the best restaurant in town. She even offered a note to be shared with the owner, proclaiming Jean and Marie receive every courtesy available.

They hurried back to the hotel to prepare for dinner. Bathed, made up, and draped in a dress straight from the fashion lanes of Paris, Marie was incredible to behold. Jean was convinced she'd never looked more beautiful.

They took a carriage ride to *Les Jardins de l'Ocean* which they found packed with diners and others waiting to be seated. Hoping they hadn't been put on, Jean apprehensively handed the note to the host, who scanned it, and smiled up at the young couple.

"Please follow me, sir and Madame."

They were immediately seated at a picturesque table overlooking the ocean under a perfect island sunset. After a lavish meal, they boarded a carriage once more, this time headed for *Le Soleil*.

Jean couldn't determine what brought him more joy and entertainment: the performers on stage or the expressions and emotions that danced across Marie's face. She was completely engulfed in the experience; laughing, then crying; laughing more, and crying once again.

Still ecstatic from the opera on their walk back to the hotel, the couple stopped in front of a busy nightclub.

Marie pulled her husband close as they reached the thriving scene out front. "Jean, let's stop here. It is still early and I would love a Bénédictine."

"Of course, my love. I would enjoy a brandy myself," he replied. However, as they approached the entrance, Jean spotted the two telltale red lanterns in the window, indicating the establishment was more than an entertainment venue. He quickly turned to steer her shoulders away from the doorway, saying "Let's go elsewhere."

"Why Jean?"

"This is a…house of prostitution. You don't belong here" he replied, hastily.

"They don't serve Bénédictine or Brandy here, you think? Well perhaps they have Cognac?" she replied, underneath a creeping smile.

"Marie, you don't belong in a place like this…" Jean began.

"Jean, these are only men and women who seem to be having a good time," she cut him off. "Is there a law against my entering such a place? Are only men and prostitutes allowed? They are women too."

"Ah, well, not that I know of—"

"Then let's go. It will be fun. If either of us doesn't like it, we can just leave." she said, making her way back to the door.

"You sure?" he tried once more, but Marie was already reaching for the handle.

"Yes, Jean. Come on!"

They entered a dimly lit, smoke-filled room that smelled of dried wine, brandy, and whiskey. The well-dressed host addressed Jean.

"A table for two? Or would you prefer our girls to join? Or perhaps join a group already seated?" he offered.

Marie surveyed the room, quickly spotting a lively group of men and women near some open seats.

"May we join that table over there?" she asked.

"What are your first names?" inquired the host

"Jean and Marie" Jean answered.

The host escorted them between the patrons to their selected table, and announced, "Jean and Marie request the honor of joining your table."

A couple of the guests waved them in while the others appeared to not care less. The two took seats on a soft couch among scattered pillows around a low table. A violin, bass, and piano trio was playing fine music accompanying a pretty French singer. Jean ordered a Bénédictine and a Cognac as he and Marie surveyed the room.

Across the table, one couple was passionately kissing. Another woman had her breast out from her loose top, conversing with and touching it to the man's face next to her. The woman in the third couple was teasing her partner with a lap dance, her lack of underwear quickly revealing itself to any observer.

These were the first floor girls, the prettiest of the brothel, and hooks to convince men to go upstairs. Most assumed they'd bed these, but upstairs were instead handed off to the harder working women. Insisting on spending their time with the downstairs girls would increase their cost by ten.

The remaining three patrons seated closest to Jean and Marie were engaged in a discussion on politics that Jean and Marie decided to join.

"The American colonies have the same problem as we have in St. Domingue," said one of the men. "They have high taxation without any representation in London. Is it not the same for our relationship with Paris?"

After their second round of drinks, Marie could feel the Bénédictine's botanical flavor of sweet honey, accented with holiday spices, stone fruits, and an herbal nuance warm her body. She ordered a third round while Jean remained engaged in lively discussion with two of the men—their female cohort clearly having grown tired of the discussion.

The woman gave Marie a sly smile and nod, then grabbed the crotch of the man next to her and began to kiss his neck in an effort to extract him from conversation. The second man immediately cut his argument short to move behind the woman, slipping his hand under her blouse.

Marie admired the power these women had over the men. She watched them chide and coax before pulling away; always controlling the tempo of seduction. She had never been in a brothel and surprisingly did not find herself revolted.

By this time, two of the original couples had left the table, likely upstairs, and two new ones had replaced them—each in the middle of their own seductive acts.

Marie felt something come over her then. Turning, she aggressively pushed Jean back onto the couch and straddled him as the third round of drinks were placed on the table beside them. Marie grabbed hers, shot half of it down her throat, and fed Jean's glass to his lips like a mother would a child. She could feel his arousal under her as he drank.

Marie began to move her hips over him slowly. She unbuttoned his shirt down to his belly button. Their fellow patrons were also becoming more openly sexual with one another, however, Marie ignored everything happening around them to concentrate only on Jean who had remained silent. She picked up her Bénédictine, poured a few drops onto his chest, and began to lick his nipples and suck on his neck before passionately launching her tongue into his mouth. She repeated the sequence again and then once more.

Jean was shocked—but completely enthralled. The liquor was lowering their inhibitions and this manner of seduction was certainly within the bounds of the establishment. He knew he was the sole object of desire for the most beautiful woman in the club and decided to fully give himself over to the night, the next day's consequences be damned. No one knew them here—they were simply new faces in the dimly lit, smokey crowd.

Marie picked up his Cognac, bringing it to his lips again. She then placed her hand behind his head, pulled down her blouse, and pressed his face to her chest so his mouth could take in her nipple.

As he sucked on and aroused her breast, she continued to gyrate her hips—grinding their clothed crotches against each other. She felt her body's natural lubrication wet her and began to pant as she arrived at the early stages of a climax. She pulled away quickly, covering her breast and regaining her composure. Just as she'd watched the other women, she was taking back control. She leaned in close and whispered into his ear "Do you want me?"

"Yes, Marie. I desperately want you" he responded, his voice strained.

"I am not Marie tonight," she answered. "Tonight, this bitch is your whore."

"I want you, whoever it is you are. Let's get out of here!"

Jean moved to get up, but Marie held him pinned on the couch with her legs.

"We haven't discussed terms of service yet, Mr. Bayard," she said.

"Anything. Name your price."

"Fifty percent of all profits from this trip to invest as I please."

"I'll give you twenty," Jean replied.

"Forty." Marie retorted.

"Twenty-five!" he countered.

"I'll split it with you at thirty-five," Marie offered, not missing a beat.

"But an even split would be thirty-two and a half!" Jean said, his mind struggling to focus.

"You have a deal, Mr. Bayard. Thirty-two and a half—and I guarantee you'll have no regrets," she whispered seductively. "Let us take our leave somewhere more private."

Marie could not help but smile, having turned the tables on her husband. What had he called it? The Indian Split?

Jean downed the remainder of his Cognac and paid the host for the drinks, leaving a handsome tip. They hurried to the hotel, nearly causing a minor scene as they stumbled up the entry steps, Jean's shirt still half unbuttoned. Arriving at their room, Marie quickly undressed him before removing her own, both impatiently clawing at each other and passionately kissing as articles of clothing flew everywhere.

Picking up exactly where they'd left off at the club, Marie pushed Jean down and slid his tall erection easily inside her. Their pure, wild sex was raw, and physical, and consumed them both. This was not lovemaking—Marie shocked Jean throughout the night as they tossed repeatedly like wild animals. She had him take her from behind on all fours, then while standing up, exploring all sorts of positions, some of which Jean had never imagined.

After what seemed like hours, their final sex ended with Marie on top and Jean deep inside her—just as they'd begun. She made a final arching of her back, head and breasts pointed to the ceiling, and arms holding the sheets to stabilize herself as they both exploded in ecstasy in a unified orgasm that shook them in spasms.

She dropped next to him on her back, panting with her entire body. She was covered in sweat from her hair to her feet. Jean lay gasping for breath next to her. Together they remained in silent shock before quickly falling into a deep sleep.

As the sun began to peer through the window, Jean woke suddenly. He was disoriented, and fearing he'd overslept, retrieved his pocket watch from the side table. It read 6:45. He looked over to Marie to find her sleeping peacefully, still naked under the sheets.

He got up and closed the shades so the rising sun wouldn't awaken her, washed, and put on a clean shirt with the previous night's trousers. Slipping out of the room, Jean walked down to the hotel lobby which was just coming to life. He arranged for a full breakfast and pot of coffee to be brought to the room and grabbed a copy of the *Gazette*, whose headline read:

AMERICAN SIEGE OF BOSTON CONTINUES
Seized Cannons from Fort Ticonderoga
Pound British Targets

Jean put the paper under his arm and ventured outside into the warmth of the early morning.

Cap-Français was already bustling with carriages full of

people, wagons full of cargo, paperboys yelling headlines, cafés filling with diners, and a rousing vibrancy that made Jean feel alive.

He went back upstairs where he found Marie still asleep. He read the front page story until a gentle knock on the door signaled that breakfast had arrived. He took the tray into the room and peeked under the covered plates to reveal a feast of piping hot eggs, sausage, smoked herrings, boiled plantains, roasted potatoes, croissants, fruits, and jams.

The smell of fine coffee filled the room and Marie's keen sense of smell began to stir her.

Jean slipped off his pants, crawled into the bed, and began to run his fingers slowly down the side of her body.

"I threw out that whore bitch you brought here last night and told her she was not allowed back unless I called for her," she whispered. "I told her that your wife is back."

"Welcome back, my love," Jean replied.

"Make love to your wife now, Jean. Fill me with your sweet love. I want to feel you but please, come into me gently, my husband" she said as she turned to face him.

Her eyes were so longing that he could not help but abide by her request. They made gentle love, nothing like the previous night. She was sore, but desperately sought to get back to their places as husband and wife which they shared before entering the brothel.

He was cognizant of her pain, her soft moans guiding his rhythm and depth. Marie felt totally safe once again, and they climaxed together and held each other—her head on his chest, his arms around her shoulders.

"I am famished" Marie finally said, after some time had passed.

"I wonder why?" Jean lightly teased.

They both looked at each other before laughing and bringing the plates into the bed with them.

An hour or so later, they devised their plan for the morning's planned departure. Jean was to go to the dock and meet with

Gerard and his brother Renald to secure payment and offload the coffee. She would stay and pack, square the bill, and take a carriage to the docks to meet him no later than 11:00 am.

Jean walked the few blocks to where the sloop was docked. Upon arriving the Captain informed him that Marie's customers had already come and retrieved their merchandise. The weather was beautiful and swells small, indicating a smooth departure from Cap-Français.

Gerard and Renald arrived within moments with two wagons, four men, and large smiles on their faces.

"Good morning Jean. How are you this splendid day?" shouted Gerard.

"Couldn't be better," Jean replied. "And you?"

"Wanting for more of your beans! I have already sold half the shipment which will be headed out to coffee connoisseurs in Paris," he replied. "When can I get more?"

"I will send you a message somehow. Give me your address for forwarding."

"It is on this bank draft—please verify that it is acceptable and the amount is exactly as we had agreed," Gerard said.

Jean had calculated the amount and presented Gerard his invoice.

"All in order, Gerard. Have your men come to take your cargo," replied Jean. "It has been a pleasure doing business with you!"

Within a half hour, the sacks were unloaded and all business concluded. At 10:30, a carriage pulled up to the dock. Marie stepped out, dressed in a light blue peasant dress and broad-rimmed hat. She was handed a basket by the carriage driver's assistant. Thanking the duo, she walked up to the sloop.

"How's it going here?" she asked.

"Fabulously well my love. Business is concluded, and with you here, we can get underway." Jean said, holding his hand out. Marie handed him the basket—which was quite heavy—before offering her hand.

The basket turned out to be filled with food not only for

herself and Jean but the crew. It included pate, chicken, bread, cheeses, and an assortment of wine. The Captain and his men were delighted to have been considered.

They set out to sea with a feeling of relief, accomplishment, and leisure. The ocean was calm and a deep blue under the bright October sun which warmed the crisp breeze. As the ship exited the harbor, they looked back for one final sight of Cap-Français.

"I like it here," said Marie.

Jean's heart fluttered with happiness. One day, he knew Cap-Français would become their home.

The sloop rounded the reef shortly after noon. The Captain estimated they would arrive in Jérémie late Sunday morning if the weather held up. They all shared a delicious lunch together, and Jean and Marie spent their afternoon doing their best to stay out of the way of the mariners as they expertly adjusted the sails and rudder to make the best of the winds.

They fell into assorted conversations, pointing to distant objects on shore or people they would see on a beach, and glancing every so often at the map to gauge which towns they passed. They anchored off *Mole Saint-Nicolas* on Thursday night, and in the town of Gonaives on Friday—where they enjoyed a nice dinner in a local seaside restaurant before spending the night in a comfortable guest house.

They had not spoken a word about the brothel to this point. However, Jean finally decided to bring it up.

"So, what will you do with the thirty percent you charged me for that night on the town?" he asked.

"That is thirty-two and a half percent, Jean. Don't try to cheat me now," she replied.

"You know, I would have paid a full one hundred percent." he smiled.

"And I would have done it for free." she countered, batting her eyes.

Jean hesitated a moment before going on. "Marie, where did you learn to do the things you did? I know I was your first man on our wedding night, for that I am sure…but where did all of that—

those things—the…?"

"You mean the sex, Jean? Don't be shy" she said, delighting a bit in seeing her husband unsure of himself.

"Yes, the sex." he relented.

"When Gustav was seventeen he began to sneak out late at night. He wouldn't tell me where he would go. One night I followed him and found out he went to a house of prostitution on the edge of town. I peeked in the window and saw…all sorts of things." Marie confessed.

"Go on," Jean urged.

"I began to Blackmail Gustav. I made him tell me everything he did and what the women taught him to do in exchange for not telling Maman and Papa," she said.

"Scandalous, Marie!"

"Yes, perhaps. I learned a lot I could never use—until the other night. I don't know whether I was doing it all right, but I improvised anything I wasn't sure of." she said.

"And the liquor pushed me on," she added quickly.

"Well, you certainly learned those lessons correctly, my love." Jean smiled at her reassuringly.

"And what of your money; what will you do with that?" he asked.

"I, I mean, *we* will find a place to invest it outside of our new business venture. I heard that talk of the American Revolution. Some of the arguments are the same we complain of with the French." her tone changed. "We have no representation in the legislature for local affairs and grievances, yet nearly half of France's revenue comes from this island. How fair is that?"

"I agree, it hardly seems so," Jean nodded.

"Jean, I believe this issue is a powder keg. Look at our own new business. If we sell crops directly to France, they set the prices. When my family buys goods from France, they set the prices. The *Exclusif* allows France to set all import and export prices. I think this island will one day revolt like the Americans, and it is best for us to put the money elsewhere for safekeeping."

"Marie Jasmine-Bayard, you have a good head on your

shoulders." Jean beamed with pride. "What if we committed to placing ten percent of our profits into outside investments? How would you feel about that?"

Marie was filled with elation, counting her blessings that she had found a man who treated her respectfully as an equal. She agreed to Jean's proposed policy and they vowed to abide by their plan.

Saturday morning they set sail to the island of *La Gonave*, halfway across the strait from Jérémie. Overnighting at *Pointe des Lataniers,* they departed for the direct shot to Jérémie early the next morning.

Arriving around 2:00 pm they headed straight from the harbor to the Jasmine compound, rightly assuming the two families would be dining together for Sunday dinner. Jean entered the dining room holding two bottles of champagne over his head.

Seated around the dining table were both sets of parents, Gustav, Marie's aunt Yvonne and uncle Victor, and little Jean Junior between Mrs. Jasmine and Mrs. Bayard. The group erupted in celebration as Marie darted for her baby, picking him up and holding him in her arms while Jean kissed his face.

"Surprise!" yelled Jean's brother Andre as he burst through the door into the room, all smiles.

Jean rushed to embrace him.

"When did you get home, Andre?" asked Jean, struggling to contain his emotion.

"Two days ago—on Friday" he replied.

"Welcome home, brother," he said, before looking at his mother and father. "Did you know?"

"He wrote to us several weeks ago informing us he'd finished his University, and was going to tour Europe—but we had no clue when he would get here." answered his mother.

"Europe is in a frenzy now." Andre said, finally breaking from his older brothers' embrace. "Talk of war is all over, especially with the revolution in the American colonies."

"Forget going to England as a Frenchman, as the gangs will chase and beat you up," he added.

"Yes, I've been reading the same. The war appears to be reaching a boiling point in the colonies." Jean said.

He and Marie were starving after their voyage, and the house staff quickly procured two place settings amongst the family. Though most had already finished eating, no one left the table. Jean's father opened one of the bottles of champagne and began pouring glasses.

"Welcome home to both my sons and new daughter! I take the Champaign as an indication of success in your new business venture?" toasted Jean-Phillippe to cheers. Jean and Marie took turns providing a full report on the trip to Cap-Français, and after all, were through with their meals, Andre related stories of his time in Paris.

From the remainder of 1776 through the middle of 1777, the young Bayard's import and export arrangement surpassed even their grandest dreams. Their coffee purchases expanded beyond the Bayard plantation to encompass the entire southern region. Any coffee grower's harvest could be brought to their warehouses in Jérémie for cash payment upon inspection. Marie not only purchased all of her father's outdated hardware but began adding to his import orders for new merchandise to sell at Cap-Français.

Soon, Jean and Marie found themselves making bi-monthly trips to Cap-Français. The time had come for the couple to move to the city and designate it as the hub for their growing enterprise. On one of their trips, they found a building across from the wharf with a downstairs office and upstairs living quarters. In the sight of their warehouses, the convenience was a Godsend. After bringing on Gerard and Renald as partners in their thriving coffee division, Jean and Marie were free to expand their sphere of influence with other goods. They soon added indigo and wood to their exports and began bypassing brokers and establishing their own accounts abroad with contacts in France.

Andre turned down his father's offer to run the plantation as his father suspected he might. Jérémie was far too rural and slow for Andre, who preferred the fast-paced city lifestyle. He joined his older brother's business in 1777, charged with developing a sugar cooperative in the northern areas around Cap-Français. The plan was to export raw sugar to France, as well as some molasses and supplies from the *Artibonite* Valley as well.

Jean's father and mother came to the realization at this time that their family was in St. Domingue, and the move to France would put far too much distance between them all—as well as their new friends the Jasmines. Besides, both Odette and Jeanne were now working hard to convince Jean and Marie to provide more grandchildren, as well as attempting to find a wife for Andre; perhaps even a relative in the Jasmine family.

One day in early November of 1778, Andrew Cabot, a university classmate of Jean's, arrived in Cap-Français. Seeing the Bayard sign in front of their office, he wandered in and inquired as to the establishment's connection with his old friend Jean-Baptiste Bayard. He was delighted to find that it was indeed Jean's business and the two caught up on the years since their last meeting by swapping stories and reminiscing.

Andrew was in town searching for a molasses connection for his new rum distillery in Massachusetts. He was fighting supply issues as the destruction of crops in the ongoing war with England had made molasses increasingly hard to come by in the American colonies. Meanwhile, Jean had plenty of molasses to sell, but finding transporters willing to make the dangerous voyage into the active war zone was proving more and more difficult.

Andrew had secured safe passage permits from the Continental Navy along the necessary routes to and from Massachusetts. He'd scoured the wharf, interviewing every ship owner he could find, looking for one willing to undergo the treacherous journey. Alas, the answer was the same: "Too dangerous."

For three days, Andrew had found nothing but disappointment. Jean related to his friend that he had come up empty in his own inquiries as well. Then, a commotion came from the front of the office.

Andre burst through the door, announcing that he'd just met a young Captain by the name of Gabriel Martin, who commanded a small schooner, the *Le Matin,* and was willing to make the trek. Upon further questioning though, the men's initial enthusiasm at the news abated. The cost was prohibitive due to the risk involved, and the cargo hold is empty on the return voyage.

Ever the optimist, Andre hatched a plan. As he had been working to procure sugar from various plantation owners throughout the area, he was increasingly asked about access to cheap, dried salted fish to feed their slaves. Andrew proclaimed he had sources for salted cod in New England, which could be shipped back and sold for a profit.

Jean was agreeable to the plan. He trusted Andrew Cabot and agreed that he would front the balance of the molasses' cost to be paid back in fish upon return. He quickly consulted with Marie who agreed to the scheme as well.

Elated, Andre quickly declared that he would personally accompany the shipment of molasses to Massachusetts, and load the Northern Cod for the voyage home.

"You will do no such thing." Jean immediately objected. "It's far too dangerous!"

"No risk, no reward, my brother" Andre responded "And I'm sure your friend Andrew Cabot will be amenable to join us and smooth out any complications with the Americans along the way."

"No, Andre. Maman and Papa would never forgive me if I allowed this. I would sooner pass on this deal than send you on such a voyage." he stated flatly.

"You worry too much my brother…but you are in charge. One day, you'll see I'm not as useless as you think. I may not be a soldier like you, but I am not afraid." Andre retorted.

"Andre, I know you are not useless," Jean protested. "I did not mean to suggest otherwise at all."

"It is just as well, as I have a business trip to the *Artibonite* Valley tomorrow. Perhaps you will see what I am capable of when I return in four weeks' time." Andre replied.

Relieved his brother had apparently given up on the notion, and as a show of confidence, Jean placed Andre in charge of making the arrangements with the young, daring Captain, and the loading of the molasses. The next morning, Jean bid the shipment, and his friend Andrew *au revoir* and *bon voyage.*

They departed on November 9th, and Jean hoped to receive good news both from the colonies and his brother's business trip in time for the annual December Christmas gathering in Jérémie.

However, Andre did not return. A week after his supposed deadline, Jean began to grow concerned. It was not like his brother to miss a grand event such as the holidays. Also worrying, Captain Martin had not returned with a load of salted fish.

Unable to wait any longer, Jean, Marie, and Jean Junior boarded a schooner bound for Jérémie on December 15th. He left instructions for Gerard and Renald to tell Andre to make haste for Jérémie the moment he returned. As for Captain Martin and his cargo, the salted fish were to be stored in the dry warehouses and sealed to prevent pilferage by cats or vermin.

The celebrations that year were as festive and spectacular as usual—but the Christmas and New Year holidays came and passed without any news from either Andre or the *Le Matin*. Jean and Marie departed on the tenth of January for the journey home on one of their scheduled cargo runs.

Back in Cap-Français, Jean sent a rider to the *Artibonite* to retrace Andre's trail. The rider soon returned with the perplexing news that Andre had never visited any of the plantations on the itinerary he'd provided Jean. Jean was now gravely concerned and contacted Georges Biassou, now head Commander for the *Maréchaussée,* who sent ten men to scour the Western *Artibonite* region for any signs of Andre Bayard.

They too returned empty-handed.

It was by now the end of February. Jean decided to write to his parents detailing the series of events, dreading every word he wrote and tearing up the letter multiple times before showing Marie the final draft. They sent the letter with the next shipment to Jérémie, dated February 28, 1779.

From then on, each shipment to and from Jérémie included pleas for updates and mournful dispatches bereft of updates in return.

Late that March, as Jean was at the warehouses, the paperboy arrived at the offices, greeting Marie with a stunning headline on the front page of the *Cap-Français Gazette*:

FRANCE ALLIES WITH AMERICAN REVOLUTION
By decree of Louis XVI, the King of France

Marie closed her eyes and the paper dropped from her hands to the floor. She knew the terms of Jean's reserve service and feared he may now be swept up into a war.

With barely any time to process the news, Jean arrived. Seeing Marie frozen in place, he ran to her. Unable to make out words, she gestured at the paper scattered across the floor under her. Jean's eyes found their way to the front page, and his heart dropped. The two embraced for a long time.

Marie eventually whispered "I'm scared Jean. I don't know if I can be without you, my love."

Before he could provide any words of support, the office door opened once more and a haggard messenger entered with a letter requiring a signature. Jean quickly signed and opened the parchment. It was a letter from Andrew Cabot.

Dear Jean,

 I regret to inform you that I have just received word stating the schooner **Le Matin** *loaded with 180 cases of dried salted cod and Captained by Gabriel Martin was intercepted and presumed sunk by the pirate Hezekiah Frith.*
 The schooner was way off course, East of where she should have been, most likely seeking a faster route to St. Domingue by taking advantage of favorable winds instead of keeping on the safe passage course I had laid out for them to follow.
 This pirate is known to ply those waters and if there are survivors, he will capture them and hold them for ransom. I know your beloved brother Andre was on that vessel, and pray that he is alive and that we will one day soon receive notice of a ransom demand.

 Your very good friend,
 Andrew Cabot

Jean did not know whether his body's trembling was a furious reaction to Andre violating his word or fear that he was now dead somewhere at sea. Or, if he were somehow alive, what dreadful acts he may be experiencing at that exact moment? He shakily handed the note to Marie who read it and put her arms around his neck, now unabashedly crying.

"*What else could go wrong?*" Jean thought to himself.

"Andre is not dead, Jean. I know it. I can *feel* it!" Marie said between tears.

The Jasmine family always had a connection with the supernatural. They felt spirits; saw and heard ghosts; dreamed of what was to come. Knowing first-hand her gift of supernatural connection, it comforted Jean to hear this from her.

Marie pulled away, leaving to pour some coffee. Unfortunately, the day's excitement was not yet done. As she filled a cup from the porcelain set she so cherished, Gerard burst in with the *Gazette* in his hands.

"What does this mean?!" He yelled to Jean.

"The same as it means for all of us, Gerard. France has joined the war in the Americas" responded Jean.

"Not for us, for *you*!" He held up a full-page advertisement on an inner page of the newspaper. It read in bold:

ATTENTION FRENCH MILITARY

ENLISTED MEN ON LEAVE
&
INACTIVE RESERVES

YOU ARE HEREBY ORDERED TO REPORT
TO
THE NEAREST REGIMENT IN YOUR AREA
BY APRIL 15, 1779

ANY ARMY PERSONNEL ACTIVE OR INACTIVE
IN VIOLATION OF THIS ORDER
WILL BE ARRESTED AND PROSECUTED

LONG LIVE LOUIS XVI, KING OF FRANCE

Six

CHASSEURS-VOLONTAIRES DE ST. DOMINGUE

Cap Français
April 1779

Jean was at a loss for words. He looked to Marie, hoping either would be able to offer some semblance of comfort to the other.

When none came, he knew what needed to be done next. He asked Marie to transcribe the letter pertaining to Andre's whereabouts and send it to Jérémie, while he composed a response back to Andrew Cabot. In it, Jean admitted he'd had no knowledge of Andre joining the journey, and to please provide confirmation of Frith's attack.

Marie composed a cover letter to Jean-Philippe and Jeanne urging them to have faith and that Jean was working on obtaining more information. She also shared her insistence that Andre was indeed still alive.

Jean and Marie solemnly went about their business for the next fortnight. This included preparations for Jean's upcoming deployment—namely getting their affairs in order should he be killed in combat. Business and personal papers were signed granting Marie unequivocal power of attorney in his absence. They discussed future business strategy as though she were already fully in charge. He ensured all his associates, from Gerard and Renald to their couriers and transporters, understood that Marie's word was law on all matters across all divisions.

After a somber and tearful farewell to his wife and son, Jean reported to the Cap-Français garrison on April 15, 1779.

His first weeks of service consisted of daily briefings, lessons in English and geography of the American colonies; and current intelligence regarding troop strength, officers, and battles. At the end of May, Jean was assigned the construction of a regiment of free *Gens de Couleur* and *Afranchi* volunteer soldiers 1,000 strong.

His men would receive an annual salary of 100 *livres* along with a 5 *livres* signing bonus, with the first 6-months advanced upon completion of training.

Jean was able to have his old friend Commander Georges Biassou temporarily reassigned to the regiment as head trainer. He requested the same for his previous lieutenant in the 110th regiment, Jean Chavannes. When word spread of the healthy salary, hundreds of men showed up within the first week. Over the next two, a total of three thousand would apply for recruitment, requiring consistent interviews and screenings to determine the best possible candidates.

The first step was a 3-day unpaid interview process in which Lieutenant Chavannes put each recruit through their paces, under the direction of 20 enlisted soldiers, to determine their fitness for the military. Those who were hired were then assigned to Commander Biassou.

Biassou brought six of his most trusted men, and requested 25 of Jean's best soldiers to become training officers under his *Marechausee* captains. Reginald, one of the officers from the plantation all those years ago, would act as Biassou's assistant and emissary. Jean approved of the Commander's methodical approach.

Strengths and weaknesses were evaluated and posts were assigned spanning from artillery to cavalry. Within a month and a half of six-days-per-week training the regiment was operating as though each man had spent a lifetime in the service. By July, the 1,000 troops were practicing war games and building their confidence for battle.

Over dinner one summer night with the Commander, Jean raised a glass of wine up for a toast.

"Georges, I commend you on the incredible work that you and your officers have accomplished with these recruits."

The two men tipped their glasses back and each took a long sip.

"As is customary for those that are not permanent regiments in the armed forces, we are granted permission to name our fighting force," Jean continued. "What shall we call ourselves?"

After a few different ideas—and more long drinks of wine— the perfect title struck them nearly simultaneously: *Chasseurs-Volontaires de Saint-Domingue*.

The Volunteer Hunters of Saint-Domingue.

Early in the afternoon of August 12th, a commotion overtook the regular activity along the Cap-Français wharf. Workers had dropped what they were doing to point out and count the massive French vessels that had appeared on the horizon. Four entered the harbor, while three remained at the mouth of the bay. Unbeknownst to the civilians along the docks and throughout the city, 18 more anchored unseen; a formidable flotilla of 25 lethal warships in total.

Shortly after the unit's arrival, Jean received orders to board a tender for the war ship *Languedoc* at six o'clock. He was to meet and dine with the Admiral—Charles Henri Hector, Comte d'Estaing. It was here he received the Admiral's decree to lead his regiment—along with several others—into the American war for independence.

What would he tell Marie?

"Jean. Jean... *JEAN-BAPTISTE!*"

Jean suddenly snapped back from his memories of the dinner with the Comte d'Estaing he'd left only an hour ago abord the Languedoc. Upon arriving home and attempting to recount the conversation to Marie, his mind had wandered; to the far off colonies embroiled in a bloody war, his brother still unaccounted for somewhere in the Atlantic Ocean, and even back to Jérémie and that night he'd met Marie…

"Where in the world did your mind go to, Jean?" implored Marie after his voice had drifted off in mid-sentence.

"I am sorry, my love. My mind took me back to the day I met you for the first time. How far we have come—you and I." Jean found it hard to focus again. "I am so in love with you, Marie." he said, gazing deep into her eyes.

"Yes, we have come a long way, Jean. And, I love you too. Now, what to do of our present predicament? You're asking me whether you should accept the Admiral's invitation to the Americas to fight in their war?" she asked.

"Yes. Your counsel has always mattered to me."

"Then the answer is yes, you will go." Marie replied.

"One, this is why you wanted to join the army all those years ago. Two, it will allow you the chance to investigate your brother's predicament as you sail north. Finally, you will learn as much as you can about these Americans and this new country, and how we can expand our business into America." she concluded.

"But you listen to me Jean-Baptiste. If you get yourself killed, so help me I will bring a voodoo priest to bring you back to life and kill you again myself!"

Jean laughed in spite of himself. Then Marie turned earnestly serious.

"Be safe, and come back to your loving wife and child."

Jean made arrangements to meet with the Admiral the following day. He relayed Andre's situation and the urgent need to locate him. He respectfully requested the Admiral's assistance should he discover Andre's whereabouts. In addition, he requested that Commander Georges Biassou and his six *Marechausee* officers assigned under him and Lieutenant Chavannes receive a promotion. In return, Jean would enthusiastically agree to join the American war.

Though unusual for a Captain to make such requests of a higher-ranking officer, d'Estaing understood the value Jean brought to their campaign and agreed to each of his terms.

Mere weeks later, Jean found himself in Savannah, Georgia—along with his new young charge, courtesy of the Admiral.

"How many cannons, Henri?"

"Twelve." said a confident Henri.

"Why do you say that?"

"The space between the cannon fire. It takes time to clean the barrel, load the powder and shot, and light the charge and fire." answered Henri. "A good team though could do it in 30 seconds, like the British. I hear explosions every two to three seconds, so I think twelve. The British are that good." he concluded.

"Henri, I was under the impression you didn't know your mathematics?" Jean responded with a mix of amusement and curiosity.

"This is warfare, not mathematics, Captain Bayard." said Henri, more quietly. "Of that I am a good student."

It was late in September, 1779. Though the air was beginning to cool, it could not overcome the humidity inherent in the Southeast of this colony. Jean and his 1,000 *Chasseurs-Voluntaries*, along with d'Estaing's 3,000 French soldiers, were under the command of General Benjamin Lincoln of the Continental Army. Their mission was to retake Savannah,

Georgia's capital, occupied for the past year by a British force numbering more than 3,200 well supplied and entrenched troops. Progress had stalled.

On the evening of October 8th, General Lincoln called a meeting with d'Estaing and Polish cavalry mastermind, Casimir Pulaski. Lincoln confided that a spy had uncovered a point of attack at the Spring Hill Redoubt. Their only resistance would be a small group of local loyalists. However, the window of opportunity was small, necessitating an immediate march on the garrison the next morning. This would prove the turning point of the battle.

"Do you trust the validity of this intelligence, General?" the Admiral asked.

"Without question. The report comes from a solid source. Prepare your officers to march before first light." responded the General. With that, he dismissed the council.

d'Estaing gathered his officers to devise a plan of attack in conjunction with Pulaski's mounted forces. The cavalry would charge from the east, while d'Estaing's infantry would strike from the center. Jean and the *Chasseurs* would tighten the noose from the west.

An hour before sunrise, Jean tasked Henri with a last minute message for Commander Biassou.

"Be back in no more than thirty minutes Henri," Jean instructed.

"Yes, Captain."

With a curt salute, Henri took off into the early morning darkness. He found Commander Biassou briefing his officers as the rest of the men made preparations to move out. The details delivered successfully, Henri quickly doubled back toward camp.

However, the sounds of voices in the woods stopped Henri in his tracks. As the entire company was supposed to be preparing for the coming battle, he crouched low and approached cautiously.

Oddly, the men were speaking English—though with two distinct accents between the two—rather than French. He snuck closer and quickly realized one of the speakers was clearly British. What was an Englishman doing mere yards from enemy ground?

"It is all set. General Lincoln believes that Spring Hill is lightly manned and will direct the brunt of his efforts there."

"Are you certain?" asked the Brit.

"He had me participate in the battle planning and advise him of the topography. The polish commander and cavalry will attack from the east, the French infantry from the center, and the colored troops from the west at dawn." explained his oddly-accented comrade. Henri deduced this to be an American colonist.

"Excellent. Our men will be ready to give them a warm welcome." replied the Brit, malice dripping from every word.

Suddenly a large arm wrapped around Henri's throat and a dirty palm covered his mouth. Before he could react, his body was hoisted from the ground by a large man, who then carried him over to the two conspirators. Henri kicked his legs and twisted his tiny body as hard as he could to no avail.

"Who are you boy?" demanded the American. Henri said nothing. The man slapped him across the face and asked again.

"Who are you?!"

"I don't understand what you are saying." replied Henri in French, cleverly masking his knowledge of English. The American's hand met his face once more, harder this time.

"What did you hear?"

"I don't know what you're saying. I speak French" Henri repeated.

"Rope and gag him so we can finish our business," interrupted the Brit. "I must alert the troops of the impending assault, so we may remain ready. The general will be pleased."

"In that case, there's something you owe me." growled the American.

"Indeed," replied the British officer, tossing him a satchel of coins.

"This is why we shall slaughter every damn one of you.

You've no loyalty to our King, and no loyalty to each other."

The man spit at the ground, turned on his heel, and left the cohort.

"Bloody git," cursed the American before looking at Henri's large captor. "Here's your share," he said, grabbing two of the gold coins from the satchel.

"Kill the kid after I leave and get your ass out of here. Have a nice life."

Henri was petrified. He contemplated pleading with his remaining captor in English, but realized his deception might further hasten his fate. He only had seconds left to figure out a means of escape—or die.

Unbeknownst to Henri however, his salvation had just happened upon him. After not returning for over an hour, and fearing for Henri's safety, Jean had mounted a small search party and ventured into the woods along the path the boy had taken. He had just caught a glimpse of Henri's head 20 yards in front of him—as well as the large man now reaching for a blade the size of a small sword with which to slit his throat.

Jean steadied himself, ignoring his pounding heart as he calculated the slight breeze, angle, and distance of his target. He lifted his rifle, found his mark, and gently squeezed the trigger. The blast echoed throughout the forest, followed almost immediately by the muffled thump of the American's body collapsing.

Jean sprinted to Henri, followed closely by his two comrades after they quickly swept the area for any other threats. Henri's clothes and face were splattered with blood and other organic matter from the fallen conspirator, but otherwise the boy was fine. Jean fought the urge to hold the boy tight in a secure embrace as Henri was clearly near hysterical with emotion. He realized how close he'd come to being killed, all alone in this cold foreign forest.

Struggling to regain his composure, Henri blurted out in a shaking voice, "It's a trap, Captain! You must stop the attack! They are planning a slaughter at the Hill of Spring! Or, the Spring of Hill…"

Jean reached out and grabbed the boy to keep him from collapsing.

"Slow down, Henri," he comforted. "Start from the beginning. What did you hear?"

Henri recounted sneaking up on the trio, overhearing their plan of deception, and how General Lincoln was playing right into their scheme. However, the sun was already breaking over the horizon, and there was precious time to spare before the assault would begin in earnest.

The party rode back to camp as quickly as possible, only to find that the regiment had already left on its way to meet Biassou on the western flank. Jean quickly procured two notes, giving one to each of his men.

"You catch up with Commander Biassou, and you with Commander Pulaski and give these to them! Ride quickly! GO!"

Jean mounted his own horse and sped to warn Comte d'Estaing, praying his men would reach Pulaski and Biassou in time. The fog was heavy in the early morning light; only the distant sounds of small arms fire could guide his path. He coaxed his steed faster.

Admiral d'Estaing was surveying the swampy landscape surrounding Spring Hill through the mist. Squinting, he could hardly make out the silhouettes of the loyalists to his northeast— just as his intelligence had promised. He sounded the march forward, and his infantrymen surged forward. To his east, Pulaski's cavalry headed into position at a slow gallop. The small group of loyalists, startled in their morning routines, immediately ran for the hills behind their settlement. Surely the mere sight of the French forces convinced them any defense was futile, the Admiral thought, as he watched the men reach the ridge. Perhaps this battle would even prove bloodless.

The last of the fog disappeared as d'Estaing dismounted from his beautiful brown mare near the front of the battle line. A victory here would win a crucial strategic position and put his legion within striking distance of Savannah itself. It was to be a good morning, indeed.

Suddenly, 200 British troops crested the hill, quickly forming a classic battle line. Those in front dropped to their knees in a firing position while those behind remained upright, also taking aim. The Admiral sounded the attack and the drummers beat their drums communicating the order through the ranks. A cheer rang out as the French forces charged up the hill. Pulaski's own charge could be heard to the east, and the cavalry stormed toward the seemingly unguarded Englishmen.

Jean had made it to the base of the valley in time to witness the Admiral leading the front line—and the first volley from the British riflemen. Men began to fall, but the attacking regiment continued forward. Jean whipped his mount's thighs hard, catching up to the rear guard. He weaved through the dead and the still-charging in a desperate bid to reach the battlefront.

To his East, Pulaski's full-on charge had nearly flanked the British line.

However, the rumble of more hooves than their own began to fill the air as they approached. Another cohort of redcoats, numbering upwards of one thousand emerged from behind the tree line, followed by the mounted British Legion, which broke off and headed straight for the Admiral and his infantry.

Pulaski could hardly comprehend the scene before hundreds of enemy combatants were on his men, efficiently cutting them down from their horses. He attempted to sound another call to charge but was struck down by the fire from several muskets. As he fell, so did his cavalry unit, as both man and horse were indiscriminately mowed down by British gunfire.

Along the front lines, the French army was crumbling in the face of incessant and overwhelming fire from the grounded shooters and mounted British Legion. d'Estaing was felled by a gunshot wound but sprang back up on the force of adrenalin and sheer willpower. He valiantly urged his soldiers forward, and the troops loyally followed his command.

Jean was only twenty yards from reaching the Admiral when his body was hit again by musket fire. The Admiral would not rise again, this time. Jean raced to his side, now finding himself in the thick of battle, savagely protecting d'Estaing from the mounted soldiers—keen to add an officer to their ledger—surrounding them. Ever the leader, the Admiral recovered his composure long enough to sound the retreat for the remaining men.

From the western edge of the battle, Commander Biassou observed the bloodshed with increasing dread. His orders were to hold back until the infantry reached the top of the hill, but not a single French soldier had reached the two front lines of loyalists. This wasn't at all what Jean had described to him. He ordered Reginald to prepare his men for battle on his signal.

Jean's courier arrived just then, forcing a folded piece of parchment into Biassou's hand. Biassou's face dropped as he read his friend's warning of the trap. He quickly redirected Reginald and Chavannes to move fast; their mission was no longer to attack, but to recover the stragglers and wounded so as to avert their capture or death by the enemy. The regiment surged forward just as the calls for retreat rose above the valley.

Jean was losing his strength. He fumbled reloading his rifle and grabbing for his sword to fend off any adversary foolish enough to find themselves within striking distance of his blade. The corners of his vision were beginning to blur. He swung wildly at shadows. He was suddenly struck by the fact that he'd missed Jean Junior's fourth birthday only days ago. Would he ever see him again? What of Marie?

A flurry of motion from the west snapped him back to the present. The soldiers turned to address the commotion occurring just past his field of view.

It was the *Chasseur* cavalry charging from their position, cutting down British horsemen as they rode. Those not on horseback were rushing to assist fallen French soldiers on the front line, protecting them as they retreated. However, the British cohort was everywhere, and the *Chasseurs* took on casualties of their own as the battle raged on. Biassou positioned his cavalry between the factions, holding off the British infantry on one side, decimating the British Legion, and blocking their retreat up the hill on the other. This allowed the retreating French army to exact their brutal revenge on the now isolated horsemen.

On Biassou's orders, Reginald and six men broke from the regiment, making a mad dash for Pulaski, who was prone on the ground. Musket fire rained down as Reginald pulled Pulaski onto his horse to retreat. The group saved another six of the fallen on their way back to the unit, knowing any who remained were doomed.

Fearing more French were waiting beyond the valley's edge, the British did not pursue the regiment. Only one hour had passed since the sun began its rise into the sky, yet the French coalition had lost approximately 1,000 men. The British suffered only 150 casualties. It was a slaughter, just as Henri had predicted.

Having escaped under the watchful eye of Biassou, Jean called a horse for the Admiral, and both quickly rode for the camp's infirmary. They found the physicians overwhelmed; many of the lesser wounded were being attended to by regular soldiers. His injuries confined to his arm and leg, d'Estaing made no fuss as Jean and another soldier extracted the musket balls from his body, cleaned the flesh, and stitched and bandaged the wounds. Upon completion, he immediately stormed off in the direction of General Lincoln's tent, Jean shadowing him closely.

Pulaski's prognosis was far more dire. Reginald rode at top speed, knowing the Polish commander had lost a significant amount of blood. They arrived at camp at full gallop, scattering soldiers and supplies. Though the surgeon removed the multiple cannon shots from his torso, Pulaski's shallow breaths and sallow complexion indicated his quickly arriving fate.

General Benjamin Lincoln had enjoyed a brilliant military career for a time; up until two years prior at Fort Edward in New York, when a stray British musket ball shattered his ankle. He was bedridden for months. When Lincoln finally emerged, his right leg was two inches shorter than his left, causing a pronounced limp—

and rumors of constant, excruciating pain. He was demoted to the lowest possible Major General ranking. This was to be his grand entrance back into the theater of battle. Instead, he was met with a furious and still bleeding d'Estaing attempting to rip into his command tent.

The two sentries posted at the entrance blocked the Admiral's entrance until ordered to allow him in by the General. Jean was forced to remain outside.

"What happened out there?" demanded General Lincoln.

"You sent my glorious army to their deaths!" roared the Admiral. "We marched straight into a trap!"

"A trap?!" repeated the General.

"Your *spy*," The Admiral spat out, "is a double agent for the British! They knew we were coming! They had a cavalry…" d'Estaing's voice quivered with rage.

"We lost over one thousand men!"

"Mind your tone, Admiral," barked General Lincoln. "You are speaking to a General of the Continental Army and your superior officer!"

"I've only just begun, General. One thousand dead. Hundreds wounded. Many may not survive the night, and others crippled for life. Their numbers are too great to overcome in Savannah. We have lost this campaign. Troops under my command are making preparations to leave come first light. I suggest you do the same before you are overrun."

The Admiral paused and stood to his full height, wincing slightly as his weight settled onto his wounded leg.

"I am an officer of the French navy, General Lincoln. I am no longer under your command."

"This campaign and your participation in it is not concluded until I allow it!" Lincoln was finding his own rage rippling just under his confusion and shock.

"No General. I will leave on my terms, not yours. I will also be taking my friend Commander Casimir Pulaski with me." d'Estaing defiantly responded.

"I do not grant him his leave—"

"Your incompetence has handed that man his death sentence!" the Admiral interrupted. "He once asked me to allow him death with the salty sea air on his last breath. If he regains consciousness before we depart, you may inquire as to his final wish yourself."

With that, he clicked his heels, turned, and exited the tent.

d'Estaing emerged from the tent and shot Jean a look that communicated it was time to leave. Just then, Henri came running up to the two at full tilt.

"He is—" Henri panted.

"He..."

"He is here! The traitor...he is in the camp!"

"Are you sure Henri? Where?" Jean put his arm on the boy's shoulders in an attempt to calm him.

"I am sure. His pouch on his belt—it is the one filled with gold given to him by the Englishman."

"Show me."

Henri hurried off in the direction he'd come with Jean. The Admiral trailed, his leg causing him no shortage of anguish.

They'd only walked a few paces before coming across a trio of American soldiers in casual conversation. One sported a rather large pouch affixed to his belt.

Jean pointed toward the man and began to approach him.

"What is your name, soldier?" Jean asked in heavily-accented English.

"I don't have to tell you my name, or anything else, Frenchie." dismissed the man.

Jean drew his pistol and pointed it directly at the antagonist's head—to the utter astonishment of the two Continental Army soldiers with him.

"Who are you, and who do you serve? I will not ask again."

"Back off, asshole! You have no command here."

"You," Jean gestured toward one of the shocked American soldiers. "Bring me that pouch on his hip."

Without warning, the accused spy whipped his pistol from his holster, shooting the other soldier in the stomach. Tossing the weapon to the ground, he pulled another, smaller firearm from

behind his back and pointed the barrel at Jean's heart.

A blast rang out, and a musket ball pierced the left side of the traitor's head. He collapsed, dead.

Jean's unfired pistol was still aimed where the dead man once stood. He hadn't had time to pull the trigger. He looked to his left.

Next to him, Henri stood, gripping a revolver in trembling hands, the rest of his body frozen in place.

Jean quickly moved to Henri, gently removing the gun from his clutches. The Admiral appeared, having hung back to monitor the altercation, limping over to check the pulse of the other soldier as the third desperately applied a tourniquet. The two locked eyes, both knowing the wound would prove fatal. Within seconds, the young man's body went limp and his breathing halted.

d'Estaing moved to the spy's body next, yanking the pouch from his belt. He poured the gold coins into his hand while shaking his head.

Turning back to the third soldier, who was still sitting next to his comrade, he asked "This man you tried to save. Did you know him?"

"Yes. We are both from the same town. We went to school together. He has a wife and a small son. What will they do now? How will they survive?" he began to sob, softly.

"What is your name Soldier?" Inquired the Admiral

"Paul. Paul Simon, Sir."

"And the name of your friend, Paul?"

"Horatio—Horatio Winters, Sir."

d'Estaing placed the pouch in Paul's hand. "Paul. I want you to honor your friend Horatio Winters by giving this money to his wife. Tell her its contents will never make up for her loss, but will help her and her child survive the next few years."

Paul looked from the Admiral, to the pouch, and back at the Admiral again.

"Put it in a safe place. Do you understand me, Paul?"

"Yes Admiral. I understand" Paul replied in a soft voice.

"Thank you. I assure you that she will get every last gold piece."

d'Estaing looked into the young soldier's eyes and knew his

word was true.

With that, Jean, Henri, and the Admiral reconvened with the rest of the regiment. Preparations were already under way for the remaining French army and the *Chasseurs* to leave Georgia as quickly as possible. 48 hours later, the company was boarding their ships, with Lieutenant Colonel Charles Tremblay handpicked by the Admiral to lead the French contingent, and Jean charged with command of the *Chasseurs*.

The French sailed east to converge with their comrades. Jean and the *Chasseurs* set their bearings south to the Herb River, a tributary of the Wilmington River, where they would find other friendly ships anchored.

The Admiral remained behind with Commander Pulaski. Despite his wishes, d'Estaing knew he would not make it to the open sea in his condition. Instead, he accompanied his friend to a Greenwich plantation northeast of Savannah, called Thunderbolt. The plantation's owner, Jane Spencer, was a pro-revolutionary woman who had hosted Pulaski and two of d'Estaing's officers several days prior to the battle. Pulaski had remarked afterward how much he enjoyed the Georgia countryside and Jane's company. He succumbed to his wounds two days later, a half-drank brandy in his hand.

Only four people were present at the burial; d'Estaing, Jane Spencer, and two French officers. With letters addressed to Pulaski's family in his hand, transcribed over his final hours, d'Estaing finally left Georgia to rejoin his army.

At d'Estaing's arrival, the armada sailed 25 miles east to the swampy waters surrounding Wassaw Sound. Protected by the difficult-to-navigate marshes, the Admiral devised the unit's next steps.

Twelve ships would join the northern French fleet, commanded by Lieutenant-General Comte Jean de Rochambeau. Colonel Tremblay would captain seven ships, along with the 470 remaining *Chasseurs*, to Guadeloupe and join the West Indies campaign.

Three ships would transport the wounded to St. Domingue and the remaining three ships would remain under the Admiral's command.

After dismissing the other captains, the Admiral requested Jean remain behind. He poured two brandies, handing one to Jean.

"Captain Bayard, I wish to express my personal gratitude to you. You fought valiantly in battle, and you saved my life."

"It was my duty and my honor, Admiral" responded Jean.

"It was unfortunate Casimir did not enjoy the same. The loss of such a man, especially to the Americans and their new cavalry, is devastating." stated the Admiral.

"My condolences, sir. I know you two were good friends."

"Indeed. I was grateful to be by his side at the end. He suffered a great deal but remained a nobleman to the end. I shall visit his family to deliver his final messages and relate his death as one resulting from deception and nothing more."

"It was a terrible day." agreed Jean softly.

The two paused momentarily, each contemplating their drinks.

"I have one final mission before I depart for France." said the Admiral.

Jean immediately shot up to formal attention. "How may I serve you, Admiral?"

"At ease, Captain. It is now my turn to serve you." replied d'Estaing.

Jean took his seat and reached for his glass, though did not take a sip.

"Select your best and most trusted *Chasseurs*. The time has come to retrieve your brother Andre from his captors."

The Admiral saw Jean's eyes light up. He knew Jean had dutifully avoided raising the subject during their campaign, but it could not have been far from his mind. A man of his word, d'Estaing planned to provide whatever resources necessary to help bring this brave man peace.

"You remembered, Admiral?"

"I never forget my commitments, Captain Bayard. Especially one to a man I respect such as you," responded the Admiral. "Here is what I have in mind."

A week had passed since the flagship *Languedoc* and two accompanying vessels began their hunt for British naval crafts in the waters off the Carolinas. It was late in the day, several miles south of Hilton Head Island, when the silhouette of a small naval ship appeared on the horizon headed toward them. The unit quickly sailed out of sight, anchoring for the night in the Paris Island inlet.

That night aboard the *Languedoc*, Jean, the Admiral, and the two other captains devised their plan. They'd split up, and ride the early morning winds east to intercept their quarry. Their target would be caught off guard, forced either to make a near-impossible about face, turn toward the shallow waters closer to land, or ram the line head-on. Strategies for each potential scenario were agreed upon, and the officers left to prepare through the night.

The sails were raised at 5:00 am the following morning, catching a brisk wind out of the inlet, and allowing them to reach full speed by 7:30 am. They'd calculated the smaller ship to reach their position by around 8:00, and there it appeared, 5 clicks south, exactly then.

Likely realizing he stood no chance against the three French ships, the British captain banked hard to starboard in an attempt to flee. The two smaller vessels expertly split to both sides, blocking her path, while the *Languedoc* approached from the front. All arrived simultaneously in such a display of force, the English were forced to surrender without firing a single shot.

The crew totaled 142 sailors, soldiers, and officers. d'Estaing ordered two of his captains to escort their captives to Paris Island, unload them, and provide a map to Savannah and ten days worth of provisions.

The captured ship was a small 20-gun Seaford Class named the HMS Rose. She was in relatively good shape, with plenty of dry powder, cannon balls, water, and other provisions onboard. The Admiral assigned twenty sailors to accompany Jean and his handpicked *Chasseurs* on their mission. Jean was granted ultimate command of the ship and expedition. Commander Biassou, Reginald, and Henri were of course by his side as well.

The following evening, Jean was invited by the Admiral for a farewell dinner.

"The time has come for my departure for France, Jean" stated the Admiral over their appetizers. It was the first time d'Estaing had referred to him by his first name rather than title. "I hope to see you again one day, and that I no longer need these crutches to support my leg!" he joked, with Jean joining in his light chuckling.

"Jean, I have a parting gift for you."

The Admiral handed him a logbook and map. Its contents consisted of all the intelligence reports the French military had gathered on Hezekiah Frith, the pirate of Bermuda.

Born in Bermuda as one of seven children to Captain William Frith and Sarah Lee, Firth was a successful captain of three cargo vessels, the largest of which being the Black Witch, with a crew comprised of both slaves and free men.

He began privateering and smuggling around 1771, from which he reportedly made a quick fortune. He was wanted by the French government for allegedly slipping into Cap Français and stealing away a captured British transport ship. He was last sighted in the Garden Grove district of Riddell's Bay, on the island of Bermuda; marked as such on the accompanying map.

Jean looked to the Admiral with gratitude and smiled.

"I never thought amid all of this that you would remember my brother's plight," Jean said.

"Ah, you continue to underestimate my sensibilities, Jean. A man of honor makes it a top priority to honor his commitments. If you learn nothing else from me, learn this lesson of honor and take it with you for life." d'Estaing answered.

The two men clinked their glasses together and each took a swig.

"Now, our final piece of business."

The Admiral slid another document across the table toward Jean.

"This document transfers ownership of Henri Christophe to you. Do not free him until his eighteenth birthday. Guide the boy until he is an adult. Find him gainful employment, and have him save his earnings. Tell him this is to purchase his freedom, but instead, the money he earns will pay the manumission tax and set the foundation for his future. Can I count on you, Jean?"

"Yes, Admiral. I will protect and raise Henri as my own." Jean replied. With that, the two parted as friends, but would never see each other again.

Seven

CHASING PIRATES

Bermuda
October 1779

Jean and his crew immediately set sail for the British island of Bermuda. Hezikiah Frith's father was known to own a general store in Riddell's Bay according to the Admiral's intelligence reports.

"How convenient to have a son in the business of stealing merchandise," thought Jean to himself.

He called Commander Biassou to his cabin to help devise a plan. As all other crew onboard only spoke French—or heavily accented English—the plan would rely upon an unusual hero: little Henri Christophe and his fluent English. Jean called for the boy to join in their meeting.

"Henri, I have an important, but dangerous assignment for you," Jean began. "After I explain the mission, you are free to refuse without repercussion. Should you decide against it, we will simply devise an alternative strategy."

"My life is yours, Captain Bayard," responded Henri. "If I die on this mission, I will be grateful to have had more adventure in this world and over my short life because of you. Whatever it is, I will do it."

So, the plan was set in motion.

Three days later, Bermuda was in sight. The ship hoisted the British flag and trimmed sail, slowing well offshore to await nightfall. Under the cover of darkness, the HMS Rose slowly made course for Horseshoe Bay on the southern side of the island.

"Furl the sails" whispered Jean, allowing the regiment to slowly creep forward in hopes of avoiding the unknown coral formations leading to the shore.

Late that night, a small tender was launched with four men accompanying Henri. He was dressed in the tattered clothes of a slave, and provided a pouch of dried meat and fish, hard crackers, and water; enough for 2-3 days of survival. Arriving at shore, Henri disembarked while the tender made a hasty retreat back to the ship. He would have one week to complete his mission and rendezvous back at the same spot the following Wednesday at midnight.

Henri pulled out the compass Jean had given him, and headed due North. Riddell's Bay was only about six kilometers across the narrow island. Moving quickly, he made it before dawn, which allowed him ample time to scout the area. Strolling through the quiet town before sunrise, he came across Frith's General Merchandise. It was a small structure, fronting a large fenced backyard. Henri approached silently, peeping through a missing wood slat. The coming dawn provided just enough light to reveal all manner of marine hardware, turnbuckles, rope, cannons, and lumber.

His observations were loudly interrupted by a barking dog running straight for the fence. Henri took off, hoping to escape before being spotted and questioned.

His next stop was the main dock, where he found a dozen different boats rocking in the lazy morning waves, and several larger vessels anchored mid-bay. By this time, the area was beginning to show signs of life. He heard a bit of commotion in front of him. Creeping closer, Henri spotted a group of eight Black boys near a couple of parked wagons. He walked up to introduce himself.

"Who are you and what are you doing here?" immediately demanded the largest of the group. Henri figured him to be a year or so older than he. The others followed behind him as he approached Henri.

"My name is *Henry* and my master sent me here to look for work," Henri replied in English, careful to provide the Anglican pronunciation of his name.

"Who your master, boy?" asked the large, mean-faced leader.

"I can't remember master's name. I only arrived yesterday and met him long enough to be told to come here. He is a very busy man." said Henri

"Where are you from? You sound British?"

"St. Christopher in the Caribbean Sea."

"Where is your master's house?"

"Up that road" answered Henri, pointing to the numerous houses lining a long, winding hill behind the docks.

One of the other boys chimed in then. "I bet he is old man Stout's slave. Sounds like something he would do."

"Yes, that may be his name," said Henri quickly.

"I don't care," said the leader. "Here are the rules: you are last in line for work. No, next to last in front of him."

The large boy gestured to the smallest of the group, standing apart from the others. The frail boy did not look up to acknowledge Henri.

"You give me one penny for every ten so long as I let you work here. Best to keep one for yourself and take the rest back to your master," he said. "You understand?"

"Yes. What is your name?"

"You call me 'Boss' and keep your mouth shut until I tell you to speak. I talk to the customers looking for slave work. Understand?"

"Yes," replied Henri.

"Go sit over there until I call for you" the boss barked.

Henri did as he was told, finding a small crate to sit on. The small boy the boss had singled out sat next to him.

"He's mean, but fair." offered the boy.

"Doesn't seem fair to me. Why does he make you last?" Henri asked.

"I get him in trouble. I cannot keep up with the rest of the crew. My muscles are not strong" he replied.

"What is your name?"

"Anderson."

"Nice to meet you, Anderson."

Anderson appeared to know everything of the town—and was eager to have a friend with whom to share. He explained how many ships docked each week, to which merchants they belonged, and even the town gossip. Henri spent the next few days gathering as much intelligence as he could, all while earning money for the odd jobs he was assigned by the boss. Knowing Anderson would receive a reprimand from his master every day he did not return with earnings, Henri would forfeit a portion of his day's wages to the young boy. The two quickly developed a strong bond.

On Monday, the boss announced an overnight job and inquired as to who of the group had permission to not return home that evening. Henri raised his hand, as did Anderson and two others.

"Let's go, then."

The boss led the group to a ship far down the dock. Henri spotted the name Sweet Witch etched into its hull.

"Have your boys load all the cargo. Come and I will show you where," came a gruff voice from the deck. Henri did not see the speaker, instead following the other boys as the boss directed them about.

It took nearly four hours without a break to load the ship. Henri was exhausted as they finally boarded the vessel. The ship untied from the wharf and began sailing toward an unknown destination. Henri did his best to note their heading as they left Riddler's Bay to the northeast, towards a group of small islands on the horizon.

Three hours hence, they arrived at a small dock. The group of boys was ordered to unload the cargo into a large thatched hut adjacent to a storage yard. Though the island appeared deserted, their freight was clearly food and supplies.

"Where are we?" whispered Henri to Anderson.

"Master Frith's island. The owner of the store in town." Anderson replied.

"What do they do here?" Henri ventured.

"No one asks." came Anderson's curt answer.

Their work was completed, and the group was given a small ration of dried fish and hard crackers and dismissed back to the ship until the following day. Nightfall came quickly and Henri and the others fell into a deep sleep born of exhaustion. Henri awoke with a start several hours later. The moon was still in the sky, and he estimated it to be around 3:00 am. He silently snuck off the ship and followed the path he'd noticed next to the hut. A short walk later brought him to a clearing filled with tents. He remained in the shadows, circling the edge, senses keen to see or hear anything. Alas, the darkness revealed none of its secrets.

Henri sat down, patiently awaiting daylight. As the shadows began to wane, he spotted another path leading away from the tents, deeper into the island. This one led to a quiet clearing as well, though instead of tents, Henri noticed what appeared to be large, tightly placed bamboo sticks coming up from the ground. The early dawn soon revealed shapes within the constructs. He quickly realized he'd happened upon an open-air jail.

One of the bamboo cells contained three naked Black girls, no more than sixteen years old. The next housed twelve Black men in good shape, bearing tattered clothes. The third held six White men in rags. The fourth was full of clucking chickens, while the final unit harbored three White women in fine, but heavily soiled dresses.

Henri looked around, spotting a water barrel, bucket, and ladle. Moving quickly, he poured some water into the bucket and walked to the first cell to offer the young girls some water. Each drank heartily. He did the same with each unit, hurrying between them. The men in the third cell were quietly speaking French.

Henri committed their faces to memory as best he could—
particularly the one who carried a striking resemblance to Jean,
albeit with a thick brown beard. He continued on to the other
bunkers, pouring the last of the barrel into a canister for the
chickens. With that, he disappeared back into the cover of the trees
surrounding the clearing.

Daylight was fast approaching now. The sun had fully crested
the horizon by the time he reached the dock.

"Who goes there?" yelled a commanding voice from his right.
Henri froze.

"It's me," replied Henri.

"Where are you going?" demanded the voice

"To the ship."

"Where were you?"

"I got off to see if there was more work, sir."

"Get your ass back on, boy! We are departing soon."

Henri crawled back into the cargo hold to find the others still
asleep. He lay down, pretending to do the same.

The ship arrived back in Riddell's Bay late that morning. The
next day was Wednesday, and Henri was due back to the tender.
After another day's work, Henri left his wages to Anderson, and as
night came, he made his way back to Horseshoe Bay. The HMS
Rose party arrived around midnight and rowed back to the ship
without incident.

Jean and Biassou were awaiting Henri's return on deck.
Genuinely happy to meet his return, the two had prepared a feast to
celebrate. Henri breathlessly recounted the week leading to his trip
to the small island owned by the elder Frith.

"Captain, there is a man there that could be your double. He
speaks French and so do the others with him."

"Do you remember where this island is, Henri?" asked Jean.

"Yes. Should we sail to the area, I can guide us."

Jean's heart lifted, and he felt a sense of relief he hadn't in
months. Andre was alive! He could never express his gratitude for
Henri's willingness to undertake such a mission, nor the gift its
successful completion had provided.

Biassou unfurled the French intelligence map, and Henri pointed out the two islands the Sweet Witch had sailed between, as well as the approximate location of the small island beyond.

The next day, the HMS Rose set sail for the northwest tip of Bermuda, careful to stay to the west so as not to be spotted by anyone on shore. That night, they set their bearings to take them just west of their destination, anchoring on the opposite side of the dock leading to the main camp.

Jean directed Biassou to take 20 *Chasseurs* with them, as well as Henri, who insisted on joining. They boarded several tenders in order to provide room for their rescues. The company relied on machetes to cut through the thick vegetation of the jungle, until Henri recognized the tent village up ahead, bathed in the pale moonlight. They doubled back to the north, which would take them to the jail cells.

The sun was now beginning to rise and they would soon lose their cover of darkness. Three of Biassou's men stood guard just before the second clearing, while five more traversed down the path to intercept any potential trouble.

Jean approached the cage with the six Frenchmen, unnerved by how rough they appeared. Still, he recognized Andre instantly.

"Andre, it is me, Jean!" he whispered.

"Jean? By the good graces of the Lord! Thank God you have found us."

"Open the doors to all cages" Jean ordered the remaining *Chasseurs*. He then turned back to the men with Andre and the rest of the group.

"I have come to rescue my brother, but we have room for all of you. I cannot guarantee where, but we will transport you somewhere safe away from here. Is there any amongst you who wishes to stay?"

The vote to leave their prison proved unanimous.

The *Chasseurs,* freed prisoners, Henri, Biassou, and Jean all retraced their freshly carved path back to the tenders, boarding quickly. The mariners aboard the HMS Rose began to haul anchor and ready the moment the first tender came into sight.

"Head north to round the peninsula," Jean ordered as the crew worked feverishly to bring aboard the additional bodies and haul up the tenders. Once aboard, Jean gathered the group of captives, inquiring as to their origins. The three British ladies were aboard a ship attacked by a group of Spanish pirates before being sold to Frith. They requested safe transport to Hamilton, the capital of Bermuda. Jean agreed to bring them near the town but refused to dock considering their need to escape from the island's waters as quickly as possible.

The dozen Black men were slaves stolen from a slave ship bound from St. Vincent to Grenada. Jean offered to bring them to St. Domingue, agreeing not to sell them into slavery, though he could not guarantee anything past that. They agreed.

The three young girls were traumatized from the continuous rape and brutality they had been subjected to by the pirates, and could hardly speak. Jean promised safety and fair treatment, but nothing further upon reaching their destination. They agreed as well.

Jean then asked the cook to furnish breakfast and water. He also provided all with fresh clothes, courtesy of the British Navy, found in the ship's lockers.

He then went to his cabin to address Andre and the others. The cook had provided a warm breakfast and a pint of rum each to lift their spirits. Upon entering, Andre ran up, hugging him tightly and crying.

After a momentary embrace, Jean pulled back.

"I love you too, brother, but you stink. Accompany these men to the bathing area and scrub yourselves as you never have before," he joked. "We will discuss your sightseeing adventures soon enough."

Daybreak the following morning found the ship outside Hungry Bay on the south side of Bermuda. Addressing the ladies in English, Jean announced "In keeping with diplomatic relations, I must say it has been a pleasure to have you aboard our vessel. My men will take you ashore." He reached into his pocket. "Here is a compass. Head due north until you reach Fort Hamilton, and announce yourselves. I bid you farewell and good luck."

The women had bathed, adorned sailor's uniforms, and were hopeful to make it back to England one day.

"Thank you, Messieurs. For a Frenchman, you are kind, indeed." said the eldest of the three. Jean helped each into the tender, watching as they made their way toward the harbor.

Shortly afterward, Andre found him on the top deck, again thanking him for saving their lives.

"You are welcome brother, but unfortunately I must now kill you for pulling such a stunt. What were you—"

A bang echoed across the water before Jean could finish. He immediately recognized it as cannon fire.

"Commander, how far is that tender?" he yelled to Biassou.

"On its way back, but halfway between us and shore, Captain. Twenty minutes. They are making good time!" Biassou bellowed back.

Another bang.

The ship's captain then called down to Jean. "Pirates! 10 kilometers southwest, Captain. These must be warning shots as they are out of range."

"How long until they are on us?" asked Jean.

"They are at full sail. Looks to be a Seaford 6th-rate class ship. Top speed of twelve clicks an hour. I estimate forty-five minutes."

Jean let into action. "Weigh anchor and ready to set sail! Commander, get your men on board as soon as they pull aside and prepare them for combat. Captain, ready the cannons for battle and set a course to intercept on our port side. We cannot outrun them in time, so we shall fight!"

Minutes later, Biassou's men were back on board and the *Chasseurs* were readying their muskets, hungry for a fight. The sails went up and the HMS Rose lunged forward through incoming swales but had a hard time picking up speed. The inbound ship was less than six clicks away, heading straight for them.

The sails of the Rose filled and the strain of stretching wood provided a soundtrack as the ship surged forward through the incoming tides of the bay. "Four clicks Captain!" yelled a sailor as the pirate ship launched another cannonball. "They are still out of range!"

"Let them waste their cannon. Ours have a range no further than one and a half clicks with dry powder" Jean instructed the captain. "Have your men fire on my command."

"Three Clicks! They are turning towards us. They intend to ram!"

"Good," Jean replied.

"WHAT!" Exclaimed the captain in surprise.

"Stay on course and ready to turn to port on my command."

"Two clicks" yelled the sailor as another series of cannonballs were launched; still falling short, but the spray of the splashes was beginning to reach the men's faces.

"Hold your fire until we begin to pass! I want us ten meters apart," shouted Jean. "Aim eight cannons at their masts. Commander, have your men take aim and kill anyone sighted on deck. Captain, have the remaining two cannons destroy the rudder as we steer behind her. Get ready to turn!"

"One click. They are within range!" cried the sailor.

"Remain on course to head straight towards her bow," commanded Jean. "She cannot fire at us on a collision course."

"Three hundred meters, sir" yelled the sailor.

"Begin your turn ten degrees to port now!" yelled Jean to the captain. "Let's hope her starboard cannons are not yet loaded as they were expecting us from the other side."

The Rose began her turn to port.

"She sees our turn and is attempting a starboard turn to ram," said the sailor.

"She's turning her nose right to us. Starboard twenty degrees now!" yelled Jean. "Hold your fire until you are certain you can hit her masts. Four cannons on each!"

"One hundred meters!"

"Commander, be ready to fire on sight!" Jean called Biassou. He barely made out a hint of a smile come across his friend's face before turning his attention back to the incoming ship.

The Rose's position gave the artillery perfect alignment to aim as both ships came within ten meters of each other. Jean was now close enough to make out the name: Night Witch.

Frith's flagship boasted 20 guns, just like the Rose. The *Chasseurs* opened fire, many of them finding their targets. The explosions emanating from Rose's cannons instantly destroyed two of the masts, causing the entire mechanism to come crashing onto her deck.

As the Rose came halfway past, Jean ordered "Port twenty degrees!"

The Rose pivoted, allowing a clear shot to the rear rudders of the Night Witch. Their aim was true, the ability of the pirate's ship to steer was suddenly decimated.

"Come about to Starboard!" yelled Jean. Hardly two minutes had passed, yet the Rose whisked away from the battle, leaving a smoking Night Witch stranded at sea. A cheer erupted from all present. The feeling of having cheated death was infectious, and delirious smiles and embraces were shared.

"Well done, all!" Jean yelled above the celebrations. "Make course south-southwest Captain, and take us home. You have the command."

"Oui Mon Capitaine"

Jean found Andre on the deck, who was gazing westward as they sailed away from Bermuda. "Thank you, brother," he said to Jean, softly. "I made a dire mistake, and only hope that you can forgive me."

"You are incorrigible, Andre. Just wait until Maman gets ahold of you. You will wish you'd stayed on that god-forsaken island." chided Jean as he looked up at a beautiful sky.

"Now, go and remove that ugly beard from your face so I can finally confirm you truly are my long-lost brother."

Andre looked at Jean with unfathomable love in his eyes. A tear dribbled down from his left eye to join a stream from his right.

He suddenly embraced Jean, bawling uncontrollably. The trauma from the past year seemed to hit him all at once. Andre could not tell whether his tears were those of joy or torment; all he knew was he was away from the hell he'd endured, and grateful to be alive.

Eight

HOMECOMING

Cap-Français
November 1779

The flotilla remained at sea for the next four days until St. Domingue arose from the horizon. The full view of the harbor came into sight as they rounded the point of Cap-Français, and butterflies formed in the pit of Jean's stomach; he was finally coming home to Marie and Junior. The vibrant sounds of the city; the scent of coffee, the smoke of charcoal, and the humid, heavy air welcomed the crew as they docked at the wharf. It was a Monday, and the dock was a typical flurry of activity.

It's good to be home, Jean thought to himself.

Glimpsing the port authorities awaiting their arrival snapped Jean back to reality momentarily. He had a lot of paperwork ahead of him, especially pertaining to the extra persons onboard not of the French registry. Fortunately, the officer on duty at the customs office that day was an old acquaintance: Mr. Morven.

Some fast-talking, a 60kg sack of coffee, and some extra cash helped grease the wheels. Nearly three hours of documentation later, Jean was able to register the twelve slaves as freed men of color, and the girls as George Biassou's nieces, also with fresh visas as freed women of color.

The ship itself required a bit more finagling. Jean promised

Morven that his wife, Florence, would receive five of the latest designer dresses on their next importation from Paris. He also offered dinner at *Chez Gerard's* for their wedding anniversary, one of the best restaurants at Cap-Français. Mr. Morven smiled widely in acceptance, and the HMS Rose received new French registration papers—albeit renamed as the *Le Matin*. Both parties parted ways delighted with the transaction.

Jean then turned his attention back to Andre. He'd observed a strained relationship between his brother and Gabriel Martin, the original *Le Matin*'s Captain over their brief return voyage. He called both into his cabin on the newly christened ship.

"Captain Martin, Andre has taken responsibility for leading you, your crew, and the ship into this mess," he began. "He told me how he coaxed you from the safe passage our friend Andrew Cabot had ensured."

"Yes, sir—but I was Captain. I bear equal responsibility." Martin replied.

"That's admirable of you, Captain. However, we Bayards do not make a habit of allowing others to bear responsibility for our poor decisions." Jean reached for the registration papers and handed them to Martin. "I hope this may go some way toward recouping your loss. Here."

The papers now listed *Le Matin* with a length sixteen meters longer than its namesake—a hearty increase in wealth for the young captain.

"You have twenty-four hours to repaint the correct name on her stern," Jean said with half a wink.

Captain Martin's eyes grew large. "I don't know what to say…"

"Of course, there are conditions, Captain. First, you will sail for my business exclusively for as long as I can provide you with enough cargo for voyages to the Americas. Second, provide your other four crew members the uniforms from the storage lockers—after removing all traces of British insignias."

Jean continued without interruption; "Third, the twelve slaves from our voyage here are now free and in need of jobs and housing. You, with your new ship and business connection, are in need of workers. You will hire them at half the normal pay rate for the first year while you train them as capable mariners. After that, you can decide whether you'd like to keep them employed or not. I want them to prove their worth."

"Lastly, sell all the cannon and other equipment and cargo aboard in order to pay your remaining crew as compensation for the horrors they have endured over the past year. As for those four who lost their lives to the pirate Hezekiah Frith, I will provide five times their annual pay—each—to their families. Do you accept these terms?"

Captain Martin looked at Jean in stunned silence. Unable to speak, he simply extended a hand, and with a quick shake, hurried to inform his crew of their good fortune. Jean tasked Andre with locating the twelve newly freed men and instructing them as to where they would meet the Captain.

Making his way back up to the main deck, Jean encountered Commander Biassou directing the debarking of his men and the French sailors.

"My friend, I cannot repay you for everything you have done for me, my brother Andre, and the *Chasseurs*."

"Not to worry, Jean. I always find a way to collect!" Biassou laughed his hearty laugh, slapping Jean on the back. "There are many fine restaurants in St. Domingue that I have yet to taste, Captain Bayard."

"Of that I am sure," smiled Jean. "Could you escort the French mariners to the fort and introduce them to the commander there?"

"Indeed. I will do so as soon as we disembark."

"Go with God, Georges. I am certain we will meet again soon."

"Si dye vle, Jean. si dye vle" - God Willing, Jean. God Willing

The two hugged, kissed each other's cheeks with the familiarity of true friends, and Biassou's hulking shoulders disappeared down the plank to the dock.

"Henri, where are you?" called Jean. No sooner had the last syllable left his lips did Henri arrive at his side, standing at attention. He provided the boy with a lengthy note.

"You will take the three girls to the *Hotel La Couronne* on *Rue Cambon*. Ask for Mr. Coidavid and provide him with this note."

Jean then walked over to the three teenage girls, clustered together and anxiously watching the bustling of sailors around them. Addressing them gently, Jean said, "Girls, you are welcome in St. Domingue. I am sending you to a safe place to stay for the night. I will return tomorrow and we will discuss your options. Please do not leave the hotel. Do you understand me?"

They nodded their heads in unison. Jean knew their flesh wounds would heal in a short time, but the emotional scars within would, unfortunately, last a lifetime. Just then, Andre returned onboard.

"Henri, guide them to the hotel and come back to the ship. I will have Andre come for you." Henri walked down the plank, waving for the trio to follow.

"Andre, come with me."

Jean walked down the plank with Andre close on his heels. They headed directly to the Bayard business offices two blocks away. Jean paused at the entrance. His time away and the fear of what he had missed—and nearly lost on more than one occasion—suddenly seemed to weigh heavily on his shoulders. A thousand emotions swirled within him. He took a deep breath, composed himself, and opened the door.

Marie was behind her desk, transcribing the day's notes in the ledger. The door opened and the warm sea air swept in, enveloping her with its salty scent. But with it, something else. Something undeniably different, yet familiar. She dropped the pen, daring not to look up yet, lest her longing heart gets the better of her. She couldn't help herself, however; her eyes darted to the entryway and landed upon her Jean.

Marie opened her mouth in delight, yet no sound came out as

she ran over to him. They embraced for eternity. Eventually, Marie realized someone else had accompanied her husband into the shop.

She let go of Jean and hugged Andre tightly.

"Tell me…everything!" she said, breathlessly. Before either of them could say anything in response, a clamor came suddenly from the stairs.

"Papa! Papa!"

Jean Junior ran into his father's arms. Jean picked him up and held him close. Marie shed a tear and wrapped her arms around them both. Pulling away, Jean placed Junior back on the floor and looked once more at Marie. She was as intoxicating as ever.

"Andre, Jean Junior will want to see the ship we came on. Take your nephew on a tour of the entire ship. I expect it will take at least an hour. Do you understand?"

Andre looked from Jean to Marie and back. Chuckling lightly and shaking his head, he took Junior's hand.

"Come Jay-Jay. Come see the big boat that Papa and Tonton Andre came in on."

"Yes, Tonton Andre. Please take me. Don't worry Maman, I will be good." Jean Junior squealed with excitement.

"On your way back, bring Henri with you," called Jean as Andre and Junior briskly walked out the front door.

Marie gave Jean a seductive smile.

"I haven't seen that look since the first night I walked you home in Jérémie" Jean whispered.

"Has it been that long, my love? Remind me."

Jean walked to the front door, locked it, and flipped the wooden "open" sign around. He turned back and scooped Marie into his arms as she buried her head in his chest, kissing his neck.

He raced with her up the steps to the bedroom, where they made passionate, beautiful, homecoming love together.

Lying naked together afterward, Jean recounted some of his stories, glossing over or leaving some parts out to instead focus on little Henri and his plight. He asked Marie whether the boy could stay with them—to which she agreed, as long as they developed a plan for his future.

A little over two hours later, Andre, Henri, and Jean Junior came back to the office, the door having been unlocked about 15 minutes prior. Jean was coming down the stairs as they arrived.

"Papa, I love the ship! Can I ride in it one day?" Jean Junior pleaded. "Also, meet my new friend Henri! He likes to play with me!"

"Of course my son, you will ride on the ship one day soon," Jean replied, smiling. "Henri, please meet Marie, my wife. Marie, this is Henri Christophe."

"Welcome to St. Domingue, Henri" Marie said with a warm smile. "Jean has spoken nothing but good of you."

"Thank you, Madame. Thank you, Captain. I am fortunate to be here." responded Henri as he respectfully bowed his head.

"I will have a room made up for you," Marie said. "Now, fetch your belongings from the ship and hurry back here," she ordered, as Jean and Jean Junior began to wrestle behind her.

Laughing, Jean picked his son up by the ankles and carried him to the couch. "Come—tell me everything I have missed that you have learned these past months."

The next day, Marie met the three rescued girls and placed them under the care of their head house servant, Madeleine. She saw to their comfort and made room for each in the servant's wing. Rather than slaves, these paid domestic helpers were provided room and board at the residence.

Madeleine enacted a training program to acclimate the girls to life on St. Domingue. Now considered free, Jean explained that after a month he would help them find employment in the city should they desire.

Despite his trying ordeal, Andre was anxious to get back to his sugar business. Since communications with the American colonies were difficult due to the war, he and Captain Martin planned a run to Massachusetts early the following year, taking their chances with a load of molasses. The risks were no fewer than before, but a successful delivery and return of dried codfish would be so lucrative as to make the dangerous voyage worthwhile. Jean agreed to again finance the expedition on the sole condition they do not veer off course this time.

Concurrently, Jean and Captain Martin established a route between Port-au-Prince and Jérémie for light cargo and coffee. He wished to test Captain Martin's business skills, hoping to eliminate his reliance on expensive common carriers for their inter-island cargo.

Jean and Marie quickly resumed a normal routine in his first week back. Jean was impressed by Marie's management of the business while he was away; particularly the loyalty she commanded from the employees. When she entered the warehouse, they treated her with respect and the dignity deserving of her leadership.

The Friday afternoon after their arrival found Jean utterly exhausted. He hadn't stopped working since they'd docked earlier that week. He and Marie had completed the final ledger audits and were more than content with the results; accounting for the losses of dried fish sunk with Andre's first expedition, the money promised to the deceased crew's family, and other expenses, they were on track to end the year with a healthy profit.

"Marie I am impressed, I must admit," Jean said. "You have done brilliantly well. I may just march down to the fort and re-enlist for the next military expedition!"

"You jackass!" she scolded, slapping his arm. "You leave me again, and a musket ball will be the least of your worries!"

The two laughed, enjoying each other's company.

"I wish to take you to a celebratory dinner tomorrow night, just the two of us. Perhaps a show? Dancing?" Jean said suddenly.

"I would love any and all of that, Jean," Marie replied. "Surprise me. Romance me all night long."

Marie chose her most sensuous gown the following evening and joined Jean on a short carriage ride to the same restaurant they'd patronized on their first trip to Cap Français. By now, however, the two were well known to the Maitre'd, and with a generous palm tip, were guided to the best table in the establishment.

They dined, laughed, and conversed for hours. It was the first time they'd been alone together, away from Jean Junior. Marie wanted to know everything of Jean's time away, and he now freely recounted the trip—though it would take many more dinners to cover every adventure.

Leaving the restaurant, the lovers attended the latest Parisian comedy show at *Le Soleil* Theater. Both laughed immensely, having the time of their lives. Afterward, the same stroll from their first night awaited them. Passing by the telltale red lights, they laughed to themselves—more than half of their business associates would likely recognize them this time around should they dare to enter again.

So they stopped in the Grand Hotel's lounge, where a voluptuous singer serenaded them with ballads of love and tragedy. Ordering her usual Benedictine and Jean his Cognac, they committed not to speak any further words of business or adventure.

Instead, they would listen to the soulful voice of the soloist, and simply revel in each other's presence. As the Benedictine and Cognac took their effect, Marie pointed out that responsible parents would head home. Jean confessed he had spoken with the nanny, Simone, and informed her they would not be coming home that night.

Marie gave him a look of seduction. "So, where are we going to sleep then, Jean?"

Jean pulled a hotel key from his vest pocket and smiled at her.

"You had this all planned out, didn't you?"

"After the great deeds she has accomplished in my absence, my wife deserves a night free of responsibility, and full of satisfaction."

"Order some cake for dessert to replenish your strength. Get me Benedictine and you a Cognac. Meet me upstairs."

Snatching the key from Jean, she hurried from the table.

What more can a man ask for? Jean wondered as he requested the drinks, cake, and a tray for both from the waiter.

The room was dim when he arrived; illuminated only by the candles Marie had lit. He found her in the darkness, wearing only a towel.

"Tonight, two women are waiting for you, Captain. You may take turns indulging in either your wife—or your whore," Marie whispered slowly, dropping the towel from her body. "Which do you wish to ravish first?"

They switched between passionate lovemaking and raw sex throughout the night. He at times was gentle or rough; she was aggressive or docile. They exhausted themselves playing out their fantasies, finally collapsing into sleep. The next morning they again came together, before washing, checking out, and arriving home before Jean Junior had awoken. The house cook prepared a lavish breakfast for all, consisting of hard-boiled eggs, smoked herring, plantains, malanga, and yucca, accompanied by warm bread, butter, juices, and coffee. The week had seemingly lasted an eon yet was somehow over in the blink of an eye.

Henri happily lived with the Bayards, quickly becoming part of their extended family. During the week he worked throughout the warehouses, ran errands, loaded ships, and helped with general maintenance. On weekends, he, along with Jean, Marie, and Jean Junior, spent every Sunday afternoon on the beach with a picnic basket of meals prepared by the cook.

Marie took immediately to Henri. She appreciated how genuinely he paid attention to Jean Junior. One Sunday, she was lying back in the sand, leaning on Jean's chest and watching Henri and Jean Junior on the shore. They played in the water, built sand castles, and ran up and down the beach. It was as though Henri, at twelve years old, was discovering being a child for the first time in his life.

She had to admit it was quite comical at times. Henri, nearly three feet taller than Junior, played with him as an equal. Even as Henri picked Junior up, carrying him to water deeper than his

head, she felt no fear. Henri would never put Junior in danger—
he'd likely lay down his life for him, in fact. Of that she was
certain. Henri was family up to and until he earned his freedom;
and would still be considered as such after.

The Christmas holidays were fast approaching. The annual
jaunt to Jérémie to meet with family was drawing near, and
naturally, Henri was invited to accompany the Bayards back home.
On December 15th, Jean, Marie, Jean Junior, Henri, and Andre
boarded the *Le Matin* for the voyage. Captain Martin had his cabin
cleaned for Jean, Marie, and Junior to sleep in, while he, Andre,
and Henri bunked with the first mate.

The trip was leisurely. Jean enjoyed observing the crew as
they continued to train the twelve freed slaves in the art of
navigation, hoisting and trimming sails, measuring longitude,
latitude, and wind speeds; and how to set the ship's course and
speed. All were attentive, happy, and engaged in their new trade.

They landed in Jérémie on a Saturday afternoon and traveled
to the Jasmine family compound. A wonderful reunion dinner
followed, with Marie's parents sharing the latest news, gossip, and
goings on in Jérémie.

Sunday morning, the cohort surprised Jean's parents at church.
Jeanne burst into tears at the sight of Jean and Andre together. The
sermon was one of thanksgiving and faith; the priest held up
Andre's rescue as a testament.

The Jasmines joined the Bayards at the plantation that
afternoon, feasting together nearly until nightfall. It was a glorious
day filled with stories and anticipation of the upcoming holidays
and the newly arriving decade of 1780. Jeanne and Jean Philippe
gave Andre no shortage of lectures, which both knew would go
unheeded as soon as the holiday season concluded.

Henri and Captain Martin were invited to all family
celebrations, which they both accepted with gratitude. Henri had
never known a life such as this existed.

The festive weeks at home were always a welcome retreat for Jean. However, he and Captain Martin stole away time to make plans for expanding their freight business. They even sailed to Port-au-Prince for meetings with forwarders, finding one they deemed trustworthy.

The New Year brought a promise for all, and each counted their blessings and their good fortune. The freight business grew to include cargo shipping schedules from Cap-Français to Jérémie and Port-au-Prince and back to Cap-Français. When the ship was to be sailing to America, two smaller vessels would be subcontracted.

In February of 1780, Andre and Captain Martin completed their trip to Massachusetts loaded with molasses, returning successfully with dried fish to sell to plantations. The 14-day journey went without incident despite the colonies' still-raging war for independence. Subsequent trips would be scheduled every four weeks, adding a lucrative food division to the family business.

Between 1780-1783, the Bayard enterprises thrived; exports of sugar, indigo, and mahogany were sent to France, and molasses to New England; while imports of hardware, luxury goods, clothing, and dried cod were received. Those years were a golden era of prosperity that would soon turn crucial for the unseen troubles that lay in wait.

Nine

❧

HÔTEL DE LA COURONNE

Cap-Français
June 1783

In the summer of 1783, the Bayards' lives were primed to change once more. Gabriel Coidavid, the owner of Hôtel de La Couronne in downtown Cap-Français, approached Jean and Marie with a partnership offer. The daily responsibilities were proving too much for the aging proprietor and his wife Christiane. The couple wished to spend more time together, and the hotel was ready for an expansion in which he elected not to invest. The time had come for a fresh direction.

The prospect was certainly an exciting one, though Jean and Marie vowed only family members and trusted confidants would join them in any business ventures. Henri would be a good choice, with the goal of training him over time in all areas of the operation.

By this time, Henri had quickly blossomed into a mature sixteen-year-old whose outgoing and cordial nature was appreciated by all whom he interacted with. To be sure, his social skills were downright infectious. He'd grown so immersed in the family that he was referred to as a Bayard publicly—to no objection from Jean or Marie. Believing the hotel might present a sound investment in their collective futures, they agreed to a 50% stake in the property.

The *Hôtel de La Couronne* attracted the best of Cap-Français. Many were owners of plantations, rich from their sugarcane and coffee profits hailing from the fertile region known as the *Plaine du Nord*. These were emigres from France taking advantage of the soil responsible for the thriving agriculture that led to their wealth. The hotel was a favorite destination in which to part with their money—and Coidavid and his staff were happy to oblige.

Its lush courtyard restaurant featured comfortable seats under the dwarf palms which encouraged patrons to gaze upon the distant mountains to the east after a lavish meal. Perhaps the establishment's main attraction was the infamous Wine Room—where glasses of superior vintages of French wine mixed with stories and songs of home, delighting the French planter class. There were tables for billiards, dominoes, backgammon, and cards. Gossip came easy as the wine and spirits lubricated tongues, and news originating from the *Plaine du Nord*—as well as France and America—spread quickly within the club.

The life of a French planter in St. Domingue was one of ease and prosperity. However, most French women did not enjoy their time on the island as much as their husbands. While the men gradually grew attractive bronze tans, their women seemed to age more quickly than back in their homeland. As such, most planters took up young Creole mistresses when their partners fled back to Europe and openly flaunted them at the hotel.

With the terms of the deal in place, Jean, Marie, and Henri traveled to meet with Monsieur Coidavid on the hotel's campus. As they exchanged pleasantries over a dark espresso in his office, Jean could not help but notice its sophisticated extravagance, likely accumulated over decades.

The office was furnished with locally-crafted mahogany furniture boasting carvings of sugar cane, oxen carts, machetes, and slaves' working fields. The solid and substantial pieces were meticulously sanded and finished in a dark high gloss stain.

The bright, framed artwork on the walls featured splashes of reds, yellows, oranges, blues, and other vibrant colors. Each depicted people of the island working or cooking; children washing laundry by a river and swimming under waterfalls, and a host of family gatherings and occasions; a wedding, baptism, voodoo ceremony, and a couple embracing.

The walls were the color of bone, the floor covered in pristinely waxed red clay tiles, and a cowhide lay under a cocktail table in the large sitting area—four heavy armchairs and a couch with thick fabric cushions beside it. Coidavid's desk, bookcase, and glass ornamental chest were closest to Jean.

"I absolutely love your decor," breathed Marie. "Commanding and formal, yet comfortable and intimate. Bravo."

"Merci, Madame Bayard. I selected each component myself over time," said Coidavid, happily accepting the praise.

"The carvings on your desk and tables are quite interesting. They remind me of the plantation," Jean added.

"Indeed, Jean," replied Coidavid. "You may have heard I was once a slave who purchased my freedom. Each scene depicts this colony's bounty, and the work necessary to realize it. I will never forget when that bounty depended upon my own hands. These engravings remind me daily of where I came from, and for what I am eternally grateful."

Henri could not keep his eyes from darting between the sights before him but paused when he heard Coidavid's admission. *What a life this man must have lived! He was once a slave just like me!*

One day, I hope to be just like him, thought Henri; Free and successful!

Marie glanced over to Henri and felt her heart swell with pride. He looked properly professional, dressed in his best suit. While he did not ever speak until addressed, she knew his eloquence and intelligence would impress Monsieur Coidavid.

Henri began his career as a server in the Wine Room and restaurant. He also sporadically assumed concierge duties in relief of the full-time employee. Henri quickly became notable at the hotel—respected by employees and customers alike. His pleasant personality was lauded by the guests and his tips quickly mounted.

Two years later, on the occasion of Henri's eighteenth birthday, Jean and Marie organized an elaborate party, inviting all of their and Henri's friends, as well as Mr. Coidavid's guests. It was a night of celebration full of music and food, lasting nearly until dawn.

Henri's most precious goal was his freedom, which he'd long worked toward. Now, on his eighteenth birthday, he'd saved more than 200 livres—though still well short of the cost he'd owe to Jean. However, he had a plan: tonight, he'd approach Jean with his savings, and graciously request a loan for the remaining balance and manumission taxes, with an interest of course.

After the partygoers had all finally retired, Jean, Marie, Henri, and Jean Junior stayed behind to help the staff prepare the restaurant for the quickly approaching morning. Knowing Jean and Henri had some business to discuss, Marie informed her husband that she was taking Jean Junior home to bed.

"I will send the carriage back for you, Jean," she said while boarding it as the driver gently carried the sleeping eleven-year-old boy.

Jean picked up a snifter of cognac. "Come, sit with me, Henri. I wish to speak with you." Jean looked lovingly upon Henri and offered him a glass. Henri politely refused, pouring himself a glass of water instead.

"You have made me quite proud over these past several years," Jean began. "You are part of our family. I consider you a brother, and trust you with my life."

"I feel the same, Captain Bayard. You have provided me a life I never knew existed; one that surprises me each day with its blessings."

Jean raised his snifter in gratitude and took a thoughtful sip, Henri following his lead.

"There is of course an unfinished matter which we will finally conclude tonight."

Henri straightened up slightly in his chair.

"How much have you saved during your time at the hotel?" asked Jean.

"I have 246 livres, which is short of the 300 needed to purchase my freedom. I also do not have the 60 livres tax for the government," Henri replied, hanging his head slightly. "It is not enough."

"Excellent. We shall draw up your papers immediately," stated Jean.

Henri was afraid he'd misspoken. Or perhaps Jean was drunk. "I do not understand, Captain. I do not have the full amount. May I owe you the balance—with interest?" Henri offered.

"Henri," Jean began. "Your years of maturity and loyalty have satisfied the only debt you have ever owed me. I made a promise to Admiral Charles Henri Hector, Comte d'Estaing, that I would make sure you worked hard, saved the fruits of your labor, and be granted your freedom on your eighteenth birthday. You are free, Henri."

Henri sat, stunned.

"You will only be responsible for the manumission tax, of which you have more than enough. The rest of your money is your own, with which you can start your adult life." Jean concluded.

Henri took a deep breath of the cool evening air. It felt different; somehow lighter. Sweeter. Fresher.

"I don't know what to say, Captain."

"From one free man to another, Henri, I wish you the very best," Jean replied. "I love you."

"This is the most magnificent gift ever!" exclaimed Henri, jumping up. "I have never said this before, but if this feeling is indeed love, then I love you too, Captain.

Jean rose to meet him, embracing the young man in his arms.

"Now, go and get some rest, as you are on breakfast duty at 6:00 am," Jean winked as the carriage returned for him. "Good night, Henri."

"Captain—" started Henri.

"From now on, you call me Jean, Henri" interjected Jean.

Henri smiled. "Jean, I want to be called *Henry*, my English name."

"*Henry*, Henri?" Jean repeated, pronouncing each with English and French accents. "Why?"

"It represents my newfound freedom. It's subtle but significant." Answered Henri. "It will remind me of where I came from as I discover where I am going. Is this agreeable for you Cap—, I mean Jean?"

"Of course, Henry", Jean said, careful to ensure the new pronunciation. "From now on, you are Henry and I am Jean."

As time passed, Henry assumed responsibility at *La Couronne*. His constant interactions with the hotel's well-heeled guests also served as education on the island's political climate. St. Domingue was a powder keg of ideas and ideals and separated by a stark caste system that Henry was still in the process of understanding.

At the time, the 23,000 White Frenchman calling the island home were separated into two groups: The *Petits* and *Grands Blancs*. The latter was the rich, planter class who frequented the hotel. The *Grands Blancs* disliked their tax obligations, particularly due to the lack of representation in the French National Assembly. Boasting approximately 15,000 plantations, the taxes derived solely from St. Domingue constituted half of the French monarchy's total tax revenue. Furthermore, they were also bound by the *Exclusif*—which predetermined favorable prices for French imports to and exports from the colony.

The hotel guests often spoke of their displeasure both openly and in hushed whispers, and it wasn't uncommon to overhear heated conversations regarding independence—something that America had just recently wrestled from the British. As time went on, more and more of the patrons identified as revolutionary; defiant to the laws of France.

The *Grands Blancs* were also constantly aggrieved with the poorer White class, the *Petits Blancs*. These were artisans, Blacksmiths, carpenters, masons, shopkeepers, merchants, teachers, slave supervisors, and various other trades of middle and lower income. The *Petits Blancs* often owned or leased slaves themselves, though not near the numbers belonging to the planters. The *Petits Blancs* were loyal to France, content with the status quo, committed to the practice of slavery, and vehement racists; viewing free persons of color, or *Gens de Couleur*, with jealousy and as economic and social competitors.

The *Gens de Couleur* numbered nearly 25,000 Blacks, mulattoes, quadroons—children or descendants of at least one-quarter of Black—and Black *Afranchi*, who had either been granted or purchased their freedom from slavery. Henry now proudly identified himself as an *Afranchi*.

Many free people of color frequented the hotel alongside the Whites. Many were also quite wealthy, usually more so than the *Petits Blancs*, and even some of the *Grands Blancs*. They saved more money, spent it more wisely, and accumulated land at a faster pace than the *Grands Blancs*.

The *Gens de Couleur* were bound by laws that limited their behaviors and were not considered citizens of France. They could not vote in the legislative assembly—though due to their wealth, the influence was bought through contacts in France to petition their issues. This ability to bypass the local colonial government irritated their White counterparts immensely.

However, the *Grands Blancs*, *Petits Blancs*, and *Gens de couleur* all equally feared the possibility of a slave revolt. The 100,000 domestic workers and craftsmen serving family households maintained a lifestyle far better than those of their brothers working the fields. Most of these aspired to one day purchase their freedom and own land and slaves themselves. The field workers on the other hand presented a potential threat, especially the *Bosals*—those newly arrived from Africa.

The 400,000 field slaves working across the island's plantations led harsh and hopeless lives. They were inadequately fed, provided no medical care, forbidden from learning to read or write, and generally treated worse than the livestock. They were expected to work for ten to twelve hours each day, six days a week. During harvests, sixteen-hour days were common, and any disobedience faced the whip of discipline. These slaves had the least to lose and the most to gain from an uprising.

The overwhelming majority of slaves imported during the sugar boom hailed from the Congo. First-generation slaves were difficult to manage, reluctant to subversion, prone to desertion, and carried the highest risk of sickness or death due to disease. Tens of thousands of escaped slaves joined colonies deep in the mountains called *maroons*. They supplemented their subsistence farming by occasionally raiding local plantations. Planter forays into the jungle were met with fierce defense systems.

Finally, there were the tens of thousands of slaves *de jure*; those neither enslaved nor free. Most lived on or near the plantations of their *de jure* owners, or outside of town, and managed their existence through daily work.

Over the years, Henry became acquainted with members of each class. Immensely popular at the hotel, even the *Grands Blancs* and wealthy *Gens de Couleur* jostled for his favor; requesting better tables, hotel upgrades, party planning, and the like. Contrarily, the *Petits Blancs* maintained a professional distance in their interactions.

Several years had passed since Henry became a free *Afranchi*. Monsieur Coidavid was rarely at the hotel anymore, and Jean and Marie's ever-expanding import and export business—along with a now teenaged Jean Junior—kept them fully occupied. As such, Henry found himself in the role of *La Couronne's* General Manager as his 21st birthday neared.

In September of 1788, Henry requested a meeting with Jean, Marie, and Monsieur Coidavid.

Entering the office that was once his, Coidavid felt a bittersweet mixture of emotions. There was a certain power commanded from this office where he, once a slave himself, lorded over others that reported to him. Now, it was headed by young Henry Christophe. Though the hotel once employed slaves, Jean and Henry had convinced Coidavid to free them and provide a decent wage. This resulted in increased loyalty and productivity— and those same slaves, now employees, reported to the 21-year-old *Afranchi* General Manager.

Henry greeted Jean and Marie as family with a customary two-cheek kiss, and Monsieur Coidavid with a firm handshake. They all found seats in the living room of the large office. Coffee was served in small porcelain cups and saucers perched upon a carved mahogany tray by a young man no older than Henry.

"May I offer anyone some water, lemonade, or tea?" asked their server.

As all were happy with their coffee, Henry thanked the server by name and dismissed him. Monsieur Coidavid in particular was keenly aware of the respect Henry had clearly earned amongst the staff.

Marie looked at Henry, barely able to contain her love and pride. She glanced over at Jean to see a similar gleam in his eye. They smiled at each other, knowing what each other was thinking. Henry had beaten the odds and found unmitigated success. He was free, talented, and respected. It was more than even they could have wished for him.

Henry began with a briefing on the hotel's finances, staff, room occupancy and other metrics. Of course the Bayards and Monsieur Coidavid already knew the hotel was well managed evidenced by their bank account deposits. Their joint investment had been producing stellar income indeed.

"I have one other agenda item to address," Henry transitioned. "I requested you all here to discuss the idea of expansion. *La Couronne* is known as the best hotel in the city—and arguably all of St. Domingue."

The Bayards and Monsieur Coidavid exchanged nods.

"We have a captive audience of wonderful, regular clients. They enjoy dining, dancing, gaming, and our overnight accommodations. Our international bookings are also on the rise due to our excellent reputation."

Henry turned to Coidavid, saying "This, Monsieur Coidavid, is due to your years of superior management." Coidavid smiled and raised his cup. Jean and Marie looked over to Coidavid and did so as well.

"We are poised once again to leap ahead of our competition through a proposed expansion, which I hope you will agree with." Henry continued. Raising himself from his chair, he walked with a sense of purpose to the side door of the office and rapped his knuckles against it. Two uniformed male staffers entered, carrying a large easel.

Thanking and dismissing them, Henry then grabbed a corner of the canvas covering the easel and whipped it away to unveil a pencil-sketched rendering of a magnificent casino.

"I present to you: *Casino de la Couronne* – soon to be the most spectacular entertainment establishment in St. Domingue!"

Marie looked at Jean with wide eyes and an open-mouthed smile, which Jean returned. Monsieur Coidavid scooted forward in his huge armchair to further study the drawing.

Henry launched into a well-rehearsed presentation, detailing table count, games, entertainment areas, food and beverage options, staffing, and anticipated revenue. Each corresponded with another hand-rendered sheet showing floor plans, accounting projections, and construction details.

"Impressive," Jean said, stroking his chin. He looked at Marie, still carrying her cheek-to-cheek smile. "What do you think Gabriel? I think I know what Marie's thoughts are."

"Spectacularly done," admitted Coidavid. "But how much capital is necessary?"

"Ah, do not worry Monsieur Coidavid, I have saved the best for last," replied Henry, a smile spreading across his face. "Total capital investment is 3,000 livres. Our reserve account is currently over 400 livres, and I anticipate an additional profit of at least 200 livres by the end of this year."

"If you each agree to forgo your dividend disbursement this year, then we can supply a 20% down payment and secure a loan from the *Banque Courtois* at a decent interest rate. The expansion will be paid off through the casino's profits in five years, and you will each enjoy an increase to your dividends and consulting fees."

The three looked at each other, stunned by Henry's incredible grasp of both their current business and the risks and rewards he was offering.

"Once paid off, the casino will double your current profits," Henry concluded.

Marie stood and clapped. "*Bravo*, Henry! *Bravo*! I love it. Jean? Gabriel?"

"As usual, you are the smartest in the room Marie. I thoroughly agree. Your thoughts, Gabriel?" asked Jean.

"Count me in," replied Coidavid, looking upon Henry with newfound reverence.

A member of the staff brought in a fine bottle of champagne for a toast. Henry felt more accomplished than he'd ever been and was in awe of the appreciation and dignity that his elder associates had bestowed upon him.

Construction on the casino began early the following January—with financing secured from the *Banque Courtois*, just as Henry had projected. Wishing to have as little effect on regular operations as possible, Henry insisted on a feverishly-paced five-month period of construction, with nearly 50 workers toiling twelve hours a day, seven days a week. The groundbreaking ceremony was set for June 1st of 1789.

Many of the Cap-Français elite were invited to the private Saturday night celebration; though several VIPs, mostly business partners and family friends, were welcomed early to a pre-ribbon cutting cocktail party at 6:00 pm. Over one-hundred guests attended the cocktail party, where champagne flowed abundantly and the conversation was lively. A string quartet performed delightful music for the pleasure of the patrons. Jean & Marie, Monsieur & Madame Coidavid, and Henry formally greeted each and every invitee at the hotel's entrance.

Andre Bayard, who had recently been named the Advocate of the Royal Parliament of Paris, was in attendance and in deep conversation with Philibert Français Rouxel, the Governor General of St. Domingue.

Commander Georges Biassou and Lieutenant Jean Chavannes, dressed in regal uniforms, were socializing with a couple of *Gran Blanc* women—and laughing loudly from a joke Biassou had expertly delivered.

Gerard and Renald Chevalier were discussing business with the sugar barons of the northern plains, and Captain Gabriel Martin was entertaining three young ladies with his stories of maritime adventures in far-off lands.

At 7:00, a multitude of waiters clanged glassware to demand the attention of the crowd. They kept up the ceremonious clanging as they approached the entrance to the roped-off and ribboned casino entrance where the Bayards, Coidavids, and Henry now stood. A hush fell over the crowd.

The twenty waiters, dressed in Black trousers, bowties, and White shirts covered by White server jackets took their places behind the proprietors.

"Good evening, and welcome to *Le Casino de la Couronne*," spoke Henry. "We appreciate you attending our opening celebrations."

The crowd clapped enthusiastically.

"Behind these ropes, lies the premier casino of St. Domingue—if not the entire French West Indies! You will find 82 tables for cards, dice, and a host of other games. We invite you to win, though we prefer you lose on occasion, and enjoy your evening of fun, food, and ambiance."

Henry paused for more applause before looking over to Marie and Madame Coidavid.

"I now ask our hosts for the evening, and co-owners of our fine hotel, Christiane Coidavid and Marie Bayard to come forward and cut the ribbon."

Marie, dressed in a magnificent sapphire evening gown, was

joined by Christiane in her shiny emerald dress. As Jean stood to Marie's left, and Monsieur Coidavid to Christiane's right, the two women simultaneously cut through the bright red fabric.

Henry announced, "The casino is now open!"

What followed was a grand celebration the likes of which Cap-Français, and perhaps all of St. Domingue for that matter, had never before experienced. The roar of conversation, laughter, and amusement nearly overpowered the full twelve-piece orchestra, and accompanying vocalists.

Now in full swing, the crowd swelled over the 300-person capacity, spilling out from the casino's entrance into the hotel's foyer, lobby, restaurant, billiard room, and club. No one, it seemed, dared to miss what was certainly the social event of the summer.

" Jean whispered to Henry, the two smiling at the success of the evening. "I am so proud of you and all you have accomplished, Henry."

"You have made me who I am, Captain," responded Henry in sincerity.

"No, Henry. I did not make you. I only guided you. You made yourself." Jean said, placing his arm around Henry's shoulders.

"What are you two talking about?" interrupted Marie, approaching them from behind.

"Of how beautiful you are, my love, and the wonderful job you did cutting the ribbon," Jean said, giving her a peck on the cheek. "I was also telling Henry how proud I am of him for putting on such a spectacular evening."

"Yes, Henry. You have been brilliant through all of this." Marie added.

"Merci, Marie. You have taught me well. Thank you for that." replied Henry.

Jean then extended his hand to Marie. They headed toward the dance floor together, Jean throwing a wink over his shoulder back at Henry.

Despite the celebration, the political going-ons in Paris remained a constant topic of conversation. The general concept of human rights, universal citizenship, and participation in government which had long been hotly contested subjects among intellectuals were now finding roots among the common people. It was even rumored a full-fledged French Révolution might erupt before the year was out.

Jean, Chavannes, and Biassou each found themselves engaged in the subject throughout their various conversations that evening. The notion that such a revolution might find its way to St. Domingue, and the loyalties that would come into play were worrisome. Over their final drinks of the evening, the three forged a pact to assist each other if trouble ever came for any of them.

The residents of St. Domingue found themselves divided into two camps: those in favor of the budding French Revolution and those loyal to the monarchy. However, the fluidity of the rights of *Gens de Couleur* as well as the moral question of slavery made discussions much more complicated. This resulted in citizens shifting from the side of the revolution to the side of the monarchy and back with neck-breaking suddenness. Rifts between families, friends, and patrons at the hotel appeared and grew more divisive by the week.

Jean and Marie were staunchly opposed to slavery; as, unlike the planters, they had no need for any in their business, they felt it was unnecessary for anyone to own any. On the other hand, Jean's father, Jean-Phillippe, insisted his slaves were well fed, provided boarding and stipend payments for jobs well done, and would likely struggle without the guaranteed work or food.

"Where would they call home? How would they earn a living? Who would take care of them if ill?" he reasoned.

Jean-Phillippe was unfortunately an exception. Far more slave owners mistreated their slaves, particularly the newly imported African *Bosals*, who were more prone to receiving harsher treatment, harder fieldwork, and death from disease. Many hardline property owners considered slaves as nothing more than property, underserving of rights at all.

Disagreements grew tense, and sides were taken among factions throughout St. Domingue. Overhearing a differing opinion while simply going to dinner or partaking in a drink at a bar was enough to spark an argument or even a physical altercation.

Hoping to reassure hotel clients, and keep the streams of revenue uninterrupted, Henry hired extra security throughout the hotel. Clients could enjoy their retreat to their favorite establishment without the fear of a fracas erupting. It proved a fortuitous solution for some time—though, outside the hotel's gates, machinations continued that would ultimately change history.

Ten

THE FRENCH REVOLUTION

Cap-Français
August 1789

In late July, the headline of the *Cap-Français Gazette* read:

REVOLUTION IS HERE
Citizens Storm the Bastille.

For some, this was expected—yet others were in utter shock. The island was abuzz with speculation of what would happen next and the resulting effects on St Domingue. The multi-week chasm between the events of France and their reporting on the island only furthered the fervor.

The revolution progressed quickly. Only six weeks after the storming of the oppressive Bastille prison, the newly convened *Etats Généraux*, or parliament of the people, passed the Declaration of the Rights of Man and Citizen on August 26, 1789.

Of particular distinction in the declaration was the stipulation that men are born—and remain—free and equal in granted rights:

'Social distinctions may be founded only upon the general good. That the aim of all political association is the preservation of the natural and imprescriptible rights of man. These rights are

liberty, property, security, and resistance to oppression.'

'The free communication of ideas and opinions is one of the most precious of the rights of man. Every citizen may, accordingly, speak, write, and print with freedom, but shall be responsible for such abuses of this freedom as shall be defined by law.'

'Since property is an inviolable and sacred right, no one shall be deprived thereof except where public necessity, legally determined, shall clearly demand it, and then only on condition that the owner shall have been previously and equitably indemnified.'

These declarations provided no clear resolution regarding the rights of people of color, or slavery. As such, in October of 1789, a faction of *Gens de Couleur* submitted a petition to the National Assembly requesting equality of rights. The petition was quickly accepted.

Grands Blancs planters were furious; launching their own campaign coercing assembly members to overturn the decree. In turn, the French National Assembly passed a powerful piece of legislation on behalf of local colonial rule.

The decree granted full legislative powers to the Colonial Assembly, allowing the colony near-total autonomy. It purposefully sidestepped the issue of mixed-race and freed Black citizens, leaving whether or not they were included open to local interpretation. It further stated that anyone attempting to undermine or incite agitation against the interests of the colonists would be guilty of a crime against the nation.

Upon news of the decree reaching St. Domingue, The Colonial Assembly in Saint-Marc, who had always advocated near-total independence from the metropolis, began issuing radical decrees and reforms, pushing the colony even more toward autonomy— deepening the conflict between the royalists and patriots.

Saint Marc planters vowed never to provide equality of rights to the *Gens de Couleur*, and expressly excluded them from primary assemblies. A new Colonial Assembly was soon installed without a single *mulatto* or free member in it.

Under the pressures of delegations of wealthy *Gens de Couleur,* the General Assembly in Paris passed another ambiguous piece of legislation five months later. While the various colonies were allowed a relatively free hand in local government, an amendment required that all proprietors of land ought to be active citizens.

The *Petits Blancs* were now enraged. Already jealous and prejudiced toward the Gens de Couleur who owned property, this now granted their prime economic and social competitors the rights of citizenship, thus diluting their exclusive White voting power in favor of a broader majority to be shared with them.

This amendment immediately divided the island between those who owned property and those who did not. The more natural allies of the *Grands Blancs* were the property-owning *Gens de Couleur*. Both supported independence and were opposed to abolishing slavery or changing the traditional control of society their wealth provided.

But instead, the Petits Blancs and the Grands Blancs planters formed an uneasy union. All Blancs began openly sporting *a Pompon Rouge,* a red cockade cap signifying support of the revolution. They published propaganda painting the French Colonial government bureaucrats of St. Domingue as being aligned with the prior monarchy. Of course, the Grands Blancs never planned to grant full rights to either the gens de Couleurs or the Petits Blancs and spoke as such openly. Theirs was a doomed alliance that did not last.

Suspicious of the *Grands Blancs* property owners, the *Petits Blancs* established a Colonial Assembly in the town of St. Marc. The planter class recognized this as one against their interests, thus withdrawing and forming their own assembly in Cap-Français.

With the White factions split, the colonial government's officials who had seemingly lost control of the colony through these various decrees, rose to fill the power void. Caught in between, the *Gens de Couleur* suffered acts of terror and violence from both sides.

Over this time, security continued to be increased across all of the Bayard enterprises. Though a favorite of the *Grands Blancs* and various government officials, the *Hôtel de La Couronne* suffered no attacks or demonstrations of unrest. In fact, despite the palpable tension throughout the island, 1790 was an extremely profitable year for the hotel. Debate required socialization—and *La Couronne* specialized in just that.

Food provided the motivation to venture into public space. Liquor lubricated the tongues for spirited debate—though barely skirting argument and outright confrontations; gambling channeled tensions into other avenues, and Henry and the hotel were happy to provide all.

Over the summer months, Cap-Français buzzed with an oscillating climate of joy, terror, anxiety, and amusement. No one seemed to know where the colony was headed—and the uncertainty materialized in all too real consequences. Every so often a dead body would appear in a back alley, or wash onto shore. Violence spread indiscriminately throughout each caste.

Many undertook the mantra of living each day as though it may be their last. This zeitgeist manifested in interesting ways: more parties, more debates, more fights, more love-making, more crime, more pleasures, and more violence. The colony was undergoing a euphoric fit of transformation, fueled by the constantly conflicting news emanating from Paris. It was as frightening as it was invigorating.

Ever cautious, Jean and Marie still couldn't help but become enveloped in the spirit of it all. It was as if their beloved town had gone mad; a sort of an alternate reality—a circus of follies unimaginable even a year prior.

Their business and profits were growing by leaps and bounds. French goods became ever more difficult to import due to the

revolution, but their early investments in American relationships quickly filled the void, providing an uninterrupted supply of popular products.

Their exports of sugar, coffee, indigo, and mahogany increased in quantity as well. The *Exclusif* had virtually collapsed, allowing for open contraband trading to any buyers, and at any price. Government bureaucrats simply looked the other way or accepted small bribes as necessary products unavailable in France were finding their way to St. Domingue from other markets.

The shipping business leased an additional seven vessels, bringing the fleet to ten. All were managed by Captain Martin, who proved a brilliant logistical mind. The company was now serving multiple freight forwarders for both imports and exports on top of Jean and Marie's voluminous cargo. Accounting for over five percent of all import and export cargo throughout the colony quickly made them one of the top shipping ventures in the colony.

Their Personal life also continued to progress. The de facto heads of both of their extended families, Jean and Marie regularly hosted Sunday dinners of more than thirty guests. Jean Junior was enrolled at the Notre Dame Catholic School, where he excelled academically and socially. Jean would escort him to the building daily under the pretense of quality bonding time, but also so he could monitor his son's safety in such turbulent times.

One evening over their after-dinner glasses of Cognac and Benedictine, Marie looked to Jean with sincerity in her eyes.

"Jean, this year has been perhaps the best of our lives," she began. "But you realize that this is unsustainable."

"I know," replied Jean in a low voice. "I suppose we should revisit those contingencies we had once discussed?"

"Yes, the time has come, my love. I feel this colony is a bomb primed to explode. What was once a peaceful coexistence has been shattered and divided between the haves and the have-nots, between the White factions and Gens de Couleur, and between the government and the citizens." ·

Jean nodded.

"Whether Black, Mulatto, or Quadroon, we all deserve the rights of citizenship but I fear that is not where this tide is taking us. Once pushed, I am certain the Whites will show their true resistance," she said.

"That deal we made to save a portion of our profits—how are those investments performing?" asked Jean, contemplating his half-full glass.

"We could leave all of this behind tomorrow," answered Marie. "We have obligations for the newly leased ships and our lines of credit on merchandise. Of course, should the worst occur, we are insured."

She turned to look Jean in the eye. "We have amassed a small fortune, Jean. Enough to set us up and live well anywhere we please."

"And where would you want to go my love?" asked Jean, smiling slightly. Without skipping a beat, Marie had her answer readied.

"New Orleans."

"I've heard great things about that city," replied Jean. "A lot of our countrymen have moved there as well."

Jean took a deep sip of his Cognac before continuing.

"It is French of course—and adjacent to America. I do believe your assurances of our future my dear, but I do not share your fear of catastrophe. Why would France or the colony put such a precious relationship at risk? After all, St. Domingue accounts for nearly half of all of France's revenue!"

Though they had their suspicions, Jean and Marie could never have predicted the fate in store for St. Domingue. The colony's future was destined for tragedy by way of one of the most violent and destructive revolutions in history. A war was set to begin, and all of their lives were about to change dramatically.

Eleven

THE UPRISING OF OGE AND CHAVANNES

Paris
August 1789

Vincent Ogé was a wealthy Creole aristocrat Quadroon G*ens de couleur* born in Dondon, St. Domingue. In Paris for business when the French Revolution erupted in 1789, he attempted to join a group of colonial planters to propose changes to St. Domingue's racist legislation. At the same time, his friend—Julien Raimond, of a similar background in Saint-Domingue—approached another group of planters with similar ideas. The *Grand Blancs* however rebuffed both.

Fortunately, the two discovered and began attending meetings held by Étienne Dejoly, a White lawyer. Dejoly was a member of the *Société des Amis des Noirs* (Society of the Friends of the Blacks); a Parisian anti-slavery initiative founded by Jacques Pierre Brissot the prior year.

Raimond and Ogé quickly united with Dejoly in leadership. Together, they pressured the French National Assembly to provide representation and voting rights for wealthy free men of color. Like others of their class, Raimond and Ogé owned slaves back in Saint-Domingue and claimed no intention of weakening the practice. Instead, they argued, equitable rights among Whites and

Gens de Couleur would strengthen devotion to France, thus making the system of slavery that much more secure.

Their argument and tactics exerted great influence over the General Assembly, resulting in the ambiguous amendment categorizing all proprietors as active citizens.

The amendment was simultaneously too much and not enough. It appeared to grant voting rights to property-owning Gens de Couleur—effectively diluting the electoral power of non-property-owning Petit Blancs; thus stoking already ingrained animosities. Arguments immediately flared up over the interpretation of the amendment.

Ogé and Raimond ventured to Saint-Domingue in October of 1790, determined to obtain explicit voting privileges for free men of color—be it through reasoned persuasion or force. Ogé in particular planned to exercise this right in the colony's upcoming elections.

On a mid-October Friday, Jean-Baptiste Chavannes, a lieutenant of the *Chasseurs* unit that had fought alongside Jean in the battle of Savannah came to visit Henry at *Hôtel de La Couronne*.

After their disastrous campaign, Chavannes volunteered to stay with the French in America and was not part of the daunting Bermuda rescue mission. Instead, he fought with the Americans in Battles across Virginia and New York, quickly distinguishing himself. Though he was more than two decades his senior, he had kept in touch with Henry over the years, and even attended the casino's opening night. However, the two had not yet had a chance to properly catch up.

The son of wealthy mulatto parents, Chavannes received a quality education which Henry duly respected. Always interested in his perspective, Henry invited Chavannes for a cup of coffee— over which they discussed Vincent Ogé's arrival on the island and intentions. Chavannes ordered a formal dinner at the hotel to host

Ogé and Raimond. Henry called for his restaurant manager and together began planning a private dinner in the secluded room next to the casino for that Thursday.

In the days leading up, Henry noticed an increase in overnight reservations from a number of *Gens de Couleur* planters. He recognized the names of several as some of the richest plantation owners in the Plaine du Nord.

Thursday evening after the delicious meal, Henry entered the private dining room to speak with Chavannes and ensure all was in order. He arrived just as the servers were being dismissed. Closing the doors, Chavannes advised Henry that he was welcome to stay as long as all topics of conversation were kept private.

Vincent Ogé then rose, addressing his guests.

"My friends and colleagues, thank you for your hospitality," he began.

"We in this room are the economic engine that drives this colony, fills the French treasury, and pads the pockets of the bureaucrats. We have done so our entire lives, much as our fathers before us—and their ancestors before them. We have done this without any voice in our local or national government. This cannot continue."

There was a discreet murmur of agreement among those assembled. Heads nodded and glances were shot around the room, testing compliance.

"It is time that we, the *Gens de Couleur* and property owners of this colony, receive our due rights as citizens outlined in the decree of last March."

Ogé held aloft a paper bearing the written proclamation.

"In Paris I spoke with members of the National Assembly. They directed me to our local government. I have since requested an audience with our Governor, the Count de Blanchelande, but he has refused my invitation. He is right to assume my intention to pressure him, the colonial government, and other authorities to guarantee us voting rights."

Ogé's voice swelled with passion. He went on, louder than before.

"We have the highest education, wealth, and largest amount of property, but are denied the ability to vote and hold public office. Is this democracy?" Ogé opined.

The murmurs grew more voluminous. "Non, ce n'est pas!" *No it is not!* one attendee near the front of the table shouted.

"I am asking you, as the most wealthy and respected plantation owners of the colony, to affix your signatures to a petition which I intend to deliver personally to the Governor— even if I must gain an audience by force!" Ogé concluded, to great applause.

"I am in total agreement with Vincent," stated Julien Raimond standing up next to Ogé and raising his hand to quiet the crowd. "I also believe that he is the man to lead this crusade on our behalf."

Raimond continued, "I now recognize this group as an official committee to pursue these rights, and have convened our first meeting tonight to vote Vincent Ogé as our leader. Do I hear a second of that motion?" Raimond said.

"Do you accept this nomination Vincent?" asked Français Abadie, a mulatto plantation owner from the *Plaine du Nord*.

"I am humbled, honored, and I do accept" responded Ogé.

"Then I second the motion," Abadie said firmly.

"All in favor?" asked Raimond. All hands were raised. "Any opposed?"

None came.

"With Mr. Ogé's permission, I now move that we each sign the petition outlining our demands to the Governor," said Raimond.

"Do we have a second?" asked Ogé.

"I second the motion," answered Renald Armand from the rear table.

"All in favor?" Again, all hands raised. "Any opposed?"

"Then the motion is carried" stated Ogé.

"And if the Governor rebuffs your overture again?" asked Joseph Jacquinette, another mulatto local property owner.

"Then he leaves us no choice!" yelled Antoine Sacalie, a Quadroon plantation owner.

"What does that mean?" asked Jacquinette, turning to Sacalie.
"It means arms!" hissed Sacalie.

The entire room erupted in a cacophony of arguments. Sides were quickly taken by those who supported potential violence and those who were strictly opposed. Ogé intensely observed the interactions, attempting to gauge the group's reaction to armed revolt. By his estimation, it appeared only eight of the two dozen guests demonstrated a true bloodlust.

Once calmed, all in attendance did agree to sign the petition. No further discussion of violence was explored, but as the group began to disperse, Ogé, Raimond, Chavannes, and Sacalie discreetly asked the most vocal and enthusiastic to remain behind. Henry then could see what was happening and elected to leave as well, wanting no part of the dangerous conspiracy in the making.

The petition containing 26 signatures—24 guests, plus Chavannes and Ogé—was delivered to the Governor's office the following day, paired with a requested audience on Monday.

Monday morning, a representative of the Governor's office arrived at *Hôtel de La Couronne* to inform Ogé the Governor would grant him an audience that Thursday at 10:00 am.

Ogé dressed that morning in his best suit, confident that his letter had swayed the Governor's favor. Upon arrival, he was escorted to the opulent room, decorated with flags of France and the colony, bookcases, and framed commendations, which served as the Governor's office.

The Viscount de Blanchelande rose to greet Ogé and gestured toward the Victorian couch in front of his desk.

"I have read your letter Mr. Ogé and noted the additional signatures affixed. Quite an impressive group of planters." the Governor offered.

"I am honored to meet your Excellency and appreciate your generous gift of an audience. The planters whose names are included in my petition are all in agreement in our interpretation of the March decree; the Assembly in Paris has granted citizenship to each of us as property owners" replied Ogé.

The Governor went on, appearing to ignore Ogé's opening argument. "These times are extremely difficult in the colony, you know—as they also are everywhere in France."

"I am aware of course, your Excellency," said Ogé. "Many issues are in need of redress, though this is one that can be accomplished locally, I presume?"

The Governor waved his hand, barely waiting for Ogé to finish.

"No Mr. Ogé, it cannot. This is an issue created by the French Assembly, as you mentioned, and requires clarification directly from that body. I have no jurisdiction to pass a resolution on this matter."

"Your Excellency." Began Ogé, straightening in his seat and meeting the Governor's eyes. "With all due respect, the issue is quite clear. The proclamation reads '*all the proprietors... ought to be active citizens.*' This legislation grants myself and the planters undersigned the right to vote in colonial elections as *Gens de Couleur* property owners—equal to any other proprietor."

"I disagree. The verbiage remains ambiguous, Mr. Ogé. If it were so straightforward, all French colonies would enact it as law, which is not the case. The Assembly must provide clarification. I suggest you bring this petition to their attention." replied the Governor.

"I have just come back from Paris," said Ogé, struggling a bit to maintain his composure. "They directed me to your judgment for implementation of the decree, your Excellency."

"Then they have erred."

The Governor stood and began to walk to the door of the office.

"I will send your letter by diplomatic pouch to the head of the National Assembly on your behalf. I will also compose a note of our conversation and we will await their reply."

The Governor opened the door for Ogé and gestured for him to exit.

"Good day, Mr. Ogé."

Ogé was furious. A year of patience, travel, consultation, and talk had resulted in nothing.

Talk is over, he vowed, storming out of the mansion and back to the hotel. Chavannes was waiting for him at the bar in the lounge of the *Hôtel de La Couronne.*

"How was your meeting with His Excellency?" He asked as Ogé arrived.

"Never a man less deserving of the title. Do not ever refer to him as such in my presence again," Ogé replied.

"I gather it did not go well, then. Where do we stand now?" Chavannes asked.

"The letter with those 26 signatures is not worth the paper it is written on. We are at a dead end." sighed Ogé, as he ordered a shot of rum.

"Is it over?" inquired Chavannes.

"By no means Chavannes. We will take this forward as far as necessary."

Ogé turned to Chavannes and dropped his voice.

"Are you still with us?"

"I am committed, Vincent," Chavannes replied. He was staunchly against slavery and viewed the granting of voting rights to *Gens de Couleur* as the first step toward eventual emancipation. As a slave owner himself, Ogé did not share this sentiment. However, Chavannes was a powerful ally, and he was content to redress this particular debate in the future.

"I will head south to *Grande Riviere.* I have shipments that have arrived from America containing a cache of smuggled arms. Enough to arm one-thousand men with rifles, fifty rounds each, as well as swords and other necessities." said Ogé.

"You will revisit the six most passionate of our allies from our dinner, and inform them of this update. We will need men to fight and money for compensation. Meet me at *Grand Riviere* as soon as you can."

With that, the two men departed upon their separate missions.

Chavannes found limited success in his meetings. Four of the original group backed out of the conflict—blaming their impassioned feelings on the alcohol they'd consumed that night. The two remaining had not wavered in their support however, and each vowed to raise 250 men as well as supply all with three months' worth of pay. A pledge was made to meet Chavannes and Ogé, accompanied by the fledgling militia, within a week.

Chavannes contacted nine veterans from his American campaigns, each of whom was happy to escape their boring civilian roles for a new fight—and the right price. Chavannes promised officer titles for any who arrived with at least 25 men. Compensation would be double what they'd earned fighting alongside the French.

When prompted as to their cause, and current levels of support, Chavannes provided the best answer he could muster.

"We are fighting for our rights as citizens. By the time word spreads, thousands will join us!"

The night before his departure for *Grande Rivière*, Chavannes stopped back at the *Hôtel de La Couronne* and requested Henry meet him for a drink.

"Henry, I am going to tell you something, but you must first swear to secrecy," Chavannes said.

"You sound serious Chavannes. Have you finally found the right woman?" joked Henry in an attempt to ease the tension radiating from his friend.

"I am serious, Henry. Look at me," Chavannes demanded, staring into Henry's eyes. "Do you believe one day all slaves should be free?"

"Absolutely," replied Henry without hesitation.

"Then help me accomplish it, Henry," said Chavannes.

"I am working toward this in my own way, my friend. I have eliminated slaves from the hotel's workforce. Every employee is a free man or woman paid a decent wage." Henry responded, somewhat evasively.

"What good is that for those who remain in chains?" Chavannes shot back.

"I am proving to our guests—those who are wealthy and with influence— that slave workers are not necessary to financial success. Free people are happier and provide a higher standard of services," responded Henry.

"Your way makes slow progress, if any at all, Henry," stated Chavannes. "Help us make a change *now*."

"Are you referring to Mr. Ogé and the *Gens de Couleur* planters from the other night?" asked Henry.

"There is a movement, Henry. One which will change history. First, the *Gens de Couleur* property owners will be granted full citizenship, then non-owners like us, and eventually all slaves will be freed!" Chavannes said, slamming his fist against the bar top with passion.

"Do you believe the local assembly will agree to that?" challenged Henry. "Most are my clients and I know them personally. They would never allow it."

"What they do not allow, we will *take*." Said Chavannes forcefully. "Their way has gone on long enough. They stay a few years, make their fortunes, and leave back to Europe. Yet they tell those who have always called this island home what we are and are not allowed to do?!"

"What do you mean by '*take it,*' Chavannes?" asked Henry cautiously.

"By *force*, Henry."

Henry waited a moment, considering his next words and hoping his friend would regain his composure and avoid the curious ears or eyes of those in the vicinity.

"My friend, I do not agree with your method. Lasting change must take place in an orderly fashion. Armed insurrection against the government? Both of the colony and of France? That is treason of the highest order and a betrayal of your oath as a military officer."

"So be it, Henry. We have not been heard. Ogé has tried every possible avenue from France to St. Domingue and back again. There will be no action unless we impose it." replied Chavannes.

This was exactly what Henry had most feared when leaving the dining room that fateful evening. Nightmares from his time on battlefields still occasionally haunted him, and he harbored no desire to find himself in the middle of another bloody conflict. Things were going well at the hotel, and while many of his clients were virulent racists, he felt accepted and appreciated nonetheless. These laws had no effect on him, and he would not risk the life of which he'd long dreamed.

"No, Chavannes. I will not join you. I do not agree with you and your revolutionaries. I will keep our conversation private, but as one of my most beloved friends, I implore you to stop before this gets out of your control."

Chavannes placed his hand on his young friend's shoulder. He knew Henry was a good and principled man, and though he'd hoped to recruit him to the cause, he also knew what he was asking Henry to put at risk.

"I am sorry Henry, truly. The way I see it, things have been out of our control for too long already. I am committed."

Chavannes picked up his glass of rum, swirled it lightly, and leaned back in his chair.

"If you don't mind, I wish to spend one more night in your lovely hotel. And, if you can arrange it, a couple of girls from the bordello would be a fitting end to my stay in Cap-Français," he said, winking.

"Consider it done, my brother. Pay them well, as I have a respectful reputation to maintain with the madame." Henry replied.

"Dinner in my suite then. Care to join?"

"I do not play where I earn my living, Jean-Baptiste."

Henry left Chavannes at the bar, knowing in his heart that his dear friend was headed toward his doom.

Chavannes arrived at *Grande Riviere* a few days later and immediately met with Ogé to brief him on his recruitment of officers, men, and money. Several days later, the two plantation owners, Sacalie and Monier, as well as the nine mercenaries and all the conscripted men had been assembled; more than 1,000 in all, with the resources to match.

Chavannes suggested Ogé issue a final warning to the local government, demanding they address their concerns seriously and under the threat of violence. He also suggested he clarify his stance on emancipation, to which Ogé obliged. A letter was thus drafted and delivered to the Colonial Assembly:

FROM VINCENT OGÉ, CITIZEN
TO THE MEMBERS OF THE ASSEMBLY

Gentlemen:

A prejudice, too long maintained, is about to fall. I am charged with a commission doubtless very honorable to myself. I require you to promulgate throughout the colony the instructions of the National Assembly of the 8th of March 1790, which gives without distinction, to all free citizens, the right of admission to all offices and functions. My pretensions are just, and I hope you will pay due regard to them. I shall not call the plantations to rise; that means would be unworthy of me. Learn to appreciate the merit of a man whose intention is pure.

When I solicited from the National Assembly a decree which I obtained in favor of the American colonists, formerly known under the injurious epithet of mulattos, I did not include in my claims the condition of the Negroes who live in servitude. You and our adversaries have misrepresented my steps in order to bring me into discredit with honorable men. No, no, gentlemen! We have put forth a claim only on behalf of a class of freemen, who, for two centuries, have been under the yoke of oppression.

We require the execution of the decree of the 8th of March.

We insist on its promulgation, and we shall not cease to repeat to our friends that our adversaries are unjust, and that they know not how to make their interests compatible with ours. Before employing my means, I make use of mildness; but if, contrary to my expectation, you do not satisfy my demand, I am not answerable for the disorder into which my just vengeance may carry me.

- Vincent Ogé, October 19, 1790

Two weeks passed without a formal response. Ogé, Chavannes, and their nine officers drew up plans to invade and occupy the neighboring towns of Bahon, Ranquitte, Bail, Pascale, Valliere, Candy, Mobin, Debuche, Madeline, and Cherry.

Each of the nine officers with one hundred men under their command would overpower local forces, preferably without bloodshed, and send the security officers to Cap-Français to inform them of the insurrection.

Propaganda would be spread, claiming all free men would be granted full citizenship once the colonial government was deposed. In order to accomplish this though, volunteers were needed to take up the cause.

Each of the nine towns was easily subdued by the new militia. The local populations were apathetic to their cause, however. The townspeople had no quarrel with the colonial government and had no desire for voting rights. Recruitment only attracted fanatics and those lusting for political power. Still, without formal acknowledgment, more drastic efforts were deemed necessary. In mid-November, Ogé ordered Chavannes to march on Cap-Français.

Unbeknownst to the insurrectionists, upon receiving Ogé's threat, the Governor had requested a contingent of French and Creole soldiers to intercept and engage the approaching militia should they march on Cap-Français. The battle was fierce and decisive. Ogé's amateur fighting force was decimated by the larger, better-trained, and equipped colonial army.

Ogé, Chavannes, and 23 of their men retreated across the border into the Spanish colony of Santo Domingo. On November 20th of 1790, Vincent Ogé, Jean-Baptiste Chavannes, and their 23 associates were captured in Hinche. The St. Domingue Colonial assembly requested extradition in accordance with the established Spanish/French treaty.

Ogé and Chavannes pled their case to the Spanish authorities, and the competent Spanish jurist Vicente Faura made a powerful plea in their favor—one so respected, the king of Spain awarded him a decoration for its presentation. However, the *Royal Audiencia* of Santo Domingo decided against the refugees, who were delivered to St. Domingue authorities days before Christmas in December of 1790.

Two months later, the revolutionaries were tried and convicted. On March 9, 1791, the sentences were carried out with the 23 militia members hanged and Chavannes and Ogé to be put to death by dismemberment in the Cap-Français public square. The two were marched past the hanging corpses of their comrades, whose bodies were strung up on either side of the main street. What awaited them at the center of the square was a gruesome contraption that would agonizingly twist and rip their limbs from attachment. It was clear the Governor was setting a ghastly example for other would-be defectors in the audience.

As they approached, Ogé caught his compatriot's eyes, and both nodded in solidarity. Their conviction had never wavered.

Ogé requested a priest administer his last rites. The French cleric unconvincingly rushed through the proceedings, never revealing an ounce of sympathy. Strapped to the machine, Ogé refused a final public statement, and the execution began. Witnessing the torment of his final moments, Chavannes wished he'd gone before his friend. The ordeal lasted over 15 minutes. The wheels continued to turn even as Ogé's moans weakened and his body was further mutilated and split apart.

The crowd of onlookers was clearly segregated between the French authorities—who made no effort to hide their pleasure with the spectacle—and the mixture of slaves, *Gens de Couleur,* and merchants who were hand-selected by the Governor and given no choice but to attend. They were here to bear witness to the perceived seriousness of Ogé's crime, and the dire punishment which lay in store for any harboring similar ideas of defiance.

This group, disgusted by the brutality administered, openly mourned the execution. Several were selected from the crowd to scoop up the dismembered limbs and entrails, furthering their repulsion and humiliation.

How could such cruelty exist in this world? Thought Chavannes to himself, as he was shoved onto the platform. A brave man, he'd never been so terrified in his life, though he struggled mightily not to betray it outwardly. He vowed to control his anguish with all his might, delaying the gratification these evil men so obviously were seeking.

Suddenly, a stunning woman with long, silky Black hair approached him. Having not requested any last rites, Chavannes was utterly confused by her appearance.

Locking her bright green eyes on his, an overwhelming sense of calm settled over Chavannes.

"My name is Cécile , and I am here to help you," she whispered.

Cécile Fatiman was a powerful mambo voodoo priestess. She'd woken up that morning compelled by what she believed a higher power to attend the execution of the insurrectionists. For several nights prior, her dreams had been inundated with proclamations by her voodoo Gods ordering her presence on this day.

She knew she was not meant to provide her assistance to Ogé; he was true to his cause, but not meant to become a martyr. Knowing that the Colonial authorities tolerated the practice of voodoo to appease their slaves, she approached the platform insisting to provide Chavannes his last rites.

She walked up to the stoic man, noticing only a hint of fear. He did not yet know the role he was to play in the future he would unfortunately never see. She looked deep into his eyes, emanating serenity, and reached for a small vial hidden in her robe. Within it was a potion handed down through Cécile 's family for generations.

It was a potent mixture of 23 herbs, berries, roots, spices, insects, and the liver of a particular fish—along with sugar and molasses for taste.

The woman began a Creole incantation and dabbed the mystery oil on her fingers. She traced a line on Chavannes' forehead down his nose and onto his lips. She opened his willing mouth, saturated three of her fingers in the liquid, and placed them on his tongue. The flavor was foreign but undeniably pleasant. A surge of warmth suddenly circulated through him. All protest and fear drained from him as his limbs felt light and numb. His quizzical look was met only with a sly smile by the priestess.

"You have started a profound movement, Jean-Baptiste Chavannes. While your body will die today, your actions now will determine whether your legacy lives on in the hearts and minds of your people."

Chavannes felt a growing sense of courage as he listened intently to the woman's words.

"I have provided you the strength to neutralize what these men will do to you. Make this your podium and rally your countrymen. The voodoo warrior God Ogoun will guide you and give you strength."

With that, Cécile bowed her head, closed her eyes, and disappeared down the platform steps.

Governor Count de Blanchelande, St. Domingue Colonial Assembly Leader Charles Bernard, and other politicians, members of the magistrate, rich planters, and businessmen all sat across from the stage on a purpose-built viewing platform. Not a single person of color or mixed race was permitted among them.

"The execution of Ogé has had the desired effect," said the Governor, leaning toward Bernard. "This should quell any notion of revolt in St. Domingue for several years to come."

"Without question, your Excellency," replied Bernard. "The man's screams on the rack were surely enough to terrify even the most ardent revolutionary. Well done."

In front of them, two Colonial soldiers led Chavannes to the machine. As was the custom, they paused the doomed briefly to allow a final address. However, where Ogé demurred, Chavannes unexpectedly elected to speak.

The crowd went silent. The Governor shifted in his seat, both curious and apprehensive.

"Today, my brothers and sisters are gathered here to witness your White, French rulers attempt to silence your voices and hold you in chains of their making forever. They insult you with this intimidation!"

The shocked crowd began to murmur amongst themselves.

"They believe my fate at this gruesome machine will douse the fire within your spirits," he went on, his voice rising to a yell. "No! It will not! You are stronger than they!"

Bernard and the Governor looked at each other. "Silence him, your Excellency. Silence him now!" hissed Bernard. On the platform, Chavannes continued.

"Today, I sacrifice my life for yours. For your freedom. For your children's freedom, and for their children as well. When I die, you must rise—take the torch from my grasp and continue this fight!"

Looking out over those gathered, Chavanness locked onto a familiar face. Young Henry Christophe was positioned in the second row, standing bolt upright and willing all of his strength and courage toward his friend. A single tear welled in the corner of Chavannes' eye. He gave a curt nod of farewell, which Henry returned. At that moment, Henry knew he would not allow Chavannes' sacrifice to go in vain.

"Silence!" bellowed the Governor. The soldier behind Chavannes procured a scarf from his pocket and rushed to gag him. With all his might, Chavannes threw his head back into the soldier's face, crushing his nose and spewing fresh blood over the platform's floor.

"Witness! These men bleed like you or me. We are stronger than them!" cried Chavannes. "We can defeat them together. Honor the men who gave their lives and still hang in this square today. We have died to free you. Freedom to you as citizens of this colony!"

"*Enough!*" screamed the Governor. The second soldier left from tending to his comrade and brought the butt of his rifle to the side of Chavannes' head, staggering him. Four others grabbed him and threw him onto the rack.

However, the crowd had become restless. Many jostled about, edging toward the soldiers isolated on the platform. Those who were able to free themselves from tying down the still-fighting Chavannes trained their muskets on those at the front of the mob, pausing their progress.

The rack began pulling at Chavannes' arms and legs. One of the soldiers was still struggling to gag him as he violently moved his head left and right. The executioner began to turn the wheels more rapidly so as to end the display as quickly as possible.

Somehow, Chavannes felt no pain. Though he was aware of the damage being done, the tearing and cracking of his limbs and sockets were interpreted through the priestess' potion as a light massage.

He smiled to himself, knowing the Governor had been embarrassed and his authority dealt a crucial blow. He'd publicly lost his composure, and his forces had appeared disorganized—and even fearful. A profound feeling of accomplishment washed over him as the rack continued its persecution of his body. His vision darkening, he gathered his final breaths and yelled:

"Claim your freedom, my brothers and sisters!"

His head dropped. A deafening hush fell over the square. Chavannes was dead.

All eyes simultaneously turned to the viewing stand. The

Governor instantly understood his gamble had gone terribly wrong. Without striking a single blow, Chavannes—eloquent, faithful, and unafraid of death—had beaten him.

"Your intent was to terrorize, your Excellency, but I am afraid these people are emboldened," came Bernard's voice, breaking the silence.

The intense stares of the crowd at their feet confirmed the Assembly Leader's assessment. They both were suddenly acutely aware of how outnumbered they were at the moment.

"Instead of exposing him as a coward, you have made him a martyr. By week's end, I predict his words will be on the lips of every man, woman, and child of color in this colony!"

"Muzzle yourself, Bernard," spat the Governor, before turning to his Sergeant at Arms. "Clear the square of this crowd!" He demanded, before swiftly leaving amid his security detail.

Chaos erupted as the soldiers burst forth in an attempt to disperse the onlookers. Two women fell to the ground and were trampled under the soldiers' boots. Seeing this, several men turned back in an attempt to help. A shot from a rifle was discharged, followed by a short scuffle and several others.

On the platform, the slaves tasked with collecting Ogé's body had returned to quickly grab Chavannes, in hopes of providing him a proper burial. They were stopped by the remaining soldiers on the platform. Two who ventured too close were impaled by bayonets.

Seven more souls lay dead in the square before the throng was cleared.

Henry had somehow managed to escape the pandemonium unscathed, though what he saw that morning would remain with him forever. Hurrying back to the hotel lobby, he nearly ran into Jean, who was discussing business matters with several acquaintances. Seeing Henry visibly upset, Jean cut his pontificating short and came to his side.

"Henry, what is troubling you so?" Jean asked.

Henry fought hard to hold his tears and steady his voice.

"It was terrible, Jean. The worst thing I have witnessed—worse than the war. It was savagery...*murder!*"

"Come, let us get you a drink."

Jean led Henry to the bar and ordered two brandies. No sooner had the glass been placed in front of Henry did he gulp it down and immediately request another. Jean stood behind him, gently massaging his shoulders and allowing him some time to compose himself.

Henry recounted the entire event in gruesome detail over the next several minutes; Ogé's lengthy macabre demonstration, Chavannes' declarations, the silent moment they shared, his last words protesting the oppression of the enslaved, and the anarchy that followed.

"His final plea was to both slaves and free people of color, Jean. He was talking to you and me—and to all of those like us. He died for us! He was my friend, and I was forced to watch it all!"

Henry could no longer hold back his emotions. He bawled as Jean had never seen him before, a different unleashing of grief than even what he'd expressed in the moments after his ordeal with the spy in Savannah.

Jean allowed him to cry—not only because he had no words, but he also knew none would suffice.

After several moments, Henry had calmed himself enough to speak again.

"Jean, this is the start of something. Or, the end, rather." Henry stated flatly, staring straight ahead. "The end of the French Colonial Government. Chavannes ignited a fire. I saw it with my own eyes. I make a promise to you now and to the memory of Jean-Baptiste Chavannes that I will continue his fight."

Jean placed his arm around Henry and hugged him tight. After some time, Henry allowed Jean to lead them into the former's office, where Henry collapsed onto the couch, instantly asleep. Jean quietly arranged for dinner to be brought to him when he awoke.

With that, he left the hotel and rode quickly home.

Marie was waiting for Jean in their upstairs bedroom. As he burst through the door, she looked up to him, cheeks stained with tears. "I heard about Chavannes. This is madness, Jean!" She leaped into his arms.

"The entire colony is rupturing, and I don't know how it will all end," she cried.

Jean guided her to the veranda, where the sun was setting behind them and the endless blue water beyond the harbor belied a false sense of calm. He gazed out over Cap-Français as she tucked her head into his chest. What was happening?

A faint, rhythmic vibration suddenly caught his attention. He instantly knew its origin; the drums in the hills were beating—broadcasting the news of Chavannes' death from village to village, and soon province to province. The entire island would soon know what had transpired on this day.

He looked back down over the city. It already appeared somehow different. The sheen had eroded, stained by blood and injustice. The activities on the streets appeared more hectic; glances were shot over shoulders, and the air he breathed was heavier. He held Marie tighter as the sky turned a dark crimson.

Jean knew not what tomorrow might bring, but realized his life would forever be defined by everything he had experienced to then, and whatever was to come. The colony was still destined for far worse if things were ever to get better.

Twelve

DUTTY AND CECILE
SPARK REVOLUTION

Bois Caïman
August 1791

Word of Oge and Chavanne's rebellion echoed throughout the colony, particularly the latter's valiant final stand and call to arms.

The brutal torture and execution of Chavannes and Oge deeply troubled Cecile Fatiman. She did not fully understand what had possessed her to attend the event, much less provide her assistance to a man she had never met. What she was sure of, however, was that her actions were necessary—and something far bigger than she, that poor young soldier, or even the sadistic Governor, had begun that day.

In the four months since Cecile had suffered alternating nightmares and visions of the future. She could see what was not yet there; what could be possible, both the grandiose and gruesome. Over time, however, her dreams transferred into hope. She began to see people of all creeds and heritage—White, Black, and *Gens de Couleur*—coexisting on an island of beautiful flowers, a blue ocean, and joy.

Each morning after another vision, Cecile would awake in a fit of anxiety. The present was hell, and she longed for the change her dreams seemed to promise. She knew Chavannes, was the catalyst. He was pure of purpose.

Finally, on the hottest day of the year in the middle of July, Cecile received a message from the respected Houngan voodoo priest, Dutty Boukman. Though she had never worshipped with him, Boukman was known for his regular ceremonies at *Bois Caïman*, southwest of Cap-Français. Yet, here had arrived a direct request for her services. Without a second thought, Cecile notified her clients, settled her affairs, and prepared for the week-long journey east.

Upon her arrival, she soon learned of the nature behind the request: the teenage daughter of the village administrator had been possessed by a demon spirit. The girl would regularly run, screaming, through the town in the dead of night, frightening residents half to death themselves. She'd eventually been corralled into a bamboo cage, and after three unsuccessful attempts of his own, Dutty had sent for Cecile's assistance in performing an exorcism.

Cecile asked to assess the girl's condition. She was not prepared for what she encountered, however. The young woman— Angelique—appeared more animal than human. Her hair was a tangled kink of knots no comb could hope to penetrate. Her complexion was pot-marked with open sores and her eyes were bloodshot, as though she hadn't slept in weeks. Her teeth were turning green and her once the White dress was stained and shredded. She was aggressive, dangerous, and horrifying.

Angelique's possession was obvious and deep-rooted—unlike any Cecile had previously known. She asked for Dutty, two additional priests, and twelve disciples to assist in the ceremony necessary to cure the girl. No one else was allowed to participate or even observe. With that, the exorcism was planned for the following evening.

The next night, Angelique was brought before the assemblage—caged, but not sedated. Cecile felt a pang of pity at what she'd become. Her father insisted she'd once been the most beautiful girl in the village; nothing like her current state.

"We will help you, my dear," Cecile said softly, even as Angelique spat and hissed venom toward her. "That poison within you, Angelique, will soon be gone."

The girl violently attacked the bars of her cage at the mention of her name, shaking them in rabid ferocity. Cecile knew that if it were let loose, Angelique's demon would certainly kill her and those gathered.

Cecile stepped back, and initiated a five-hour ceremony, consisting of prayer, dance, songs, drums, fire, sacrificial offerings of chicken, goat, and pig; and chants summoning the voodoo Gods *Papa Legba* and the supreme creator *Grand Mèt Bondye*.

"You maintain the world order and are universal Papa Legba and Bondye. We beg you to remove this demon from your servant Angelique and restore her sanity so she may serve and worship you once again my Gods."

Cecile chanted the refrain over and over after every dance, every song, and every sacrifice.

Angelique had gone feral. She jumped up and down, rocked the cage from side to side, and growled and screamed in an unidentifiable, animalistic roar. The longer the ceremony continued, the more viciously she revolted.

Lightning and thunder erupted from the sky suddenly, and a deluge of rain opened up over the ritual. More timber was thrown into the fire to keep it ablaze amid the downpour. The rainwater ran together with Cecile's sweat, creating a sheen reflecting the flames. Boukman continued to pray, the dancers danced and the drummers drummed, until all fell into an uncontrollable trance. Their pace increased to a feverish pitch.

A sudden bolt of lightning struck a nearby hut. The accompanying blast of thunder shook the earth and the thatched roof of the structure ignited just as the rain came to an abrupt halt. The trance had broken, and all stood silent and still amid the crackling of the fire.

The cage door burst open. Cecile gasped, fearing the demon had escaped. However, only Angelique stirred, stumbling forward and confused.

Cecile hurried to the cage, motioning for the girl to remove her tattered dress. Once naked, Cecile waved her to come forward out of the cage. The bewildered and disoriented Angelique nonetheless obeyed her directions. As soon as she was free of the door, Cecile signaled several of the men to slam it shut, raise the cage, and toss it into the fire. The flames surged nearly twenty feet into the sky.

"Your demon is no more, Angelique," said Cecile. "God *Papa Legba* and *Grand Mèt Bondye* have expelled it from you, never to return again. Let us pray and give our thanks."

Song erupted, and the dancers began once more as the drummers beat their rhythm. Cecile nodded to several young girls to take Angelique's hands and lead her away to the still-smoking hut, followed by the dancers who encircled it once they were inside.

Cecile looked to the sky and smiled. "You have again blessed us, my Universe. Thank you, Thank you, Thank you."

Finally giving in to her fatigue, she collapsed onto a blanket set out for her. Two older women wiped her sweaty face with a mixture of herbs and water and caressed her sore muscles.

The fire had dwindled significantly by the time Cecile regained her composure. Dutty Boukman sat in front of the dying flames, taking swigs of rum. He'd been impressed by the mambo priestess. Of all those he'd encountered in his travels, she appeared the truest and most pure.

Cecile sat down next to him, gazing into the fire, blanket wrapped around her shoulders. He offered her the bottle, of which she took a deep gulp and spat into the fire. The blaze jumped briefly before dying down once more.

"For you, my Gods," she said, taking another long draw and swallowing.

"Cecile, you have accomplished what I could not," Boukman intoned. "You are indeed the great Mambo Priestess your reputation suggested. I attempted to exorcize the demon on three occasions but only made it stronger. You have vanquished it in one ceremony."

"I am a true believer, Dutty. You may practice voodoo, but you do not live it" she responded, matter-of-factly.

"What do you mean by that?" asked Boukman, miffed at the allegation.

"You sit here drinking your rum, without making an offering to the Gods. However, when you offered me the same just now, I first offered it back to the Gods as thanks, before I indulged myself."

"That means nothing, Cecile."

"It means everything!" Cecile fixed an intense gaze upon him. "Gratitude is a cornerstone of our voodoo religion, Dutty. *Always* remember that."

Cecile looked back to the fire.

"This is why I live it, and you simply practice it."

Boukman was caught off guard and embarrassed. She was right, of course. He'd taken his gift for granted and leaned on it to his own advantage for some time. Perhaps he had lost his way. Prayers of forgiveness would be necessary beginning that night.

"You are indeed wise, Priestess Cecile. I have learned tonight and have much to repent for. For that, I thank you." Boukman bowed his head.

"What of the girl, Angelique?" he asked.

"My girls will bathe and clean her over a period of seven hours. We will nourish her for the next several days with a balance of proper nutrition, potions, herbs, and essential oils. They will pray together, and the healing process can begin. She is saved, Dutty."

"How can I and her father repay you?"

"I am too tired to discuss anymore. Allow me to sleep and

dream about what should be." Cecile said, rising to leave. "I am going now after one last taste of rum." She took a final long swig of the bottle.

"Thank you, Priestess. Good night."

Cecile fell into a deep and peaceful slumber, dreaming of wonderful sights and sounds. She awoke late the next morning and decided to observe Angelique's progress after breakfast.

The overnight transformation was remarkable. The young teenager's wounds had already begun to heal. She was exhausted, but resting peacefully among the other girls who took turns gently and lovingly stroking and caressing her body and face.

Cecile then went to visit Boukman to discuss her repayment for the exorcism. Upon seeing her, Boukman jumped up and embraced her as though they'd known each other their whole lives. They exchanged pleasantries and Cecile provided an update on Angelique's state. She then shifted the conversation to restitution.

"Name it, Cecile. Nothing within reason will be refused." Boukman insisted.

"My requested compensation is for the Gods, Dutty, not me. Her father will throw a celebration for the entire town and the surrounding villages. He will provide pigs, chickens, and goats for meats; as well as rice, beans, corn, and rum." Cecile began.

"You are to invite at least one representative from no less than one-hundred plantations, all townspeople, and ten military men of your choosing. The feast will be held one week after the next full moon—August 14th. The honoree will be Angelique, who will join the Gods in celebration here on earth."

"I will make sure it happens," Boukman responded.

Cecile went on.

"Dutty, the Gods have spoken to me," she said, her eyes locking with his. Boukman felt his next breath catch in his throat.

"They have selected you to lead a revolution against the French slave owners and free our people."

Boukman blinked, waiting for a punchline. The look on the priestess' face quickly put away such a notion.

"Cecile, I am not a military man. Prior to my adoption of

voodoo, I was a peaceful Muslim. I am no warrior and I have never felled a man—."

Cecile shushed him. "Be prepared to listen for the Gods. They will speak to you soon. Pray that you hear them well, Dutty. I will leave tomorrow morning, and will return to *Bois Caïman* the day before the celebration."

She turned and left without another word to a confused Boukman.

The constant beat of drums echoed nonstop throughout the countryside since Chavanne's execution. Folk songs were written; stories crafted; and a mixture of anxiety and excitement beset the population—particularly amongst the slaves.

On the night of August 14th, with the drums' continuous beat as the backdrop, the air was festive at *Bois Caïman*. Hundreds had gathered to drink rum, eat food, dance, sing and mingle. Angelique stood at the center of the clearing, where all could admire her. She was dressed in White; with flowers in her hair and a necklace bearing an amulet to ward off evil spirits which Cecile had crafted for her. Cecile, Boukman, and her parents stood by her side.

The evening's guests were in disbelief at the girl's transformation. A curse had seemingly been lifted from the entire town as the story of the exorcism spread. Many extended their congratulations to Angelique, her father, her mother, Boukman, and Cecile.

Halfway through the celebrations, Angelique was asked to lie upon an altar constructed to show gratitude to the voodoo Gods. She lay on her back atop a large flat stone in front of the fire as men threw extra wood into the flames.

"Observe your creation, our Gods! Your daughter, Angelique." Cried Cecile to the cheers of the crowd.

The music swelled, the drums picked up in cadence, and the dancers swayed in rhythm. They circled round and round the stone and Angelique, in a near hypnotic state, for an hour.

Carafes of rum circulated amongst the crowd as more and more joined in the dancing and folksongs.

Suddenly, a gasp ran through the crowd, and all but the dancers at the stone came to a halt. Angelique had begun to levitate above the hard stone.

At first only inches, then higher, until she was floating several feet in the air. The drums continued throughout as the girl rose higher and higher until suddenly Cecile threw her hands up and commanded: "SUSPANN!" - *STOP!*

The silence was immediate, and deafening. "The Gods wish to hear from your new leader, Dutty Boukman!" yelled Cecile.

Dutty Boukman made his way to the front of the crowd, still marveling at Angelique's hovering body. Though he had heard tales of such a thing, in all his years as a Houngan priest, he'd never witnessed anything like this. Just then, he felt a warmth in his chest, and words that were not his own burst forth from deep within him:

"God who made the sun, who brings us light from above;
who raises the sea, and who makes the storm rumble.

That God is here!
Do you understand?
Hiding in a cloud,
He watches us!
He sees what the WHITES do!

The God of the WHITES pushes them to crime.

Now our God who is so good orders us to vengeance;
He will direct our hands, and provide us with aid!

Toss away the God of WHITES who thirsts for our tears.
Listen to the liberty that speaks in ALL OUR HEARTS!"

The skies violently erupted with lightning and thunder, yet no rain fell. Angelique slowly descended from the air, landing on her feet, though her eyes remained closed. The crowd hushed and the lightning and thunder ceased.

A Black pig was led to the stone and a knife was placed in Angelique's hand. She kneeled and expertly slid the stiletto into the pig's heart, who uttered a faint squeal and collapsed dead.

Covered in the pig's entrails, Angelique then took the knife and slit her left arm. A wooden chalice was placed forth, capturing the mixed blood of both. The chalice was then filled with rum. Taking a long swig, Angelique then handed it to Cecile, who held it close to her chest.

The young girl then opened her mouth to speak, though the voice that emanated forth was deep and vociferous.

"I am Ogoun, the Voodoo warrior. This girl, pure and connected to the Gods, is my vessel. You have heard God *Grand Mèt Bondye* through the High Priest Dutty Boukman. You will go forth and seek stark justice from your White oppressors."

The group remained in rapt attention as the possessed girl continued.

"Dutty Boukman is your supreme leader. He is respected by all in the Northern plains. He is to assemble a great army to pursue your cause."

Angelique's eyes snapped open and fixated on a man to her left.

"This army will be led by Jean-François Papillon, who possesses unmatched leadership and military skills."

Papillon was stunned. How could this girl know his name or his experience as a soldier?

Angelique then turned toward the middle of the crowd.

"Commander Georges Biassou is also called to lead. He is a skilled tracker, fighter, and pure of spirit."

Biassou was equally perplexed. He'd only accepted the invitation to the ceremony as a favor to an acquaintance—yet now he had been singled out to lead a rebellion?

Angelique then turned to face the other side of the group.

"Jeannot Bullet is chosen for his brutality and callousness. He will be effective and necessary; cruel as the Whites are, but kept in control by this tribunal."

The man Angelique identified shrugged, unsure whether to be insulted or proud.

Angelique turned once more to face Cecile and Boukman. Her eyes closed, and her body went limp. Boukman caught her and carried her to her father. The spirit of Ogun had departed, leaving only an exhausted teenager.

Cecile raised her hands. "The Gods have spoken! We shall follow their command!"

She turned to face the still-stunned crowd.

"Tonight we celebrate and worship—tomorrow we will rise and take back our freedom!"

As if on cue, the drummers took up their beat and the dancers began to leap and wail.

The four men who had been named by the spirit quietly excused themselves and congregated in a nearby hut. None had ever met the others prior to that moment, yet each agreed with the concept of revolution—and quickly vowed their loyalty to each other.

Boukman introduced himself first.

"My name is Dutty Boukman. I am twenty-four years old and born in the proud nation of Senegambia in Africa. I was captured in my country, sold, and transported to the island of Jamaica. When my British owners caught me preaching the teachings of Islam, I was sold to a French plantation owner here on St. Domingue. I was a *commander*—a slave driver—but I was not very good at it. I later became a coach driver."

He went on as the three others listened intently.

"The English called me a 'Book Man' for my reading. I prefer the variation of *Boukman*. I healed many with my understanding of Syncretism and medicinal sciences. I received my freedom after healing the daughter of my grateful master. I am now a devout follower and Houngan high priest of voodoo."

Boukman finished with the strongest statement he could muster.

"I believe all slaves should be freed, and I pledge my life to achieve that goal!"

The man to his left cleared his throat and began.

"My name is Jean-Français Papillon. I am thirty-two years old, and I was also born in Africa before being taken in captivity to the North Province of this colony. I worked the plantation of Papillon, before escaping and becoming a Maroon in the mountains, where I learned the ways of guerrilla warfare. I am now free, and vow to liberate the enslaved and make St. Domingue a free nation."

"I will serve the cause well with my learned ability to surprise the enemy and disappear just as quickly."

"I am Georges Biassou, and as you can see by my signs of gray, I am older than you all at fifty," began Biassou. "I was born a third-generation slave in this colony. My Grandfather was kidnapped, sold, and brought here many decades ago. Our White master was a noble one, and I was lucky to be freed upon his death."

"I spent my years in the *Marchuasse* as a hunter of escaped slaves. I later discovered returning slaves to their masters was not always good. They would be beaten, tortured, or even killed in front of me upon their return—to my infuriation."

Biassou slammed his fist on the table, emphasizing his last words.

"For several years, I would hunt and capture slaves, and instead of returning them to their masters, take them into the hills to join the Maroon colonies. I pledge my military experience and ability to lead men.

Bullet sighed and shook his head. "My name is Jeannot Bullet. And, as that girl pretending to be possessed said, I am brutal and have no heart. My motto is *koupe tèt et boule kay"* - Cut off heads and burn houses.

"I stop at nothing in pursuit of my own ends. I seize quickly on chances and do not care for honoring my word or yours. I fear no one and nothing. I look forward to drinking the blood of all Whites and any *Gens de Couleur* who dare to stand in our way."

The others looked upon Bullet with curiosity. A small, thin man, he had an undoubtedly forbidding nature. Any man willing to out himself as this despicable would surely be dangerous to not only the enemy but possibly his allies as well.

Boukman quickly took back control. "Enough of the introductions. Let us arrive now at an agreement. If I am the commander and supreme general of our forces, then you three shall be my subordinate Generals. Is this clear and agreeable?"

Papillon, Biassou, and Bullet looked at each other, nodding their agreement.

Bullet spoke up suddenly.

"What is our payment? What do we stand to gain from this war?"

"Honor, accomplishment, and gratitude, Bullet" Boukman responded.

"You can keep that. I am intent upon the spoils." Bullet shot back.

"In the chaos of war, there will always be the spoils," said Boukman, measuring his words. "Once the French leave, hundreds of abandoned plantations will be left without owners. You will have your pick of land and all its promises at that time."

The two men locked eyes for what seemed an eternity. Boukman hoped this necessary evil would quickly outlive his use. Bullet was certainly capable of that which the three of them were not, but he hoped the Gods had chosen their devil wisely.

Bullet finally broke the tension. "Don't ever double cross me, Boukman, or any of the rest of you for that matter. I will slit your throats as easily as I slice a mango and suck its fruit. I pledge that—and my allegiance—to you," he spat.

The four retired for the evening, each falling into a restless sleep.

The generals met frequently over the next three days, hatching and organizing a military campaign. The revolt would officially begin one week from their coronation, on Sunday, August 21, 1791.

Word had spread rapidly of the prophetic religious service, and voodoo priests and priestesses across the region foretold of the pending uprising. Messages were conveyed through the drums which beat throughout the hills, their language alien to the French.

Those invited to the ceremony from the hundred plantations surrounding Bois Caïman would initiate the war; organizing the workforce of each and subduing the overseers and families of the owners. The main house would be burned as a sign of success, and to ensure the plantation was uninhabitable—forcing the owners to leave or face death.

Once these first plantations fell, the mob would move to those neighboring, repeating the process, gathering strength and momentum.

Generals Papillon and Biassou were dispatched to the mountains to gain the support of their Maroon comrades and raise the call to arms. Drums would carry the word throughout the hills from one Provence to the next. The Maroons would converge at the outskirts of Cap-Français to join the main army and be split into four regiments—one under the command of each general. Their weapons would be the same tools the slavers had expertly trained them to master: machetes and axes.

They believed ten thousand men could overpower the well-armed professional French forces, which currently numbered twenty-five hundred in Cap-Français. Two regiments would take the city, while the others would split east and west to continue the purging of plantations.

On the morning of the revolt, a tropical storm battered the island with the roar of thunder and flash of lightning. It was perceived as an omen. On that star-filled, moonlit night, drums began to beat throughout the Northern plains. A great slave uprising had begun. Within four hours the northern plains surrounding Cap-Français were engulfed in flames.

Owners and overseers were overwhelmed and became targets of brutality in retaliation for their treatment of their slaves.

Many were murdered, their wives and daughters raped and killed, and children slaughtered. It was a savage outburst of horror and bloodshed—decades of rage finally unleashed all at once. Some owners attempted to defend themselves. Others immediately fled. Few were spared. However, those masters who had treated their slaves humanely became protected by them, hidden and taken to safety.

Within a week, more than one thousand Whites were killed, and the northern plains were little more than smoldering ruins.

The few spared were rewarded in recognition of their years of proper treatment and perceived kindness to their workers and became unwitting benefactors of their past gestures.

Slaves and Maroons rallied to the banner of the revolution. Of the estimated 170,000 slaves of the North Province, nearly 80,000 had escaped and joined the cause. The generals' plan and ingenuity proved overwhelmingly effective, and the rookie army quickly set up camps of thousands of dwellings, multiple infirmaries, a civil government, and fields of confiscated crops, livestock, and supplies. They were well prepared for the siege of Cap-Français.

Meanwhile, Jeannot Bullet became increasingly insubordinate. He exhibited brutality far beyond even what they felt was warranted, torturing prisoners for his own enjoyment; hanging those he captured by hooks under their chins, and personally putting out their eyes with red-hot pincers. His men feared him, and this seemed to give Bullet even more confidence and strength, only matched by his contempt for his fellow leaders.

The revolution had begun. However, the other generals would soon reach an inevitable conclusion; Bullet must be eliminated.

Revolts against slavery and rights restrictions ignited in pockets throughout the island. In *Mirebalais*, north of Port-au-Prince, *Gens de Couleur* and slaves began to attack plantation owners throughout the region. A contingent of colonial soldiers was dispatched from Port-au-Prince to suppress the violence but was soundly defeated.

However, it was a time of chaos and uncertainty as the fledgling rebellion struggled to find direction amid long-simmering tensions and conflicting ideologies. In a twisted turn of events, the free *Gens de Couleur* staged an abrupt about-face. Realizing the absence of slave labor could ultimately result in economic collapse; many reasserted their loyalty to the colonial authorities and joined the *Grands Blancs* in opposition to the growing uprising.

The colonial government assumed this to represent a successful template to pursue. Ironically, during a heated emergency session of the Colonial Assembly, representatives moved to recognize the March decree of 1790, thus granting all property owners the right to vote and hold political office. Against Governor Blanchelande's wishes, the motion was put to a vote and passed unanimously on September 20, 1791.

This infuriated the Governor. Blanchelande had been humiliated by the botched execution fiasco, and now came vindication for those he'd ordered executed. Further damaging his credibility, the Assembly then recognized the citizenship of all free *Gens de Couleur*, regardless of their property status or ancestry.

This flurry of legislation resulted in clear battle lines and a calculated political wedge between the free, regardless of skin color, and the revolting Black slaves and Maroons of the colony.

Despite what the Assembly presumed an ingenious bout of political maneuvering, French Whites in the south and west were outraged by the measures and demanded a revocation of the newly granted rights. This immediately led to the fracturing of the already fragile alliance between the free *Gens de Couleur* and Whites.

The region quickly divided into three competing factions; Black slaves, freed *Gens de Couleur*, and Whites.

Meanwhile, machinations continued in Paris. Word of the uprising and subsequent spells of violence had spooked the National Assembly. Fearing the decree had caused more trouble than intended, with increasing pressure from the Grands Blancs residing in France and not wishing to lose the colony to a civil war, the controversial March decree was annulled on September 23, 1791—rendering the Colonial Assembly's ratification three days prior null and void.

In an attempt to restore order, three new commissioners, along with 6,000 soldiers, were dispatched to St. Domingue. Their intent was to re-establish French control of the island, restore slavery, and squash any hint of insurgency.

Again facing a common enemy, the rebellious slaves and *Gens de Couleur* collaborated once again—this time in a full-fledged violent uprising. Their forces lay siege to Port-au-Prince, cutting off its water supply and blockading access to incoming supplies.

The arrival of French forces managed to subdue the campaign with a massive counter-offensive, though the city was nearly burnt to the ground in the process. Vowing to restore Port-au-Prince to its former glory, the emissaries' focus turned to reconstruction, and away from the still-burning embers of revolution.

Thirteen

TOUSSAINT GUINOU BREDA

Ennery
August 1791

Toussaint Breda relished his first-morning cup of coffee on the outdoor porch of the sprawling Habitation Sancey plantation in the town of Ennery. The sun had just broken the eastern horizon and the air was still cool from the night before.

"Suzanne, your coffee is splendid as it is every morning," he declared. "Where is it from?"

"It is the latest crop from our *Roufittier* plantation, my darling," his wife answered, gently rubbing the back of Toussaint's neck. "It is a promising crop this year—one that should yield a pretty penny from the French connoisseurs."

"I would have guessed it from *Sancey* or *Beaumont*. This is far more refined than what the *Roufittier* soil yields." jabbed Toussaint with a sly smile, knowing *Roufittier* had been in Suzanne's family for generations.

"Toussaint!" Suzanne scolded. "Great Grand-Papa Alix will haunt you tonight if you keep chiding me this way!" She shot him a sour look before betraying a smile of her own. The two had been married for nearly ten years; their daily banter was a cheeky demonstration of the deep love and respect they both still carried for one another.

Of course, when it came to coffee, the line between offense and poking fun was somewhat fine; the daughter of wealthy Black planters who had successfully run coffee plantations for decades, the liquid was Suzanne's lifeblood.

Toussaint however, was born a slave of the *Bréda* Plantation in *Haut du Cap*. The name of Guinou, he proudly used from his African ancestry, and the name Breda he adopted from the name of the plantation. While growing up, he displayed a particular skill with horses, eventually rising to a position as the Plantation's coachman and trainer of horses. He was educated and baptized Catholic by his godfather Pierre Baptiste, an older free man who lived and worked at *Bréda*.

Baptiste and various Jesuit missionaries fostered a well-rounded education, resulting in Toussaint's command of both French and Creole; a philosophical knowledge of Epictetus, the Stoic philosopher who lived as a slave, and familiarity with Machiavelli and Enlightenment thinker Abbé Raynal—a critic of slavery. He also learned to read and write in the French language.

He'd also developed an interest in medicine, combining African and Creole herbal techniques with procedures commonly found in Jesuit-operated hospitals.

During his time on the Plantation, Toussaint grew loyal to the head overseer, Bayon de Libertad. It was Libertad to whom he owed his freedom, earned over thirty-two years of handwork and loyalty. Toussaint knew Libertad wished him to stay on in compensated capacity, but he had eyes on heading an operation of his own. Afraid to completely lose his influence and friendship, Libertad granted Toussaint ten slaves and ten hectares of land. The two established a repayment plan, and Toussaint suddenly found himself a Plantation owner.

Shortly after, he met Suzanne. Their love grew in tandem with their family and business—eventually developing multiple estates and farms.

The warm wind unfurled from the west on that splendid morning late in August of 1791. The birds sang along to the gentle humming of the Mahogany leaves shifting in the air.

Nathalie, the Ennery's house servant, appeared with two glasses and a pitcher of cool water. "More coffee, *Monsieur et Madame?*"

"No Nathalie, not for me." Suzzane answered. Toussaint?"

"I will have another cup of my wife's delightful family roast," Toussaint said, exaggerating the final words in loving hyperbole.

"And breakfast?" inquired Nathalie.

"Are the boys awake yet?" asked Suzanne. She and Toussaint were the early risers of the family. It was typically the only private moments they could share before their three sons, Placide, Isaac, and baby St. Jean stole their attention.

Toussaint looked out beyond the porch. Moise, his 21-year-old nephew, was already working in the field. In charge of organizing the daily workforce, his leadership-by-example and fair treatment of the Plantation's slaves resulted in high productivity. Though always pleasant and respectful, Moise harbored a deep hatred for Whites; his mother, Toussaint's sister, had been raped and beaten by a mob of drunken French sailors, eventually succumbing to her wounds several days after the attack. Toussaint and Suzanne took the then 13-year-old under their care, raising him on the Plantation ever since.

Toussaint felt no such ill toward Whites. He'd been treated well by Libertad; and Placide, Suzanne's ten-year-old firstborn, was a mulatto as a result of her prior relationship with a White Creole. At times, Toussaint would attempt to curb Moise's rage when it sprang forth, though he was rarely successful. He often feared such passion might one day spiral out of the boy's control, leading to an untimely demise.

"Not yet, *Madame.*" Nathalie's answer disrupted Toussaint's thoughts. "You may enjoy your coffee and breakfast for a while longer."

"Eggs with smoked pork then, for me, Nathalie. My dear?" asked Suzanne.

"Perfect. I'll have the same, Nathalie. Thank you."

No sooner had Nathalie left to prepare their dishes did the rapid clomping of hooves break the early morning peace. The noise grew louder and closer with each passing second.

"What possible emergency could there be this early?" wondered a slightly irritated Toussaint. "Lost chickens? A missing cow? Wild dog? Perhaps a hawk swiped some eggs? What minor inconvenience would dare break our solitude, Suzanne?"

Without slowing, the young and fit Black horseman skillfully guided his steed around the final curve of the path and continued on to the residence at full gallop. Nearly before the beast had fully come to a stop, the rider had dismounted and hurried to the front steps. Neither Toussaint nor Suzanne recognized him.

"I have an urgent message for Toussaint Breda of Ennery," said the rider laboring for air.

"I am Toussaint Breda, and this is the Ennery Plantation. What is your name - who are you, boy?"

"I am Emmanuel Rochet from the Breda Plantation. My Master, Bayon de Libertad has sent me to deliver an urgent letter to you." Rochet was still struggling to catch his breath.

"How long have you been riding, son?" asked Toussaint.

"All night, sir"

"Richard, come!" called Toussaint to a teenage boy tending the garden.

Richard immediately bolted up the steps. "Yes, sir?"

"Take Monsieur Rochet, to the kitchen and ask Nathalie to prepare a hearty breakfast for him."

"Right away, sir" answered Richard. He then turned to Rochet. "Please come with me, *monsieur*."

Toussaint waited for them to depart before opening the mail pouch. What awaited his eyes shocked him to his core.

My Dear Friend Toussaint,

I do wish this letter bore better news than the reality it must. To be brief, the Northern Plains of St. Domingue is in flames and the devastation is moving North-East towards Breda and Cap-Français.

A massive slave uprising has broken out, and its brutality is beyond any description I am able to provide.

I am currently packing Monsieur & Madame Breda for a trip to Cap-Français to assure their safety, before returning to the plantation in hopes to save it from the destruction that has befallen hundreds like it.

Toussaint, you simply cannot believe what is happening. I ask whether you can find it in your heart to join me and assist. If so, I would be eternally grateful and heartened.

I understand if you cannot leave Ennery, and hope to see you once again under better circumstances.

My fondest regards,
Bayon de Libertad.

Toussaint handed the letter to Suzanne. She placed her hand over her mouth. She too could not believe what she was reading. Finishing, she looked up to him with an odd expression he could not decipher.

"Well, what are you waiting for Toussaint?" she finally asked.

Moved to action, Toussaint called out "Richard!"

The boy appeared before him instantly.

"Bring Monsieur Rochet's horse to the stables. Have two stallions readied—one with Monsieur Rochet's saddle—for immediate travel," commanded Toussaint.

"I will pack your things and have food prepared for the journey, my love," added Suzanne, hurrying to the kitchen. Toussaint left for his quarters to wash and dress. Several minutes later, he found Rochet in the dining room finishing breakfast. The young man stood as he entered.

"Sit, Rochet," Toussaint said gently. "Tell me everything you know about the goings on in the Northern Plains."

Nathalie emerged from behind Toussaint to deliver a hearty plate of breakfast in front of him.

"It is like nothing I have ever seen, Master Breda," began Rochet.

"It started last Sunday night. The dark sky lit up in red and orange, and the sounds of explosions rolled across the hills. We believed it to be a wildfire at first. By the next morning, however, horses and carriages appeared carrying people and possessions running from the area. They were escaping to Cap-Français. Master Libertad directed us to set up stations on the road with food and water so they could refresh on their journey."

Rochet lowered his voice and paused a moment to gather himself.

"They told of murder and rape. Pillaging. Even beheadings and the mutilations of children. Entire plantations and many homes were set aflame. It was horrific, Master Breda!"

Toussaint allowed the young man to regain his composure before speaking once more. "I wish to depart immediately for Breda. Are you up for the journey?"

"Yes, sir" responded Rochet. Just then, the stableman arrived out front with two of the plantation's strongest and most surefooted horses. They swayed somewhat impatiently, snorting and pawing at the ground. Suzanne and Nathalie accompanied the two men outside with saddle bags of food, water, and Toussaint's smallest garment bag.

"I know you can find plenty of clothes at Breda, Toussaint," Suzanne said, pulling herself into his arms. She then glanced over to Rochet. "Keep each other safe and be careful."

"My medicine bag?" inquired Toussaint

"Packed, my dear" replied Suzanne, pulling away.

Toussaint walked her to the far edge of the porch. "Do you remember where all of the important papers are, Suzanne?" he asked.

"Yes, my love."

"Everything is in your hands now. You have a limitless power of attorney in my absence which I had drawn up with our notaire. Do whatever you must." stated Toussaint.

"This is 'au revoir' Toussaint, not goodbye," Suzanne said, bringing her lips to his and embracing him one final time.

Turning to leave, Toussaint found Othello, the large plantation overseer, awaiting him by the porch stairs.

"I have saddled another horse, boss," Othello said, his voice deep and measured. "I must accompany you."

"No, Othello," Toussaint replied, shaking his head. "You must remain here. If things progress, trouble may come here next. I need you to construct a fortress that can be properly defended. Your obligation is to this plantation and the people on it. Do I make myself clear?"

"Yes, sir!" Othello was heartened to receive an assignment of such importance. "I have procured weapons and ammunition for you both from the armory."

Othello handed two rifles and two pistols each to Toussaint and Rochet.

"Let us make haste, Rochet. We should reach Breda well before nightfall."

Toussaint jumped onto his stallion. He gracefully controlled the large animal, performing a brief canter and roll of its front hooves. Less than a minute later, he and Rochet were already out of sight, a trail of dust the only hint of their presence.

They arrived at Breda late that afternoon, exhausted from the pace of the day's ride. The horses were bathed in sweat and their movements were slowing. They arrived to find the refreshment stations Libertad had set up a few days ago were abandoned, but the sounds emanating from further up the road seemed to indicate the property was vibrant with life.

Toussaint's appearance was met with a not insignificant amount of fanfare; once a slave and now a plantation and slave owner himself, a crowd quickly gathered and followed he and Rochet as they neared the main house. Toussaint noticed all work on the plantation had ceased, and the remaining slaves milled about without purpose.

Libertad awaited on the porch with a mix of slave overseers and freed workers. "Toussaint!" he cried out, racing down the steps to greet his old friend and protégé who had by now accumulated dozens of admirers in tow. The two men embraced.

"Good job Rochet!" He exclaimed, turning to the young man. "You have managed to pull Toussaint Breda from Ennery and Suzanne – no small feat! Now, have the cooks prepare a fine meal for our distinguished guest, and help yourself to some as well."

He then placed his hand on Tousaint's shoulder and led him into the home. "Come with me, Toussaint. Gentlemen; carry on without me."

The two left the group of men and the anxious crowd behind.

"I managed to get Monsieur & Madame. Breda to safety yesterday." Libertad began. "They understand things will never be like they were before. This uprising may be permanent—or if not, reversing it would require a long and bloody war. The Breda's elected to free their slaves and work out compensation for work in exchange for housing, food, and stipends. I need your perspective and help in order to devise the proper system."

"My perspective?" ventured Toussaint.

"Yes, Toussaint. You know slavery better than I," answered Libertad.

"As you can see, the slaves know what is happening. They do not return to the fields. Within weeks crops will die and the harvest will be lost," he added.

Toussaint was exhausted but knew that time was of the essence. "Give me a moment to wash up and I will meet you in the main study. Let us get right to work, my friend."

Libertad asked his men outside to gather the entire workforce for a meeting the following morning. Until then, the kitchens would continue work, and all should eat as normal.

The two talked and worked intensely for the next several

hours. It was nearly midnight by the time they finalized their plan. Workers who lived off property would be paid 10 livres each month. Those for whom the plantation provided room, food, clothing, and medical care would receive 5 livres per month.

Furthermore, all wages and plantation expenses incurred over the year would be deducted from the harvest's revenue, and one-third of that profit would be shared among those workers who had been under employ for at least one year.

Libertad provided some estimates from prior years to ensure this model would still yield a viable profit for the Bredas, as well as an acceptable income for workers—and even the potential for bonuses.

The two friends looked at each other and smiled through sleepy eyes. Why this was never put in place before they had no clue. Implementing such a system throughout the colony may have prevented the revolt from ever taking place. Alas, they could not change the past—but they could possibly save Breda from a terrible fate.

The plan was presented the following morning to a mixed reaction from the workforce. On the one hand, was incredulity and excitement. On the other, distrust and skepticism.

"What if we do not wish to work the fields at all?" asked one burly slave directly in front of Toussaint.

"Then you are free to leave," replied Libertad. The man appeared shocked by the answer.

"Yes, that's right," Libertad continued, turning to address the broader crowd. "You are free to leave—as are any of you. You are no longer slaves, but free men and women. However, with that will come the responsibilities of finding work and taking care of yourselves."

"This is a trick!" yelled a man from the middle of the audience.

"I assure you it is not," stated Toussaint, stepping forward. "All freedom papers are being prepared as we speak. I stand before you a free man from this very plantation. Do I look like a trick to you?"

"What do they want from us?" the man responded, cautiously.

"Masters Libertad and the Bredas wish for you to continue your work in exchange for a living wage. Otherwise, you are free to go. It is that simple." answered Toussaint.

"I accept my freedom and wish to continue my work!" yelled one man. His sentiment was echoed quickly by another. Chants of 'Freedom!' and 'Long live the Bredas!' rippled through the crowd.

"Celebrate your freedom today! Work can wait until tomorrow!" Cried Libertad to more cheers. "Cooks; slaughter enough pigs, goats, and chicken for a day-long feast. Quartermaster; break out the rum and provide partitions to all. Today we mark the first day of your FREEDOM!"

Drums began to beat and the women broke out in song. While several turned and made their way toward the path leading from the plantation, the majority remained for merrymaking—signaling their intent to stay. The affair was lively and lasted into the late afternoon. Eventually, all had exhausted themselves and retired to their quarters to sleep off the effects of the rum and repast.

That night, Toussaint and Libertad sat together on the veranda, glasses of rum in hand, and stared into the night sky. Despite their triumph that morning, the distant plantations still aflame were a stark reminder of their good fortune.

"Toussaint, I could not have done this without you." sighed a weary Libertad. "I believe you have helped me save this plantation. I only hope that others may find solutions for their own upheavals and that the colony's economy can withstand such changes."

"It is a process that can only occur on a case-by-case basis, my friend. Your genius behind this plan should be handsomely rewarded by the Bredas—you have ensured their livelihood without bloodshed." Toussaint replied.

"My brother, it was only your brilliance that allowed for it," Libertad stated. "I, and by extension the Bredas, are forever in your debt."

The next day, production picked back up as though there had been no interruption. All were back at work—and Toussaint even noted an improved pace and demeanor. The plantation's newly minted and now highly motivated employees were content, and their work reflected as much.

Toussaint and Libertad decided to venture toward the burning they'd observed the night before. They guessed it to be a half-day ride to the west. They departed late that morning.

During their journey, they encountered many others heading in the opposite direction on the main road towards Cap-Français. They paused briefly to hear several of their stories—each seemingly more horrific than the last.

"The Plains are in ruins…"

"We've lost everything, our life's savings…

"My family was tortured and killed. I was lucky to escape…"

"Any slaves who would not join were immediately and publicly slaughtered…"

A common name emerged as the tales of brutality and carnage accumulated: General Jeannot Bullet.

Not wishing to breach the contested region unprepared and lightly armed, Toussaint and Libertad turned back to the plantation before nightfall. All appeared in good order, just as they'd left it, and both retired to bed.

Toussaint was exceptionally fatigued, as the past two days of constant riding finally caught up to his fifty-year-old body. He was no longer the young lad who could seemingly spend every waking second on horseback. He collapsed into a deep slumber, his dreams tinted in the red and orange glow of fire.

Over the next week, Toussaint leisurely toured the plantation, quite enjoying a brief respite—though he missed Suzanne immensely. Libertad had left to inform the Bredas of their new business deal and arrange for supplies. He requested Toussaint stay through November to help coordinate supply shipments amid the current turmoil.

Toussaint corresponded the turn of events to Suzanne, and they both agreed that he remain at Breda to assist Libertad in the restructuring process.

One morning in early November, Toussaint, Rochet, and four overseers liberated through the Breda deal were enjoying breakfast and speaking of business in the main dining room. Their discussion of newly found positive attitudes and plans for expansion was suddenly interrupted by the bellowing thunder of horses pounding down the path to the plantation's entrance.

The men hurried to the front porch, only to be greeted by a fearsome sight: a contingent of nearly 1,000 men, mostly barefoot and clothed in rags, raising their machetes and axes high. The slave army, with very few horsemen, had finally come for them.

The dust obscured the front line of horsemen until they came to rest in front of the main house. There the particles eventually settled, covering the finely trimmed grass and garden.

"I command the Master of this plantation to step out before me!" barked one of the mounted men.

Toussaint stepped forward. "Master Breda, the owner of this plantation, is not here," he answered in a measured though authoritative tone.

"And who are you?" Demanded the horseman. Toussaint noted the tattered remnants of an old French uniform. Behind him were two dozen horsemen, and foot soldiers stretching as far back as the eye could see.

"I am Toussaint Breda, though I am not a relative of the owner, sir. Who, may I ask, has come calling?"

"This is no formality, old man," sneered the leader. "Round up your slaves, and bring them here immediately!"

"There are no slaves at this plantation, sir" Toussaint responded.

Suddenly, from behind the contingent, three new horsemen arrived at a gallop, nearly trampling several of the soldiers who were slow to move. Their uniforms appeared far cleaner, likely stolen from defeated colonial officers and denoted a higher rank in the makeshift platoon.

"Where are the slaves?" the lead officer asked the man who had been speaking with Toussaint.

"This man here says there are no slaves on this plantation."

Toussaint considered the new officer. His face harbored a stern, permanent scowl, accented by a long scar running from his cheek to his jaw. Despite the early hour, sweat poured from his face and his eyes were bloodshot with what likely were the remnants of the previous night's cheap rum. Brutality oozed from his very core.

"There are no slaves here? Who is it I see working the fields and the crops then?" he demanded, turning his ire toward Toussaint.

"All workers on this plantation are free men, working for fair wages, sir," answered Toussaint. "Your lieutenant has not yet introduced himself or shared the purpose of your visit, so may I ask who you are?"

Toussaint already knew before the man could finish his answer. His muscles tensed unconsciously and his right hand moved instinctively to where his sword normally sat on his hip.

"You may call me General Bullet of the revolutionary army. Who are you?" replied Bullet.

"My name is Toussaint Breda, and I am currently in charge of this plantation. What may I do for you, General?"

"I want all slaves to assemble here immediately! That's an order, asshole!"

"My name is Toussaint Breda, General. And as I told you before, there are no slaves on this plantation," responded Toussaint, keeping his voice calm.

"Get everyone here now!" roared Bullet. His horsemen immediately headed off in all directions to gather the workers.

"If I find out that you're playing some game, I swear I will cut your old tongue from your gray head." Bullet snarled through clenched teeth.

Toussaint decided silence would best serve him at that moment. Within twenty minutes, workers began to appear, being herded toward the house like animals.

The entire workforce was finally present, and Bullet spoke again.

"My name is General Bullet and I wish all slaves step forward to claim your freedom!"

None of the workers moved. Bullet repeated himself, this time more forcefully.

"Again, I command all slaves to come forward, claim your freedom, and join our army of rebellion against those who have enslaved you!"

"None of us are slaves, Monsieur General" yelled out one of the workers.

"What do you mean? Are you not working in the fields?" demanded Bullet.

"We are. But not as slaves. We are paid for our work." the man responded.

Bullet's intimidating frown broke momentarily. This was an unanticipated turn of events. Unsure of what to do, his base nature took over.

"Confiscate all livestock, grain, beans, and coffee for the cause! Burn the fields and main house. Leave the slaves'—or freed men's—quarters untouched!"

He let loose a wicked laugh and turned his head over his shoulder, shooting Toussaint a look of pure malevolence.

"Wait, General!" yelled Toussaint. "Why injure those you claim to liberate?"

Bullet's and Toussaint's eyes locked. At that moment, each man knew in their bones they'd met a lifelong enemy. Bullet suffered no sympathies for Whites, G*ens de couleur*, or Blacks he deemed loyal to the planter class. His judgment was swift, brutal, and final.

"Hang him."

Toussaint quickly found a noose wrapped around his neck as two horsemen jumped off their mounts and ran to him without a second's hesitation. A 3rd horseman dragged the struggling Toussaint by a rope behind his steed to the large tree several yards from the porch they intended to hang him from.

Their progress was impeded suddenly by a swell of workers who had rushed forward. Hands grabbed at the rope, attempting to

loosen it from his neck, while several of the largest workers stood shoulder to shoulder in an attempt to block the huge horse from advancing forward to reach the tree.

"Back! I will shoot the lot of you!" Bullet screamed. He turned and shouted toward the other mounted men, "Ready your rifles!"

Unbeknownst to Bullet, a small detachment had arrived to the area amid the scrum. As Bullet trained his rifle on his first would-be victim, a shot rang out, instantly quieting the crowd.

"I command you to stand down!"

None other than General Jean-Francois Papillon himself appeared between the henchmen, crowd, and tree. The horsemen lowered their weapons. Bullet's face contorted in a mixture of rage and disgust.

"How dare you interrupt my military operation, Papillon!" "You shall address me as General Papillon, and you are under arrest, General Bullet."

Ten of the newly arrived soldiers all turned to aim their rifles at Bullet, who stopped in his tracks.

"On what charges?!" he howled.

"Murder, torture, rape—and undoubtedly more that will be unearthed before your trial," responded General Papillon. "Now, drop your rifle, or my men will drop you from your mount."

"I will *kill you*, Papillon," Bullet sneered, every inch of his skin burning with rage.

Unfazed, General Papillon turned to his men.

"Secure the prisoner until I decide his fate."

Bullet struck a blow to the first officer to reach him but was quickly subdued by several others. It appeared more an act of pride than genuine resistance, but one which emphasized the danger he constantly posed.

General Papillon turned his attention to Toussaint next.

"You are clearly held in high regard here. These men would have given their lives for you. I am General Jean-Francois Papillon of the revolutionary army. Who are you, and what is your position at this plantation?"

"My name is Toussaint Breda, and I have come to assist friends in difficult times. This plantation is owned by the Breda family and managed by Bayon de Libertad. I was once a slave here, just as these men were. We have all been set free by the Breda family."

"Accept my apologies for the behavior of General Bullet, Monsieur Breda. You may take leave to tend your wounds and compose yourself," responded Papillon, bowing his head slightly in respect. "Now, I wish to meet with General Bullet's officers. May I utilize a room within the home to do so?"

"Yes, of course, General. Rochet will show you to Master Breda's study."

With that, Toussaint headed to the main quarters to wash up and address the rope burns around his neck.

General Papillon interrogated Bullet's officers for over an hour, finally identifying and arresting three who had enthusiastically participated in the torture, rape, and murder of civilians. The others were determined to be soldiers following orders and admitted to being disgusted by the actions forced upon them.

General Papillon also quickly deduced Bullet had not provided training, strategy, logistics, organization, or any real military skill to his charges. Instead, he ruled through fear, intimidation, and terror, subverting them to his will. He sent a request for General Biassou to take command of the division as quickly as possible. He would personally remain on the plantation in the meantime, assessing the readiness of the fighting force, before moving to their next campaign.

Unfortunately, the outlook was bleak. Bullet's troops were demoralized, dehydrated, malnourished, and ill. Often while walking amongst the contingent, the General would spot Toussaint tending to the injured and sick. One afternoon, he approached him as he was treating a soldier with a mixture of his famed herbal healing medicines he had long ago mastered and perfected.

"How are you feeling after your ordeal, Monsieur Breda?"

"Much better, General. Thank you for allowing our workers to return to the fields and crops. It is important the economy continue to have access to viable products." replied Toussaint.

"Hard to believe it has been only a few weeks since this all erupted," the General offered.

Toussaint finished bandaging a wounded soldier's ankle and stood up.

"May I ask, General, what is your goal? Why such a bloody rebellion? What does a possible victory and future look like? I have so many questions and have received no answers."

"You are receptive Monsieur Breda," allowed the General. "These are confusing times and there are no simple answers. The slaves want and deserve freedom, but do not know how to exist as free people. Myself and General Biassou wish for *Gens de couleur* to enjoy citizen's rights, but the Colonial and National Assemblies disagree on this. White landowners want their slaves, but cannot maintain peace under the present system. Of course, once bullets are fired, it only gets more complex."

"I fear there is no end in sight," sighed Toussaint.

"Any conclusion will be made all the more difficult by an unfit fighting force. These men are in far worse condition than I imagined."

The General paused suddenly, stricken by a thought.

"Can you help us?" He asked.

"Help with what, General?"

"We have no doctors, yet we have legions of sick and injured. I have seen you tend to them and have heard praise for your medical knowledge and healing. I ask that you assess and report back as to our general health and how we can improve it." finished General Papillon.

"I would not have good news, General. Malnutrition is rampant. However, we have large corn and kidney bean stocks high in fiber and protein which can help nourish your troops, as long as we can find an organized team to prepare it all."

The General nodded.

"We can then train a core group of your finest as field medics, thus expanding my abilities tremendously. Finally, all must be bathed and provided proper sanitation facilities to reduce the risk of disease." Toussaint concluded.

"You are skilled indeed, Monsieur Breda. General Biassou will be arriving today. Let us plan to meet with him after I debrief him tomorrow morning." the General replied.

However, Biassou did not arrive that afternoon. It was not until the following Tuesday, in the middle of a deluge, that the burly officer finally found his way to the plantation. While the weather was gloomy, his first report was even grimmer. Dutty Boukman had been ambushed and killed by a faction of French colonial soldiers and planters. He was beheaded on the spot, his remains transported to the Cap-Français main square, '*Head of the Rebellion*' inscribed under the pole impaling his skull in a display to shatter his reputation of invincibility.

The two Generals had much to consider. Boukman was their leader and commanded the utmost respect of most of the rebels. Meanwhile, Bullet still awaited his fate, and the movement was weak of any real leadership other than themselves.

The next morning, General Papillon arranged the meeting between General Biassou and Toussaint, who instantly took a liking to each other. It was quickly decided that all of Toussaint's recommendations would be implemented, providing nutrition, sanitation, and hygiene for Bullet's soldiers.

Later that day, the military tribunal for Bullet convened on the plantation. General Papillon called upon Bullet's own men to recount the atrocities of the prior two months. Three hours later, Bullet and three of his associates were found guilty of multiple crimes and sentenced to death. The execution by firing squad was carried out at sunrise the next morning.

Generals Biassou and Papillon departed the Breda plantation

shortly afterward to rejoin their armies. Without the cauterizing leadership of Boukman however, the rebels began to falter in the following weeks, unsure of how to proceed. With wavering loyalty and outbursts of anarchy amongst their troops, the remaining officers chose to open negotiations with the colonists.

Their demands centered on improved quality of life on the plantations; less working hours and days, and amnesty for themselves in exchange for an end to the hostilities.

The slave and maroon coalition on the other hand, would entertain no surrender. They vowed to continue their fight for freedom, even if it meant sacrificing the former leaders who they now deemed traitorous. Their commanders were already free men, and could not understand that any compromise constituted defeat and a return to bondage. But at the end of November, the Colonial Assembly had refused all the rebellion's demands anyway, thus ending any hope for immediate peace.

General Papillon, Biassou, and the other leaders agreed to return to war.

In early January of 1792, Governor Blanchelande led a march including the newly arrived 6,000 French soldiers against the slaves encamped outside of Cap-Français. Short on supplies and outnumbered, the rebels abandoned the camp, retreating into the mountains. In their haste, they left behind a group of noncombatants; several hundred women, children, elderly, and injured whom they expected would be treated leniently by the French.

Instead, the French troops massacred all of them, cutting off heads and slashing bodies. Women were torn to pieces as they ferociously fought to protect their children. 3,000 captured slaves from the campaign were returned to their masters, where many were promptly tortured and killed. The colonists celebrated this as a victory—though the atrocious actions only served to further steel the resolve of the strongest and most determined of the opposition, biding their time in the green mountains overlooking the city.

Bullet's army had remained at the Breda plantation under Toussaint's management. The officers, lacking any leadership experience, grew to trust and respect him over his daily visits. Their situation had improved markedly over the browbeating and scare tactics employed by their former General.

Toussaint had nourished them back to health with his expert medical skills and herbal medicines, organized firearm and combat training, and taught officers various drills and war games to help develop a strategy. Having only read books on the subject and without any formal military training of his own, Toussaint had turned the ragtag group into a cohesive and capable force.

Early March had arrived. Toussaint embarked upon a long overdue trip to Ennery to reunite with Suzanne. During the course of their rendezvous, he confessed his anguish at the situation, and the love he'd developed for the soldiers and officers encamped at the Breda plantation. His heart could not allow them to be sent back into slavery.

He and Suzanne also implemented the same compensation plan he and Libertad had established at Breda and officially freed all of their slaves.

"I feel good about this, Toussaint" smiled Suzanne. "How did we not think of this sooner?"

"My love, we have all been accustomed to the ways we have lived for so long, we never ventured thoughts towards change," Toussaint replied. "Even I who was once a slave worked to become a slave owner myself."

"Do you think others will follow?" she asked, looking up at him.

"Some, perhaps. But most I think not. Slaves are viewed as property; not as people. They would sooner lose their livestock." Toussaint sighed.

"What is happening to the colony, Toussaint?"

"Revolution, Suzanne. Change through arms and violence. It is the only way these things happen."

"How is it you've become so invested in this?" Suzanne

asked, suddenly.

"I am not certain, Suzanne. Has God put me in a position to help or hinder this movement? He has charged me with nearly 2,000 men who know not what to do without my direction. If they disbanded and returned to their plantations, it would be to assured death or torture. But they have no leadership or guidance otherwise."

"What of the Generals you told me about; Papillon and Biassou?"

"They are stretched quite thin. They anticipated 20,000 slaves would join the fight. Now, 80,000 have escaped from plantations and are actively fighting with and without any organized leadership. It is more than an army—it is a large movement that they are incapable of managing. On top of that came the killing of Dutty Boukman, and now everything is in disarray."

Suzanne encouraged him to search his heart and, as a devout Catholic, pray to Jesus for guidance. While she had not yet reached the same conclusion, Toussaint had already recognized an undeniable calling to serve his people. The actions of the Governor and the colonial authorities could simply not be abided. He felt destined to be part of this revolution.

Toussaint spent a month at Ennery before heading back to Breda in April. Upon his return, he found Libertad had grown weary of the rebel army's occupation and disruption of the plantation—though he acknowledged the debt he owed to Toussaint for saving it. Toussaint agreed to march the contingent east and rendezvous with General Biassou and General Papillon at Ouanaminthe, near the border of Spanish Santo Domingo.

The army arrived in June of 1792. The Generals were heartened to observe the condition, organization, skill, and morale of the soldiers under Toussaint's command. General Papillon particularly noted the transformation of the same officers who were once brutalized by Bullet. Toussaint was immediately appointed and accepted to be Commander of the division.

During their encampment, a message arrived bearing a request from Matías de Armona, the retired governor of California, sent under the auspices of the Spanish government intending to invite the rebels to fight alongside the Spanish Colonial army. General Papillon agreed to an audience.

De Armona entered the camp in a brilliant dress uniform and an entourage of twenty mounted Spanish soldiers riding beautiful Paso Fino horses—originally imported by Christopher Columbus and known for their smooth-riding gait, beautiful appearance, and spectacular presence.

Two thousand barefoot and mostly shirtless fighters of the slave army greeted them, standing at attention shoulder to shoulder, lining the road as far as the eye could see. At the end of the path, General Papillon awaited, flanked by General Biassou and Commander Breda.

The Spanish emissary and his officers dismounted with grace and precision and walked toward the three men without saluting.

"*Bienvenidos*, Governor de Armona," greeted General Papillon. "We are honored by your visit."

"The honor is returned, General Papillon. I also bring you salutations from His Majesty Charles XIV, King of Spain" replied de Armona.

"May I present General Georges Biassou and Commander Toussaint Breda."

"My salutations, gentlemen. I present in turn my Officers; Santana, del Fuego, Chavez, and Muniz."

Each officer bowed his head briefly in respect and was returned in kind by Papillon, Biassou, and Toussaint.

"May I offer you some Rum? Coffee? Water?" asked General Papillon, gesturing to the large tent behind them. "I will have all three brought to us."

After several more moments of pleasantries and small talk, de Armona raised his hand to command the attention of those gathered. "Down to the business at hand, if you don't mind?"

"Please," answered General Papillon.

"Spain will soon be at war with France," de Armona began. "We are in the process of bolstering our forces throughout California, Mexico, Cuba, and our other colonies. As those preparations continue, we foresee a potential alliance between Spain and your efforts in St. Domingue."

"Your country is still sore over the French taking Western Hispaniola 100 hundred years ago?" Papillon ventured with a smile.

"It was and should have continued to be, a Spanish possession after all" replied de Armona, content to charm his hosts for the time being.

"How do our interests align, exactly? Spain still tolerates slavery in its colonies and our cause is emancipation for St. Domingue," Papillon went on.

"Our goal is a unification of the colony," stated de Armona. "The crown will accept members of your army as free on the united soil of Santo Domingo."

"And beyond our freedom, Commander," Papillon responded. "What do we gain from this partnership?"

"Consider our troops, side by side." Said de Armona, rising from his seat and walking toward the entrance of the tent. He pulled a flap aside for a moment, shook his head, and turned back towards the table.

"We have proper attire and arms, and your men barely have shoes. We will supply uniforms, boots, munitions, food, and money to your army. You will in turn become an auxiliary force subordinate to the Spanish Colonial Army. You will attack French installations in St. Domingue on behalf of Spain and allow our army to occupy the conquered facilities. Over the next several years, we will conquer the entire island and your army will have achieved legitimacy under Spanish rule."

General Papillon remained stone-faced, but he knew there to be no choice. Of the 2,000 troops present, 1,200 were Toussaint's men—fit and healthy—while the rest were far less viable. Another 8,000 were starving and destitute and had to be hidden from sight. They were desperately in need of a well-funded and supportive alliance. Without much further discussion, a deal was struck.

Papillon, Biassou, and Breda were given six months to prepare their armies for renewed confrontations with the French. During this period, they enjoyed Spanish protection from confrontations and planned to be officially absorbed as the Spanish Colonial Army's Black Auxiliaries in February of 1793.

That November, Toussaint prepared to return to Ennery with the intention of settling his affairs and preparing for an extended period of battle. He also planned to relocate Suzanne and their three sons to Santo Domingo for their own safety. As his soldiers were still the most capable, well-equipped, and nourished, General Papillon and General Biassou felt confident Toussaint's leave would not jeopardize any preparations.

The night before Toussaint was to depart, he called a meeting with his most cunning officer, Jean-Jacques Dessalines. Dessalines was a 32-year-old, field-savvy, and fierce commander of nearly five-hundred men, the largest of the army's platoons.

Dessalines exhibited unmatched organizational skills, likely derived from his enslaved years as a foreman of the Cormier plantation in *Grand-Riviere-du-Nord.*

Having refused to whip another slave under the orders of Henry Duclos, owner of the Cormier plantation, Dessalines himself received the punishment of the whip and was then immediately sold to a cruel Afranchi owner, whom he derived his surname from. Having been present at Boukman's voodoo ceremony, Dessalines was one of the original supporters of the uprising after strangling to death his cruel master and running away with others to join the new army. He kept the Dessalines name as a trophy.

Assigned under the even more evil Bullet, however, Dessalines was gradually growing disillusioned with the cause. He bemoaned the cruel irony of first serving a callous master and now a brutal free man. He was quite relieved when Commander Breda was appointed. He admired and respected Toussaint, vowing to follow him to death.

Toussaint in turn appreciated Dessalines' abilities, although he was wary of the younger man's confrontational nature.

"Dessalines, I am placing you in charge of this division while I am away" Toussaint stated as the soldier arrived to his tent. "Do you accept this appointment?"

Dessalines was immediately taken aback. His shock quickly turned to humility, however, as he recognized the high regard in which his respected Commander held him.

"Yes, Commander Breda, I accept and will not disappoint you."

"Good, Dessalines. Please call for the other officers, so I may announce your promotion. They will report to you, and you will report to Generals Papillon and Biassou in my absence."

With that, Toussaint finally felt comfortable taking his leave home.

Arriving at Ennery, Toussaint was overcome by the casual ease and serenity his home always provided. A pang of remorse entered his thoughts for how this ordeal would affect his family. Their lives completely revolved around their farms; displacing them from all they'd known was regretful, but he knew the move was necessary.

He was rather surprised to find that Suzanne agreed with him. Of course, she firmly insisted that when the time was right, they would all return to the lives they left behind on the plantation. Within a month, they were ready for the journey to Santo Domingo.

While he'd hoped Moise would remain and commit to maintaining operations at Ennery, as soon as he learned of the revitalized campaign, he demanded to join the battalion. Eventually, Toussaint was forced to relent and instead appointed Othello to take charge of Sancey.

Before embarking on the journey to Ouanaminthe, Toussaint

decided to allow the party a few pleasant days of relaxation in Cap-Français. They would spend time enjoying the sights and sounds of the city prior to continuing their journey east.

Toussaint selected the finest accommodations the city had to offer and set their course for none other than the acclaimed *Hôtel de La Couronne.*

Fourteen

THE BRITISH ARE COMING

Cap-Français
April 1792

That morning in early April began like any other. Marie and Jean shared their morning coffee together and headed downstairs to their Cap-Français office. There, they were greeted by a surprising headline emblazoned across the morning's *Gazette:*

ALL FREE PEOPLE ARE CITIZENS
King Louis XVI Affirms French Citizenship
Regardless of Skin Color

According to the article, the French government had determined the 6,000 troops of the First Civil Commission could not settle the uprisings throughout St. Domingue. As such, the authorities decided the solution was to encourage the unification of Whites and free *Gens de Couleur* against the rebelling of Black slaves. King Louis XVI himself issued the decree on April 4, 1792.

In addition, the French National Assembly was deeply concerned with the burgeoning independence movement among White planters, the rebel army which by then controlled much of the rich northern plains, and the constant besiegement of Cap-Français. Hundreds of Whites had been killed, plantations were in ruins, and the slaves were quickly advancing in their military skills.

The Parisian assembly had deployed a second Civil Commission to St. Domingue in a further attempt to restore order. This commission was to be led by Léger Félicité Sonthonax.

"Wow," said Marie, softly. "We are citizens now, Jean!"

"Indeed, Marie. I guess you can finally run for the Colonial Assembly now!" Jean chided.

"Women can't do that yet—but one day, my husband, we will," she replied.

"And on that day, this colony will be the better for it, my love," Jean smiled. His brow then furrowed.

"Very diplomatic, Jean", Marie sarcastically asserted.

"There will still be a constant struggle between free *Gens de Couleur* and the *Grands Blancs*, Marie. I think the time has come to discuss our plans. We are in a good place—we transformed our shipping business for the better, and the hotel and restaurant are constantly over capacity, particularly with planters who have lost their homes."

"But the turmoil has also disrupted our supply routes," argued Marie. "We can only secure a fraction of our sugar, molasses, coffee, indigo, and mahogany. We've adapted as best we could, but have made no headway since all of this uprising began."

Jean nodded. "It is just and inevitable that the slaves will be free. It is only a matter of time. I fear it may only get worse, my love. We should divest from the hotel—it is susceptible to damages or even total destruction should violence reach it. You do remember our insurance doesn't cover acts of war or rioting."

"We should include Henry in these discussions. Let's meet him for lunch at the hotel today," Marie suggested.

"Excellent idea, Marie," replied Jean.

Bringing Henry up to speed on their perspective and plans over lunch, the three agreed the best course of action was to find a buyer for the property as quickly as possible. While some of the debt incurred for the casino remained outstanding, the hotel's popularity and consistent revenue still made for an attractive investment.

Henry would offer to stay on as manager if asked; if not, however, Jean and Marie would incorporate him into another division of the family enterprise. If Mr. Coidavid did not wish to sell, then the pair would only divest their share.

Félicité Sonthonax and Étienne Polverel, leaders of the second Civil Commission, arrived at Cap-Français on September 17th of 1792.

Their arrival in Saint-Domingue was met at first with hostility; the *Grands Blancs* feared their mission was to abolish slavery. As a result, Sonthonax and Proverel turned to the *Gens de Couleur* for support which proved the only reliable group with which to ally.

Both men were Freemasons and members of the political Jacobin Club. Like many Jacobins, they were fervent supporters of the French Revolution. Both were also nationalists and primarily committed to upholding the laws of the Assembly. In the Jacobin view, those who dissented from passed laws were not in opposition but were to be considered counter-revolutionaries—and dealt with harshly.

The two men checked into the *Hôtel de La Couronne* and quickly began to enjoy the establishment's various amenities. Henry greeted both and worked to ensure all their needs were met. Next to the Governor, these men were now the highest-ranking officials in the colony.

During the Bayard's traditional Sunday dinner, Henry recounted his experiences with the Commissioners, as well as his belief that they were good and reasonable men.

Suddenly, an idea struck Jean. He suggested their arrival may prove an opportunity for a change of plans. Requesting a meeting with Coidavid, the four set about formulating a strategy that would remove any risk facing the hotel—while still retaining their control.

A week following the arrival of the Commissioners, Jean invited Sonthonax to lunch. After the requisite small talk—which included high praise from Sonthonax in regard to the hotel's accommodations—Jean hatched his plan.

"Commissioner Sonthonax, you will require office space, accommodations, private meeting areas, food, and support during the pursuit of your mission in St. Domingue, is that correct?"

"Indeed Mr. Bayard, we will. However, with the influx of citizens from their ravaged estates outside the city, it has resulted in a shortage of real estate," Sonthonax lamented. "I hadn't accounted for such an issue, and now it may delay my mission. I have staff prepared to depart from Paris, but no way to house them."

"I am pleased to inform you that I have a solution," smiled Jean.

"And what might that be, Mr. Bayard?"

"We are prepared to lease seven rooms of the hotel for use as accommodations and working space. Food services will be available on the property, and you'll also maintain the fringe benefits that come with a luxurious and stylish location." Jean offered.

Sonthonax eyed Jean for a moment.

"And what would this cost me?"

"The rooms will be discounted by half; a total of one thousand Livres will be due in advance for the first year, with an option to renew the agreement at the same rate for the next, if you so choose," Jean answered.

"The Commission does not distribute cash advances like that, Mr. Bayard," Sonthonax said, shaking his head.

Perfect. Jean prepared to spring the final hook.

"We neither desire nor need cash, Commissioner. I have a simple suggestion for how you can provide compensation."

"Which is…" Sonthonax ventured.

"We have a one-thousand Livre loan due to the *Banque*

Courtois. The French government of course does quite a bit of business with the *Banque*. The government will assume our note, without recourse, and you will be granted the rooms for one year," Jean continued.

"Of course, you will be responsible for food and beverages, and any additional rooms needed from time to time—at half of the posted rate."

He could sense Sonthonax was intrigued by the prospect of maintaining the same accommodations he was currently enjoying for the next year.

"And if this cannot be arranged, Mr. Bayard?" hesitated Sonthonax.

"You still have your rooms reserved through the end of the week, which should provide time to explore the viability. Though we cannot accommodate you and your entourage past that, I do know of some boarding houses which I can arrange for you," Jean responded.

"However, the prices are rather steep. Higher even than my offer of the seven rooms," he added.

This was Jean's negotiation skills at his finest; confidence, demonstrating value, creating excitement, identifying the compensation plan, and creating urgency. A classic performance by the seasoned businessman.

Naturally, the contracts were drawn, bank notes transferred, and suddenly Sonthonax was Jean's newest best friend and most enthusiastic customer.

Sonthonax was still in a festive mood a week after their discussion. His ideological dream had been brought to life via the headline of the morning Gazette:

FRANCE A REPUBLIC
The Monarchy is finished

Sonthonax immediately requested Henry organize a celebration. He sent invitations to the elite *Gens de Couleur* of the colony, while purposefully ignoring the White royalists bemoaning the Monarchy's fall.

During the party, Sonthonax planned to open a dialog with those attendees in contact with the rebel army, and offer to broker a peace deal. All 300 rebel officers would receive full amnesty, while the slaves would return to their plantations and await a new, more lenient, work system.

Sonthonax's olive branch seemed to calm the island. Reports of slave attacks in the wake of the negotiation decreased as rebel leadership contemplated the offer—while still quietly strengthening their ranks. The tense ceasefire allowed planters to visit what remained of their properties and assess damages and consider whether or not to rebuild.

The holidays of 1792 found the Bayard family back together in Jérémie, save for Henry, who remained at the hotel to host lavish holiday parties to further bolster revenue. All told the proprietors were on track for a record year despite the unrest.

Jean Junior was now seventeen and a promising young man. He studied enthusiastically at school—where he was quite popular—and toiled in his parents' various businesses, slowly being groomed to one day take full control.

Awaiting the company ship *Marcelle* to arrive at the dock in Jérémie, Jean, and Marie each took a deep breath, intoxicated by the aroma of a booming coffee harvest. They caught each other's eye and laughed heartily at what their lives had become.

Though they knew themselves inside and out, there were still opportunities to surprise. On Marie's fortieth birthday, for example, Jean commissioned a private room at *La Maison* restaurant, with a special dinner featuring her favorites: grilled shrimp, rice and beans, asparagus, and a host of trimmings. A violinist had serenaded them through dinner. Later, they went to a nightclub for an after-dinner drink of Benedictine, accompanied by dancing and a romantic overnight at the Grand Hotel. They were still crazy in love after all these years.

"It's been twenty-one years since we met in this town—our hometown," Marie said, interrupting Jean's reminiscing. "It is incredible that we had never met until that one day."

"Yes, it is remarkable. You somehow made me the clumsiest man in town" Jean laughed. "I was a real piece of work back then."

"That you were! You made a mess of things the first couple of times we met," she chided. "It was only your sheer determination that I decided to go out with you after all that."

The two retired to the family compound, still laughing and discussing their memories. They took the time to relax under the shade of the plantation's mahogany trees and enjoy the sweet and simple flavors of life.

Jean's mother and father were nearing seventy but in good health. Enjoying the later part of their lives immensely, they seemed oblivious to the turmoil that had been rollicking the colony. Julien and Rene had finally fulfilled their father's dream and were doing a fantastic job of managing the plantation, increasing both the yield and quality of their products.

On a lazy Sunday afternoon, the family was finishing a wonderful family dinner in the outdoor courtyard amongst the company of nearly thirty relatives visiting from Port-au-Prince, Jacmel, and Cayes. Feeling overloaded by the heated conversations and wild predictions on the prospect of war between France, Britain, and Spain, Jean excused himself for a walk around the yard.

Here, he encountered the rambunctious gang of children, ranging in age from a year into their teens. Several were playing tag; a trio of young girls compared their dolls; the teenage girls were giggling over stories of boys.

Each was attended to by a slave, who would gladly have given their life to protect the brood, he knew. Jean furrowed his brow. So loyal were the slave servants to the children that it joked that some would actually take a spanking for their child in care over having the child receive the corporal punishment themselves. These servants were loved by both the children and parents alike.

During his time home, he'd taken the opportunity to speak with his father and brothers about freeing the slaves and implementing a workforce payment system. He explained what was happening in the northern plains, and how it was only a matter of time before the idea of revolution—or worse—would reach their region.

Julien and Rene understood the situation and their father to get ahead of any potential conflict.

"We already provide room, board, food, clothing, medical care, and all else needed to care for our slaves, Papa" Julien had said. "If they shared in the profits, would they not be motivated to work harder and keep expenses low?"

Jean then relayed a novel financial model a friend of his, by the name of Libertate, had implemented at the Breda plantation several weeks prior. He'd reported increased morale and higher production and even claimed the plantation was achieving higher profits than ever.

Their father finally relented to the pressure a few days after the family dinner. The new process would begin on New Year's Day, 1793.

On January 1st, all slaves received their papers all at once. The surprise prompted a grand day of celebration and merriment. Not a single worker decided to leave the plantation and all enthusiastically went back to their jobs the following day. Jean and Marie stayed in town the first few weeks of the year, assisting Julien and Rene with meetings and providing clarification on different aspects of freedom to the curious workforce.

It was the dawning of a new era for all. There were questions of housing, food procurement, healthcare, taxes, and a myriad of issues the newly freed employees were unprepared to face if they chose to live off the plantation. The four helped each navigate the complex issues and educated them on the management of finances and how to structure their new lives.

After a wonderful final Sunday on the Bayard plantation, Jean, Marie, and Junior finally departed for home on Monday, January 28, 1793.

The *Le Matin* was now captained by Captain Gabriel's former first mate Roger Lafontaine. Captain Martin was also on board this trip, heading back from a business trip in Port-au-Prince, and was immensely pleased to catch up with Jean and Marie.

During the voyage, Jean marveled at the performance of the crew of former slaves rescued from Bermuda who had grown into capable mariners. Captain Lafontaine expertly called out orders, and lines were pulled, sails hoisted, and steering engaged in time with his direction. The crew had learned French as well, easily conversing with one another. Their smiles and happiness were not lost on Jean.

The itinerary included an overnight stop at *Pointe des Lataniers* on the Northwest side of the unpopulated Gonave Island. Marie looked forward to the warm waters, powdery sand beach, and starlit night their trip home promised.

The following morning, Marie packed a picnic basket and boarded the tender for shore with Jean, Junior, and half the crew. The family quickly found a shady patch of coconut trees on the beach, and Marie spread out a blanket.

Junior started to relax on the sand with his parents until Jean reminded him that the day's duties included the harvest of coconuts.

"It is certainly nice to be the boss sometimes, Jean," said Marie, as she watched their well-built son grab a machete and disappear amongst the coconut trees. "We can lounge about, romance, and snack as the staff works."

"It's taken us years to build this business, my love. Why should we ignore the fruits of our labor?" Jean responded.

"Come swim with me, Jean."

The water was warm and the sun was nearing its midday high.

Jean and Marie frolicked like children before enjoying a leisurely lunch of dried fish, cheese, and wine.

"My Grandpapa used to tell me stories of his exploits with that pirate Montbars while drinking rum and coconut water," sighed Marie. "I wish to taste one of those drinks tonight for the first time with you."

Junior approached then, providing a brief report of the morning's work, and sitting for a spell to eat.

"We've about concluded the harvest on this side of the beach," Junior said, hurrying to eat and rejoin the team. "I'm taking half the men to the east, and Hector is going west with the rest."

"We should be back by four to begin loading the tenders. The captain says we'll anchor here overnight and depart first thing in the morning," Junior concluded. Just as quickly as he'd arrived, he was leaving once more to continue his mission.

Jean and Marie watched as the cohort disappeared out of site once more.

"I suppose we have the beach to ourselves, Jean," said Marie softly, shooting him seductive eyes.

Jean stood, extended his hand, and offered her an afternoon swim.

"Only if you make love to me in that pristine blue warm water, Jean."

They spent the next hour warming their bodies under both the afternoon sun and each other. Finally collapsing back under the shade, Marie panted, "What a wonderful day it is on this piece of paradise."

Around the eastern point of the island, however, the seemingly perfect oasis was about to be shattered by a dangerous discovery.

Junior and the crew had worked a good portion of the new beach on the far side of the shore when the group suddenly stopped dead in their tracks. Junior placed his finger to his lips and motioned the party to crouch down.

A warship was anchored only a few dozen meters from shore and two tenders were patrolling the shoreline as another dozen men walked the tree line. Beyond on the beach, four others were gathered around a table drawing a map.

Junior moved stealthily toward the rocky shore to investigate the ship's stern, hoping to make out a name or nationality. No flag was flown on the mast, and the men on shore had no discernible uniforms.

The sharp crack of a rifle suddenly rang out, and a bullet narrowly raced past Junior, ricocheting off a nearby rock. He'd been spotted.

The men near the tree line were yelling and came charging toward him, clumsily continuing to fire their guns even though they were well out of range. But Junior recognized the British tongues during their shouts.

"GO!" Junior yelled. The group tore off back west where Jean and Marie, having heard the terrifying bark of bullets, were hastily packing.

"Take the tender and tell Captain Lafontaine to ready for departure," yelled Jean as the other crew drew near. "Get things ready here Marie, I'll go find Junior and the rest."

"Be careful, Jean!" Marie pleaded as the first of the men reached her, grabbed their things, and hurried her toward the small boat.

Jean sprinted east, spotting Junior and the other four running flat out toward him.

"Papa! British!" shouted Junior. Reaching him, Jean quickly stole a look back down the beach. They had a solid lead on their pursuers, but one which was quickly evaporating.

Reaching the tender, the sailors frantically began rowing back to *Le Matin*. As they closed in on the vessel, Jean turned to look behind them. The other men had turned around, heading back in the direction from whence they appeared.

Back onboard, Captains Fontaine and Gabriel were swiftly making preparations to depart—hauling up the anchor as the mariners raised the sails.

"Those are likely spies charting invasion paths. They'll be keen to keep their secrets." Jean suggested. Captain Gabriel knew his coded language was intended to mask their grave situation.

"Jean, we will follow your direction," Gabriel said. "Fontaine, your crew will take orders from Captain Bayard moving forward!"

"Are there arms on board?" asked Jean.

"Indeed Captain—and we're prepared to use them." He turned and bellowed out, "Fontaine, MAN THE CANNONS!"

"Cannons?" asked Jean, slightly stunned. "I thought I'd ordered all cannons to be dismantled and sold?"

"Forgive me, Jean, I thought it prudent to keep four onboard— just in case. You can reprimand me later."

Jean smirked in spite of himself. "If they get us home safely Captain, we'll call it even. Have the men ready them and prepare for battle."

Turning to Captain Fontaine, he ordered "Captain; full sail ahead—get us moving west before those British bastards are able to move!"

The sails immediately caught the wind, lurching the ship forward. The *Le Matin* picked up speed rapidly as it headed out of the harbor. However, the British had reacted quickly as well— leaving their comrades marooned onshore—and had already given chase.

"They're two clicks out and approaching with foul intentions," yelled Jean to the crew. "All hands on deck and fully armed, *NOW!*"

The crew whooped and assembled across the deck, loaded rifles at the ready. Junior hustled below, retrieving the new rifle Uncle Gustav had given him for Christmas. Returning topside, he found his father sermonizing, motivating the crew.

"Remember our encounter with the pirates all those years ago, my brothers," yelled Jean. "You were all just slaves then, and we triumphed together. Now, we find ourselves in the heat of battle once more—but as free men!"

"These British invaders seek to conquer our colony. Their success will mean the end of your survival or worse; YOUR

FREEDOM! Our fate is in our hands alone. I choose for us to survive and live free! Do you agree?"

Primal cries of war ensued. The men were being whipped into a frenzy, just as Jean had intended. They were outmanned and outgunned, but he'd experienced enough battles to know tenacity, utter fearlessness, and luck would sometimes carry the day.

"You will fight for your freedom again at this moment. This will be the fight of your lives. LET'S GIVE THEM HELL!"

The HMS Trident, a large and lethal 64-gun Ardent Class ship captained by the capable Brock Holmes was bearing down on them.

"Captain Fontaine," Jean called out. "Mark a course for a head-on collision! When we are 100 meters from ramming, steer port, then be ready to steer starboard on my command."

"Oui Capitaine," Fontaine responded.

"Gabriel; you and the crew aim your rifles true and as we pass. Kill anyone within sight. Are we clear?"

"Oui Capitaine!" roared Gabriel, staring down his barrel.

Jean looked around briefly, spotting Marie steadily cradling a rifle as well. His wife could expertly mark a duck at fifty meters. Junior was untested, and Jean hoped his nerves wouldn't betray him.

A cannonball shot toward *Le Matin*, splashing thirty meters short. Another followed, landing within twenty. Jean could tell the crew was rattled.

"That was damn close, Jean," shouted Gabriel. "We can't let them board us with lines."

Jean caught Marie casually turning to Gabriel and by the smirk on her mouth knew she would launch one of her classic verbal grenades - and with that, she didn't disappoint.

"Don't worry, Gabriel. If we are boarded, I won't let them rape you or steal your pretty little ship," Marie quipped, rifle still at her shoulder.

Gabriel seemed taken aback momentarily, but suddenly let out a deep belly laugh. The crew joined in, a welcome breaking of the moment's tension.

"We will outmaneuver them and counterattack with force," said Jean bringing the focus back. "Maintain course to their bow to nullify their cannons. We'll execute a zig-zag at one hundred meters. Position yourselves on the starboard side!"

Jean knew the British navigator was likely watching them through their spyglass. He hoped to fool their combatants into loading up on the wrong side.

"All of you switch to port when we turn, and fire as we pass. Once behind, fire all cannons at the rudder. Is everyone ready?!"

"Oui Capitaine!" yelled Fontaine and Gabriel in unison.

The HMS Trident was close enough now to nearly block the horizon. They were out of time. Jean hoped all were as prepared as they looked.

"Steer thirty degrees to port NOW!"

Fontaine threw the wheel and *Le Matin* rolled left. Without hesitation, the British ship expertly corrected course to intercept.

"Fontaine, starboard correction sixty degrees NOW! Everyone to port!" Jean bellowed. The *Le Matin* banked right. Still engaged in its opposite turn, the heavier Trident could not correct course fast enough to launch a shot.

The bow of *Le Matin* was nearly in alignment with the enemy ship.

"Ten degrees port!" Jean called Fontaine. Turning to the crew, he ordered, "Hold your fire—make it count!"

The ships passed each other close enough that Jean could make out the surprised expressions of their enemies.

"FIRE AT WILL!"

A dozen rifles rained hell upon the deck of the HMS Trident. Several British soldiers fell instantly as others hurried to reposition the cannons. Alas, after being caught off guard their countermeasures were slowed, and the forward half of *Le Matin* was now passing their stern.

"Sixty degrees to port Captain!"

Fontaine expertly whipped the wheel once more, and the ship began its turn. However, two of the Trident's cannons had been readied, their payload bursting forth and taking out *Le Matin's* mizzenmast and rear sails. The crew ducked, shielding themselves from the shower of wood.

Jean remained focused on the rear of the enemy vessel. The rudder was in view.

"Fire cannon!"

Two of the four cannons found their mark. The Trident began to wildly spin in the heavy winds, unable to steer to control its direction.

A wild cheer rang out as *Le Matin* sailed away, damaged, but serviceable. Fontaine remained careful to keep the sterns in alignment so as not to provide another opportunity for a British offensive volley.

"Do not correct course for home until we are out of cannon range," called Jean to Fontaine.

Onboard the rudderless Trident, Captain Holmes called out; "Furl the Sales! Helmsman - keep Jury Steering the ship until you can get it under control. "Surgeon - how many killed or injured? Lieutenant - get me a damage report!"

The Master of the ship, Charles Holbrook, arrived at his side and said "That was one crazy maneuver by that ship, Captain"

"Yeah, they caught us off guard and we are way too big and heavy to turn as quickly as they did. They're lucky they didn't get blown to pieces by us. Did you catch her name?" asked the Captain.

"Le Matin - means The Morning, Captain" answered Holbrook. Looks like one of our old 20-gun sixth-rate ships to me."

"For a moment I thought I saw a ghost. When I was but eighteen back in '79 I served on a ship named the HMS Rose, a twenty-gun sixth-rate just like her. I could swear that was her."

"How could you tell?"

"The taffrail on her stern afterdeck had 3 rails missing the last time I sailed on her. That ship has 3 different styled rails replaced in the exact same spot where the HMS Rose had hers missing. I could swear that Le Matin is the old Rose. We were captured off of Savannah, Georgia and she was stolen by the French" Holmes said.

"If that is truly the case, well then, it's a small world indeed" answered Holbrook.

Onboard Le Matin, Jean quickly surveyed the crew, heartened to find no one had been injured or killed. His eyes eventually found Junior, who appeared to be in slight shock. He arrived at his son's side simultaneously with Marie; her maternal instincts had picked up on the boy's torment as well.

Junior was undoubtedly shaken, but not hysterical. Marie put her arms around him in an embrace.

"I—I think I killed someone today, Maman," Junior said, shakily. "I aimed, shot, and saw him fall. What if I did? What if I did kill a man today?" His resolve breaking, Junior began to sob uncontrollably. "Did I kill someone, Maman? Did I really do it with the rifle Tonton Gustav gave me for Christmas?"

Marie put her hand behind his head, held him close, and looked at Jean. "It is not your fault, Jean Junior. It is not."

"You did not choose to be in this position, Junior," counseled Jean solemnly. "You did what you had to do—just as that man was doing what he had to. It was kill, or be killed on this day."

Jean looked down at the bowed head of his son.

"You were brave, Junior. You did not waiver and you pulled that trigger without hesitation. I would rather console you than bury you. I am so very proud."

Junior raised his head to see his father's wise smile and a glint of moisture in one of his eyes.

"Always protect your loved ones, son. Your actions today may have saved your mother's life, or mine, or one of the others on this ship."

Junior's tears dissipated. It dawned on him that this was all a part of growing into the man his father wanted him to become.

"Now, go to the tender and look under the center row. Bring me what you find," said Jean.

The ship had turned northwest to round the tip of St.

Domingue, and the sun had begun its descent toward the open ocean.

Junior returned quickly, two coconuts under each arm. "Did you mean these Papa?"

Marie turned to Jean, mouth open and fists on her hips. "You sneak! You didn't tell me you smuggled any coconuts off the island!"

"Can I not still surprise you every now and then, Marie? Junior, fetch a machete."

Jean then called to the bow of the ship, "Captain Gabriel—please bring our best rum from the galley." He then turned back to Marie, saying, "I think we deserve a little of your Granpapa's magic after today."

Jean cut a hole and poured some rum into each coconut before handing one to Marie, Gabriel, and Junior, keeping the fourth for himself. He then extended his arm for a toast.

"Today, we drink to my son, Jean-Baptiste Bayard Junior. He proved himself a mighty warrior and helped save us from certain disaster. To Junior!" The others followed. "TO JUNIOR!"

Captain Fontaine knew the waters well, sailing through the night to arrive at Cap-Français the following afternoon. The damage had slowed them, but all were grateful to have arrived at all.

Renald and Gerard Chevallier were waiting for them at the dock. No sooner had the gangway been dropped were the two brothers barreling up the platform with a newspaper in hand.

"What the hell happened to the ship?" asked Gerard.

"Never mind that—what is the emergency?" Jean retorted.

"This," panted Renald, shoving that morning's edition of the Gazette toward Jean.

KING FOUND GUILTY AND EXECUTED
Former Louis XVI Guillotined at Place de la Concorde

Fifteen

THE ESCAPE OF TOUSSAINT

Cap-Français
January 1793

Jean turned to Marie. "I must get to the hotel and confer with Henry on this, as well as what we encountered on that island."

Marie nodded.

"Commissioner Sonthonax, as well." She said.

"Of course. Will you join me?"

"I prefer to go home. I need to wash this sea salt off my body. Give Henry a kiss for me. I'll have a wonderful dinner prepared for all of us" responded Marie.

Jean arrived quickly at the hotel, finding Henry in the main dining room. He was sitting with Bayon de Libertate, Sonthonax, and a couple with their backs toward him.

Seeing Jean, Henry immediately rushed to him. "Jean! You look battered—what's happened?"

"I came straight from the ship, but I am alright, Henry. I need to speak with Commisioner Sonthonax right away."

"The Commissioner is just over here, with Libertate and a friend of his—Toussaint Breda and his wife Suzanne."

Henry guided Jean toward the group. "They're a lovely couple; owners of some small plantations around Ennery. Libertate wanted them to meet Sonthonax."

Henry proceeded to make formal introductions as they arrived at the table. Sonthonax and Libertate greeted Jean warmly. Wishing to get ahead of any inquiries regarding his obvious dishevelment, Jean quickly explained their encounter with the British Naval ship.

"I am glad you have made it home safely my friend, but unfortunately I cannot say I am surprised to hear of the incursion. We have gotten several similar reports from other parts of the coast," Sonthonax said. "I fear that the winds of war are stirring. Fortunately, the British had no idea who they were up against, this time," he smiled.

"Yes, there are many issues to be resolved yet," Libertate said, looking directly at Sonthonax. "I understand the Spanish are not at all pleased with the beheading of the King. After all, he is, or should I say he was, the King of Spain's cousin."

"Not my doing. Quite frankly, I have more pressing issues to deal with in the colony," said Sonthonax, waving his hand.

"You dismiss such concerns at your own peril, Commissioner. You may soon be dealing with both the British and the Spanish right here in this colony," Libertate responded. "Toussaint knows the Spanish are amassing, arming, and training runaway slaves at the border."

He broke away from his stare to look over at Toussaint.

"Tell them."

Sensing the direction of the conversation, Suzanne stood, prompting the others to do as well. "Toussaint, I must tend to the children. Gentlemen; I bid you goodnight. It was a pleasure to be in your company and to meet you, Mr. Bayard."

Toussaint leaned over and kissed Suzanne on both cheeks. They all then found their seats once more and turned their attention to Toussaint.

"What Libertate is saying is true. A slave army was encamped at the Breda plantation for weeks before they left and marched to the Spanish border," replied Toussaint, careful not to divulge it was he who had led them.

"I have sent messages to their leaders requesting they put down their arms and come home. I even guaranteed amnesty to their officers and fair treatment of the slaves to return and resume work on their plantations," stated Sonthonax matter-of-factly.

"They will not resume work until they are freed," responded Toussaint. "Of that, I can assure you."

"That is an issue for a later date, Toussaint. For now, if the planters are open to negotiations on better working conditions and even land for them to farm on their own, would that convince them to surrender their arms?"

"The execution of the King has complicated things somewhat," Toussaint replied, taking a sip of his drink.

"You appear to know more than you let on, Mr. Breda. How familiar are you with the rebels?"

"I have met General Papillon and General Biassou. Both are quite capable leaders. We met when they saved my life from the brutal General Bullet."

He turned to fully face Sonthonax. "In fact, it was I who led the army off from the Breda plantation to the border."

Sonthonax eyed Toussaint momentarily, considering this information.

"Would you then carry a message to the encampment for me, Mr. Breda? Ask them to throw down their arms so we may save this colony for France."

Jean could feel the tension building. It was as if all the other diners surrounding them had suddenly disappeared. An uneasy silence hung over the table as Sonthonax and Toussaint stared each other down.

"The King of Spain bestows rewards and provides us sustenance," began Toussaint. "We have lost the King of France. Consequently, we are unable to acknowledge you, Commissioner, or your requests, before you have found a new King."

Sonthonax shot up from his seat, shocked and dismayed by Toussaint's reply. Sonthonax was a Jacobin—a revolutionary. How dare this man prefer a King over the revolutionary government of France?

"I could have you arrested for your actions," he hissed.

"What actions are those, Commissioner? Libertate can attest that I am no rebel. I performed a service, and removed the slave army from his property."

"I bid you all *adieu*," Sonthonax spat, storming out from the dining room.

Jean and Henry looked at each other, then at Libertate, who sighed and reached for his drink.

"Here I thought you were making a friend, Toussaint. Sonthonax is in a precarious situation, you know." Libertate stated to his old friend.

"I imagine so. The British are invading, the Spanish are waiting at the border to attack as well, the South acts as an independent state, slaves in the North are in rebellion, the Grands Blancs despise him—and his only allies are the free Gens de Couleur," Toussaint conceded. "It must be incredibly difficult."

He rose to leave. "Good night, gentlemen, it has been a pleasure."

With that, he turned and departed from the dining room.

"We must unite this colony before all hell breaks loose," Libertate said, finishing his cognac with a final swig. "I'm getting way too old for this."

The next morning, Henry awoke with a sense of unease. He didn't trust Sonthonax to easily forget the verbal exchange from the night before. He was a powerful man with near-unlimited authority in the colony. Toussaint had insulted him, and the French revolutionary government, publicly. That alone was perhaps cause enough for Sonthonax to flex his power and label Toussaint a counter-revolutionary – essentially making him an enemy of the state.

Henry genuinely admired Toussaint's conviction, comparing him to his good friend Chavannes, who had given his life for the same cause a year earlier. He decided to find and intercept

Toussaint to voice his concerns regarding Sonthonax.

Passing by the front desk, the overnight receptionist, Nathalie, greeted him warmly.

"Good morning Mr. Christophe. Where are you rushing to so early this morning?"

"Just checking up on operations, Nathalie. When is your replacement arriving?" asked Henry.

"Yolande will arrive at eight this morning. She needed to attend an appointment at her daughter's school, so I am staying on a bit later."

Just then, six French soldiers and an officer entered the hotel lobby, heading straight for Henry and Nathalie.

"Say nothing, and agree with everything I say," Henry whispered to her, keeping his eyes on the incoming group.

"Which room is the man Toussaint Breda in?" demanded the officer.

"Mr. Breda and his family checked out early this morning, sir" replied Henry.

"How early?"

"A couple of hours prior to sunrise, sir."

"Which room were they in?"

Henry glanced over at the keyboard, seeing the one for the room furthest down the second-floor corridor hanging on its hook. "Room 28, sir. But that room is already cleaned and made ready for the next guest to arrive."

"Give me the key."

Henry calmly handed over the key without any protest.

The French officer rudely swiped the key from his hand and loudly stomped up the stairs, his men in tow.

Henry turned back to Nathalie. "When they return, they will ask for Mr. Breda's destination. Tell them they departed toward the southwest road to Ennery."

Henry bolted down the opposite first-floor corridor, knocking rapidly on the door to room 19. Toussaint appeared at the entrance, already fully dressed.

"Mr. Breda, soldiers are looking for you. I fear they are here to arrest you" stated Henry.

"On what charge?" Toussaint asked, confused.

"I do not know. I believe the Commissioner didn't take too kindly to your conversation last night. Where is your family?"

"We have the two adjoining rooms. They are all getting dressed," answered Toussaint.

"May I come in?"

Toussaint glanced down the corridor behind Henry and opened the door to allow him in. Toussaint then followed Henry to the interior door connecting the rooms. Toussaint knocked and opened it.

"Come here, all of you, immediately!"

Moise, Placide, and Isaac burst into the room, giving Toussaint their full attention.

"We are all going to listen to Mr. Christophe, the manager of this hotel. No questions – just follow instructions. Do you all understand?"

"*Oui, Papa*," answered Placide and Isaac.

"*Oui, Tonton*," answered Moise.

"Please follow me," said Henry. "Leave all of your belongings here. Do not bring anything—I will ensure they find their way back to you. Mr. Breda, please hand me your room keys."

Toussaint complied, immediately knowing he could trust Henry with his family's life.

"Now, let's go—quickly, and quietly please."

Henry took them down the hallway to a side corridor leading to the kitchen, and out the door to the exterior warehouse.

Back at the front desk, the soldiers had returned to question Nathalie.

"Where did Mr. Breda say he was headed?"

"Back to Ennery, sir. They packed their things in a carriage and left, I think, on the western road."

The soldiers quickly turned to leave, Nathalie shouting after them, "Sir, please return the key to the room!"

The French officer flung the key towards the desk, hitting it hard and landing on the floor, as he rushed to catch up to his men.

The rear loading dock was abuzz with deliveries of fruits, vegetables, meats, and other hotel supplies. Henry scanned the street and spotted a number of *de jour* slaves looking for work. He looked back at Toussaint and his family, saying, "Wait here."

Henry approached the group of slaves dressed in old tattered clothes and looked them over. Pointing to the ones he wanted, he commanded "You, you, you—the young one there—and that one. Come with me."

Two men, one woman, and two young kids smiled and followed him. Toussaint and his family were waiting for Henry at the far corner of the warehouse, out of sight.

"You slaves, remove your rags. You must be well dressed to work in this hotel. I will provide you with new clothes in exchange for these. You may keep them after your workday is complete," stated Henry.

They quickly undressed and handed the soiled garments to Henry.

"I will return shortly with your uniforms," Henry said.

Henry walked over to Toussaint. "I need you each to undress, give me your clothes, and change into these rags."

"When will we get them back?" asked Moise. "My uncle just purchased these fine garments for us yesterday as gifts."

"You will never see them again," snapped Henry. "But if you follow my instructions, you will stay out of prison. I consider it a fair trade."

They all looked to Toussaint who gave a curt nod. Once they had stripped down, Henry gathered the expensive ensembles and brought them back to the slaves.

"Get dressed and wait here. I will return with your assignments."

Toussaint's family seemed totally uncomfortable and disgusted with the soiled, ripped, smelly, and ill-fitting outfits.

"Perfect," commented Henry, to grimaces of disgust. "Suzanne, cover the baby with this potato sack and keep it on him. Now, follow me."

Henry exited the warehouse and turned down the street,

entourage in tow. Along the way, he stopped briefly to grab loose dirt, rub it in his hands, and smear it on the face of little Isaac, who giggled. "All of you do the same. You are far too clean."

Henry hired a wagon and driver, telling the family to sit in the back. "Say nothing. You are slaves now."

He then approached Toussaint separately.

"There is a church, east of town, named *Sacre Coeur*. The priest is Father Jerome. He will provide you with food and shelter. Wait for me there." Henry instructed.

As Henry began to turn to the driver, Toussaint whispered, "Thank you, Henry. I will never forget this."

Henry nodded and approached the driver. He knew it would be an uncomfortable ride, but surely preferable to whatever the French had planned for them.

"Take these slaves to the *Sacre Coeur*. They will be working for Father Jerome today and give the priest this note."

He reached into his pocket. "Here—a bonus to make no stops as I want them to get there quickly and begin work. Do you know the way?"

"Yes, sir." answered the driver. He whipped the reigns and the carriage lurched forward.

Hurrying back inside and finding one of his most trusted employees, Henry instructed him to discreetly collect the Breda family's bags and deliver them to the carriage and wagon they had originally arrived in. That evening, amidst the afternoon rush, Henry and his aide drove the carriage out of town with two saddled horses in tow to meet Toussaint at the church.

As relieved and happy as the family appeared to see him, Henry couldn't help but feel they were even more excited to get back into their normal clothes.

"Henry, I believe you saved myself and my family from a lengthy bout of trying times," stated Toussaint. "But why? We only met last evening."

"I am not completely certain myself, Mr. Breda. I do know that you remind me of a dear friend of mine—Jean Chavannes."

"Ah yes, Chavannes. A brave and honorable man."

"Indeed. We served together in the *Chasseurs*. He died for his cause of freedom. I think helping you today was an honor to his memory."

Toussaint paused, looking deeply into the young man's eyes.

"Join us, Henry. We can ensure the freedom of our people, together."

Henry hesitated before answering.

"I am not yet ready to leave everything behind me, Mr. Breda. Not yet," replied Henry.

"Well, so be it." sighed Toussaint. "For now, I am thankful that you saw it in your heart to help my family." The sincerity in his voice filled Henry with pride.

"*Aux revoir* Toussaint. May God be with you." Henry said. He was unsure whether he'd ever see him again. He and his aide climbed back aboard their horses and then departed for the city.

Three days after the daring escape, Henry, Jean, and Marie were having lunch in his office, reviewing the past year's performance reports. The thick mahogany door suddenly burst open. All three leaped to their feet in surprise. Jean quickly cased the office for a weapon of some sort.

"Henry Christophe, I am here to place you under arrest."

It was the same French officer who had been pursuing the Bredas.

"What is the meaning of this intrusion?" roared Jean, stepping between the officer and Henry. "Under what charges?"

"Treason." Answered the smug officer. "By order of the Commander of the Northern Colonial Army. " The officer motioned for his men to seize Henry.

"STOP! I am Captain Jean-Baptiste Bayard - Retired, and I demand to speak to Commissioner Sonthonax," ordered Jean, not moving from his position between the men and Henry.

"The Commissioner departed for Port-au-Prince yesterday, and is not due to return until the end of the month."

"You have no evidence that Mr. Christophe has committed any crime," snarled Jean. "I warn you, do not advance your men."

The officer looked towards his men and made a nodding motion with his head. A soldier appeared from behind him, clutching Nathalie by the arm. Her once beautiful lip was bruised and stained with fresh blood.

"I am sorry Mr. Christophe! I am so sorry—" she cried.

"This is not your fault, Nathalie," Henry said in a soft voice and stepped forward. "You only did what I asked of you."

"This bitch provided false information as to the whereabouts of the fugitive Toussaint Breda. We wasted two days of time riding to Ennery and back. Mr. Christophe obviously helped him escape, and he will pay for his crime," said the officer, his voice rising.

Henry put an arm on Jean's shoulder. "It's alright, Jean. I will be fine." He then turned to the officer; "Sir, this woman knew not what I told her concerning Mr. Breda to be false. She believed it was the truth and should not be held accountable for my actions," Henry stated.

Jean locked eyes with the French officer. It had been years since he felt anything akin to the malice that was now burning in his heart. Snorting, he shifted his stance slightly, allowing the soldiers to reach Henry and let Nathalie go free.

As soon as the cohort escorted Henry off the property, he rushed to the Commander's headquarters of the Northern Colonial Army. His pleas for mercy were to no avail; Henry would be locked up and await a trial. His efforts over the next week to reach Henry were defeated at every turn. As the days went on, Jean's hopes of ever seeing Henry—a man he considered a brother— outside of the gallows, grew fainter and fainter.

FRANCE AT WAR
St. Domingue Risks Invasion from Britain & Spain

A week later, the headline of the Gazette announced that the world had further entered uncharted waters. The colony was again embroiled in turmoil.

Jean arrived at the dock that morning to board his company ship, the *Laura*, which was preparing for a run to Port-au-Prince. He would find Sonthonax and convince, beg, or bribe him to release Henry.

Marie was already waiting for him, a tear running down her cheek. He put his lips to hers. The gentle kiss escalated into a heated embrace of passion and longing on the crowded docks of Cap-Français. They knew not whether the dangerous trip would be a success or not. The British were still plying the waters off the coast, and the Spanish were sure to join them soon. No ship was assumed safe.

Jean focused on the moment, feeling the need to hold her close. Marie needed the warmth and security of her husband's arms. They looked deeply into each other's familiar eyes. No words were necessary or adequate. Jean pulled away and began his ascent up the gangway, but was unable to resist one last look back at the love of his life; his bride, his woman, his lover, the mother of his child—and the best friend he had ever known.

Sailors bustled about him, but Jean ignored them as he walked over to peer over the railing of the ship. He dared not look away from her, fearing he may never get another chance. His eyes remained on hers—and hers on his—as the ship cast off from the dock and maneuvered toward the mouth of the harbor.

Just before he disappeared out of sight, Marie raised her arm in a desperate final wave. The *Laura* was too far away for her to see whether it was returned. She remained anxiously at the dock, daring the ship, mentally ordering it to turn around and bring Jean back to her. It was now a speck on the horizon,

Finally breaking away from her trance, she realized nightfall was upon her. How long she'd been standing there, she did not know. Her stomach was in knots and her throat was raw from the tears and emotions boiling inside her.

Junior appeared at her side and put his arm around her shoulders.

"I love you Maman. I am here for you."

Marie allowed her son to turn her around and lead her to the awaiting carriage. She resisted shooting one last look back. Marie trusted Jean and knew in her heart he would let nothing stop him from returning to them.

The ride home was silent. High above, the stars had been extinguished. The ocean wind had hushed. The island was bathed in darkness and foreboding. A fertile breeding ground for fresh terrors.

Marie's thoughts drifted from Jean to Henry, to the slaves hidden somewhere above them in the hills. A faint drumming rhythm could be heard from high in the mountains overshadowing the deafening stillness of the night. She sighed and squeezed Junior's arm.

Thank God she still had her son.

TO BE CONTINUED.

Subscribe to our Newsletter
For History and News of Haitian People

www.TriumphToTragedy.com

EPILOGUE

The entire colony of St. Domingue will soon explode into an all-out slave rebellion, foreign invasion, and class warfare which will lead to a bloody civil war, followed by a revolution.

Follow the fates of Jean, Marie, Jean Junior, Libertate, Sonthonax, Toussaint, Papillon, Biassou, and many more larger-than-life figures as they march toward Triumph, and fall into Tragedy.

In the follow-up of the series, Book Two, Toussaint Breda will rise as General Toussaint Louverture as he strives to vanquish the colony's imperial enemies of Spain and Great Britain and unite the island to secure its successful future. He demonstrates incredible military and political skills as he tackles the issues of the day.

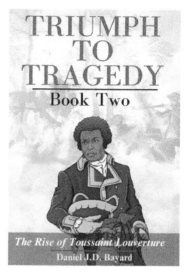

Historic revolutionary leaders will emerge to include Henry Christophe, Jean-Jacques Dessalines, and Alexandre Pétion as well as many brave women in battle, including Marie-Jeanne Lamartinière and Sanite Bélair on the front lines.

Future Books in the Triumph To Tragedy saga will chronicle the colony's civil war named The War of Knives, Napoleon Bonaparte's defeat of his invasion to re-enslave its citizens, and the tumultuous formation of ruling governments.

The first and only successful slave uprising in history will eventually give birth to the independent republic of Haiti – the subject of future novels in the Triumph To Tragedy Series.

AUTHORS NOTES
In Order of Appearance
in the Triumph to Tragedy Series

HENRY CHRISTOPHE

Christophe (1767 – 1820) began his military career as a drummer boy in the famed Chasseurs-Volontaires de Saint-Domingue and reportedly worked at the Hotel la Couronne, albeit for an unknown period of time. As an adult, he became a key leader in the Haitian Revolution and ascended to be a monarch of the Kingdom of Haiti. Christophe set out to improve all aspects of life in the Northern Province focusing on building defense mechanisms for his country, expanding agricultural production and educating his people.

JEAN BAPTISTE CHARLES HENRI HECTOR, COMTE D'ESTAING

d'Estaing (24 November 1729 – 28 April 1794) was a French general and admiral. Following France's entry into the American War of Independence in 1778, d'Estaing led a fleet to aid the American rebels and participated in the failed attempt to oust British troops from the city of Savannah, Georgia. He was executed by guillotine during the Reign of Terror. Before his execution, d'Estaing wrote, "After my head falls off, send it to the British as they will pay a good deal for it!"

ADMIRAL JOHN BYRON

Vice-Admiral John Byron (1723–1786) was a British Royal Naval officer and explorer. He earned the nickname "Foul-Weather Jack" in the press because of his frequent encounters with bad weather at sea. As a midshipman, he sailed in the squadron under George Anson on his voyage around the world, though Byron made it only to southern Chile, where his ship was wrecked. He circumnavigated the world as a commodore in 1764–1766 and fought in battles in the Seven Years' War and the American Revolution. He rose to Vice Admiral of the White before his death in 1786.

HENRI-LOUIS DE BOULAINVILLIERS DE CROY

De Croy (unknown birth/death) was a French Navy officer who joined the Navy as a Garde-Marine in 1735. He was promoted to Lieutenant in 1751 and to Captain in 1757. He served in the War of American independence. He commanded the 80-gun Languedoc as flag captain to Estaing. He took part in the Battle of Rhode Island, the Battle of Grenada and in the Siege of Savannah in 1779.

BENJAMIN FRANKLIN

Franklin (1706 – 1790) was an American polymath who was active as a writer, scientist, inventor, statesman, diplomat, printer, publisher, and political philosopher. He served as the first United States Ambassador to France from 1776-1785 and was instrumental in securing aid of the French government for the American Revolution.

LOUIS XVI, THE KING OF FRANCE

Louis XVI (1754 – 1793) was the last King of France before the fall of the monarchy during the French Revolution. He was referred to as Citizen Louis Capet during the four months just before he was executed by guillotine.

GENERAL MARQUIS DE LAFAYETTE

La Fayette (1757 – 1834) was known in the United States as Lafayette, a French aristocrat and military officer who fought in the American Revolutionary War, commanding American troops in several battles, including the siege of Yorktown.

GENERAL BENJAMIN LINCOLN

Lincoln (1733 – 1810) was born to one of the first dynastic American families and obtained much success during the revolutionary war until wounded and had to take a hiatus to tend to his recovery. When he returned in 1778, Washington placed Lincoln in charge of the Southern Department. In 1780, Lincoln was forced to surrender over 5,000 men to the British—the largest surrender of American troops during the war. Lincoln served from 1781 to 1783 as the first United States Secretary of War.

GEORGES BIASSOU

Biassou (1741 – 1801) was an early leader of the 1791 slave uprising in Saint-Domingue. Although I place him as part of the Maréchaussée of St. Domingue, though there is no evidence he served in that force.

He withdrew from Santo Domingo in 1795 to St. Augustine, Florida and at one time owned the historic Salcedo House. There he served as a Spanish general, fought Indians, owned a plantation, retired, and died at age 60 in 1801 during a drunken bar brawl. He was buried with honors by the Spanish military.

DANIEL MONTBARS AKA
'MONTBARS THE EXTERMINATOR'

Montbars (1645–1707), better known as Montbars the Exterminator, was a 17th-century French buccaneer. For several years, he was known as one of the most violent buccaneers active against the Spanish during the mid-17th century.

CASIMIR PULASKI

Pulaski (1745 – 1779) was a Polish nobleman and military commander born in Warsaw, Poland. His family was an old and influential branch of the Polish aristocracy. In 1771 the Polish government implicated Pulaski in a plot to abduct Stanislaus II, the Russian-controlled king, and accused him of treason. Pulaski sought protection in France and in 1773 briefly commanded an international force during the Russo-Turkish War.

He is credited with aiding the American Revolution and has been called, together with his counterpart Michael Kovats de Fabriczy, "the father of the American cavalry."

HEZEKIAH FRITH

Frith (1763 – 1848) was an 18th-century British ship owner with the reputation of a "gentleman privateer", who engaged in piracy during the 1790s. One of the richest men in Bermuda during the late 18th and early 19th centuries, he built the Spithead House in Warwick, Bermuda.

JEAN-BAPTISTE CHAVANNES

Chavannes (1748 – 1791) was an abolitionist from St. Domingue and a rebel soldier. He was the son of rich mulatto parents and received a good education. He distinguished himself when fighting with the Chasseurs-Volontaires de Saint-Domingue Savannah and later during military operations in Virginia and New York for American Independence. Chavannes returned to Saint-Domingue and joined Vincent Ogé in a failed insurrection, later to be publicly executed by dismemberment.

VINCENT OGÉ

Ogé (1755 – 1791) was a Creole aristocrat from St. Domingue who instigated a rebellion against the Bourbon Regime in French Saint-Domingue that lasted from October to December 1790 in the area outside Cap-Français, the colony's main city. The failed insurrection cost him his life by execution by dismemberment along with his co-conspirator, Jean-Baptiste Chavannes.

GOVERNOR, THE COUNT DE BLANCHELANDE

de Blanchelande (1735 – 1793 guillotined in Paris) was a French general. He served as Governor of Saint-Domingue at the start of the Haitian Revolution.

DUTTY BOUKMAN

Boukman (1767 - 1791) was an early leader of the Haitian Revolution. According to accounts, Boukman, alongside Vodou mambo Cécile Fatiman, presided over the religious ceremony at Bois Caïman, in August 1791, which served as the catalyst to the 1791 slave revolt which is usually considered the beginning of the Haitian Revolution.

Boukman was a key leader of the slave revolt but was killed early on by the French planters and colonial troops just a few months after the beginning of the uprising. The French then publicly displayed Boukman's head in an attempt to dispel the aura of invincibility that Boukman had cultivated. It was rumored that neither bullets nor cannonballs could hit him.

CÉCILE FATIMAN

Fatiman (1771-1883), was a Haitian voodoo priestess, a mambo. She is famous for her participation in the voodoo ceremony at Bois Caïman along with Dutty Boukman which is considered to be one of the starting points of the Haitian Revolution.

TOUSSAINT GUINO (BREDA) LOUVERTURE

Also known as Toussaint L'Ouverture or Toussaint Bréda; (1743 – 1803) was a Haitian general and the most prominent leader of the Haitian Revolution. During his life, Louverture first fought against the French, then for them, and then finally against France again for the cause of Haitian independence. As a revolutionary leader, Louverture displayed military and political acumen that helped transform the fledgling slave rebellion into a revolutionary movement. Louverture is now known as the "Father of Haiti".

In 1802, Toussaint was captured and deported to France on the 74-gun French ship the Créole. He warned his captors that the rebels would not repeat his mistake, "In overthrowing me you have cut down in Saint Domingue only the trunk of the tree of liberty; it will spring up again from the roots, for they are numerous and they are deep."

During his imprisonment at the frigid Fort-de-Joux in Doubs, France, Louverture, who was a bona fide French General, attempted to gain an audience with Napoleon who refused. He wrote a memoir and died in prison on April 7, 1803, at the age of 60.

He was reported to have buried a treasure near his plantation in Ennery, which Napoleon had men hunt for but was never found.

SUZANNE SIMONE BAPTISTE LOUVERTURE

Suzanne Louverture (1742 – 1816) was the wife of Toussaint Louverture. When in 1801 the constitution appointed Toussaint as governor of Saint-Domingue, she received the title of "Dame-Consort."

In 1802, Charles Leclerc's troops captured her along with her husband and the rest of her immediate family and shipped them to France. Madame Louverture survived her husband, who died in a French prison the following year. She was the mother of three boys, her youngest of which, Saint-Jean, died in 1804 in Agen, France. She died in 1816, in the arms of her sons, Placide and Isaac in Agen as well.

FRANÇOIS ANTOINE BAYON DE LIBERTAD

Libertad (1732 - 1802) was believed to be the one who freed Toussaint Louverture as the head manager of the Breda Plantation in St. Domingue. It is also believed that he developed a strong bond with Toussaint and assisted him in launching his own plantation business.

MOYIZ (MOYSE, MOÏSE, MOISE) LOUVERTURE

Most commonly "Moise" (1773 - 1801) was a military leader and one of the most ardent leaders of the first uprising in 1791 and acted as the second-in-command to Toussaint. There is universal agreement that Toussaint L'Ouverture adopted Moise as his nephew. Originally allied with Toussaint, Moise grew disillusioned with the minimal labor reform and land distribution for Black former slaves under the L'Ouverture administration and lead a rebellion against Toussaint in 1801. Though executed on order of L'Ouverture, the insurrection he directed highlighted the failure of the Haitian Revolution in creating real revolutionary labor change and ignited the movement that eventually contributed to driving L'Ouverture from office.

PLACIDE LOUVERTURE

Placide (1781 – 1841) was born before his mother's marriage in 1782 to Toussaint Louverture, who accepted the boy as his legitimate son. He was sent to school in France under the scholarship of Napoleon

Bonaparte. Placide and his brother Isaac were charged with delivering a letter to their father from First Consul Napoleon Bonaparte strongly suggesting he retire as Governor General of the colony and cede his power to General Leclerc, his designated replacement.

Upon returning to St. Domingue, he sided and fought with his father against the French government. When Toussaint was arrested and deported on June 8, 1802, by order of Napoléon Bonaparte, so was the entire family along with his mother and his brothers—Saint-Jean and Isaac.

ISAAC LOUVERTURE

Isaac (1786 - 1854) was the son of Toussaint and Suzanne Louverture. He and his half-brother Placide were sent to France in 1797 to be educated. They both returned with General Charles Leclerc to St. Domingue in the failed expedition to seize control and re-establish slavery in the colony. Placide and Isaac were charged with delivering a letter to their father from First Consul Bonaparte.

MATÍAS DE ARMONA

de Armona (1731 – 1796) was a governor of Las Californias, serving from 1769 to 1770, during the Spanish Empire's colonial rule of New Spain. While in Santo Domingo, he negotiated the recruitment of the Black slave army to fight under the Spanish Colonial army as the Black auxiliaries.

JEAN-JACQUES DESSALINES

Dessalines (1758-1806) was a leader of the Haitian Revolution and on January 1, 1804, became the first ruler of an independent Haiti under the 1805 constitution. Under Dessalines, Haiti became the first country to permanently abolish slavery. Initially regarded as governor-general, Dessalines was later named Emperor of Haiti as Jacques I (1804–1806) by generals of the Haitian Revolution Army and ruled in that capacity until being assassinated in October of 1806. He has been referred to as the father or one of the founding fathers of the nation of Haiti.

GENERAL CHARLES BELAIR

Belair (1760–1802) was Aide-de-Camp and lieutenant of Toussaint Louverture, Head of the 7th demi-brigade, Commandant of l'Arcahaye and Former lieutenant of Biassou. He was also said to be a nephew of Toussaint Louverture. In 1796, he married Sanite Belair, a female hero of the revolution.

SANITE 'SUZANNE' BÉLAIR

Sanite Bélair, (1781 –1802) was a Haitian revolutionary and lieutenant in the army of Toussaint Louverture. Born free from affranchi parents in Verrettes, Haiti, she married Brigade commander and later General Charles Bélair in 1796. She was an active participant in the Haitian Revolution, became a sergeant, and later a lieutenant during the conflict with French troops of the Saint-Domingue expedition. Her portrait appears on the Haitian 10 gourdes banknote.

MARIE LOUISE COIDAVID

Coidavid (1778 - 1851), was the Queen of the Kingdom of Haiti from 1811–1820 as the spouse of Henri Christophe. She was born into a free family; her father was the owner of Hôtel de La Couronne in Cap Francais, St. Domingue. Henri Christophe was a slave purchased by her father and he supposedly earned enough money in tips from his duties at the hotel that he was able to purchase his freedom before the Haitian Revolution.

They married in Cap-Francais in 1793, having had a relationship with him from the year prior. They had four children: François Ferdinand, Françoise-Améthyste, Athénaïs, and Victor-Henri. She was exiled for 30 years after Christophe's death. Shortly before her death, she wrote to Haiti for permission to return, however, died in Italy.

FRANÇOIS-THOMAS GALBAUD DU FORT

du Fort (1743 – 1801) was a French general who was briefly governor-general of Saint-Domingue and exiled by the authorities from there. When Galbaud reached Paris in the spring of 1794 he was at once arrested and thrown into Abbaye prison. In 1799 he was released and rejoined the army, assigned to Egypt, with the rank of brigadier-general but died of the plague in 1801 in Cairo.

BENOIT JOSEPH ANDRÉ RIGAUD

Rigaud (1761 – 1811) was the leading mulatto military leader during the Haitian Revolution and the civil war in the colony. Among his protégés were Alexandre Pétion and Jean-Pierre Boyer, both future presidents of Haïti. Rigaud, like many mulatto's of the day, was a racist who hated the Black population of the island. He returned to Saint-Domingue in 1802 with the expedition of General Charles Leclerc to unseat Toussaint and re-establish French colonial rule and slavery in Saint-Domingue

ALEXANDRE PÉTION

Pétion (1770 – 1818) was the first President of the Republic of Haiti from 1807 until his death in 1818. He is acknowledged as one of Haiti's founding fathers; a member of the revolutionary quartet that also includes Toussaint Louverture, Jean-Jacques Dessalines, and his later rival Henri Christophe.

Pétion distinguished himself as an esteemed military artillery officer and commander with experience leading both French and Haitian troops. The 1802 coalition formed by he and Dessalines against French forces led by Charles Leclerc would prove to be a watershed moment in the decade-long conflict, eventually culminating in the decisive Haitian victory at the Battle of Vertières in 1803

NAPOLEON BONAPARTE

Napoleon (1769 – 1821) and later known by his regnal name Napoleon I, was a French military and political leader who rose to prominence during the French Revolution and led several successful campaigns during the Revolutionary Wars. He unsuccessfully attempted to re-enslave the most valuable of the French possessions, St. Domingue, from 1801 to 1803.

CHARLES VICTOIRE EMMANUEL LECLERC

Leclerc (1772 – 1802), of small stature, was a French Army general who served under Napoleon Bonaparte during the French Revolution. He was husband of Pauline Bonaparte, sister to Napoleon. In 1801, he was sent to Saint-Domingue (Haiti), where an expeditionary force under his command captured and deported the Haitian leader Toussaint L'Ouverture, in an unsuccessful attempt to reassert full imperial control and slavery over the Saint-Domingue. Leclerc died of yellow fever during the failed expedition.

COLONEL CHARLES HUMBERT MARIE VINCENT

Vincent (1753 – 1831) entered the French military service in 1773. In 1801, he delivered the new constitution established by Toussaint Louverture to First Consul, Napoleon Bonaparte in France. Vincent warned against making the doomed Saint-Domingue expedition, but his advice was not heeded. First Consul, Napoleon Bonaparte, exiled him to the island of Elba. After his exile in 1803, Vincent went on to serve a brilliant military career until his retirement in 1815 at age 62.

PAULINE BONAPARTE

Bonaparte (1780–1825), the youngest of Napoleon's three sisters, was the most frivolous one. She possessed magnetic beauty and charm. Whenever she went, the eyes of men turned after her. Men loved her and she loved them. Pauline was a nymphomaniac and much to Napoleon's chagrin, she made it very public.

LOUIS DAURE LAMARTINIÈRE

Lamartinière (1771 - 1802) was a participant in the Battle of Crête-à-Pierrot. Lamartiniere was a small, thin, man of thirty years during the battle who by all appearances was. He was the illegitimate son of a White father and a sacratras - a quadroon - mother. Lamartiniere's father owned a sugar plantation and refinery near Léogane. He had recognized his mulatto son but left his property to his legitimate, White son. He was the husband of Marie-Jeanne Lamartinière.

MARIE-JEANNE LAMARTINIÈRE

"Marie-Jeanne" (unknown - 1802), was a Haitian soldier and reportedly a "dazzling beauty." She served in the Haitian army during the Haitian Revolution and in at the Battle of Crête-à-Pierrot (March 1802) with her husband Louis Daure Lamartinière. She fought in a male uniform standing along the fort's ramparts bearing both a rifle and a sword.

CATHERINE FLON

Flon (unknown birth-death) was a Haitian seamstress, patriot, and national heroine. She is regarded as one of the symbols of the Haitian Revolution and independence. She is celebrated for tearing off the White portion of the French flag and then sewing the first Haitian flag in May 1803 and maintains an important place in Haitian memory of the Revolution to this day.

MARIE SAINTE DÉDÉE BAZILE

Bazile (unk. birth-death), known as Défilée and Défilée-La-Folle, is a figure of the Haitian Revolution. She is remembered for retrieving and burying the mutilated body of Emperor Dessalines after his assassination at Pont Rouge, at the northern entrance to Port-au-Prince. Dédée Bazile was born near Cap-Français to enslaved parents and made a living serving as a sutler to the army of Dessalines.

EMPRESS MARIE-CLAIRE HEUREUSE FÉLICITÉ BONHEUR

Félicité (1758 - 1858) became Empress of Haiti (1804–1806) as the spouse of Jean-Jacques Dessalines and they had seven children together. During the siege of Jacmel in 1800, she was applauded for her work with the wounded and starving. She managed to convince Dessalines, besieging the city, to allow roads to be opened for food, clothes, and medicine which she personally delivered.

She is also credited for saving many French colonists by hiding them under her bead during the revolutionary war.

FRANÇOIS CAPOIS

Capois (1766 – 1806) military career began in 1793 after a visit with independence leader Toussaint Louverture. Capois is mostly known for his extraordinary courage and especially his herculean bravery at the Battle of Vertières in which the French general Viscount of Rochambeau, commander of Napoleon's army even called a brief cease-fire to congratulate him.

He was nicknamed "Capois la Mort" for his numerous episodes of defying death during battles.

JEAN-PIERRE BOYER

Boyer (15 February 1776 – 9 July 1850) was one of the leaders of the Haitian Revolution, and President of Haiti from 1818 to 1843. He reunited the north and south of the country into the Spanish Haiti (Santo Domingo), which brought all of Hispaniola under one Haitian government by 1822. Boyer managed to rule for the longest period of time of any of the revolutionary leaders of his generation.

Chasseurs-Volontaires de Saint-Domingue

Originally, the regiment was to consist of 10 companies of light infantry organized into two battalions, each company consisting of 79 men. It was open to all Gens de Couleur, not just free Blacks of mixed race, but also slaves who were promised their freedom on their return if they joined. In 1779, the regiment received authorization for an expansion. Each of the companies would now number 100 Gens de Couleur, plus three White officers. The military regiment distinguished themselves at the battle of Savanah, Georgia in 1779 helping the American colonies fight for their independence.

Hessian soldiers from Germany

Hessians were German soldiers who served as auxiliaries to the British Army during the American Revolutionary War. The term is an American synecdoche for all Germans who fought on the British side since 65% came from the German states of Hesse-Kassel and Hesse-

Hanau.

Maréchaussée Force

The Maréchaussée was responsible for hunting escapees of the slave population. All enlisted members of the maréchaussée of Saint-Domingue were of African ancestry. These were important men in their communities and formed part of a group of free people of color defined by their lack of family connections with Whites and by their frequent use of military service to advance socially, build networks with each other and White patrons, and get access to capital to permit economic advancement

BATTLES OF THE REVOLUTIONS

Battle of Savannah
Spring Hill Redoubt
United States - September 16 - October 18, 1779

The Battle of Savannah, Georgia, which occurred between September 16 and October 18, 1779, became one of the bloodiest battles during the American Revolutionary War with troops participating from Saint-Domingue (later Haiti) and other French Caribbean colonies. In 2007, a memorial statue was unveiled in Savannah dedicated to the Chasseurs-Volontaires de Saint-Domingue to pay tribute to the significant role that these brave soldiers played in the American Revolution.

The Battle of Vertières
(in Haitian Creole Batay Vètyè)
The Battle that Ended the Revolution
November 17th - 18th, 1803

The last major battle of the Haitian Revolution was fought 0n November 18, 1803, between the St. Domingue Revolutionary army and Napoleon's French expeditionary forces. Vertières is situated a few miles south of Cap-Français

General Rochambeau sent Duveyrier to negotiate the French surrender and was given ten days to embark the remainder of his army and leave Saint-Domingue. The battle occurred less than two months before Dessalines' proclamation of the independent Republic of Haiti on January 1, 1804, in the town of Gonaïves.

The Other Major Battles of the Haitian Rvolution

Battle of Croix-des-Bouquets – March 1792

Siege of Port-au-Prince – January 1793

Battle of Cap-Français – June 1793

Capture of Fort-Dauphin – January 1794

Battle of the Acul – February 1794

Battle of Gonaïves – April 1794

Battle of Port-Républicain - May 1794

Battle of Jean-Rabel – April 1797

Battle of Ravine-à-Couleuvres – February 1802

Battle of Crête-à-Pierrot – March 1802

Siege of Port-au-Prince – October 1803

Battle of Vertières – November 1803

Siege of Santo Domingo – March 1805

FORCES AND VESSELS

Languedoc, A Warship of the French Navy

The Languedoc was an 80-gun ship of the line of the French Navy and the flagship of Admiral d'Estaing. She was offered to King Louis XV by the Languedoc province in France.

She took part in numerous battles including the Battle of St. Lucia in December 1778, the capture of Grenada in July, and Savannah in September of 1779. She was later refitted and went on to further conquests until her last log in 1798 prior to decommissioning.

HMS Rose, a Warship of the British Navy

HMS Rose was a 20-gun (Seaford-class) sixth-rate post ship of the Royal Navy, built at Blaydes Yard in Hull, England in 1757. Her activities in suppressing smuggling in the colony of Rhode Island provoked the formation of what became the Continental Navy, the precursor of the modern United States Navy. She was based at the North American station in the West Indies and then used in the American Revolutionary War. She was scuttled in the harbor of Savannah, Georgia in 1779.

ABOUT THE AUTHOR

Daniel Jean-Dominique Bayard

Mr. Bayard was born in Port-au-Prince, Haiti, and raised in the United States when his parents moved to New York in 1958. He returned to Haiti for the first time at 18 and has been fascinated with Haiti's culture, people, and historical significance ever since. He lived and owned a business in Haiti for a short period of time and came to love it.

While researching his family's ancestors dating back to the 17th century, he became intrigued with the complexities and drama of St. Domingue, the colonial precursor to the Republic of Haiti. In-depth research into all aspects of the period's history and aspects of colonial society led him to write this thrilling, enlightening, and entertaining story.

Mr. Bayard is a Chief Marketing Officer for a major company, married with 4 children, blessed with 5 grandchildren, and resides in South Florida.

Ancestors of the Author

Philippe Bayard (Lille, France DOB 1689)
(Arrived in Saint Domingue circa 1710)
Married Marie Debreuse

Jean-Philippe Bayard (Son) 1725
Married Jeanne Guillemette Bachelier

Jean-Baptiste Hyppolite Bayard (Son) 1750
Married Marie Jasmine

Jean-Baptiste Bayard (Son) 1775
Married Marie Victoire Georges

Achilles Othello Bayard (Son) 1823
Married Elizabeth Pressoir

Georges R. Bayard (Son) 1850
Married Marianne Clerie

Thomas Bayard (Son) 1879
Married Alzire Sansaricq 1881

Daniel Thomas Bayard (Son) 1912
Married Marcelle Elisabeth Oriol 1921

The Author:
Daniel Jean-Dominique Bayard (Son) 1957
Married Lily Anne Marie LaPlace 1957

THE REPUBLIC OF HAITI

Haitian Creole: Ayiti

The country of Haiti is located in the Caribbean on the western third of the island of Hispaniola. It is bordered by the Dominican Republic to the east, the Caribbean Sea, and the Atlantic Ocean.

Haiti's terrain consists mainly of rugged mountains interspersed with small coastal plains and river valleys. The government system is a republic; the chief of state is the president, and the head of government is the prime minister.

Haiti has a largely traditional economic system in which most of the economy relies on subsistence farming, and government regulation is widely constrained. Haiti is a member of the Caribbean Community (CARICOM)

In color, the flag of Haiti's top section is Blue and the bottom section is Red. The inserted image in the center of the flag consists of Blue, Red and Green in a White background.

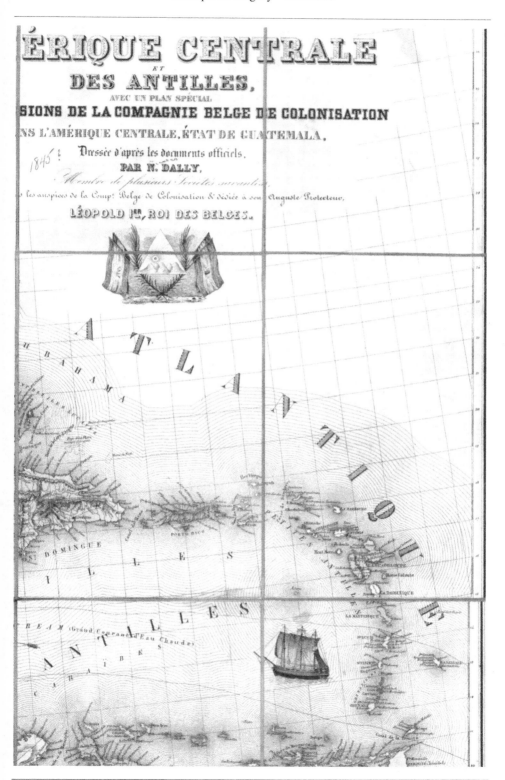